T0168091

Advance praise for *Crossing the Street*

"Molly Campbell's *Crossing the Street* is a funny, warm, and charming novel. It was such a pleasure to get lost in this world, and in Campbell's capable hands."
– Julie Klam, *New York Times* bestselling author of *The Stars in Our Eyes*

"*Crossing the Street* is a compelling story about all the different people in our lives who become family. Campbell draws us into her characters with heart and humor and with a unique voice that will stay with me for a long time. I can't wait to read her other books!"
– Camille Di Maio, author of *The Memory of Us* and *Before the Rain Falls*

"I am crazy about Molly Campbell's writing. Her characters are funny and real. Her storytelling is fresh and poignant. She breaks the rules and looks fabulous doing so. *Crossing the Street* is a surprising and unpredictable, thoroughly enjoyable read!"
– Amy Impellizzeri, award-winning author of *Lemongrass Hope* and *The Secrets of Worry Dolls*

"*Crossing the Street* is a quick, entertaining, and original story about the challenges of knowing what to want in a world filled with expectations and pressure. Molly Campbell in her signature irreverent humor has written a novel that is funny, warm and sure to get readers thinking about how both fate and choice create our lives, as long as we are open to both."
– Ann Garvin, *USA Today* bestselling author of *I Like You Just Fine When You're Not Around*

"*Crossing the Street*, Molly Campbell's funny and endearing novel, is about the intersections of our lives, mapping characters as they cross from childhood to adulthood, from middle to old age, from isolation to community, and from sadness to joy. We find connection, humor and love in the oddest, strangest and most gloriously unexpected places, as *Crossing the Street* illustrates with warmth and generosity."
– Gina Barecca, author of *If You Lean In, Will Men Just Look Down Your Blouse?* and *Babes in Boyland*

Crossing the Street

Molly D. Campbell

CROSSING THE STREET

Molly D. Campbell

The Story Plant
Studio Digital CT, LLC
P.O. Box 4331
Stamford, CT 06907

Story Plant Paperback ISBN-13: 978-1-61188-248-3
Fiction Studio Books E-book ISBN: 978-1-945839-05-4

Visit our website at www.TheStoryPlant.com

First Story Plant paperback printing: May 2017

Printed in the United States of America

For my husband,
With intense positive regard

PROLOGUE

The Saturday I babysat for Ginny Dawkins changed my life. I was fifteen. Ginny was four. She had scabs absolutely everywhere because Ginny was a menace to herself. Ginny had a buzz cut due to a lice scare at preschool. She had dirty fingernails, blazing blue eyes, and she shrieked like a banshee. During the four hours she spent in my charge, Ginny tore her shorts on a rusty nail, and I had to put a Band-Aid on the scratch. The scratch that I figured would probably give her lockjaw. She insisted on five different sugary snacks. I could not get her to stop long enough to sponge her down, so I envisioned Mrs. Dawkins absolutely shitting when she saw the strawberry jam fingerprints all over the eggshell white wainscoting in the formal dining room. Ginny somehow managed to shove an M&M deep inside her ear. Again, I wagered that Ginny would require medical intervention—Mrs. Dawkins would *never* hire me again. In between those activities, Ginny kicked me in the shins twice, ran into the street after a basketball, and was nearly hit by a car, ironically driven by my father.

It was that day I decided I never wanted children.

CHAPTER ONE

My life isn't exactly bright and shiny. My name is Rebecca Throckmorton. I live in a small town, and I muddle along as best I can. Four scenes from my world:

Scene one: I am at the grocery store. Aimlessly wandering down the produce aisle, looking at the grocery list, as usual, in my mother's elegant hand. *What the hell is a rutabaga, and why do we need one?* Suddenly, I see my father, who is long gone from our family—divorce. He is wearing a gold golf shirt, his khaki slacks, crisp and unwrinkled. His hair from the back is a bit silvery, as I am sure it would be after being away from our family for all these years. My heart lurches— *He's back! He came back!* I abandon my cart and nearly bowl over a woman studying kiwis, knocking the one in her hand to the ground. I don't even stop to apologize, because *my dad.* I come up behind him, breathe in his cologne—*yup, Eau de Sauvage.* I reach out to touch his shoulder, and he turns around. I gasp. The man is definitely *not* Dexter Throckmorton. Instead of a Roman nose, this guy has a schnozz. There is awful hair growing out of his nostrils. His eyes are not velvety and black, like my father's—they are a watery gray and clouded with cataracts. He hears me gasp and asks, "Do I know you?" I abandon the rutabaga and rush out of the store, grocery list still crushed between my fingers.

Scene two: My sister's wedding. I am wearing a sleeveless, misty green satin dress with two small lines of silver sequins along the bodice. The misty green is reflected in my coloring and makes me look slightly vomitous. I *feel* about to vomit, since my sister Diana is marrying my former boyfriend, Bryan Dallas, who stands at the end of the aisle, beaming, his horn rims polished so highly I worry that he might start a fire with their refractions into the balcony. As D comes down the aisle on my mother's arm (see divorce, above), my mother looking for all the world like an aging Audrey Hepburn in a slender tube of taupe silk, I look down at my bouquet and stifle the impulse to hurl it in my sister's smug, highly-made-up-with-false-eyelashes-and-dewy-lip-gloss face.

Scene three: Me and my girlfriend, Ella Bowers. I sit with her in front of the TV. We like to watch really old reruns of Lawrence Welk that I found for her on the Family Network. Ella pats down her soft, fluffy lavender white hair, and *every time Myron Floren comes on* comments how much her mother "just loved that man and his accordion." I nod and agree, because I don't intend to hurt her feelings—Ella is eighty-three, and I don't want her to get riled up and have a stroke. I notice my cut glass tumbler of iced tea is empty, and I offer to go into the kitchen of her cozy bungalow and get us each some more.

Scene four: My day job and what really pays the bills. I get home from my part-time job at Starbucks at four. I stretch, try to do the downward facing dog, and fail, as usual, about three quarters of the way down. My cat, Simpson, ambles over for a purr, and then I go and pee, change into sweats, and sit down at my computer, where I pound out a scene in which four orgasms occur within the space of twenty minutes between Travis and Crystal, who are extremely talented genitally. My latest book, *Boys on the Beach*, is under contract and due at my publisher in two months. When I think about this, sweat pools into the cups of my bra, because I am behind schedule, and erotica pays the bills, not venti lattes.

There you have it.

▷◁

Today at Starbucks, in the slate gray late winter, as I made my zillionth mocha latte, I got a text from my mom. Old school, using no emoticons and complete punctuation:

Hello, honey! How is it going? Big news! Your sister is pregnant! Due in July!

I hit "delete message," my heart pounding. I stuffed my phone back in my apron pocket, spilling scalding milk from the frother down my front in the process.

"Shit!"

At the other end of the counter, Joe, the nerdiest of the nerds, but a great barista, despite his bifocals and saddle shoes, noticed. "Hey, are you okay?" He intoned, looking around to see if any of the customers had heard the *s-* word.

I felt my ribs tightening. For some reason, there were a few tears in my eyes, and I had the urge to fling a ceramic coffee mug into the wall behind me, but I replied, "No." Then I had the urge to smack poor Joe for noticing.

He shrugged and continued to wipe down the counter, which he kept immaculately clean with Clorox and soapy water, not in the employee manual, by the way. "You look like all the blood just rushed into your head. Sort of like you might explode, if you know what I mean."

I knew what he meant, because right at that moment, I figured that my face was probably the color of a tomato. My skin throbbed to the drum of my erratic pulse, and I could *hear* my heartbeat pounding in my ears. I shut my eyes for a second, and who should float into my head but my sister.

D, at aged seven, her blonde hair in an adorable fringe, skipping into the dining room carrying my favorite book, Tuck Everlasting. *She flaps the pages flagrantly. They're covered with large, red splotches, drawn on with magic marker. I shriek in alarm, and both my parents look up from their tuna salad plates.*

"What's wrong, kiddo?" Dad, concerned, between sips of ice water.

"D HAS RUINED MY BOOK! She marked all over it with marker! Look at it! It's ruined!"

My mother springs to her feet and hugs me, at the same time chastising D. "Diana, that isn't your book! Did you use a permanent marker?"

She did. It was indeed ruined. The outcome was one less cherished book for me, a smirk of victory on D's felonious little face, and a request for Tums from my father.

So now Mrs. Bryan Dallas was pregnant. I poured myself some ice water from the fridge, told Joe I needed a break, and bolted for the "associates' lounge." I flung myself into a rickety chair, and swept all the *People* magazines off the breakroom table in front of me. I laid my pounding head onto the table, covered my sweaty head with my hands, and smacked my forehead up and down onto the Formica. *FUCKETY, FUCK, FUCK.*

So why was the fact that Diana was pregnant so offensive to me—the least maternal person in the world? I, Rebecca Throckmorton. The last person on the planet who would want to wrestle with loaded diapers and night terrors. The woman who just the week before had watched a woman wrangle a twin stroller through the front doors of Starbucks, her lips in a tight line, her screaming toddler and drooling baby writhing in their restraints, only to arrive at the counter to request a container of apple juice and a blueberry muffin *for her kids*, not once glancing at the menu of the new "sip into Spring" coffee drinks. At that moment, I wanted to make her a free venti latte and give her a hug. A smug, *thank God I knew enough not to turn into you* hug.

I sat up and pushed my hair away from my face and took a long drink of the ice water. Restored a bit, I looked around at the break room, with its corkboard full of inspirational sayings, some of them so old that they were faded, yellow, and tattered at the edges. So this was the first day of the rest of my life. I glanced at the fridge in the corner with our lunches in it—marked with things like **This is Eric's. Don't touch, you morons.** And the alliterative **Louise's lunch.** The thrumming in my head had let up a bit. So I stood and threw my remaining water in the waste can that hadn't been emptied in what looked like weeks, spilling over with sour yogurt in half empty cups, pizza crusts, and other stinky detritus. Then I squared my shoulders and went back out there to serve caffeine to the sluggish masses.

It was a long day. Not many customers in the late afternoon—boring. The image of my sister, pregnant and glowing, would not leave my head. By the time I left, Joe seemed convinced that I was either having a stroke or planning a murder. He must have asked me "Are you sure you are okay?" a hundred times.

I got home and choked down some leftover Skyline chili for dinner. The deadline loomed over me like a noose. I deleted five paragraphs from Chapter Twelve of *Bad Boys* and wrote what I hoped were steamier ones. In between paragraphs, I ran my fingers through my dry, Pepsi-brown hair, split ends crying out for a conditioning treatment. I re-read what I'd typed so far, and suddenly I wanted to jump right into bed with Travis, replacing Crystal in his arms. I wanted to feel his fingers as they gently stroked my back, sending chills down my spine. I wanted to bite his lips as he kissed me, causing us both to moan. I wanted him to push me back against the slippery cushions as he whispered my name. I felt a rush of heat between my legs. I snapped to attention with pain and realized that in my gush of pent-up passion, I had knocked my mug of chai tea directly into my lap, nearly scorching my lady parts. My life right then sucked.

CHAPTER TWO

Spring in Framington, Ohio. Lots of buds. That sheeny bright green that is so fleeting. Magnolias. Dogwoods. I sat on a bench in front on the bank of the Green River, which flows along the west side of town. A light breeze blew, ruffling my collar. I sat, waiting for my friend Gail, trying to resist opening the box lunches I bought us, to eat the chocolate chip cookies inside. Futile.

As I chewed, the dark chocolate chips melting in my mouth and probably all over my face, I remembered when I met Gail Boatwright in first grade. She stood proudly at the top of the monkey bars, proclaiming herself "SUPERGIRL!" and waving regally to the crowd of boys below her, not realizing that they were her minions only because that was the day she wore a dress and tights, but no underwear. Mrs. Boatwright was a hippie mom who apparently felt that vaginas needed air.

There Gail stood, her pigtails bouncing as she turned, waving to those below, her legs spread-eagled on the bars for balance. I squinted up at her as I approached, my heart filled with envy at this powerful personage, her sneakers untied, her grin triumphant. But suddenly, it all took a nasty turn. Bobby Dickerson yelled, "I see London, I see France, but Gail's not wearing UNDERPANTS!" All hell broke loose below as the boys jostled one another for a good view, and Gail nearly fell off trying to get down in a hurry.

"Go to Hell!" I kicked Dickerson in the ass. He fell down on his knees in the gravel, howling. Miss French hustled over and broke up the whole thing. But not before Gail punched Timmy Eagleston and gave him a bloody nose, and I elbowed John Parker in the eyeball.

Gail and I bonded in the principal's office while waiting for our mothers to come in for a talk.

"Thanks for hitting those boys."

"Welcome. How come you aren't wearing underpants, anyway?"

Gail blushed. "I get itchy. So Mom said today I could air out. I forgot at recess."

I grabbed her hand in consolation and unity. "That's okay. One time I jumped into the pool and my bikini top came off. I don't wear two-pieces any more. It was so *humiliating*."

Gail herself interrupted my trip down memory lane. "Hey, kiddo—how's the orgasm business?" She glided up, her teal silk blouse highlighting the blue of her eyes, her blonde hair in a stylish crop, frosty spikes and gamine bangs that accentuated her high cheekbones and plush eyelashes. Gail's long legs were encased in a flowy, gray paisley skirt that swirled around her espadrilles. I wondered briefly if she was wearing underwear.

I grinned and motioned for her to sit. She first examined the bench for bird droppings, brushing it off with her Coach bag before dropping down beside me and grabbing one of the box lunches. "I am ravenous. Oh, shit. You already ate the cookies." She reached out and wiped a smear of chocolate off my cheek.

"Damn, Gail. I never get away with it."

She laughed. "It's fine. I'm on a diet, anyway."

Gail spread the napkin in her lap and delicately peeled the waxed paper off her tuna sandwich. She munched one small bite, and took the bottle of water I held out for her. Setting her sandwich down carefully on her lap, she wrested the cap off the bottle and said, "If only this were vodka."

"My God. What's wrong? Did you lose a listing?"

Gail is a realtor. High-end. She gets the listings for the McMansions on the outside of town that sell to the bankers, the doctors, and the hot-shit entrepreneurs that move to Framington because they don't want to live and work in Columbus. Framington became a bedroom community when urban sprawl first took over. Despite the long commute, people of affluence like to live in Framington, and Gail is their go-to gal.

Gail capped her water and put it on the bench beside her. She re-wrapped her sandwich and put it back in the box, setting that down, too. She leaned back against the bench and tilted her head to the sun, closing her eyes. "I am so damn sick of being single. All I *have* is listings, for God's sake."

"Whoa."

"Beck. We are in our thirties. We are unmarried. We have no children." She opened her eyes and looked at me. "Okay. You hate kids. But my biological clock is ticking the crap out of me."

"Gail. Today isn't about you. It's about ME." I wiped my mouth with my napkin.

Gail raised one beautifully waxed eyebrow, grimaced, and indicated with a manicured nail that I had something between my front teeth. "Damn, Beck! I had no idea you were in crisis mode. Your text didn't warn me that we couldn't even have any conversational foreplay. Okay. What does this meeting *all about you* concern?" Gail lifted her dill pickle out of the lunch box and crunched off a bite. She chewed and made the "go on" motion with her other hand.

"I have been in denial about this for as long as I could, but it is no longer something I can try to ignore. Diana and Bryan are having a baby, due in July."

Gail spit out her pickle, appropriately thunderstruck. It landed on the front of my brand new Ralph Lauren polo that I paid *full price* for at Nordstrom in Columbus. Bright orange. A gift to me from me. I picked off the pickle piece and looked at the wet spot. "This will probably be permanent. Of course it will, because my whole life is in the dumper right now. I don't deserve nice things." I brushed at the spot, then held it out, fanning the shirt in a futile attempt to dry the spot off.

"D is preggers? And you have kept this to yourself for how long?"

I looked down at my sandwich. The turkey/avocado combo suddenly smelled a little off. I scrunched the whole thing up into a waxed paper ball and put the whole box lunch on the bench beside me. "Mom told me a few weeks ago. I have been in stunned disbelief. Or denial. Or both."

Gail shrugged. "I mean, this isn't actually a surprise, you know. D always said she wanted to have—how did she used to put it—'Six kids and a rich husband?' So yeah. It is just starting to pan out. You know. Married people do tend to have children eventually. But I get it that you are blown away by this, because well—Bryan. But certainly you don't envy her being pregnant? You, the child-hater?"

I drew myself up and poked Gail in the ribs with my elbow. "I have never said I *hate* children. Not exactly. I just don't think I have the talent for enduring them. You know. Patience. Being able to tolerate their turbo-charged enthusiasm levels. Arts and crafts. *Row, Row, Row Your Boat.* It's a gift that I just don't possess."

Gail actually chortled. "So you are upset by this whole thing because you are jealous of what? You walked out on Bryan for this exact reason: kids and the white picket fence. You don't get to have it both ways."

I had a brief flashback to the day I left the loft in Chicago. *Boxes packed, the burly Two Men and a Truck guys hefting the last of my possessions into the truck. All that was left in the center of the room was that one tarnished brass lamp that Bryan found at the estate sale around the corner for a dollar. Its moth-eaten, rose-colored shade with the tassels, and the claw footed base—we thought it must have come out of some brothel during prohibition, it was that cool looking. Bryan had one fist hooked around that lamp, white knuckled. Claiming it. I shook my head with pity and said something like "Go ahead. Keep it. They like stuff like that in suburbia. Antiques that give the home 'character.' I wish you well." And as I walked out of the loft to climb into my Prius to follow the movers, I stubbed my toe on the concrete and sobbed.*

"Right? Beck. Hey." Gail put her arm around my shoulders. "You knew this was coming, eventually."

I nodded. Jesus, I just had to *buck up.* "I know. And Mom is over the moon about it. It just isn't sitting well at the moment. I will come to grips. Really." Ha. There was a little bile stinging the back of my throat. I took a slug of water, gulped, and turned to my steadfast friend. "Enough about me. What is this about biological clocks?" There was a pause as I watched Gail's face go gray beneath her makeup.

18

"I want Will back." She sighed.

Horrid history: Gail was engaged right after college to the love of her life, Will Garnett. Will had an absolutely open face, an honest heart, dimples, and a Harley. Will was starting medical school in the fall after Gail and I graduated, and Gail planned to move to Columbus to get a job. The traditional "put him through medical school and then focus on your own career" scenario.

Will and Gail were right out of the romance novels. He finished her sentences. She and Will's mother laughed at each other's jokes. Mrs. Boatwright promised Gail that she could have the family silver and the wedding china. Gail and I discussed at length the pros and cons of full-length veils. Will presented her with a small but flawless emerald-cut diamond.

My phone rang at two in the morning on a Saturday in August. I struggled out of a dream to answer my phone, and heard screaming at the other end. I awoke instantly, with the crushing knowledge that something was terribly wrong.

All I could make out was Gail saying the word WRECK over and over. I dropped the phone, shoved my arms into my bathrobe, and ran barefoot from my mother's house the three blocks to the Boatwrights'. By the time I got there, my feet were bleeding and Gail was keening on her front porch, wrapped in her mother's arms.

He wasn't wearing a helmet. They always say "killed instantly," but I know it's just a very kind lie. But I repeated it over and over to Gail, during the horrific three days before the funeral, and I whispered it to her as I stood, grasping her hand tightly, at the funeral home after the service. "He didn't suffer. It was instant. No pain."

Gail stayed in Framington as I moved with Bryan to Chicago. She stayed to remember. She stayed to recover, and she did. Gail knows her corbels and her columns. She can see potential in the ruins of a century-old farmhouse. Gail is a nester. So it came naturally to her to become the best realtor in Framington and the surrounding environs. I thought that Will was just a tiny little achy memory. But I looked at my friend's face and watched it crumble. I laid my head on Gail's shoulder.

"I am so sorry I ate the cookies."

We both started to laugh, but you know how laughing quickly degenerates into crying—like the two emotions are packed so closely into your emotional repertoire that they spill over onto one another. We sat on the bench, Gail and I, our lunches baking in the sun, our heads together, our eyes wet and our noses running. Best friends in the midst of it all.

Gail was the first to sop up her tears with a napkin. She handed me one and I blew my nose, honking like a goose. Gail stood, gathered up all the uneaten catering, and stuffed it into the bin. It was for "BOTTLES AND CANS ONLY." That was printed in huge white letters against the green plastic.

I looked at Gail and pointed to the lettering. "You never do things like this."

"Dammit, kiddo! This is going to be the summer of CHANGE." And with that, Gail leaned over and spit into the bin. She beckoned me over. I leaned over and spit into it as well. Solidarity for the two of us.

"To change!" We both walked back to work, me to make mochas, and Gail to show granite countertops to the nouveau riche. When we parted on the corner to go our respective ways, Gail whispered, "Scared of blood. So we're spit sisters . . ."

CHAPTER THREE

A beautiful afternoon for porch sitting. In late spring, Ohio, flowering trees are in their full glory, their delicate whites and pinks a backdrop to neighborhood sounds of *arfing* dogs, bouncing basketballs, and lawnmowers. Ella and I sat companionably, people-watching. In our neighborhood, most of the residents know one another's backstories so well that when somebody celebrates a wedding or a birth, we all do. Ella gently fanned her face, the ivory pleats of her fan ruffling her cloud of newly permed hair. I dangled my legs off the porch swing.

"You know that Fred Danvers has started dating. He is going out with Myra Ellson." Ella stopped fanning and tilted her head in the direction of Mr. Danvers, in his early nineties, who had just come out of his front door. Wearing his toupee, a white patent leather belt, and snazzy seersucker trousers, sporting his tripod cane, he looked frail but jaunty. He waved to us cheerily as he inched down his front steps carefully.

I waved back to him as he stutter-stepped towards the bus stop on the corner. He waved again, adjusted his hair, and shouted, "Lovely day, and you two are lovely women!"

"He reminds me of Robert. So courtly." Ella's smile dimmed slightly. "I have been a widow for twenty years, but it doesn't get any easier."

I hate to see Ella shrink into herself. She is already as small as a mouse, and when she mourns Robert, she diminishes even further. I always try to rush in to change the subject. "It seems like everybody is dating these days, but me." The swing stopped moving, so I shoved my feet against the concrete to set it going again

21

as I flipped the hair out of my face. "Not that I am begrudging Mr. Danvers, mind you."

Ella squinted at me through her cataracts. "Dearie, is this a change of heart? You have seemed so independent since we met."

I laughed. In one of my chapters, I would describe it as "she laughed ruefully." I looked down at my legs, which I hadn't shaved for a month. "Oh, Ella, not really. But it does seem like I've been going solo for an awfully long time. You know our friend, Gail. She keeps reminding me that we are not getting any younger. And you know all about my sister expecting. All this is"—I poked a finger into my temple—"messing with my brain a little."

I watched a mourning dove swoop down and land gracefully in Ella's driveway. It wobbled along, pecking for whatever doves peck for. A horn honked in the street behind us. I pressed my toes against the insides of my Vans. "I am independent. I made my choice. But Gail makes me wonder."

Ella nodded. "So she is having a hard time? I know how much she mourns for dear Will."

Ella, Gail, and I spend time together. I know. Three best friends, one of whom is eighty-three. I watched the dove poke around in the mulch beneath the oak tree in the tree lawn. "You know how lonely Gail is, and lately she harps on this biological clock business. Ticking, ticking. I don't know how many times Gail has pointed out happy couples pushing strollers lately, but it is a *bunch.*"

Gail and I. Sitting in the window of Beth's Bistro, having delicious cheese soufflé and talking about how much we dread swimsuit season, when suddenly, Gail's smile disappears as she stares out the window wistfully.

It's a vivid young family. The hottie husband pushes a jogging stroller containing a chubby, bald baby, arms waving some sort of lime-green lizard, his tubby legs churning. Somewhere along the way, he has lost a sock. His mother, auburn hair caught up on top of her head in a black chopstick, her firm thighs encased in black bike shorts, a tight red tank top accentuating her admirable biceps, laughs along beside them, bending over twice to pick up the lizard her baby tosses to the ground. The three of them absolutely gleam.

Gail stares, rapt. I watch them, wondering how soon before the baby gets a gas pain and starts to scream, and the wife tenses up, annoyed by the shrieking. I wonder how long before the husband stops smiling and hands the stroller off to his wife so he can walk ahead and pretend that he doesn't know either one of them. Ugh. The rest of the lunch consists of me talking about current events and Gail staring off into space.

Ella cleared her throat with a croaky moistness. "Oh, goodness. Well then my news might not be exactly welcome."

Ella straightened up in her wicker chair and adjusted her flowered housedress to cover her bony knees, smoothing out the wrinkles. She reached inside the sleeve of her pink cotton cardigan, drew out an embroidered linen handkerchief, and gently wiped her nose. Stalling.

"Ella. What is your news?"

I watched Ella fidget for a few seconds, her papery cheeks flushing. Her knotted fingers closed and unclosed her Chinese fan. She put the fan in her lap, wiped her nose once more, and leaned forward. "I am having a visitor."

This didn't sound like bad news. "Wonderful! Who is it?"

Ella looked at her lap and took a deep breath. "You know that my grandson, Charles, is deployed over there?" She spread her arms in two directions, but I knew what "over there" meant. The Mideast. Horrors, children slaughtered, terrorists, and blood.

"You have mentioned that, yes."

Ella looked at me with widened eyes. "He is on his final tour. He's due back, as I probably told you, in February." Her forehead creases deepened. "You know he has a little girl. She's eight."

The visitor. A child. My head filled with visions of Ella trying to keep her delicate balance as a whirling dervish of a kid jostles into her as she tears down the stairs and out the door. I pictured devilish red hair in greasy pigtails, filthy fingernails, and a deafening howl.

"Oh, really? Your great-granddaughter is coming for a visit? How long will she be here?"

Ella once again unfurled her fan and waved it weakly. "Actually, she will be here until her father comes back from . . ." Ella waved her arms again in the direction of "over there."

This was worrisome. "I see." I hesitated, but then just blurted, "Why is she staying with you? Are you sure you're *up* for this?"

I watched the blue veins in her temples pulse. Ella waved the fan more briskly as the color rose in her cheeks. "Rebecca, there is simply no other option."

Ella's explanation was long and winding. Charles Bowers, a young Marine stationed at Camp Pendleton, met and fell in love with Rowena Chilton.

Think passion, a wayward and headstrong girl trying desperately to escape her abusive family. Drugs. An unwanted pregnancy and a stalwart soldier who vows to stand by his girlfriend. Tumult. A number of overseas deployments, and a mother in and out of rehab. Custody papers signed over to the father.

As Ella went on, I could see the story unfold just like a reality show. Rowena, her arms dotted with track marks, looks down at her sleeping toddler, reassures herself that all will be well for a short while. She runs her fingers through her own ratty hair, pulls on a hoodie over her sweats, grabs a fistful of bills, and snatches the house keys. She hardly notices the peeling paint around the doorframe of the squat she calls home as she locks it behind her. She *needs* to get some more stuff. The kid will be all right. She is always all right, even on the days when Rowena returns and the child is crying in fear. A hug will reassure. She is starting to shake as she heads down to the bus stop to meet her supplier.

"... So now that Roberta's grandparents in Iowa can no longer take care of her—they are in poor health—Charles asked me if I could take Bobby."

I raised my eyebrows.

"Charles calls her Bob. Well, I guess everybody in the family does but me. She hates being called Roberta, because it sounds too much like Rowena, I guess."

Ella began to falter. Her voice dropped to almost a whisper. "Rebecca, I am *not* sure I am up to this, but I have no choice."

I heard myself talking from somewhere outside of my body. "Of course! You are up to it. *WE* are up to it! I can help you with ...

Bob, is it? Right. I am home a lot, you know, in the afternoons and on weekends. This will be fine."

Meanwhile, my stomach churned as I thought about how much children like to shriek. I remembered my playground days, with endless games of freeze tag, hundreds of episodes of bullying, and the myriad ways that kids can injure themselves. Ginny Dawkins, for God's sake. Sweat ran down behind my ears, and I pulled up my shirt to blot my drips.

"How soon is Bob coming?"

Ella's fan stopped waving. Her dear, filmy eyes glistened. Her lips parted in a brave smile. "Two weeks. She will be here in two weeks."

I stopped breathing for what seemed like a full minute. "Okay then. We need to get a move on. I'll call Gail."

▷◁

There was a flurry of activity. The Framington Target checkers got to know us by name as Gail, Ella, and I purchased a mountain of Goldfish crackers, Kool-Aid, Popsicles, and healthy stuff like whole milk, American cheese slices, apples, oranges, and broccoli florets. We also bought a new pillow and crisp white sheets for the twin bed in the spare room at Ella's that originally belonged to Charles' father, Robert Junior. As we perused the aisles for bubble bath and sunscreen, Ella reminded us that her son, Robert Junior, died of a heart attack when Charles was only twelve, and his mother Connie succumbed to breast cancer when Charles was fifteen. Charles had lived with Ella until he left for college. So Charles was Ella's one and only.

That made Gail tear up, thus she insisted that we go immediately to the beauty aisle to get some nail polish for Bob, because "all girls like to get pedicures."

I mentioned that not *all* girls like pedicures. I have never liked for anybody to touch my feet. Gail waved me off dismissively. "You're an oddball. We all know that."

Ella chuckled and pointed to the bottle of OPI *Mod About You.*

"This is a nice pink, don't you think? Bobby will like this one." Ella placed it carefully on top of her black patent leather pocketbook in the cart. "Do you think we should get her a doll?"

"Whoa!" I stopped pushing the cart and put one hand on Ella's shoulder and one on Gail's. "Let's stop with all the girly things. We don't know this child well. Maybe she isn't the type to play mommy. Let's just get to know Bob better before we foist any more girly stuff on her. As a matter of fact, I think what Bob needs is a SCOOTER." My mind's eye conjured up a little skinny sprite, knobby knees pumping as she skimmed the pavement, her arms akimbo, covered with mosquito bites and the scabs of liberation.

That day, we got the scooter. We went back four more times for other necessary equipment such as a helmet, two boxes of Band-Aids, a tube of antibiotic ointment, Shout stain remover stick, Clorox, assorted cereal (Gail vetoed anything sugary, but I snuck in a box of Honeycombs), and Children's Tylenol. I chose the Tylenol, because naturally, there would be fevers. All kids get unexplained fevers, right?

Ella supervised the rearrangement of Bob's bedroom. It had not been touched since Charles lived there. After we cleared out all the old pennants, basketball trophies, and the stack of hockey sticks propped up in the corner, she sent me up to the attic for a worn but serviceable yellow-and-blue quilt. While I was up there, I discovered a very distinguished looking teddy bear with one eye missing, his head nearly threadbare from probable hugging, and a faded red bow tie.

"Oh, that was Rob's. He loved that bear. He named him Teddy, of course." Ella stroked Ted's ears and gently squeezed his torso, the stuffing now brittle with age. "Charles inherited him from his father. So now there will be another Bowers to love Teddy. Let's put him on her pillow."

We finished off the room by dusting off all the books in the bookcase, among them The Hardy Boys series, some books about aviation, and a few ancient games. Gail sighed and vowed to bring over the first Harry Potter book, *A Wrinkle in Time*, and a Barbie doll. I nearly protested, but kept my peace.

We three surveyed our work. The room was neat, clean, and soulless. "This wallpaper is okay," I gestured to the slightly grayish pattern of circus animals. "But what this room needs is a couple of bright pictures, or posters, or something. Wait! I have an idea!" Ella and Gail looked expectant as I ran out of the room, down the stairs, and across the street to my apartment. At the back of the closet in my bedroom were two framed pictures of my cat Simpson that Bryan had taken when we got him at the shelter. In one, his kitten eyes were closed, his gray tiger stripes just starting to mark the tiny "M" on his forehead. In the other, he was about six months old, and he stared at the camera, his amber eyes like magic orbs. I took them with me when I left Chicago, but I had never wanted to hang them here. I put one under each arm and hustled back to Ella's.

Gail was handy with a hammer. Realtors do all that staging. We hung one photo over the bed, and one over the bookcase.

"I hope Bob likes cats," Gail murmured as she closed Ella's toolbox.

"How could there be any doubt?" I exclaimed. "We are talking about the world's most charming animal."

We were pooped. Well, Ella was pooped. As we followed her slow progression down the stairs, one arthritic hand gripping the handrail and the other touching the opposite wall for balance, I wondered how on earth Ella was going to survive the coming ruckus.

CHAPTER FOUR

Ella had insisted on going to the airport to meet Bob by herself. She called the cab a *day* ahead of time, and Simpy and I watched from our living room window as Ella, dressed in a soft, green linen shirtwaist, pearls, and a brand new pair of white Keds, paced back and forth waiting for the taxi. When it pulled up, she adjusted her white/lavender perm, straightened her shoulders, and marched down the steps, her arthritic knees probably cracking, and lowered herself into the car.

Simpson and I did our own pacing after that. I strode from my living room window, which had a clear view to Ella's front porch, to my kitchen window, where I drank glass after glass of water as I looked out the window over my sink, craning my neck for a view down the block. Simpy followed me everywhere, twining between my legs, nearly tripping me.

Finally, I heard a car door slam. I jumped up from the sofa, where I was on patrol hiatus. Simpson fell unceremoniously off my lap, protesting with a squawk. "Sorry, sweetie!"

I rushed over to the window to see. Ella was assisted out of the back of the taxi by the cabbie, who held first her hands, and then pulled her out gently by the elbows. Ella straightened and turned to watch as a child *shot* out of the backseat and hurtled up the steps of Ella's porch. A blur of skinny legs, pale skin, nut-brown curls in a froth around her head, and black high tops. She stopped suddenly, turned, and watched as her great-grandmother paid the driver, wiped her forehead with one frail hand, and slowly trudged up the steps. They paused at the top, a skinny, lightening bolt of a child and a delicate, unprepared little old woman. My head pounded with a sudden rush of dread. *How was this going to go?*

I picked up Simpson and pointed his furry head in the direction of the Bowers' house. "Well, guy, there they are. And this is our immediate future." Simpy purred. I put my head against his fuzz and gained a bit of calm from the vibrations. We watched Ella and Bob disappear into the house, the door shutting behind them.

A few hours later, as I walked past my window, I caught sight of the child sitting on Ella's front steps. She didn't stray from the spot, although she knocked jittery knees together. Most children, I would think, would want to wander around and explore a new place. Look around for friendly neighbors, other kids, or at least a dog or two. Cars drove by, and at least three people passed her on the sidewalk, but this child just stared at the ground, biting her nails and banging her knees. A kid rode by on a bike, and he looked over at her and swerved in her direction. She didn't seem to notice. Watching her there, all alone in the swirl of activity, I felt sad, and once again I worried how Ella would deal with this. The door opened and Ella shuffled out. The girl looked up without a smile. Ella reached out to take her hand, but the kid shrugged it off. They went into the house.

Oh, man.

I put my cat down and shook myself off. There was cat fur all over my Josh Groban tee shirt. I blew a few stray hairs out of my nostrils and walked over to the door. I turned to Simpy, who sat, inscrutable, beside my stack of old issues of *The Atlantic*. "Wish me luck, fuzz ball. I'm going in."

I rang the doorbell. Ella's chimes were the first strains of "America, the Beautiful."

Before it even got to *spacious skies*, the door was flung open, and there stood the urchin—sharp, wide hazel eyes, short coils of dark hair, a frown etched into her oval face. She wore wrinkled black cargo shorts that looked about two sizes too big, a greasy looking gray tee shirt that was so small it revealed an inch of her tummy, and I noticed that both of her Chuck Taylors were untied, the laces frayed and uneven. She looked at her feet. I was forced to blink and clear my throat.

"Hi. My name is Beck Throckmorton. Rebecca, really, but everyone calls me Beck. I live across the street. I know you might not believe this, because of my age, but I am your grandma's best friend. We have been friends for a long time. She has told me all about you . . ." *My God, this kid made me so nervous, I was BLATHERING.*

She stood still, blocking the door. Slowly, she shifted her eyes to my face. "Hi." It was barely a voice. More like a loud whisper.

I wanted to turn and run back across the street, up the stairs, into my apartment, bolting the doors and then hiding under all of the covers for the rest of the day. But I resisted. I unclenched my fists because my fingernails had begun to cut into my palms. I took a breath. *Get ahold of yourself. This is just a little girl, for heaven's sake.*

Bob took a step back, opening the screen door.

I stepped into Ella's hallway, nearly bumping into the child's stiff shoulder. She moved out of my way in a flash, backing into the wainscoting.

"Bobby, who is it?" Ella's voice from the living room sounded tired—raspy with what probably was a noble effort to make conversation with this kid on the way home from the airport. I stepped into the living room.

Ella's house is just like the ones in the old movies I like to watch. You know the kind, like in the original *Father of the Bride*: chintz overstuffed furniture. A little dark. Wallpaper in every room. Persian rugs and curtains with tassels. Books, candlesticks, and African Violets on the windowsills. Ella's house is a haven, as far as I am concerned.

Ella sat, sunken into the chintz chair opposite the sofa, looking as if she might dissolve into it completely before long. Her shiny pocket book was in her lap, her hands clasped over it, one of them clutching a linen hanky with a lacy pink edge. Her eyes were nearly closed. My God, the poor thing looked exhausted.

"Come in, Rebecca. Sit down. This is Bobby. Oh, dear, I guess you know that." Ella blotted her forehead with the hanky, shaking slightly. "Well, sit down, everybody! Let's get to know one another."

Bob slunk into the living room and slowly lowered herself onto the very edge of the sofa. Again, no eye contact. Her fingers played nervously with the hem of her shorts, pinching and rolling it again and again. When she did look up fleetingly, her eyes skimmed the room, as if she were looking for a corner to hide in. She reminded me of those terrified abandoned dogs you see in the animal rescue videos. The ones who squeeze themselves into the very back of their enclosures, trying to disappear so that nobody will touch them.

Ella also looked strained, a fixed smile on her face. She blew her nose loudly into her hanky, as if to get her granddaughter's attention.

Nobody was comfortable. Desperate to make *something* happen, I clapped my hands like a fool. "What we need is refreshment! Something reviving! Shall I make us a drink? Ella, would you like some tea, or some ice water? Bob? I know there is some Kool-Aid. Your grandmother got it just for you. Orange or Grape?"

She looked at me. Well, not exactly *at* me. She sort of looked through me, as if I wasn't really right in front of her. "Okay. I don't know what Kool-Aid is, but I like orange. I'll pick the orange."

I could have sworn I heard Ella groan under her breath. "Just a glass of ice water would be delightful, Rebecca."

I poked around in the cupboards, looking for something unbreakable to put the kid's Kool-Aid in. The words "stray dog, refugee, Oliver Twist, and outcast" went through my mind. I discovered an aluminum tumbler, and poured in some Kool-Aid and a few ice cubes. I put that and two tumblers of ice water on a tole tray and carried them into the living room, where neither Ella nor Bob looked any more at ease.

I handed Bob her drink. She peered down at it suspiciously, then sniffed at it, as if she had tons of experience with being poisoned. She took a wary sip, and swirled it around in her mouth like a sommelier, for God's sake. But wait. She swallowed, and suddenly her timid little face broke out in a smile. It transformed her. She took a glug, put the cup down on the coffee table, ignoring the coaster. "Gran, that Kool-Aid stuff is the most delicious drink I think I have ever tasted. I do not like drinks with *bubbles*. Did you know that?"

Ella beamed. I relaxed. And this was my introduction to Roberta Charles Bowers.

Mom and I have lunch every couple of weeks or so. Our favorite place is Beth's Bistro, where the salads are to die for, Mom knows everybody, and we often share dessert.

We were discussing the new addition to my neighborhood. Mom sipped her iced mango tea as I enumerated all the ways that I thought Bob might crush Ella.

"First of all, you know how much energy eight-year-olds have. Thank God we got her that scooter. She certainly takes advantage of it. Of course, she never wears the helmet we got her, and I swear she is going to mow down Mr. Danvers one of these days. Secondly, she seems to be ready to bolt at any second. Wound up tight. Understandable under the circumstances, but STILL. She will probably have trouble making friends, so poor Ella will be stuck with entertaining her all the time that she isn't terrorizing the neighbors on that scooter. And third, she is here for God knows how long. Poor Ella."

Mom wiped the condensation from the side of her glass and raised her eyebrows. "She sounds like a needy little girl to me. You are the one who said she has had all sorts of trauma in her short life, Rebecca."

I reached over and pulled a piece of croissant off Mom's bread plate and put it in my mouth. Heaven. Mom pushed the whole plate towards me. "Go ahead. Have the whole thing. You might as well break down and order one next time; you always end up eating mine."

I spread some butter on the remaining croissant and ate the whole thing in nearly one bite. She was right, who was I kidding, pretending not to eat carbs? We chewed for a while in companionable silence, me still thinking about the challenge that was Bob Bowers.

Mom ate another few bites of her Caesar salad, then put her fork down diagonally across the plate. She pushed the plate away slightly, so that she could clasp her hands on the tablecloth in front of her, her bangle bracelets clinking together, her French manicure perfect as always. "While we are on the subject of children, we need to talk about your sister. Diana is getting a bit stir crazy, being at home and pregnant. You know that she had to go on hiatus at work, because of the morning sickness. She can't seem to shake it, and the Zofran they prescribed for the nausea makes her so constipated."

I smiled as I chewed my "Field Greens with Strawberries and Candied Pecans in a Light Citrus Vinagrette." Diana and constipation had a nice ring to it. "So? Maybe she should try prune juice."

Mom swatted my forearm, and I dropped my fork. It clattered to the floor. I started to lean down to get it, but Mom *tsked* loudly. "Stop it, Beck! They will bring you another one. Now listen to me." She wadded her napkin and set it beside her plate and cleared her throat. "I have invited her and Bryan for a visit. Diana needs a break. I am having a little brunch for her on Mother's Day."

I snorted. "You just told me she is sick all the time. Why a brunch? She'll just vomit."

My mother is an elegant and calm woman. She doesn't swear. Her voice is gentle and well-modulated. I am not sure if she even knows what the F word actually means. So her response was a huge surprise.

Mom actually shouted. Albeit softly: "Damn it, Beck—it is high time you stopped all this sibling rivalry nonsense!"

The force of it pushed me backwards, and I nearly tipped my chair over. I shifted in my seat and tried to make it look as if I deliberately leaned back that far, in order to indicate that I was finished with my lunch. As I scrambled around, I stepped on the tines of the fallen fork, sending it flying up in the air. Luckily, it didn't hit anyone, but landed with a clink on the marble floor a few feet away. But attention was drawn. Ugh.

Mom waved gaily at the assembled patrons. "She's a writer! Always so dramatic!" She chuckled and turned to me with a pasted on smile. By this time, I was sweating.

"Mom." I looked around, pulled my chair closer to the table, and lowered my voice to a near whisper. "Let me remind you of a couple of things."

Picture a family, seated around the television on a normal, Midwestern Saturday night. Friends or Seinfeld is probably on. Everyone is happy, laughing. Suddenly, the younger of the two preteen children gets up and leaves the room. Nobody pays much attention, because something hilarious is transpiring. Popcorn is being consumed, and the father tips his head back and roars with laughter.

Suddenly, the younger daughter appears, carrying a little blue book, a tiny brass key attached to it with a twisted pink cord. "Listen to this, everyone: 'Dear Diary, tonight I actually got my very first kiss! It was at Marcella Pruitt's party, and her parents weren't there. There was beer! So Tommy Connell and I went in the laundry room and made out. I didn't like the tongue—so I kept my teeth clamped shut.'"

She waves the diary over her head. "Beck was drinking and French kissing!"

I pointed out to my mother how humiliating THAT was. She rubbed her temple with one hand while taking a large sip of tea. "A long time ago, Beck."

I held up my hand to stop her. I reminded her of another tableau from the past.

Our family of three—because divorce. Claire, Beck, and Diana gathered around the Christmas tree. My mother has outdone herself. Her loft is decked with garlands over the fireplace, a huge silver-and-gold tree in front of the picture window; fairy lights strung all over, a homemade wreath on each side of the front door, and even a tiny crèche on top of the toilet in the powder room. We are opening gifts. Mom carefully unwraps the shiny red paper from a small box and exclaims enthusiastically over the perfume from Diana. The Mormon Tabernacle Choir thrums in the background. "This is lovely. I have never heard of Fancy." Mom sniffs at it gingerly.

"Oh, it's Jessica Simpson. Actually, it's a re-gift. I don't love the scent. Hey, are we out of champagne? I want another Mimosa."

Mom shut her eyes, her eyeballs fluttering beneath the lids. "Your sister has her own issues, but doesn't everyone?" I watched her lick her lips and take a deep breath. She opened her eyes and looked at me through her mascara, the edges of her eyes crinkling with concern. "We are a family. So as I said, Diana is having difficulty with this pregnancy, so I have invited them to come visit. That is what you need to focus on, not the past."

I gave up and flashed Mom what I hoped was a confident smile. "All right. No. You are right. The past is the past."

As we left the restaurant, Mom waved to various friends, her elegant legs flashing as her skirt swirled around them, her bangles tinkling with her fluttering arms. I stumped behind her, trying not to look resentful or grumpy. I probably failed.

CHAPTER FIVE

As a matter of fact, Ella was doing better with her great-grand-daughter than I expected. I noticed that they had established a habit of sitting on Ella's porch in the evenings, Ella crocheting, and Bob swinging wildly on the porch swing, the two of them deeply in conversation. I had not noticed Bob playing with any neighborhood children, and I worried that she was monopolizing Ella.

Bob had finished third grade in Iowa. So she wouldn't be going to school in Framington until the fall. I told Simpson that I was worried about how Ella would deal with Bob all summer by herself.

"Simp." I hefted him onto my shoulder to look at Bob and Ella on the porch. The porch light was on, and Ella sat, fanning herself with one of the fans from her extensive collection. Bob sat on the steps, looking bored, scraping the concrete steps with a stick. "I guess I have to go over there. Ella looks as if she needs a break. This kid needs to make some friends."

Simpson butted me with his head in assent. I set him down, tried unsuccessfully to brush off some of his fur off my front, stepped into my flip-flops, and headed out to meet the enemy.

As I approached, Bob looked up with a smile. It dimmed when she saw that it was me. Ella, on the other hand, stood up and waved me forward. "Oh, Rebecca! It is so good to see you! Isn't this a beautiful evening? I was just telling Bob about how her father used to ride his bike up and down the street with his buddies! This is such a nice, flat neighborhood."

Bob moved aside so I could come up the steps. She dropped her stick and put her small, white face into her palms, still gazing blankly outward.

I sat down in the wicker chair opposite Ella. I sank down into the soft, old cushion, lifting my thigh to pull out a sharp down feather that poked me. "Bob, you seem to like the flat street—you sure go fast on that scooter."

Bob turned and leaned against the pedestal supporting the concrete railing. "I do like the scooter a lot. It's fun. But I have to ride by myself. Gran, are there any kids that live around here?" Bob picked at a scab on her knee, dislodging it and watching the blood form a droplet in its place. She dabbed it up with her forefinger and put it in her mouth. My stomach turned.

"You will make a lot of friends when school starts, I bet." Ella smiled, but I sensed just a little desperation around the edges of her grin.

It was my turn, and I knew it. "Bob, there are kids around here. As a matter of fact, there is a new family that just moved in behind us. The Davises. I met Mrs. Davis when she came to Starbucks for coffee the other day. Her husband is the new football coach at the high school, and they have a daughter your age. If you want to, we can walk over to meet them sometime.

Bob leapt to her feet. "Tomorrow? Can we go tomorrow? Gran, is tomorrow okay? Like right after lunch?" Bob vibrated.

"Certainly, honey. But maybe you shouldn't just drop in. Maybe you should call them, Rebecca?"

"Here's the thing, guys." Two pairs of eyes looked at me expectantly. "I don't know them well enough to call them. I am not sure I even told Mrs. Davis my name, actually."

Bob sat down immediately and picked up her stick again, stabbing it against the concrete until it splintered.

"But, Bob, I have an idea. Do you know that I have a cat? He is a very nice, fuzzy guy, and he likes to take walks on a leash."

Bob looked startled. "Really? A cat on a leash? They can do that with cats?"

I nodded. "Absolutely. And I have found that cats on leashes are great conversation starters. So if we just happen to walk by the Davises house, the three of us, it may be just the thing we need to get acquainted!"

Bob clasped her hands around her knobby knees. Her eyes shone with excitement. "Did you know that I almost had a cat once? My Dad was going to get me one, but then he was deployed, and I had to go to stay with my grandparents in Iowa, so he said we couldn't get one. I really like cats." Her gaze turned outward, and I could almost see a cloud of sadness descend on her.

"Welp. That's decided. Tomorrow, after lunch?" I looked at Ella, who nodded. "Simpson and I will pick you up tomorrow at one. Okay?"

Bob said nothing, but her lips moved. They formed the word *Simpson* over and over. I stooped on my way down the steps to touch her on the head. She startled at my touch, her bony frame stiffening. I snatched my hand away. *What a nervous kid.* Then Bob resurfaced, wiped her nose, and smiled.

"See you tomorrow!"

When I got home, I sank onto my bed beside Simpson, who had been dreaming of tuna, probably. He opened one golden eye and purred. "Fuzzball, we have our work cut out for us."

Simpson purred. I worried.

▷◁

Simpson's harness was made out of lime green cotton mesh. He was very patient as I put it over his head and threaded his legs through the openings for them. Then I pulled the "girth" under his tummy and fastened the Velcro on the other side. Just like a miniature saddle. He purred during the procedure.

"He looks so cute! OOOOH, he has a matching leash! And it has little blue fishes all over it! A fishie leash!" Bob clasped her hands and squatted beside Simpson, reaching out to stroke his head. Simpson mewed at her. "I think he is rarin' to go, don't you?"

I laughed and attached the leash to the clip on his harness. "Well, *rarin'* may be overstating it. I think Simpy is pretty tolerant. I would say he is *willing* to go."

"Can I hold the leash when we walk?"

"Yes." I put a restraining hand on Bob's shoulder. "But you have to promise not to let go. Because Simpson is most definitely NOT a dog, and if he gets away, we can't just say 'Simpy, COME!' and expect him to run right back to us. I know this from experience. Once I dropped the leash, and he ran away from me, and he didn't come back for a few hours. I thought I had lost him for good."

Bob put her left hand over her heart, "pledge of allegiance" style.

"No, Bob. Other hand. Your heart is on the other side of your chest. Use your right hand."

"Oh. Okay!" She switched. "I solemnly promise."

We headed out of the apartment in single file. First, a very kind tiger cat, all his stripes in a row, tail held high; followed by one little turbo-charged girl, tangled curls and freckles flashing, clutching the fishie leash proudly; followed by me, smiling my best insincere smile, wondering how I got myself into all of this wholesome activity.

It was a beautiful afternoon for strolling. The sun was warm but not sizzling. Lawns sparkled, wet from sprinklers. Those little mineral specks in the concrete shone like diamonds. I felt liberated after six hours of serving coffee to strangers.

Simpson padded along with dignity, stopping to take a delicate bite of grass here and there. Bob stepped behind him carefully, clutching the leash for dear life; my warning must have made her very nervous. I waved at Mr. Granville, weeding his rose bed.

"Hello, girls! This is quite a procession." He wiped his forehead with his forearm. "Who is this new friend, Rebecca?"

Bob shaded her eyes with her free hand. "Hi. My name is Bob Bowers. I just moved in with my gran."

Mr. Granville motioned us to join him on his lawn. Simpson trotted up to Mr. Granville and rubbed against his legs. Bob stuck out her hand in greeting. "I am very pleased to meet you."

Mr. Granville shook hands with her gravely, and then twinkled at me. "Taking a little constitutional? I hope the Duncans' dog isn't out!"

"Yes, we are hoping to meet some of the neighbors."

He nodded. "Nothing like a little tiger cat on a leash to break the ice! Would you two like some lemonade?" He gestured to the wide front porch with wicker furniture and a very inviting porch swing.

"Thank you, but we just got started."

Bob flashed a freckled grin. "Maybe we will see you on the way back." She bounced.

As we made our way back to the pavement, Bob observed, "He was very nice. I bet he has a whole bunch of grandchildren."

I winced. Mr. Granville's wife died very young, and he had never remarried. "He should have, but he doesn't. He lives alone since his wife died many years ago."

Bob looked stricken. "Well, I will have to go and visit him sometimes. He could pretend that I am his grandchild, right?" We continued down the street, but before we got much further, Bob turned and waved goodbye to Mr. Granville, who returned it with a salute. Bob nodded to herself, as if making a pledge.

We walked past Mr. Havens, who also offered lemonade, the Reeders, who welcomed Bob to the neighborhood and told us that the Starks had a new Pit Bull named Triscuit, who might not like cats. We hobnobbed briefly with the Teeters, the Stricklands, and the Prices. Simpson seemed to be getting bored and tried to turn for home.

But then we drew even with the small, immaculate brick bungalow that had featured a "SOLD" sign just a couple of weeks ago. Jumping rope in the driveway was a brown, plump little girl in bright pink sneakers, orange shorts, and a red-and-white polka-dot shirt. Her hair clattered with what looked like hundreds of multicolored beads and barrettes.

Bob gasped. "She's beautiful! Like a rainbow!"

The girl dropped her rope at the sight of us and hurtled down the driveway towards us, flapping her arms in excitement. "Oh, hi! What a cute cat! I have never seen one on a leash! Can I pet her? Do you live on this street? I just moved here. I don't have any friends yet. My name is Hallie Davis. My dad is going to be the new football coach at Framington High next year. My mom is a housewife."

She took a breath, knelt down, and stroked Simpy, then stood and clapped her hands. "Do you want to play? I have a swing set in the backyard and everything! My dad went to Home Depot and built it just for me and my friends. When I get some."

Bob looked to me for approval. I nodded. We walked into the Davis's backyard, where the grass was manicured within an inch, the swing set looked very inviting, and the flowerbeds were thick with mulch. I sat on the back steps and watched as Bob and Hallie frolicked.

Hallie seemed like a kind child. That was apparent from the first, when she offered Bob the best of the two swings "This one is too low; your feet will drag. I'm used to it—you can use the high one." She also was quick to laugh. She told Bob a series of knock-knock jokes that were hilarious to both of them, and they swung and giggled, their legs pumping and their heads dipping backwards and forwards as they gained momentum. It occurred to me that maybe I ought to introduce myself to Hallie's mom, since we were making ourselves at home in her backyard. I stood and knocked on the screen door. I heard footsteps, and Mrs. Davis came into the immaculate kitchen towards me, smiling.

"Hello. I am Beck Throckmorton. We met the other day at Starbucks. I am so sorry to have barged into your yard like this. I live down the street, and that is Bob Bowers, my little friend. We met your daughter a little while ago, and they came back here to play. Oh, and this here is my cat, Simpson." Simpy sat calmly at the end of his leash, gazing into the shrubbery.

I stepped back, so that Mrs. Davis could come outside. This was a very stately woman. She was taller than I, nearly six feet, I reckoned. Her soft hair floated around her face in a mahogany cloud. Her skin was like a mocha latte. She glanced over at the girls and smiled, motioning for me to sit at the picnic table along with her. "Of course! I remember! My name is Marva. So nice to see you again. We have only been here for a few weeks, so it is so nice for Hallie to meet . . ." there was a pause. "Bob, did you say?"

"Her name is Roberta, but she prefers Bob."

Marva raised her eyebrows. I guessed that a bit more of an explanation of Bob and me was in order. "Bob is living across the street from me with her great-grandmother, Ella Bowers. Her father is deployed in the Middle East. Bob and I are new friends, too."

The girls were now swinging and holding hands. It looked as if they had been buddies forever.

Marva smiled. "Well, then. We are all new friends!" She called out to the girls, "I bet you're thirsty! Would you all like to come inside for some Coke?" They shrieked with enthusiasm.

"Oh, I just LOVE Coke!" Hallie said to Bob. "And Mama won't let me have it except on special occasions!"

This was the start of a beautiful relationship, I thought. And I almost never had Coke, either. Nothing is better than a new friend and an ice-cold cola. I watched as Bob took a small sip of the Coke without letting on that she hated bubbles. Wow. And even Simpson approved, because Marva Davis offered him a bite of string cheese.

CHAPTER SIX

Pizza night. The gloaming in northern Ohio. The sounds of the neighborhood settling down: garage doors humming closed, screen doors slamming, the final thumps of basketballs in driveways. Gail and I sat on my front stoop, a double cheese pizza between us, along with plastic cups and a bottle of wine.

Gail and I had each devoured three large slices—calories be damned. I was on my second cup of merlot. Gail poured herself a third. Gail had listened patiently to my tale of woe concerning Diana—tutted and nodded in all the right places—reminded me of all of the reasons I needed to wake up and smell the coffee, let bygones be bygones. But when I sighed and launched into the story of Bob and Ella, Gail began to twitch with boredom. She sighed loudly three times, and when I failed to pay attention, she raised her hand as if in class.

"May I interrupt, please? Enough info about you and all of your issues—Beck. I get it. You still resent your sister and Bryan. Tough beans. A little girl with emotional baggage has sort of fallen into your lap. Ironic. I can't wait to see how that turns out. HOWEVER"—Gail waved her hands dismissively—"we need to change the focus here. Let's talk about *us*. I need a man, and so do you."

Although I like cutting to the chase, in this instance, Gail was pushing things. She needed the man, not me. I leaned back against the steps, the concrete digging into my elbows. "Gail. I am not interested in another one of your 'friend of a friends.' These guys you hook us up with are never my type. Or they are other women's cast-offs, or simply losers. Relationships and I don't go together, apparently. I do fine on my own with my writing. And I have a vibrator, for God's sake."

Gail rolled her eyes. She ran a manicured hand through her artfully streaked spikes. "Beck. Everybody needs to have a partner. A companion. You have been in total denial since you walked out on Bryan. How much longer do you think you will be able to fool yourself into thinking that a cute apartment and a cat will do keep you happy for the rest of your life?" She picked a cat hair off my shoulder. "God. This place has 'spinster' written all over it."

Usually I use a tape roller before Gail comes over. But this afternoon was a bit fraught—no time. "Gail. Spinsters are women who have never had sex, been married, or lived with a man. I am most certainly not THAT."

"Hair splitting. You write erotica, for God's sake. Any therapist would tell you that your writing is a substitution for real life. If you had an actual man, you might be writing the next great American novel right now, instead of *The Wicked Warlord*, or whatever you are calling this one."

I winced. "There may be a modicum of truth in what you're saying. But let me also remind you of Art Viscup."

"Art Viscup was not all that bad. So he had a few pocks on his face, and he played Frisbee Golf. There are worse things."

I nearly choked on my wine. "Right. Worse things. Like that guy named Winthrop? The house flipper wannabe? Even you, Miss eHarmony, saw the futility of that one. And of online dating. We are getting to an age in which all the good men are already taken. The ones that remain are the leftovers. And I despise leftovers."

A sigh from Gail. We have this conversation, or variables of it, nearly every week. She never gives up. "Beck. Just let me tell you about Theo and Rick."

My God.

"Theo Blackburn is the new manager of Framington Title. I met him at a closing a month ago, and we have since worked on three others. He is, I would say, about forty, and yes, divorced."

I clenched every single muscle in my body.

"But wait, Beck! His wife left him for her chiropractor. He is a really nice person. Very sincere. He never got over his divorce."

"And so you think I would see this as a plus?"

"Hear me out. Anyway, Theo is good looking in an average kind of way. Not slick, but you know what I mean. Brown hair and eyes. Sincere smile. Honest. People trust him. All of my clients have raved about him."

"And who is Rick? His twin brother?"

Gail rolled her eyes. "Honestly, Beck, you get more jaded by the minute. No. Rick Ramsey is on Theo's softball team."

"Are we in a sitcom? How on earth did you meet somebody on somebody you sit with in the occasional conference room's *softball team*?"

At this point, Gail was getting frustrated. I knew this, because when she's frustrated, she bites at the gel on her nails. Her thumbnail was nearly gel-free. "Beck, for your information, I have extracurricular activities that you know about but seem to ignore. You know that I joined the Framington Business District Softball Tournament in the spring. I asked if you wanted to do it, but you just laughed."

I dimly remembered scoffing.

"And that is where Rick and I became friends. And Theo is on Rick's team. So we have had beers together a few times after practices. And despite your lack of interest in anything other than your cat and your porno, I have spoken highly of you to them. Well, to Theo, because Rick and I kind of have a thing."

"First of all, it isn't porno, and you know it. Women's erotic fiction is not porno."

"Splitting hairs, but go on."

I took another gulp of merlot for fortification. "I am not dead set on living alone for the rest of my life. Good God. And leave my cat out of this! Simpson is a pet. Just about everybody but you has pets. But I am still getting over the massive dumping that Bryan and Diana did all over me, thank you very much."

Gail sneered. "That was years ago. And as I recall, you walked out on Bryan first. How much time do you need? A decade?"

Point taken. "Gail, what do you want me to do? I am sick and tired of blind dates. It would be nice to have a great and delicious man in my life. But meeting him in an orchestrated fashion has NOT worked. One final flashback: remember Del Hicks?"

Gail stifled a snort.

"Yeah, Gail. How could anybody named DEL HICKS be cool in any way, shape, or form?" I reached over and pinched her upper arm. "Let me take you back to that wonderful evening at Bill's Taproom. Yes, it was August, the height of allergy season. We sat around the high-top, sipping our brews. You were asking Del about his job as a meteorologist. He described it in *great* detail, as you recall. But right in the middle of his explanation of isobars, he *sneezed*. Is this coming back to you, Gail?"

Gail rolled her eyes and flapped a hand at me. "Get this over with."

"Yes, Gail. Del Hicks SNEEZED. And copious amounts of what I will politely call *mucus* spewed out of his nose, cascading down his face and onto his shirtfront. Remember this, kiddo?"

Gail brought her lips together tightly but said nothing.

"Yes. Poor Del. A victim of the pollen count. But the worst part, as you know, is that Del picked up his napkin and WIPED HIS FACE."

Gail burst out laughing. Tears came to her eyes.

"Right? He mopped his face. He didn't realize that there was SNOT all over his shirt. And I nearly vomited. And you suddenly announced that you had to go to the ladies' room and YOU ABANDONED US."

I leaned forward and put my head between my knees.

Gail, who hates to be reminded of past failures, moved on. "That was then and this is now. I learned from that. Theo is nothing like Del Hicks. I give you my word." Gail rubbed my back soothingly, but giggled again.

I sat up and shot her a look. "I am just fine with the way things are."

Gail stopped laughing. She wrinkled her nose. "You are completely out of touch with reality. Completely. So I am going to override your stupidity and arrange drinks for us with Theo and Rick. Period and end of story."

Did I really want to stick with the status quo? I tried to imagine myself at Ella's age, clumping through my apartment on my walker, trying to sort through my murky gray matter to remember why I needed to come into the living room. I pictured the hairs growing out of my chin, my sagging breasts, and orthopedic shoes. No family—all dead. Alone, except for a parrot that would probably outlive me.

I nodded weakly. "Okay. I will give you and this Theo guy one final chance."

I have never been very good at standing up to the tsunami that is Gail on a mating mission. I wondered if I needed to buy some new black pants and perhaps shop for Spanx.

That night, sitting on my sofa in my underwear, the fan blowing directly in my face, my hair puffing gently against my neck, I shut my eyes. A boyfriend. I tried to picture Theo. But all I could see were the pale, watery eyes, the flushed cheeks, and the greenish slime remaining on Del Hicks' beige sweater after he wiped his face.

▷◁

The blind date. Gail had set up this meeting at Hugo's, a trendy eatery that was newly open. But just for Saturday lunch—Gail's version of "failsafe."

Hugo's was the newest restaurant in Framington. Just a dozen or so tables, mismatched chairs at each, set with candles and fresh flowers. I am not sure if there is actually a Hugo—I heard that the owner named it after a dog in a poem.

The small, hip place looked very New York. The walls were bright yellow, dotted with abstracts. It smelled faintly of rosemary. I walked in and immediately spotted Gail with two guys. I knew that the one wearing Chuck Taylors, tattered cargo shorts, a red tank top, and a man-bun had to be Rick. Steamingly attractive. The one in penny loafers with socks had to be Theo. Natch.

It was too late to turn back. They had already spotted me. Gail waved coyly. I wandered over reluctantly, an insincere smile pasted onto my face.

They all stood. This was getting worse. Gail began the sales pitch.

"Beck, I'd like you to meet my friend Rick Ramsey. (She indicated hottie man-bun, of course). And this is Rick's friend, Theo Blackburn.

Theo stretched out his hand, and we shook. I have to admit, it was a quietly firm and manly shake. But it lasted just a couple of beats too long, and I was forced to retract my hand. Awkward. I think Theo must have felt it, too, because he knocked his chair over as he scrambled to sit down. The four of us nearly bumped heads as we all attempted to right the chair, reassemble, and finally sit. Ugh.

I tried; I really did. "Gail tells me you two met playing baseball?"

Theo cleared his throat. He looked very earnest. "Well, no, actually, Gail and I met via work. I manage the title company where she does a lot of real estate closings. Rick and I play softball together." His eyes were cocoa brown and they did sparkle a little. And when he smiled, I took note of the fact that he probably knew about Crest Whitening Strips.

"Oh, yes, I knew that." Brilliant comeback.

Gail pointed to the menus. "Shouldn't we order something? I absolutely adore the egg salad here. And the roast beef sandwiches on pretzel rolls are great!" Gail was really pushing; her voice was an octave higher than normal—a telltale sign of anxiety. She often squeaks when things get really uncomfortable. I felt a squeak coming on.

"Theo, Gail is right. The roast beef is delicious. But they are huge—would you like to split one?" A feminine ploy. I could eat two of them without taking a deep breath, but I was on my best behavior—for Gail's sake.

He smiled. Again with the white teeth. And with the smile were dimples. "That sounds just about right. Would you like a beer with that? Oh, can we get beers here?"

So he wasn't a wuss. He liked beer at lunch. Not as bad as I thought. Rick and Gail also split a roast beef, and we all had beer. Well, beers. Actually, we all had a few. Gail told her best dirty joke, the one I always laugh at about the guy who has pockets full of condoms, and we all had tears streaming down our cheeks. It turns out that Rick was as smart as he was good looking, and Theo could match Gail's condom joke with one that was even funnier about a short man at a circus. Before we knew it, it was three o'clock, and the manager kicked us out to get ready for the dinner crowd. Not a bad afternoon.

Gail and Rick mounted his Harley for an afternoon cruise, and that left me and Theo standing on the pavement, soaking in the heat. My armpits trickled. Using the take-out menu I took from the restaurant as a fan, I tried to air out my midsection without looking too ridiculous. I failed.

Theo, as crisp and dry as I was soggy, asked "Would you like to sit over there on the bench where it's shady?" He had taken note of my moisture.

Before we sat down, he brushed some stray twigs and what looked like fresh bird poop off the bench with his handkerchief. Note: handkerchief. Not Kleenex. I wasn't sure about this—the only men I knew who used handkerchiefs were over eighty. But it was a very thoughtful thing to do, as the bird poop was fresh, and it defiled his handkerchief. But Theo popped it back into his back pocket without hesitation. I was impressed with that, to be sure.

"So you write books. Gail says you're really talented."

Shit. I wondered just how much of my talented subject matter Gail had shared. I fanned a bit faster. The menu wilted. "Yes. I write for women." *Let's just leave it at that, please . . .*

"Women's fiction? Wow. Would I have heard of any of your titles? Or maybe my mom has read some of your books?"

Shit. I had a choice. I could lie, and then get muddled up in that same lie later, as always happens, or I could go for broke and just hit him right between his innocent Midwest eyes with the truth. I hesitated, licked my dry lips, and went for broke:

"Actually, Theo, I make my living writing erotica. That, and selling coffee at Starbucks. But I bet you know which one of those occupations pays most of the bills."

There was a pause, in which Theo's baby browns bulged slightly and he caught his breath. But then his eyelids relaxed, and he took a breath. "Wow."

I waited for something more. But Theo just smiled fixedly and crossed and recrossed his legs. His yellow linen Bermudas rode up his thighs a bit. He had firm thighs. I wanted to stroke them, almost.

"Yes. Well. The reason I write what I write is that it is lucrative. These days, there are about a million books written every month. The competition in the publishing world is cutthroat. It's very hard to sell fiction. I'm a good writer, but after having my novel rejected a hundred or so times, I realized that I will probably never be a Nora Roberts. So I began writing erotica. And it sold. It keeps selling. There is a growing market out there for it. So this is what I do. For now. I still want to rewrite my novel and get it out there. But in the meantime, this pays the bills."

The menu by this time was worthless. I crumpled it up and set it next to me on the bench. Theo recrossed his legs yet again. I felt a huge impulse to split and run.

"I get it." He grinned, dimples blaring. "I bet they are just like that *Forty Shades of Grays* book. It's a movie now and everything."

Okay. This Theo guy might just be a prince in Bermuda shorts and an alligator polo. I grinned back and settled into the bench. Just then, a cool breeze ruffled his mouse-brown hair. It was thinning, but not in an unpleasant fashion.

▷◁

When I got home, I told Simpson all about it. We sat on my bed, with the Lumineers on iTunes for atmosphere, and I described Theo to Simpy. "Actually, he's fine. He has those sort of good looks that nobody really notices, if you know what I mean." Simpy blinked. "Like Jesse Eisenberg. Unprepossessing."

I petted Simpson against the grain, which Mom always told me was a complete sin against all felines, but then again, Claire Throckmorton is not an animal person. Simpy absolutely adores it. He leaned into my hand and purred like a locomotive.

I continued, waving cat fur out of my face. "He is very polite. Pulled out my chair. Opened the car door. Bryan never did that." Simpy seemed bored. He laid his chin down flat on the duvet. "You, see, that is

EXACTLY what I am talking about! There isn't a whole lot to say about this man. No undercurrent of excitement. No frisson of slightly dangerous sex. I can't imagine him with handcuffs, for example." I threw myself down on the pillows and stared up at the cracks in the ceiling. "I know, honey." I gently ran my hand down the cat's tail. "Safe men are good men. Nobody marries an outlaw. Too dicey. No. People marry the nice guys, and then they have a nice, safe life."

I shut my eyes and pictured myself safely married. *Wearing sweatpants and a loose fitting, left-over-from-pregnancy maternity top, I wearily push a shopping cart down the Kroger cereal aisle. The four-year-old, let's call her Lizzy, reaches out her grubby little hand to grab the Alphabits. I wrest the box out of her hand, setting off a litany of whines. Dragging his feet behind me, alternately calling, "Mom, Mom, Mom, Mom, Mom, Mom!" or "Tell Lizzy to shut up! She's hurting my ears!" is my seven-year-old son, Theo Junior. His nose is running, and he stabs at his sister through the bars of the cart with his* Star Wars *light saber. I ignore them as I try to decide if macaroni and cheese from a box is an acceptable side dish for leftover meatloaf.*

As we check out, the harried woman at the scanner, purple circles under her eyes and a ballpoint pen behind each ear, smiles wanly at my kids as they continue to grizzle at one another. Theo Junior tries to snatch one of the free lollipops out of the plastic container next to the conveyor belt, sending it crashing to the linoleum, multicolored suckers flying all over. Blushing with humiliation at my feral children, I bend to gather up the candy, apologizing profusely to the floor. The checker reassures me. "Hon, those damn things get spilled about forty times a day. Don't know why the hell—pardon my French—we have to give those things to kids. Rots their teeth."

I straighten up and grin at her. "They have been acting up all day. I had to haul off and smack Theo over the head with a pack of Twizzlers a few minutes ago. You know how it is."

She nods. "It's all just snot and fury until they grow up."

Simpson rose, stretching. He sat and began to wash his face. "Simp. Snot and fury. What do you think about that?"

He jumped down off the bed. I shut my eyes. That image of myself as an old lady, stumping around in my apartment with my walker and a parrot floated back into mind. Me, chatting dementedly to a bird. No family. No friends. A loose housedress, tatty house slippers and the distinct odor of urine and mothballs in the air. I rubbed my throbbing temples. *Okay. safe it is.*

CHAPTER SEVEN

Sleeping in is such a luxury. I had gotten up at eight, stumbled over to close the blinds against the glare of the sun, and I was just dozing off again when my doorbell rang. Damn. Simpy jumped down and headed into the kitchen. I swiped my fingers through my tangled hair, realizing the futility, and hobbled over to the door. I looked through the eyehole to see a pair of sparkly barrettes, freckles, and a huge grin. Bob, the Saturday sprite.

I swung the door open to the full glory of Bob wearing an electric-blue tee shirt, melon orange and shamrock green plaid shorts, pink socks, and red sneakers. She was holding a notebook. "Gran said that I could come over and show you my cat pictures. I'm doing a portrait of Simpson."

I stepped aside and motioned her in. "I'm glad you came over. You are just the ray of sunshine I need right now. I slept in." (Obviously—she picked up on that one immediately.) "Would you like something to eat? Simpy and I need breakfast."

Bob hopped in on one foot, holding her notebook high in the air. I shut the door behind her, wishing I still had even a trace of her energy and optimism.

"Yes. I would love a Popsicle for breakfast dessert. But you should have something nutritious. Like oats. Gran says breakfast is the most important meal of the day, and she makes me eat oats, even though I told her they taste like glue. But she puts raisins in now, and that helps some."

"I have to agree about the oats. Mostly I just have coffee for breakfast. With milk, for protein."

I opened the cat food cupboard, and Simpy wound around my legs, purring extra loudly. He adored his cat kibble. I poured some into his bowl, and he began crunching in earnest. Cat crunching can make even kibble sound delish.

Bob slid into one of the two chairs at my little café table. Setting her notebook carefully down on the glass top, she drummed her fingernails, swinging her legs underneath her like pistons. We listened to the coffee as it dripped through the filter into the carafe. "I love your house. It is so much more cozy than Gran's. You have old-fashioned stuff in here, but it doesn't look old-fashioned. I like your stove and the black-and-white checkers on the floor. Gran's house isn't cozy, even though she has cozy-type things. But her house is always dark. And it is so hot; Gran is cold all the time. She says air conditioning gives her arthritis. So it is hot and dark and kind of smells like mushrooms. But it is safe there."

I tried not to react to Bob's insecurity. I poured myself a mug of coffee, added milk, and sat down opposite Bob. She beamed back at me. "Well, I think as people get older, they lose some of their ability to regulate their body temperature. So they get cold." I sounded like an infomercial—my God.

"Gran is nice, though. But she says that she is out of practice raising children. She says that she is running low on patience at times, like when I make a racket." Bob sighed and looked longingly at my freezer door.

"Oh, kiddo—I forgot!" I set my mug down, pushed off the table like the crone I felt I was, and opened the freezer door. "Oh, gosh. I need to put Popsicles on the list. All I have is one orange pop left."

Bob nodded enthusiastically, and I gave her the pop and sat back down, stifling a groan.

"Beck, what is the matter? Are you sick? Do you have a 'sick headache?' Gran gets those."

"No. I know. I look sick. I was up very late last night, writing. I have a deadline. But that's not important. Why don't you show me what you drew?"

Slurping, Bob opened her notebook. The first drawing was of a tiny gray-and-black blotch behind a lot of black vertical lines. "That's Simpson in the shelter, sad and lonely and scared. Somebody just dropped him off there. He doesn't have a mother."

I nodded gravely.

Bob wiped a sticky finger on her tee shirt and turned the page. Now the blotch was bigger, and had stripes. He was sitting on what looked like a brownie, "Your sofa cushion," she explained, and he had very long whiskers sticking out from both sides. His front legs looked like Q-tips. He smiled.

Bob turned to another picture, this one of a tall woman with brown hair, which was overlaid with black shading. The woman resembled me, which was remarkable. Bob was a talented artist in the making. The woman had an expansive red grin, and in her arms was what looked like a tiger-striped marshmallow with pointy ears. Simpson exactly. Blue squiggly lines radiated from both sides of the woman and cat. I pointed to them.

"Happiness. The cat is purring, and your heart is popping like popcorn with love."

She stopped, wiped the orange drippings from her chin, and looked up at me.

"That is very interesting. How did you know about the animal shelter? I actually *did* get Simpson at one."

"I guess I just *figured* that you got Simpy at a shelter. My dad and I used to go to the shelter, back in Iowa, before he was redeployed. He told me that he wanted us to have a pet. But just as we were deciding, he got his notice. I cried when I found out. But he said that I shouldn't worry, because when he comes back this time, he will be finished going overseas, and we will definitely get a cat.

This kid and her hard knocks. My God. "Bob, this is something to look forward to! But can I ask you about the *popcorn* thing?"

Bob grinned. "My dad said that the first time he saw me, when the nurse at the hospital put me in his arms, he took one look at my little face, and his heart popped like popcorn with love. He said that when your heart does that, it means you will love that person forever."

Of course.

"And I am glad my pictures are the real truth, because I love Simpson, and he deserved to get out of that shelter."

Naturally. I watched as Simpy wandered over and rubbed against Bob's scuffed little legs. He purred as she reached down to stroke his head. As she whispered something that sounded like *goody boy good* into his ear, I felt quite buoyant all of a sudden.

And I was so relieved that my house had no mushroom odor.

▷◁

Second date with Theo. We went to see a foreign film with subtitles at the Framington Art Cinema. Old, Victorian theatre that used to host vaudeville. Restored in the early 70s, but now once again musty and dank, with sticky floors and stale popcorn.

Theo chose seats in the exact middle of the theater. We settled down and watched previews of some film festival's short subjects. Then a preview of a movie about drug deals gone wrong.

I munched my popcorn, but kept getting whiffs of lime. Candy? Air freshener? No—of course: Theo's aftershave.

The film that had something to do with Nazis and Jews living in the woods, foraging. Of course, the ending was tragic. Theo at one point tried to hold my hand, but I pulled away. No public displays of affection are appropriate watching people being brutalized, in my opinion.

Afterwards, we strolled up Main Street towards the Icee Crunch, where I adored the "Perfectly Peach" ice cream cones. Theo took my hand again. I have to say that I am not a big fan of handholding. It reminds me of preschool and street crossing. I never feel like an adult doing this. However, to pull my hand away once again might seem rude, so I did nothing. Theo's hand was warm but moist. I tried to ignore that. I focused on his smooth hair and flawless complexion.

He looked over at me, just as I stumbled on an uneven strip of pavement and stubbed my toe, nearly face-planting right there. It was his moist grip that saved me. Chagrin. I scrambled to regain my balance, and blushed with the embarrassment of it all.

Diversion: "Theo, what did you think of the movie? I found it utterly depressing and gratuitous."

He took it as a challenge, I guess. Stopping and abruptly releasing my hand, he retorted, "Gratuitous? World War Two was *gratuitous?*" He looked incredulous. As incredulous as a mild-mannered banker with perfectly cut hair and dimples could look.

"Let's get our ice cream, and then we can sit down and talk about the film." This might prove to be our first in-depth discussion. He ordered a vanilla cone—one scoop, cake cone. Telling. I ordered two scoops of peach on a chocolate-coated waffle cone. The only choice for people with passion. Vanilla???

We sat at a little table by the window, where we could see folks wandering by, enjoying the Midwestern summer evening, chattering and chuckling. They all looked so incredibly white bread. I bet none of them had read any of my books.

"So how do you think the film was gratuitous? The Holocaust?" Theo looked riled. His brow furrowed and he ignored his cone.

"Well, I just think that the filmmakers replayed the same old tune. We all know the Nazis were butchers. We all know the horrors. This film just rehashed them. I would expect this from American movies, but a foreign film? They are usually so much more nuanced."

The vanilla was melting down the cone and onto Theo's hand. He ignored it. This made me want to hand him a napkin. I restrained myself.

"You know that there are some people who say that the Holocaust never happened? This film serves as a reminder to those people!" In his passion, he shook his cone, and the scoop of vanilla nearly fell off. He righted it just in time and took a few discreet licks.

"I get that. But do you think that people who don't believe that there was a mass extermination of the Jews would really go see this movie? I don't think Holocaust deniers would seek out foreign films about World War Two and the Nazis, do you?" I demolished the last three bites of my cone. Theo's was still nearly pristine.

Theo, apparently overcome, pulled a napkin out of the dispenser, set his cone down on it, and proceeded to give me a lecture involving Hitler, Americans with short memories, the entire history of the Nazi incursion across Europe, and the need for us to REMEMBER. I watched with fascination as his ice cream dissolved and saturated the napkin, forming a viscous puddle in the center of the table. Theo rambled on. I felt the way I always did in World History class in high school. Bored.

The ride home in the car was uncomfortably silent.

I called Gail as soon as I got home.

"My God. Theo is nice enough. But could he be more diligent and accountable? A more decent guy? Any more well groomed or fragrant? Gail, he is really nice. But I have to admit that there isn't any chemistry. Shouldn't there be chemistry? Why isn't there any *chemistry?*"

Gail, who bestows the benefit of the doubt around like manna, was indignant. "This was your second date. YOUR SECOND. Do not write this man off so quickly! And Beck—the sort of chemistry you are talking about only happens in the kind of books you write. Come ON! These things take time."

"He has a fine and detailed knowledge of history. At least of World War Two. Gail, it was a lecture! Took me right back to the back row in Mr. Miner's history class! My God!"

"Beck, you are impossible. This is a really good man. You have to give him a chance! You are critical of things that any other woman would find completely admirable. He is good looking, well educated, loves foreign films and history, and he smells good. What on earth is wrong with you? Plus, you haven't even slept with him yet. He may be dynamite. You of all people should be willing to wait for this. Chemistry—shemistry! You call yourself an erotica expert?"

She made good sense. I rolled my eyes and remembered the parrot.

"Gail, you win. You are right. I will give him another chance. That is, if he is even remotely interested in me after this evening. And I will bet you a million dollars that his sexpertise is lacking. Speaking of that, what about the *Man-Bun*? I feel sure that he has a light touch, if you catch my drift."

Snorting at the other end. "Honey, your drift is right on. However, as you know, I don't discuss my sex life with you, because I don't want to end up in one of your books. And his name is Rick. As you *know*. And he only wears a man-bun when he is working out."

A pause to let that sink in. "Gail. Sex. Working *out*."

We both snorted.

But after I ended the call, I felt a surge of envy. I grabbed Simpson, buried my nose in his neck and inhaled. He smelled a little spicy. "Oh, Simpy, if you were a man, I would marry you." We padded back to the bedroom. The lights from across the street made shadowy patterns on the walls. The curtains puffed in the breeze. I pulled down the covers and placed my kitty on the top of my pillow, where he loves to sleep. The sheets were cool and crisp. I love newly laundered sheets, especially in the summer. I fell asleep with a tabby vibrating on my head and a tiny thrust of hope in my heart.

I dreamed I was leaning over a crib, winding up a Muppet mobile. I woke up in a cold sweat. Shit.

CHAPTER EIGHT

My writing lately lacked oomph. Maybe Gail was right. An infusion of a new sexual partner might be called for. But Theo? Could I really develop a sexual relationship with Theo? I contemplated how to even get Theo going. Would it be tricky? A see-through blouse? Oysters for lunch with champagne? New perfume? Ugh. So much work. For such an iffy payoff.

It was a Sunday evening, and I had been pounding away at my latest, *Bad Boys on the Beach*, (for the summer reading crowd—I seem to have to write seasonally; my books come out about a year after I write them, so it works out), and no matter what I did, it had begun to sound mediocre. I might as well change the title to *Mindy Does Malibu*, for God's sake.

I tried to work the Theo dilemma into my chapter. The main character's friend, Mindy, would use all sorts of inventive foreplay to get her dud of a boyfriend, Brad, to heat up. Delete. I tried again, this time having Mindy do a strip tease while Brad watched from the bed. Better. But getting Brad from his office at the accounting practice and into Mindy's bed proved problematic. Delete. I tried the oysters. Didn't work. I shut down my computer and went to bed, frustrated. Kind of like Mindy and Brad. I pictured myself churning the sheets with Theo. The picture was pleasant, but murky. I tossed and turned, trying desperately to picture the two of us engaged in steamy foreplay. I began to drift off before Theo even got my bra unfastened.

I slept for about an hour, but then a horn honked right outside my window, jolting me awake. I sat up in bed, eyes grainy with sleep, my tee shirt riding up, my stomach suddenly clammy. I adjusted my clothing, lay back down, and shut my eyes, but sleep eluded me. I started another internal conversation instead.

What is WRONG with you? A perfectly adorable man presents himself in your life, and all you can do is find fault?

I know. I know. Theo is what every other woman on earth dreams of. So I am obviously defective.

You don't think you deserve happiness. And you dwell on the fact that most marriages end in divorce. Relationships tend not to work out. You hate to feel vulnerable. So you stay alone to preclude being hurt.

By this time, my armpits were slimy, my hair was what the romance novelists call lanky, and my fingertips tingled. I got up, turned on the light, and shuffled to the kitchen. I grabbed a glass out of the cupboard and filled it with water, which I chugged. Rehydrating seems to be the first line of defense when things go south. I stood looking out the window, waiting for my body to get normal again. The moon shone on a green sedan as it drove by, making it look like absinthe. Good line for a book. I made a mental note.

Returning to my room, I surveyed the books in the bookcase beside my desk. All my well-worn childhood favorites lined up on the top shelf: *Little Women, Anne of Green Gables, The Five Little Peppers and How They Grew.* All books in which hapless children were raised with love, and all conflict was overridden with patience, all problems resolved with spiritual resonance. I thought of Anne overcoming the stereotypes of "orphans" that surrounded her and piercing the ironclad heart of the stoic Marilla. I thought about Marmee's devotion to her dear husband, ministering to the Union Army on the front. People who were saved by the good and true love of others. Family. I put my head in my palms. I dug my fingernails into my forehead. The pain felt good.

When I got back into bed, Simpy purred without stirring.

▷◁

I went to work the next morning, still thinking about this dilemma. Joe, the faithful back-up barista, greeted me as soon as I put on my apron. "We are all out of blueberry muffins, and five people have called me names already this morning. And the cinnamon container spilled behind the counter, and did you know that in large concentrations, it is actually highly spicy? And it BURNS your eyes when you try to clean it up? Shitty start of what will most likely be a shitty day!"

Joe is a little weak. Nervous. Nerdy. But a nice guy. He used to have dandruff, but I gave him the T-Gel suggestion and that seemed to have solved that. I watched him fuss around up front; swabbing the work area, with his dark bangs dangling in front of his watery eyes, owly spectacles and pale face like an empty paper plate. He twitched with annoyance.

"Joe. I will finish up. Take a break to calm down."

He smiled, pushed up his glasses by putting a finger directly on the left lens, turned, and went into the break room. Sweet guy—easy to work with. I bet *he* never taunted his siblings.

I began to wash the few mugs and plates. Not enough to put in the dishwasher. I added a capful of bleach to the water to meet health department requirements. I threw in some spoons and the milk frother. Just as I was getting into the Zen of cleaning, I had a customer.

"I would like a mocha latte, sugarless syrup please, but with whole milk and whipped cream."

"Oh, hi, Mom. What brings you here so early? More family news?"

Claire, wearing her latest Net-a-Porter.com ensemble, ran a red gel fingernail through her thick, stylish waves. I have always wanted her hair, dammit. She set her Burberry bag on the counter and leaned in. "Honey. Can't you take just a small break and have a coffee with me? We need to talk. And since you never answer my texts, I had to come all the way down here." (Mom lives about five minutes away from here, tops.)

Poor Joe. I yanked him back up front, told him it was all up to him for the next half hour, unless we suddenly got a logjam of caffeine junkies in here. I poured myself a venti latte and joined her, where she was elegantly draped around a seat at a corner table. I plunked down. I lack her grace, obviously.

"I see you have *your* coffee. Did you forget about my mocha latte?"

I sighed, dragged myself back to Joe, and supervised Claire's drink. I didn't tell Joe about the sugarless part. Spite. I carried it back to her with a napkin. I knew enough to tell Joe she needed it in a mug.

We sipped. Not exactly companionably. Mom seemed tense. I burned my tongue on my first sip. Awkward.

"Mom. What would you like to talk about? War? Health care crisis? Gay marriage?"

Claire raised a silver eyebrow and gave me the stink-eye. "I am here to remind you that Diana and Bryan are coming Friday. The Mother's Day weekend brunch. You know."

I shifted in my seat, crossing and uncrossing my legs. A pain stabbed me behind my left eye. I dropped my spoon, and it dinked into my mug, displacing some of the coffee onto my mother's hand. She recoiled. "Rebecca, do you have ADD for heaven's sake? Be still!"

"So you want me to calm down and be very still about the fact that D and Bryan are coming. This, you understand, means a forced face-to-face with these two. Is this what you just dropped into my workplace to 'share a coffee' with me and talk about? So what are your expectations, Mom?" I shot her a stink-eye right back. "Well, it's been lovely sharing this bonding time. But I have no plans to see either one of them."

Then my mother did a very characteristic maternal thing. She stood up, leaned over me, and enveloped me with her pipe stem arms in what I would have to classify as a hugging gesture. Being as slender as she is, a hug is more a matter of banging together elbows and collarbones than melding of bodies. But it had an immediate calming effect. My shoulders dropped about two inches, and the tightness in my chest eased. This is what happens when a mother hugs you. The mother-child bond just kicks right in.

I reciprocated in a self-conscious fashion by patting her three times on her shoulder and pulling away. There we were: me—negativity wrapping me like a shroud, all anger and angst; and Mom hovering over me, with her pashmina nearly knocking both mugs of coffee off the tiny table. It didn't last but for a couple of seconds before Mom smoothed my hair and sat back down.

"Truce, Rebecca. Truce. What can I do to convince you that we all need to get over this? I want a grandchild. A happy one. I want two happy daughters, not one happy one and one sour, bitter one. Let me put it more strongly. I *need* this to happen. Because, Rebecca, I have skin cancer, and it might be serious."

Wait. Before you react in any way. Because *skin cancer.* Claire Throckmorton did not say *breast cancer, pancreatic cancer, lung cancer, or brain cancer.* None of the actual huge, deadly, scary, and truly "family back to the fold" cancers. No. Because all of those cancers have to be very real and very provable. Skin cancer? Not so much. She will go to the dermatologist, have something removed from her face so we can all see it, and she will keep us all in suspense "waiting for the test results." Isn't this the way mothers work? When all else fails, haul out the guilt? And notice also that she did not say the word *melanoma.*

"Mom. What kind? Did the doctor say it was melanoma? My God! Will you have to have chemo after the surgery? When is the surgery scheduled?"

She took a long sip of her latte, wiped her lips with the napkin, gave me another, slightly less stinky eye, and cleared her throat. "Its basal cell. But it can still be dangerous—they told me it was locally invasive. So don't be so bitchy."

"Where is the spot?" I peered closely at her smooth, lovely face.

She pointed to a spot I could barely discern next to her left eyebrow.

"That's *it*? Looks pretty small to me. I'm sure it won't leave a scar."

"Of course not! I go to the best plastics man in Framington! None of this is the *point.* The point is, I am not getting younger, and I am starting to have health stuff happening. You two girls aren't getting any younger, either. All you have is each other, because Lord knows what all and where all your father is. He may be dying of a tropical disease or Ebola or something right now."

Sidebar: Dad was in Africa, we thought. He doesn't write. Mom gets an occasional missive from his attorney.

I was hit with a sudden wave of fatigue. My head still hurt from the eye-stabbing pain earlier (maybe *I* had cancer). I was beaten. Beaten down. "Okay, okay. What exactly do you have in mind?"

Claire Throckmorton had triumphed once again. Her hazel/blue/green/amber eyes (depending on the light and what she was wearing) flashed. She smiled, her whitened teeth gleaming. Her cheeks bloomed with the expensive blush that she wore, and there wasn't a noticeable pore anywhere. She straightened in her chair, clasped her hands, her gold cuff bracelets clinking, and pronounced, "Rebecca, I love you more than ever. You won't regret this, I just know it!"

And with that, she readjusted her summer-weight pashmina, stood up, slung her Burberry bag over her shoulder, handed me her mug, and turned to sweep dramatically out of the store. As she pushed through the door, nearly hitting a college student on his way in, she turned and left me with an "I'll text you the details!"

She left a waft of Chanel in her wake.

▷◁

Theo had arranged a picnic for the four of us. Gail and Rick were to bring wine and cheese. Theo was "doing everything else." I offered to make cookies, but he insisted that I just "show up and look beautiful."

So far, we had been out to dinner at Beth's Bistro one more time, and the four of us had met for cocktails after work at The Green Gate, a local bar. I had three vodka tonics and felt buzzy. Theo and Rick drank some sort of artisanal beer. Gail stuck with the standard glass of merlot. When Theo suggested the picnic, Rick put his arm around Gail and said, "We may need an extra blanket." Then he growled. Gail smoldered. I was uncomfortable. But I made a mental note to include growling in my next chapter of *Bad Boys on the Beach*. Then I looked at Theo, who didn't seem to notice the growling, because he was absorbed in brushing the spilled peanuts on the bar into the palm of his hand and placing them carefully in a cocktail napkin, wrapping them snugly in it and putting the whole thing into his empty beer glass. I had to restrain myself from ordering a fourth vodka and tonic. Normally, I don't have to do this. But nothing about double dating with Gail and Rick the Man-Bun was normal.

▷◁

The day of the picnic arrived, irritatingly perfect. It would be in the low eighties with partly cloudy skies and low humidity. I was sure that Theo could barely contain his excitement. I wondered what delicacies he was preparing. Once again, that inner voice kicked in with a vengeance: *What is wrong with me? Here is a perfectly pleasant man, with kind eyes and a totally coordinated wardrobe!* A banker. Or sort of—whatever people at title companies do. Good prospect. Probably exceeded Claire Throckmorton's code of standards. I gave myself a mental kick in the ass and decided to shower and do some extensive personal shaving. Just in case.

Bob just happened to stop by as I was contemplating whether the denim cutoffs or the gray linen drawstring pants were "lovely" enough. I held them out to her with raised eyebrows.

"Well?"

She bit her index fingernail, looking concerned. "Is that all you have? Don't you have a sundress or something? They have them at Target. Gran says that she might get me one before school starts."

"These aren't good?" I noticed a little rip in the seam of the gray pants. They *were* kind of old. I got them the summer before I met Bryan, when I needed something "suitable," in Mom's words, for a luncheon she was having for her garden club. I was bartending. So these were actually bartender's clothes. I got Bob's point.

"It's too late to go shopping." Bob disappeared into the back of my closet and rummaged. She reappeared holding a bright yellow cotton sundress that I had forgotten I had. I wore it when Bryan and I were together. I thought I had gotten rid of all of the clothes from that segment of my life. But somehow, this had survived. It had apparently been crumpled into a ball on the floor—it was covered with wrinkles, cat hair, and a small, desiccated patch of Simpy barf.

"This is pretty. There's time to wash it. It's wrinkly, but Gran says all you have to do is put it in the dryer and take it out the minute it's dry, and the wrinkles will be gone. She does that with all my tee shirts. I think you should put this in the washer right now. Do you have any yellow flip flops?"

"No. But I have brown ones. Those will do. But a dress? For a picnic? Isn't that a little over-the-top?"

Bob looked at me and sighed. Believe me, when a child who just turned eight sighs at you with disappointment in her eyes, you pay attention. "Okay, okay. I will wash this. And we can sit and wait for it to dry so we can snatch it out of the dryer. Maybe we can play a game in the meantime."

Bob followed me to the hall closet that contained my stackable washer/dryer. We put the dress in along with a couple of towels to make it a balanced load. As I was closing the lid, Bob suggested we add some fabric softener. Okay, then.

"What game do you want to play? I have Uno, I think." We sat down on the sofa, Bob tightly hugging one of the flowered throw pillows.

Bob shook her head. She heaved a loud sigh. "I am not really in a very good mood today." I thought she looked worried. Her nails were bitten down to the quick, despite the bright pink nail polish. Her freckles bunched on her forehead. "Today I am missing my dad a whole lot. He doesn't send as many emails or letters now. Gran says he is probably fighting hard." She crumpled the hem of her tee shirt with both hands.

"Gran says to say extra prayers and have faith . . ." Bob faltered. "I don't know how. He might die."

Tears formed in her dear, brown eyes. My heart. "Oh, Bob, honey!"

I gathered her into my arms and held on as she cried, smashing the pillow between us. Her breathing was jagged, and with every shudder, I held her tighter. I rested my head on the top of her dark curly one, and we both swayed until I felt Bob wind down. I stroked her wiry hair.

Finally, she snuffled, sat up, and wiped her nose with the back of her right wrist, still clutching the pillow with her left arm. "Gran says when you get worried or scared, the best thing to do is to keep busy."

"I agree." I let go of Bob, and she straightened her spine and ran the back of her hand across her nose again. She nodded with great dignity. With a juddering breath, she said, "Remember how you said you couldn't cook, so I should teach you how Gran makes grilled cheese sandwiches?"

"Great idea. I am totally in the mood for grilled cheese. And guess what? I bought Velveeta just the other day, with Bob Bowers in mind!"

Her little face brightened, and I wiped the tears off her cheeks with both hands, resisting the impulse to kiss her. Bob stood with dignity, smoothed down the creases in her tee shirt, and smiled. "Do you have real butter? 'Cause Gran says margarine is absolutely awful. And since you're with me, we can use a frying pan. When I make them at Gran's, I have to use the Foreman Grill. Gran thinks the stove is too dangerous for me. I've been using the stove *for years*, but it doesn't matter—Gran doesn't want me to get hurt."

I wondered about Bob cooking for herself. Once again, it felt like a shadow had briefly passed over us. "She's right. It's better to be safe than sorry." I opened the fridge. Butter, coming up! I read on Facebook that nowadays, it is healthy to have stuff like butter and whole milk again. So I switched from margarine back to butter. And I have tomato soup, too! Have you ever dunked grilled cheese soldiers into tomato soup? Divine."

Bob stopped in front of me, turning with a confused scowl. "Soldiers? Like my dad?"

I smiled. "You've never made toast soldiers? Well, then—you can teach me how to make the sandwiches, and I will show you how to cut them into soldiers!"

Bob opened the refrigerator and found the box of Velveeta. She held it out. "This is so good. But it is hard as anything to slice.

Gran has a special tool for it. It has a wire thing. I bet you don't." She tapped the box with her index finger.

"No, I don't. Can we just use a knife?" I rummaged around in the pantry cupboard, shoving cans of chicken noodle and beef barley aside, noting that the box of baking soda was probably way out of date. I found the tomato behind a can of cream of mushroom.

Bob pulled out the drawer with all my knives in it. "We will just have to use one, but it won't be easy."

Bob opened the box of Velveeta. "You haven't even had any of this! Me and Gran eat about a ton of Velveeta every week! We eat it on crackers and things, and sometimes Gran puts it on corn chips and melts it in the microwave and it makes nachos. How come you haven't eaten some of yours already?"

Bob struggled to open the foil wrap. I stopped her before she used her teeth. "Let me use the scissors—your gran would *not* like it if she saw you biting the wrapper!"

Bob giggled. I was relived that she seemed to have forgotten her father for the moment. I chipped off a corner of the brick of cheese and put it on her nose. "Okay, kiddo! What next?"

She picked the morsel off her nose and placed it carefully on her tongue. "You have to savor it." She rolled her lips around as if tasting wine.

"I know. This stuff is gourmet, right? The cheese the world awaited?"

"Yes!" Bob was too young to remember the wiener reference. "It is SUBLINE!"

"Yes, SUBLINE. How thin do we need the slices?" The knife kept getting stuck in the brick—I was producing wads, not slices. "This cheese is not cooperating! Bob, can we make the sandwiches with chunks of Velveeta, since I don't have that special tool? Ugh!" The cheese was sticking to the knife, my fingers, and the cutting board. "This stuff is sort of gluey. Are you sure that it is actually *subline*?"

Bob chortled. "Let's chop up the chunks small. It will work. We need a frying pan and bread. Do you have the good kind of bread, not whole wheat?" She looked around.

"Bob. Do I look like a person who would eat whole wheat bread? Of course I have the good kind." I opened the fridge and showed her the Pepperidge Farm family white. I took my large cast iron skillet out of the oven where I keep it. "But before we start the sandwiches, we need to start the soup. Do you like tomato made with water or milk?"

Bob was incredulous. She gasped. Her curls seemed to stand on end. "Does anybody make tomato soup with WATER?" She put a hand against her chest to steady herself. "Making it with water would just be like having *hot tomato juice.*"

With that, I died. We both nearly prostrated ourselves with laughter, and I grabbed Bob's bony shoulders and pretended to shake her. "I will have you know that I grew up having it the *hot tomato juice* way! It was just fine. However, I learned about making it with milk from a food blog, and it is a lot better that way." I put my finger on her nose. "But just so you know. The tomato juice version is totally acceptable."

"I will tell Gran that some people have it with water. She won't believe it!"

I opened the soup, dropped the glop of red stuff in a saucepan, added one can of milk, and turned it on to warm up.

Back to the task. I took out four slices of bread. I laid them on the counter next to the cheese and began piling the sorry chunks on two of the slices. That done, I opened the fridge and got out the butter dish. I cut a generous slice of it and plopped it into the frying pan and turned the burner on the stove to medium.

Bob was apoplectic. She grabbed my arm. "What are you DOING? NO, NO!"

"What?" I nearly dropped the pan on my foot.

"You have to butter the bread! You don't do it that way! If you put the butter in the pan, the sandwiches are greasy!!"

How a sandwich using Velveeta could be anything *but* greasy entered my mind, but I was the student, here. "Oh, sorry, Bob." I set the pan on the counter, turned off the heat, and plopped the hunk of butter back on the butter dish. "So how do you spread the butter on the bread without tearing it to pieces?"

Bob, aghast, said patiently, "Beck, this is what microwaves are for. You soften the butter in there." She padded over to my microwave and pointed to one of the buttons. "Didn't you ever notice this one? It says 'soften butter.' You use that button. Put the butter on a little plate and do it on 'soften' for about twenty seconds."

Oh. I have to admit that buttering the bread that way was easier. We stacked up the sandwiches and put them in the pan. They browned up beautifully, and the Velveeta melted like a dream.

When they were done, I showed Bob how to cut the sandwiches into strips. "I don't know exactly why these are called soldiers, but they are especially good for dipping. I put our soup in mugs, steaming. Each of us had four soldiers. I used green-and-blue paper plates.

As we sat down to eat our gourmet lunch, garnished with garlic dill pickles and potato chips, Bob pronounced that dipping grilled cheese in tomato soup was "scrumptious." Bob noted that the sandwiches were far superior to the ones she made in the Foreman grill. We chatted about the news of the neighborhood: Hallie's new electric blue sparkly scooter, and how Bob was sort of envious; school coming up and how relieved Bob was to have a friend who would also be new there; and Hallie's dad, who once played football with Andy Dalton, but he didn't have red hair, so it must not have been Andy Dalton.

The time flew. We had Popsicles for dessert.

▷◁

I was exhausted. The picnic loomed. I hoped Gail would bring numerous bottles of wine. The washer dinged, and I pulled out the sodden yellow dress. I remembered when I wore it to a wine tasting at the Bridge Hotel downtown. What a great party. We all got drunk, and Bryan took flowers from a bouquet in the lobby and put them in my hair. I felt like a princess, until Bryan said I looked like a bride. That was the night I started feeling claustrophobic about our relationship.

I rolled up the dress and stuffed it into my kitchen trashcan. I decided to wear the cutoffs to the picnic. To hell with it.

▷◁

We trudged through Framington Public Gardens, looking for the right spot. Gail fell off her platform espadrilles twice, managing to squelch her usual impulse to say "Fuck!" out loud. Rick slapped at mosquitoes, waving away the insect repellent I offered. I was quite comfortable, actually, in my cut-offs. Much more practical than the billowy hot pink flowered mini dress that Gail kept having to push down whenever the breeze blew under her skirt. Theo carried the huge picnic basket, his biceps bulging with the effort. His polo sleeves were just short enough to reveal the fact that he had a glorious farmer tan.

I was relieved when Rick pointed out a good spot under a maple tree. Flat and shady. I shook out the canvas drop cloth, which was the most acceptable thing I could find to sit on—it had lived in the trunk of my car for at least five years, but I felt it was serviceable—after all, this wasn't a scene from one of my books.

Sitting down for Gail was awkward. She had to manage her legs, her skirt, and her dignity. After tossing and turning on the canvas for about twenty seconds, she settled for a very uncomfortable looking sideways leg arrangement that I knew would cause her lumbar region to scream after about a half hour. Rick sprawled beside her with his glorious legs splayed in front of him, leg hair gleaming in the sun. *Just* like a scene from one of my books.

Theo carefully set the basket down, and began to pull out the delicacies. Ugh. Just like in one of my books, I have to admit it. Cold fried chicken. Potato salad. Cherry tomatoes "Much easier to eat outdoors," Theo informed us. Carrot sticks (I hate carrot sticks), mini blueberry muffins, and WAIT FOR IT—*wet wipes.*

Finally, Theo pulled out a gallon jug of lemonade. Smiling, he held out his hand and said, "No worries. I also packed an insulated bag of ice we can use in the cups" (which he had also thoughtfully included); "I think staying well hydrated is critical. I drink as much fluid as I can every day."

Okay. *Fluid*. Not on my list of favorite words, perhaps because the characters in my books exchange bodily fluids at every opportunity. I never use the word in real life, and here was Theo declaring his belief in their importance. I stifled a shudder as I took the cup of *fluid* that he offered me.

Gail looked around optimistically. "This all looks delish, Theo. Where did you buy the food? At Beth's Bistro? She does terrific picnics!"

Theo shook his head, frowning. "Oh, no. I made this myself."

Fried chicken? The man *made* fried chicken? I happen to know that frying chicken is an elaborate procedure that only people like Ina Garten actually ever do, because it involves making batter, soaking the chicken pieces in buttermilk or some such, an electric frying pan or deep fryer, a lot of time, and the willingness to clean grease splatters off your kitchen walls for days. I know this because this is what Claire always told us when we asked for it—right before she put us all in the car to go to KFC.

"Wait. Theo, you made this chicken? From SCRATCH?" I couldn't stop the disbelief; I had to ask.

Looking slightly smug, Theo picked up a drumstick and ran it under his nose, appreciating its fragrance. Yeah. Thyme, probably. "My grandmother's recipe. She taught me the summer I had the Cocksackie virus, then pneumonia. I was sick for three weeks, then weak for another two. I spent a lot of time with her. We cooked. She also taught me how to make pecan pie."

I looked over at Gail, certain that the Cocksackie virus would have sent her over the edge. But she was focused on Rick's legs, and I don't think she even heard Theo's comments about his invalid summer. Oh, boy.

There was nothing to do but take a plate of food and eat. The chicken was crunchy on the outside and very tender and moist. Despite my misgivings about Theo and his grandmother, I ate two pieces. Gail picked at a drumstick and sipped her lemonade, all the while eating up Rick with her eyes. Rick, on the other hand, inhaled his chicken and potato salad with zeal, not even noticing the mayonnaise on his chin. Theo cut the meat off his drumstick with a plastic knife and ate it with his fork. Of course.

The rest of the afternoon was uneventful. Theo proved to be excellent at throwing a Frisbee, and Gail proved to be unable to participate, due to her shoes. She sat, rapt, as Rick, Theo, and I tossed it around. I am sure she was paying full attention to Rick's flowing brown hair and his bulging calves. Hell, I certainly was.

We called it a day at around six. We waved to Rick and Gail as they climbed into his Jeep and drove off, Gail waving as they disappeared from the parking lot. Theo put his arm around my shoulders and we ambled towards his sea green Prius. He opened the truck, deposited the almost empty basket, and as I went to open the passenger door, screamed, "NO, NO! I will get that!" and sprinted around the side of the car to open the door for me.

We drove to my house, Theo humming what I swear was the theme from *The Golden Girls*. I said nothing.

"It's still early. Do you want to see what movies are playing? Or we could just hang out and have some wine or something…"

"Oh, Theo, thank you so much. But I have a deadline to meet. This has been a …" (I groped for a gracious adjective) "really nice" (I failed) "afternoon. But I have to get to work on my manuscript."

Theo leaned in for a kiss, and our lips met. Mine were closed tightly.

I patted him on the arm, smiled insincerely but I hope not noticeably, and got out of the car before Theo could run around and get the door for me.

As soon as I got inside, I grabbed Simpy and hugged him. "Oh, Simpson, why can't I meet a guy with your animal magnetism, hmm?" Simpson gently kneaded my boobs and began to purr.

"Oh, Simpy. What a day. Theo is absolutely the perfect man. He can cook. He looks good in shorts. He is extremely nice. Why am I not head-over-heels for him?"

Knowing that the question was hypothetical, Simpy began to wash his right front leg. Indifferent. "But wait, Simp. There's more."

Simpson stopped grooming momentarily and looked at me with his owl-eyes. I buried my head in his delicious, almost-cinnamon-smelling fur. Very soothing. "I want to have a relationship. I don't want to be an old lady who writes dirty books and pours coffee for the rest of my life. I don't want to acquire a parrot to talk to after you're gone." Simpy licked my thumb with his sandpapery tongue. "So I just have to fake it, right?" Simpy squirmed, and I set him down on the floor. He curled up in the meatloaf position on top of my feet. I looked at my hands, wondering how soon they would resemble Ella's, with prominent veins and papery skin. I wasn't getting any younger, and my options for happiness were limited. I pictured myself sitting in restaurants at tables for one for the rest of my life, ordering the small plate version of the featured entrees. I vowed to try harder with Theo. Because what woman in her right mind wouldn't want to have a guy like him?

Simpson, obviously bored with the entire subject, slowly shut his eyes and went to sleep, laying his adorable head down on my right instep. I rubbed my eyes and groaned.

CHAPTER NINE

As I was making a venti latte, my phone vibrated in the pocket of my apron. I served the latte to the harried-looking young mom, her two toddlers wailing at being strapped tightly into their twin stroller, screaming "OUT, OUT, OUT!" at the top of their tiny, little lungs. Both the mom and I couldn't wait for her to get out of there. As she wheeled them furiously out of the store, spilling her latte on her wrist, I wondered if she would slap them as she unstrapped them from one piece of equipment and restrapped them into another for the car ride home. For a second, I wanted to run after that woman and hug her.

I pulled my phone out of my apron. There it was, the text from Mom:

Sunday. The brunch. Diana and Bryan. Be there at eleven. No need to bring anything but a good attitude.

They were coming to town for sure. I replaced the phone in my pocket. My neck muscles seized up. I bit my lip. I needed a quick break to get my shit together. I told Joe I felt sick, which was not a lie, and I nearly ran out through the back to the parking lot. Fresh air. Not. It was a humid seventy-five degrees out there, but I gulped a few lungfuls of the saturated air anyway.

The pulse in my temples was banging like a metronome. I leaned against the wall, rubbing my palms against the brick, and imagined what Sunday might be like.

Diana, looking aglow, her bulge attractively set off by some designer skin-tight top, still lithe, still gorgeous. Bryan, with his great cheekbones and kind eyes, hovering over her. Mom, smiling and beaming, serving spicy Bloody Marys.

Or, and I grinned evilly, this: *Diana, her belly bulging, two double chins and jiggly thighs, reaches for her tenth canapé, as Mom and Bryan look on with concern—her excessive weight gain was both unexpected and out of character. Twins had been ruled out, so why was D so fat???*

I felt so much better. Keeping the image of a fat and miserable Diana in my head, I went back inside to finish my shift.

I was wiping the counters when Gail breezed through the door, cool and collected in peach linen slacks and a white silk top, nary a drop of perspiration anywhere on her body. She glided up to the counter, and I grinned at her. "You never break a sweat, do you? Meanwhile, we minions toil away making ridiculous, boiling hot coffee combos, sweat dripping down into our underwear. How do you do it?"

Gail waved my question away with a manicured hand. Orange Sherbet, I think that color was called. Her nails always coordinated with her clothes. "One iced coffee, STAT. And Beck, clinical strength antiperspirant works wonders. You might want to visit the drug store. But forget sweat for a moment. I just got a call from Rick. He has tickets to the Gathering Dusk concert on Saturday night. I don't know how he managed it—it's been sold out for months. Great seats, too. The man is amazing. Anyway, put it on your calendar. I know you don't actually *have* a calendar…"

I interrupted her with a huge sigh. "Shitballs. Remember who is in town for a family intervention? For Mother's Day, no less. I told you this, but of course, you have much more important things on your mind."

I shoved her iced coffee towards her. "I am to show up ready to embrace Diana, clap Bryan on the back, and let bygones be bygones. Hey, where can I get a legal firearm in this town?"

My comment drew stares from the customer standing behind Gail. He shifted uncomfortably in his wingtips and cleared his throat.

Gail glanced behind her. "Be quiet. Call me tonight." She grabbed her coffee and a napkin and turned to go, waving her orange manicure at the guy behind her. "Don't worry—she's just a barista with a grudge, but she wouldn't ever kill anyone!"

And with that, she floated out. I gave the guy a free Flat White. He didn't even smile. He will probably start going to Saxby's from now on.

Bob was sitting on my front steps when I got home, her knees scabbier than usual, her tee shirt ripped on the right shoulder. I sat down on the steps beside her and pulled on the torn sleeve. "Did you have a run-in with a bear?"

Bob grimaced. "I hit a rock on my scooter and fell off. My scooter got bent up, and Gran says she can't fix it. So now I don't have anything to ride around on, and the rest of the summer won't be any fun at all. And Hallie has her new cool one. So we won't be able to ride around together."

She leaned her head on my shoulder, and I put my arm around her. "You can always come visit me. We can draw pictures and play games."

"Well, being with you is fun. But you work all the time, and that's when I ride my scooter."

This child. "Honey, I bet we can find someone who can fix your scooter. A handyman or someone."

I had never in my entire life known a person who made a living as a handyman, but right that second I determined that I would find one. "I will call my boyfriend, Theo. I bet he could fix it—or if not, know somebody who could. Come on upstairs. I think I have ice cream sandwiches in the freezer."

Settled onto my sofa with a dishtowel in her lap for protection and licking the drips off the edges of her ice cream sandwich, Bob looked content. "I hope your boyfriend can fix it. I didn't know you had a boyfriend. His name is Theo? Have I ever seen him? Does he have a cat? Is he handsome, like my dad? Are you going to marry him?"

"Whoa, Bob! Too many questions! But here goes: No, I am not ready to marry him. We just met this summer. Yes, his name is Theo—short for Theodore, I guess. And he is very nice. He does not have a cat."

Bob smiled through her ice cream mustache. "You didn't say if he is handsome."

I pictured Theo in one of his coordinated outfits. "Well. Let's see. Theo is tall. He has light brown hair." I was stumped. "I would have to say this: He is not handsome like a movie star, no. But he is nice looking."

Bob savored the last bite of her treat, wiped her mouth with the towel, then draped it over her head. No explanation. "What does that mean, 'nice looking'? Does that mean he is nice to people and smiles at them? Or does it mean that he isn't ugly or anything?" She pulled the towel down over her eyes. Again, no explanation.

"Bob, you ask very intelligent questions. I have to think about this." I pulled the towel up so I could see Bob's eyes. "Are you hiding?"

She giggled. "I saw Mr. Havens mowing his lawn this afternoon, and he had a rag draped over his head, kind of like this. He told me it keeps him cooler. I am just testing. But what about your boyfriend? Tell me what he is like."

I sat back against the throw pillows. I considered this. There was certainly a lack of sexual chemistry there. We had not progressed beyond kissing. And the kissing was, at best, lukewarm. I marveled at my own lack of enthusiasm.

"I guess I maybe shouldn't call Theo my boyfriend, yet. He is a very nice man that I am dating. We don't know each other that well. But I bet he could fix your scooter."

Bob looked skeptical. "Your heart didn't pop like popcorn when you met him? If it didn't, then he shouldn't be your boyfriend."

Good heavens. "Bob, you are one of the wisest women I know. You are right in many ways. The closest I ever came to popcorn was when I met my former boyfriend, Bryan. My sister is married to that man, though." Shit. I was spilling my guts to an eight-year-old.

Bob sat upright and pulled the towel off her head. "Oh, no! That's terrible!"

I had already jumped off the deep end here, so I figured I had to keep going. "It all happened a long time ago. I'm fine. You don't need to be worried."

She looked totally worried. Her eyes widened, and she put her grubby hands over her heart. "Your sister? Married your boyfriend? But why?"

This was the perfect end to a fucktacular day. How could I distill my disastrous romantic history down to a story fit for a precocious eight-year-old? How could I protect her, already maimed emotionally by her own family situation?

I did my best to deflect. "Bob, you know that life is very complicated. My family isn't perfect. He and I didn't agree on a lot of things. After we broke up, he started to love my sister. It was just all mixed up. You know how that is. Your mom and dad loved each other, but there were so many problems that they had to face. Your dad was gone overseas so much, and your mom was so sad and took drugs in order to deal with things. They just couldn't make their relationship work out. But they had you, and they both love you."

Bob twisted the towel into a tight roll. She seemed to pull inwards. Even her freckles seemed to dim. It was a whisper: "My mom doesn't love me. She loves drugs."

We were very still. I watched Bob wring the towel, helpless. My platitudes were ridiculous here. This child seemed desperately in need of a love story with a happy ending. So I manufactured one, right on the spot. "Bob. You know what? I bet you're wrong about your mother. If your dad loved her, she can't be a bad person, right? She's just sick. Drugs make people sick. Your father is going to come home, and he will be just fine. And you, your dad, and your gran are going to live right across the street from me. And maybe your mom will get better and come, too."

Bob threw the towel on the floor. She leaned towards me, glaring, dry-eyed. "My mother will never get better. She is a selfish witch. We are not going to have her live with us. Ever. You are wrong about that."

We sat quietly as my heart shattered.

▷◁

Just as the afternoon waned, as I sat on my sofa brooding about lost loves and twisting my hair, there was a knock on my door. I schlepped over and peered out the peephole. There stood Theo, in a grass green polo shirt and madras Bermudas, holding in one hand a bottle of what looked like merlot, in the other a bunch of bright orange Gerbera daisies. He looked a little delicious, in spite of my previous judgments. I gave myself a tiny little mental pep talk about not judging books and covers, and I swung the door wide.

"Hi, Beck! It's going to be a beautiful evening. I love it right before it starts to get dark, don't you? I know I wasn't invited," and he held out the bottle and flowers sheepishly, "but I thought you might enjoy some wine and conversation. Oh, and flowers."

I curtsied, motioning him in. "This is just exactly what I need right now." I sniffed the daisies, which had no odor whatsoever. "Let me go get a vase and some wineglasses." Feeling nobler than I have in a while, and really wanting to give Theo the full benefit of all the doubts in my head, I kissed him. A breezy kiss, but it took him by surprise, and he fell back a step, then beamed. He marched behind me into the kitchen.

"Let me get this open so it can breathe. Corkscrew?" He set the bottle down and opened my junk drawer.

"No, no, not there. Just a sec." I pulled the corkscrew out of my implement crock. "Here you go."

The flowers looked beautiful in the turquoise vase that Bryan brought me home from one of his business trips. Bryan. I stopped myself from comparing Theo to Bryan. Okay. I *tried.*

We sat down on the sofa, twirling our wine. It was delish. I perhaps should have restrained myself from gulping down half of my glass all at once. Theo's eyes widened.

"Hard day?"

I wanted to swig down the rest of the merlot, but I set my glass down on the coffee table and took a deep breath. "You might say that. Let's see—where do I begin? With the imminent arrival of my horrid, selfish, and evil pregnant sister, whom I am expected to hug and kiss this Saturday evening, or the little child from across the street who has been abandoned by her druggie mother, left with her sweet but frail great-grandma, and who fully expects her father to die in the Middle East, where he is deployed to some secret location to fight Muslim terrorists?"

Theo set his glass down. His face sagged. "My God. Go on."

It all came out in a rush. "I haven't told you about my bitch younger sister, Diana. Diana, the beautiful and self-involved. Oh, yeah. She married my former boyfriend. Not just a casual boyfriend—we had lived together for years."

Theo gasped. "She broke you two up?" Lines of concern formed across his forehead.

"Well, no. We had broken up. But still. There are the unwritten rules. Sisters don't touch one another's property—present or former."

He nodded. But I could tell by the baffled look in his eyes that he had no idea about this very important unwritten rule.

"Now she's pregnant, and despite the fact that she crapped all over me, my mother expects me to forgive and forget, *for the sake of the baby and the family.*" Hell and damnation—I drank the rest of my wine in one swallow and poured myself a second glass.

Theo swallowed. He looked deeply into his glass of wine, and then back at me. He shrugged, tilted back his glass, draining it as well. He grabbed the bottle away from me, filled his glass, and held the wine bottle up to the light. "We are going to need at least two more bottles of this."

Right then and there, I began to appreciate Theo.

"Can you tell me exactly what happened? You know, so I can hate your sister, too. And get up to speed on the unwritten rule." He winked.

I told him the whole sorry story. He sat, rapt, nodding in all the right places, keeping his mouth shut. When I ended with, "And that is why I despise her," Theo ran a hand through his hair, shifted in his seat, and then stood up slowly. As he walked towards the bathroom, he said, "I held it in until you finished. I will return to digest all of this with you."

I watched his orange shirt disappear down the hall, his sandals flapping. Theo was calm, quiet, and deliberate, all things that I was not at the moment. Or anytime, really. I listened to his muffled tinkling—endearing, really— and wished that I were in love with Theo. I wondered for the millionth time what was wrong with me.

"I like that soap you have in the bathroom. It smells like flowers." His face was so kind, but in that bland, Theo-ish way. He picked up the bottle of Chardonnay that we had finished after we polished off the merlot. "Empty."

He ambled into the kitchen, and I heard him depositing the empty bottle in the trash, carefully, so it wouldn't clank into the merlot bottle and shatter. He rustled around in there for a few minutes and emerged, carrying two glasses of ice water. "We don't need to get any drunker," (I was *so* not drunk) "so I brought some water. We need to stay hydrated." (I mentioned Theo's obsession with hydration already, right?)

I was too weak to argue, so I took the ice water and glugged some down. Theo drank his entire glass while standing, made the "time out" sign with his hands, and went back for a refill. Then he settled back down on the sofa beside me, rubbed my shoulders, and offered up a solution.

"I think that if I went with you to this brunch thing, it might be helpful. You know, moral support."

Backup. Yes. "Oh, Theo. This isn't your problem." But I said this with very little conviction.

He patted my shoulder. "I know. But think about it. If I'm there, first off, you won't seem like the poor, injured party, all alone and sad. And second, with me there, maybe everybody will be on their best behavior. You know how that is."

I did. Awkward. But there are times when awkward is good. I imagined Mom, passing around tiny biscuits filled with strawberry cream cheese, her face set in a paralyzing smile. Bryan would be over-polite, enthusiastically cramming the biscuits down his throat, despite the fact that he hates cream cheese. D would patronize Theo, treat me like dirt, and run her hands all over Bryan, but she would keep her insults to a minimum, because THEO.

"Theo, it just isn't right to put you in the center of all of this. But my God, having you there *would* be so helpful." I tried to smile, but it came out as a grimace.

"Then it's settled. But we still haven't talked about the little girl." Theo glanced out the window.

It was my turn to get up and pace. I did three laps around the living room, my hydrated guts churning.

"This little girl. She hates her mom? Do you want to sit down and tell me about it?"

I didn't want to. I didn't want to breach Bob's trust. I went over to the window and looked over at Ella Bowers' porch, Bob's broken scooter lying on the cement floor, as if someone had carelessly thrown it up there. Bob was nowhere to be seen. "Theo, are you handy at all? Do you think you could fix a broken scooter?"

Theo got up and came over to stand beside me at the window. "That one over there? Is it the little girl's? I might. Should we go over and have a look?"

What the hell. "Sure. I have some tools."

I got the toolbox I kept under my bed. Theo tried to hold my hand as we walked through the front yard, but I pulled away. Then I thought better of it and reached out to him, but the moment had passed. Awkward.

Luckily, the porch light was on. As Theo squatted, examining the scooter, and I settled on the top step of the porch, Bob emerged from the side yard, her hair festooned with twigs, her face smudged. When she saw us, she jumped up and down twice and raced up the steps. "Hi!"

She grinned through her freckles at Theo and stuck out a grimy hand. "I'm Bob Bowers. Nice to meet you. Oh, sorry I'm dirty—I was digging a grave for the moth Gran killed with the flyswatter before it gets too dark out. It was really big. I hated for her to kill it, but Gran said it was as big as a bird, and it scared the hell out of her. Well, she didn't say 'hell,' but it's the truth. I don't have a good shovel, so I was just using my hands."

She stopped to take a breath. Theo put down the screwdriver he was using to bang ineffectually at the bent axle, and took Bob's hand. "Nice to meet you, Miss Bob. I don't think I'm going to be able to fix your scooter. I'm not really much of a handyman."

Bob sat down cross-legged beside the scooter and frowned. "I figured that it is a dead dog. Gran said the same thing. But soon, she is going to take it over to the hardware store and ask Mr. Tillis if he can do something about it. She says those men at the hardware store are all retired janitors and mechanics and stuff, and between

Mr. Tillis, Mr. Swift, and Mr. Franklin, somebody will be able to fix it. And they have all the right tools," (Bob scowled at the screwdriver) "so I'm not worried. Thanks, though, Mister. "

"Oh, sorry, Bob. This is Theo Blackburn."

Bob somehow managed to bounce while remaining seated. "Very nice to meet you, Mr. Blackburn. Are you going to marry Beck?"

Theo reared back, his head smacking against the porch railing with a thud. I flinched. Bob gasped and flew up to squat directly over Theo's head, leaning over to study it. "Did you get a goose egg? I have always wanted one of those! Should I get you some ice?"

Before Theo could reply, Bob zoomed into the house, calling, "Gran! Gran! Beck's boyfriend smacked his head! We need ice!"

"At least that got her off the subject of matrimony. My God." I helped Theo to his feet.

We set the scooter against the far wall of the porch, as Bob returned, holding a paper towel filled with too many ice cubes, some of them spilling out and breaking on the concrete. Bob held out the towel, losing more ice in the process.

Theo took the towel, wadded it around the ice, and put it against the back of his head. "I don't really need this, but it was very nice of you to get it for me. I think Beck and I should mosey on back to her house. Bob, it was very nice to meet you, and I hope you get your scooter fixed."

As we walked across the street, I looked back and saw Bob picking up shards of ice and putting them into her mouth with gusto.

When we got into my apartment, Theo deposited the paper towel and ice into my sink. "I better get going. Cute little kid. But kind of nutty. No wonder, with all of that family drama going on."

"You're wrong. She's brilliant."

Theo looked puzzled. "I thought you said you weren't a fan of kids?"

I took the wet paper towel and put it on top of my head. Just like Mr. Havens when he mowed the lawn. Just like Bob. "I have no real experience with children. They scare me with all that energy and innocence. But Bob isn't really a kid. She's just an adult trapped in a child's body. Kind of like I was at her age, actually."

Theo shrugged. "I want to change the subject." He stepped closer. His lips were really quite soft. Plump. "You know what? I read one of your books. *Rhett and Reba.* Downloaded it onto my Kindle. You are a fantastic writer." He gently took the wet paper towel off my head and leaned in for a kiss. A fine one, at that. I might have misjudged Theo in the sexuality department.

What followed wasn't quite as steamy as the chapters I write, but nothing is in actual life. Theo had gifts that I would never have imagined. He had gifts that he demonstrated three times, actually.

By the time we reassembled ourselves and dragged out of the bedroom, it was completely dark, and I had to push Theo towards the door. "I have writing to do, and you have been a true inspiration. Let me get to work while I am still, (cough cough) *hot.*"

He grinned, again with those soft lips. "My pleasure entirely. But you know how they say writers write from real life? Can you just make sure that none of your readers recognize me? I have my clients to consider."

"Don't worry. You will be totally obscured. But I thank you for this afternoon. Whew! Oh, and seriously, for Sunday." I shoved him out the door and blew him a kiss.

After he left, I realized that I had never in my entire life blown a kiss, so I sat down on the sofa and questioned my sanity.

CHAPTER TEN

"Why don't you wear nail polish? Dark pink would go good with that dress."

I had broken down and gotten a sky-blue-and-white striped dress at Old Navy for the Mother's Day "festivities." Bob had showed up just as I was starting to get ready. She supervised the entire process, charging back and forth, surveying me from all sides, commenting on every move. She rummaged through my jewelry box, selecting a pair of filigreed hoops, whooping with approval when I put them on. We studied my sandal assortment, and Bob held up every single pair against my dress, finally selecting the tan gladiator sandals with bronze studs. "They match your earrings, almost." Appropriately attired, according to my small wardrobe consultant, I stood in front of my bedroom mirror, putting on my "makeup," which for me is some blusher and lip gloss. My hair was pulled back in a ponytail, per Bob—"It looks more sophisticated." I had managed to find a blue hair tie to put it back with, so I matched, sort of.

"Bob, I am not a girly-girl. Nail polish always smears when I try to wear it."

Worn out from all of the supervision, Bob had come to rest on the edge of my bed. She studied her own bitten-down nails critically. "At least you don't chew them. Gran says if I keep on biting my nails, I won't get a boyfriend. But I don't want a boyfriend. Are you going with Theo someplace?"

"Yes."

"Is it fun having a boyfriend?" Bob continued to study the stubs of her nails.

I was as good as I was going to get, makeup-wise. I turned from the mirror and sat down on the bed beside her. "Fun? I'm not sure you'd call it fun, exactly. But it is nice to have someone to go out with. Especially today." I squeezed my eyes shut and envisioned D holding court and both Bryan and Theo panting after her.

"What's the matter? Are you going someplace awful today?"

I opened my eyes. Bob grabbed my forearm. "Are you going to a horror movie? Gran won't let me go to those—she says I'll get nightmares. Or are you going to a movie about war? I can't go to those, either—because of my dad." Bob looked down at the floor, keeping her back very straight. She squeezed my arm tighter. "The war movies; they stink."

I wanted to hug her, but that ramrod little back told me otherwise. So I put my hand over her small one on my arm and squeezed back. "No, I am not going to the movies. I am going to my mother's house. But I don't want to go. Theo is going with me for moral support. Do you want to hear the story?"

Bob lifted her head and looked at me with such clarity, her dark eyes filled with concern. "Oh, yes. I want to hear about your mother."

"Okay, then. Let's get comfortable." I punched my pillows and smoothed the wrinkles out of the quilt. "Here. Lean on these." We lay on the bed, our legs outstretched, thighs touching companionably. Simpson padded in, leapt onto the bed, and curled up against Bob, his paws kneading the air. Bob stroked his stripes.

"This is not really about my mother. My mother is part of it. But it's mostly about my sister. And my ex-boyfriend."

Bob lurched, sending Simpy hurtling sideways off the bed. "Is this going to be like the movies on Lifetime? Gran makes me watch those with her. I hate them. They aren't true at all. Happy endings are stupid."

"Bob, this is a long story. And we don't have *all* morning. So I will just give you the important details." I wondered at this point if I was doing the right thing, sharing all this ill will about my sister with Bob, but it would take her mind off war movies, and her father out there in peril. But the happy endings? Bob's jaded eyes made me shiver. I plunged ahead, anyway.

"My sister Diana is a selfish person. She is kind of like those bad princesses in fairy tales. She is very beautiful, and she only thinks of herself."

Bob nodded.

"Diana and I have never gotten along very well. As we got older, it got worse. In high school, she had all the boyfriends, and if a boy seemed interested in me, she made sure that she flirted with him, so that he would fall for her instead of me."

"She sounds mean." Bob scowled, drawing up her lips against her teeth.

"She is, kind of. No. She just IS!"

I hesitated, not knowing where to go next with the saga. Bob motioned for me to go on with one hand, while stroking the cat's head with the other.

"So while I was in college, I met a boy named Bryan Dallas. Bryan was very smart and funny. He was also handsome. He seemed just perfect. I just liked him right away."

Bob clapped her hands. "Popcorn?" This was too much for Simpson, who leapt off Bob's lap in a huff.

"I wouldn't go so far as to say that, kiddo. So anyway, Bryan and I got together. We lived in Chicago. It should have been happily ever after, but he and I just didn't agree on a lot of things. It didn't work out, and so we broke up. But after that, my sister swooped in and she and Bryan fell in love and got married." Bob looked at me, her eyes widening in confusion. "I know. Diana didn't actually steal my boyfriend. But it kind of still feels like it. Even though I am a grown up, I guess I have to admit to you that I am jealous."

Bob looked over the edge of the bed for Simpson, but he had departed the bedroom in disgust. Sighing, she righted herself. She swiped her nose against her palm, wiped her hand off on her shorts, sighed, and leaned against me. I took a long whiff of her wiry curls, which smelled like a combo of cut grass, mud, and Ivory soap. We stayed companionably in sync for a few seconds. I swung my arm around her shoulders and patted her hard little arm.

"So you are always mad at her now?"

I sighed. "Yup. I felt that my sister ruined my life, and I had a very rough time. I moved back here, and after a while, I got better. But I have never forgotten what my sister did. And so I am dreading this brunch. Especially since Diana and Bryan are going to have this baby." *Why was I telling this garbage to a little kid?*

I felt Bob's body stiffen. Her eyes blazed. "You should be excited about a baby! Babies are so much fun! *Everybody* should love babies! And it wasn't just her fault, was it? You shouldn't be mad and jealous of the baby!" She looked down into her lap and whispered to herself, "*People are so mean to babies…*"

This sank in. Coming from an eight-year-old. I felt nauseated all of a sudden. I remembered how Bob flinched the first time I touched her. Some intimations I had entertained about Bob's past suddenly snapped into place in my mind. "Bob, was your mom mean to you when you were little?"

She crossed her arms on her chest and gazed into space. There were three scabs on her forearms, and her face was dirty. She reminded me of the feral kittens that showed up in the parking lot at work—lost, helpless, and yet fierce. "Gran says I mustn't think that my mom takes drugs because of me—because I'm not good. Gran says that my mom had something called poor impulse control. So that is why she…" Bob hung her head. "Punished me so much."

She lifted her hands and covered her eyes. "Because I wasn't good enough for her to stop taking drugs to look after me. Because I was a bad baby. Gran says that isn't true. She says I shouldn't think I was a bad baby. Because babies aren't bad."

I gently pried Bob's hands away from her eyes. "Honey, look at me."

Bob turned her head. Eyes dry, she stared past me, seeing things I didn't want to imagine. Rowena, damn her.

I touched her cheek. "Bob, you are the smartest person I have ever met. I am going to go over to my mother's house today, and I am going to give my sister a hug. And I am going to think of you all afternoon—every time I feel angry or jealous, I am going to think of you. Even if my sister flirts with Theo. Even if he flirts back. I will think about what you just taught me. I will think about the baby coming into our family. I will think about goodness. About you. Because *you* are not just good, you are absolutely superior. In every way."

I wrapped her in my arms very tightly. Bob took a deep, jagged breath, then relaxed into my chest. I stroked her back, one little knobby vertebra at a time. Then I did it again, and again, and again—until we both stopped crying.

Babies aren't bad. I tried to get that out of my skull, but it remained, a throbbing earworm.

▷◁

Claire Throckmorton's loft apartment is as stylish as she is. Eclectic. All white walls, dark hardwood floors, built-in bookcases, geometric rugs, and strategically placed houseplants. Books. Mom answered the door wearing a caftan made out of an antique gold, red, and teal sari. Silver hoop earrings. Barefoot. She held a Bloody Mary in one hand. Central casting: Audrey Hepburn in her sixties. As soon as she caught sight of Theo standing behind me, holding the forty dollar bouquet of multicolored roses we had bought to impress, Mom gasped, spilling half of her drink onto her left foot.

I took the Bloody Mary out of her hand and stepped in, motioning with my head for Theo to follow. He smiled weakly and entered, looking around for enemies. "Mom, this is Theo Blackburn." I took a swig of her drink for courage.

We walked through the entry hall, past the chrome kitchen. Theo didn't seem to know what to do with the roses. He looked around for help.

"These are lovely! Let me get a vase!" Mom got down a tall crystal vessel and proceeded to arrange the roses, only pricking herself once. We stood awkwardly and watched her. "Go on in, you two! There are homemade cheese biscuits out there!"

I braced myself as we entered the living room, the centerpiece the sea blue and sunset pink Murani glass chandelier Mom got on her last trip to Italy. Posy bouquets on seemingly every surface, the glint of sun from the huge picture window highlighting the lone figure slumped on the creamy suede sectional.

I stopped abruptly, Theo banging into me from behind. Mom swept around us and set the vase on the coffee table in front of the dejected wreck that was my sister, clutching her distended belly. Diana, my God. Her hair was dull. There were dark circles under her eyes. Her red nail polish was chipped, and she had no makeup on. She had a pimple on her right cheek. Bryan was conspicuously absent.

"Mom, what is going on?" Brilliant opener, but I was in shock. "Diana, what happened? Mom, where is Bryan? What on *earth* is going on?"

For an awkward few seconds, we shuffled around each other. Mom ended up dropping heavily down beside D on the sofa. After colliding against the coffee table and each other, Theo and I ended up perched uncomfortably on the two Windsor chairs at either side of the fireplace. Theo cleared his throat at least three times.

Diana looked like somebody had hit her. She hardly seemed to notice that we were there. But of course, that was a misperception, because no sooner had we all settled into our seats, D began:

"Oh, hello, Beck. And I guess this is your newest boyfriend?" She glared at Theo. "I am sure you have heard all about me from Rebecca, right? I am the horrible slut of a sister that stole her *boyfriend*? Despite the fact that they had broken up months before that? The bitch-sister? Well, guess what?" D reached for what looked like a gin and tonic, and took a huge gulp. Alcohol and pregnancy—not apparently on D's taboo list. She thunked the glass back down, of course, not on the coaster Mom had thoughtfully provided. The condensation would make an indelible white ring on the lovely table Mom had brought back from London. D caught my glance. "It's *sparkling water and lime,* for God's sake."

I reached out and put her drink on a coaster and shot my sister a snotty look.

"So guess WHAT? I am in an advanced state of pregnancy, and my husband and I just had the monster fight to end all monster fights. I am hugely pregnant with a child who keeps kicking the crap out of me, I can't sleep because of it, my arms are flabby, and I can't go to my yoga classes anymore because I vomit when I smell incense, and Bryan gets his feelings hurt when I don't feel like making dinner, and I slap him away when he tries to be *romantic*! Romantic, my fat ass!"

Mom leaned towards us. "It's a boy." Sotto voce.

Theo, bless him, tried to turn the tide. He leapt out of his seat, grabbed the tray of cheddar biscuits, bending to offer them first to me, and then to Mom. I saw him nearly extend the tray to D, but then he thought better of it, popped one into his mouth, and set the tray back down on the coffee table next to the bowl of cashews.

"A boy. That is wonderful." Spoken with a mouthful of bread, but sincerely. "How exciting."

We all stared at Theo. Diana, I swear, picked her nose a little. My God. Theo seemed to lose the will to live and sat back down.

My sister, miserable because Bryan called her on her own personality. My mother, at a loss. Me, staring at both of them, my new boyfriend beside me. In a room containing the two women who had always made me feel mediocre. I grubbed around in my head for something to say, but came up empty. So I babbled, "Well this isn't good, is it? Not good. Just a terrible thing. Does anyone want anything? Another gin and tonic—*sparkling water*, D? Some cashews?"

I scuffled over to the coffee table and picked up the nut dish. Both women looked at me as if I had just offered them a bowl of eyeballs. I set the nut dish back down and looked wildly around for ideas. My armpits began to drip. This was going nowhere. I decided to just go for broke. I sat down on the other side of D, our shoulders touching. Diana's felt spongy. I glowered at my sister.

"Bryan is unhappy because you wouldn't cook dinner or have sex? Come on. This is ridiculous. What else weren't you doing—well, besides the starving and the rejecting? And why did you come here without him?" Diana just stared at me with those cold, blue eyes. So I poked her on the cheek. "Wake up, D! What else did you do?"

Mom reached across Diana's bulging front to slap at me, but she missed, her blow ending up on D's abdomen with a thump. This seemed to bring Diana to consciousness, and she lashed out.

"I didn't do anything! In case you didn't notice, I am *gigantic*! Being like *this*"—she indicated her belly—"is horrible! I feel bloated, sick, ugly, and tired all the time! You can't blame me for being just a little self-centered at the moment!" Diana teared up. Mom continued to pat Diana's arm helplessly. "Bryan wouldn't come. He said he needed a *break.*"

My God. I looked over at Theo, who seemed intent on escape. He turned longingly towards the entryway. The poor guy—dragged right into the scene from a reality show. He crossed and uncrossed his legs, checking his watch.

I couldn't help myself. "Jesus, D. It's all about you, isn't it? The Diana Dallas show! My God. You have a handsome husband, you are going to have a baby, you have a beautiful apartment in Chicago, and just because you don't feel tip-top, you push away one of the greatest guys ever," (I wished I hadn't said that part—poor Theo) "and you still manage to blame him for your own disgusting self-centeredness?" I punched her on the arm.

"OW! Mom! Did you see that?"

By this time, Theo had stood and begun inching toward the door. It was just too much. Diana, rubbing her arm and pouting, moaned, "You don't understand! You have never understood me!"

With that, I dragged myself off the suede, stomped over to Theo, turned to D, and snarled: "Nope. I don't understand you, D. I guess I need to Google *narcissism.*"

I hated to leave Mom holding the bag (literally), but it was just too poisonous in there. I grabbed Theo's arm and dragged him out the door, slamming it in our wake. We both gulped the air in the hallway, as if we had just escaped drowning.

"I don't know about you, but I need a huge cheeseburger and some beer. Do you by any chance have any more siblings?" He put his hand over my mouth. "Wait. I'm not sure if I want to know the answer." Theo grinned.

The cheeseburgers were restorative. Later on, after a brilliant sunset, Theo demonstrated his skills two more times before falling into a deep sleep. I on the other hand, stayed awake the rest of the night, imagining Bryan alone in Chicago, sitting on the sofa, drinking brews and watching sports on the big screen. Ordering his favorite Moo Shu Pork from the Chinese delivery just down the block. Choosing not to come because his wife was fat and didn't want sex. Having "me time." I stared at the streetlight, flickering through the leaves outside the bedroom window, trying to remember to blink. The covers seemed to strangle me. My elbow hurt. I got up, leaving Theo breathing evenly, drooling slightly onto my best pillow.

I ran the water in the kitchen sink for about a minute, waiting for the ancient pipes to send up some cool water. I filled a mug, drank it down, and looked out the window over the sink. The Bowers' house looked settled, solid, the porch light beaming softly. I thought of Ella, probably snoring softly in her batiste nightgown, probably talking to her dear Robert in her sleep. And Bob, the nightlight illuminating all those freckles, her scabby legs lashing out in a dream about chasing butterflies or racing down the sidewalk on her scooter. Or worse, limbs churning due to nightmares about a hopped up mother, track marks on her arms, raising a fist in anger. I held the coolness of the mug against my cheek and thought of the promise I had made Bob. The promise I broke as soon as I set foot in my mother's apartment.

I set the mug in the sink. I felt the softness of Simpson as he wound around my legs. I bent down to pick him up, burying my nose in his neck. I held him tight.

"Simpson, I am a liar and a horrible role model." Simpy merely purred, kneading my throat gently with his dear old paws.

CHAPTER ELEVEN

The three of us hadn't had lunch in a while—too much going on in our lives. Ella had invited Gail and me over for a "picnic" one afternoon while Bob and Hallie were at the movies with Marva. Mom and D were also otherwise occupied—luckily for me, I hadn't been called upon to deal with my little sister since the brunch.

Ella sighed, as she had been doing repeatedly for the last hour. We sat on the comfortable old lawn furniture in Ella's back yard, surrounded by soft grass, hostas, and Ella's very disciplined boxwood hedge, thanks to Mr. Danvers and his pruners. Ella had served us triangular egg salad sandwiches with dill springs and iced tea, which she had put on an antique tole tray. It sat between us on Ella's glass-topped table. I had eaten three already. Ella just nibbled hers. Gail bent toward Ella with concern. "Are you okay? You seem tired."

Ella sat, holding her sandwich with both spotted hands. "Bobby has been having a hard time lately. She worries about all sorts of things. She wakes in the night after bad dreams, and so I have been sitting up with her. I am just a bit behind on my rest."

Gail, always the fixer, urged Ella to eat. "Nutrition is very important, Ella. Especially when you are burning the candle at both ends. Don't just stare at your sandwich, dear. Eat some."

Ella took a small bite, chewed, and then took a sip of tea. "Bobby is so fragile. I worry about her."

I had never thought of Bob as particularly fragile. Her energy seemed boundless, her inner springs always wound very tight. She rode her scooter like a gladiator. She loved Simpson with an all-consuming fervor. "Bob? Fragile? Really?"

Ella set her sandwich on her napkin and put it back on the tray. "She is always worried about something. She is afraid Charles won't make it home. She worries that I might die. She has nightmares about her mother." A sudden cloud floated over us, turning Ella's face gray in its shadow. "She is better during the day, when there are things to do outside. She *loves* being outside. And Rebecca, I am so glad you are across the street, because Bobby so enjoys your company. And the cat. And, Gail. You are such a wonderful, encouraging friend to all of us."

I felt as if someone had just gut punched me.

Gail jumped in again. "Ella, you can't handle this all by yourself. Have you thought about finding a nice camp or maybe a youth counselor?"

"Bobby was in counseling in Iowa. But the counselor was ineffective. She made Bobby feel guilty for disliking her mother. She tried to get Bobby to forgive." Ella's face flushed with the memory. "Imagine—asking an eight-year-old child to understand the concept of forgiving an abusive mother? That woman just made things worse! No, I will not put Bobby through that again. And camp? I couldn't send Bobby away." Ella made a bony fist and drummed the arm of her chair. "No. Bobby needs to have stability. She has been shuffled around enough."

Gail looked abashed. I felt the egg salad curdle in my stomach. My internal organs felt as if they were rearranging themselves, my mouth was dry, and all I could think about was how terrible it is to be a person who feels lost in the world. I knew how that felt. The winter after my father left, I had recurring dreams. I often woke in the night, absolutely sure that he had just kissed me on the forehead and left the room. I remember scrambling out of bed, running down the hall and into my parents' bedroom, only to find Mom sleeping alone on her side of the bed, her hand resting on my father's pillow. I remembered being alone on Dads' Weekend at Ohio State, High Street clogged with fathers and daughters strolling companionably, eating Jeni's ice cream and looking happy as I stared at them with both envy and loathing.

I jolted out of my chair and knelt by Ella. "Don't you worry. I am right across the street. I work part time. I have all kinds of hours free. Forget camp. Bob can hang out more with me, and we will stay busy! Right, Gail?"

Gail, who actually *had* a full-time job, and one that demanded lots of extra hours for stuff like open houses and scouting around for listings, looked at me with wide eyes. "Right, Beck. *You* certainly do have the time to spend with Bob. But I am right there with you, *emotionally.* And of course, whenever I am available."

Ella relaxed into her chair, fist unfurling, and she looked first at my hot face and then over at Gail's soothing one. She seemed to sense that the two of us had just reached over to lift the burden off her little, osteoporotic shoulders, and she smiled with great relief, picked up the rest of her egg salad triangle, and put the whole thing into her mouth with gusto. As she chewed, she patted me gently on the head. I wanted to put my face in her lap.

Instead, I stood up and began to wish that I had been to camp. Or at the very least been a Girl Scout. If only I possessed those skills!

▷◁

Three a.m. Dammit. Real life drama and deadlines just don't mix. Heartthrob Press was expecting the first draft of *Bad Boys on the Beach* in just weeks, and I was only a third of the way through. My heroine and her pals weren't nearly satisfied enough with just one lover each—I had to invent at minimum one other hottie and throw in at least a smattering of plot.

I wondered if this was a sign from the universe that I should stop phoning all this crap in and start to actually craft a novel. Lord knows there had been enough inspiration so far this summer: a bitchy pregnant sister, a heroic little girl, a drug addict mother, a slightly boring boyfriend with a heart of gold, a weary granny, the war in the Middle East. I stopped typing to think about this. Just as I was envisioning a new work of literary fiction by Rebecca Throckmorton hitting *The New York Times* bestseller list, my phone beeped. A text at three a.m.?

It took me a while to find my phone. It wasn't in the pocket of my sweatpants. I swept my feet under my desk, thinking I might have dropped it. Nope. I lifted the scrambled mass of papers and bills on the desk. Not there. It beeped again. The beep sounded like it was coming from my armpit. Oh. I reached into my bra and pulled out the phone.

I need to talk to u

Wake up

It was from Bryan. My heart flopped in my chest. My ears burned. Suddenly, my hands shook so much I could hardly type.

I am awake. What's up?

He texted back immediately.

Let me in.

My heart stopped flopping. It just stopped altogether. I realized I needed to inhale, and then my thoughts ran amuck:

Oh my God! He is outside the apartment, and I look like shit. uick, comb your hair; no time to brush teeth, just eat some toothpaste. my God, he is outside. what the hell is going on? Spray some perfume down your front and get a hold of yourself, Beck, take five deep breaths . . .

I opened my door, and there stood my one-time lover.

He looked awful.

Compare and contrast: The Bryan I fell for had deep coffee-brown eyes and lush eyebrows. This guy had dull eyes underlined with purple circles. Had he plucked his eyebrows? The old Bryan had gladiator muscles and ramrod posture. This sad sack was slumped over and flabby. To top it all off, he gave off a pungency that reminded me of Limburger cheese.

I waved him in. For all I knew, the guy was dying.

"Bryan. Sit down before you drop over. What are you doing here? And what in God's name is going on? You look and smell like garbage. Wait. Do you want something to drink or eat? Maybe a hot shower?"

Bryan smiled ruefully as he sank down onto the floor. It was nice of him not to sully my furniture with his nastiness. My prince.

"Hi." He rubbed his eyes and pulled something out of the left one and rubbed it on the front of the tee shirt that looked as if Bryan had been sleeping in it for about a week.

"Wait. Don't say anything yet. You need a Coke." I pulled a cold can out of the fridge and popped it open. By the time I had settled down on the floor, a safe distance away from him to avoid asphyxiation, Bryan had glugged the entire can dry.

He set the can down on the floor beside him. Meanwhile, Simpson had wandered sleepily into the living room to investigate, and as soon as he got a good whiff of Bryan, he yowled in either protest or disgust. I sympathized and shooed him away. Good cat. He complied.

"Okay. Spill it. You came to beg D's forgiveness? So why do you look like someone tried to murder you?"

Bryan put his head in his hands for a few seconds. I thought he might just fall asleep like that. I cleared my throat. He dropped his hands and looked at me with those hollow, inflamed, yet gorgeous deep, dark eyes.

"Well, first off, I haven't slept since the eruption between Diana and me. Secondly, I have been drinking for about three days straight, and third, I nearly had a car accident on the highway on the way here from Chicago. I think I may have fallen asleep at the wheel or something." He wiped his nose, and then looked at the back of his hand. I nearly gagged.

"Bryan."—I pushed him toward the bathroom—"Take a shower, then let's talk. Clean towels are hanging in there. Just go wash."

While he showered, I got a hold of myself. Sort of. I reminded myself that Bryan was no longer mine, and that he was in some sort of crisis, and that I needed to be calm and listen. No old Beck agendas. I found a tatty OSU tee shirt and a pair of sweats that I thought would fit him, and I opened the bathroom door and threw them in, shutting the door so the steam wouldn't escape.

A few minutes later, Bryan wandered out, looking drippingly woeful. He followed me into the living room. I motioned for him to sit. His hair dripped onto the back of the sofa. I sat cross-legged on the floor. Didn't want to get too close.

"I need the whole story. And I don't care how pitiful you look or how execrable you feel. GO."

"Shit, Beck." He took a deep breath. I held mine.

"Your sister has been a complete mental case since she got the pregnancy hormones."

"This is old news."

He held up his hand. "If you want the whole story, don't interrupt. I know how you feel about her, so just shut up and listen."

He put me in my place. I nodded, making the "lip zipping" motion.

"We both wanted to have a baby. At least that's what I thought. Diana was taking her temperature and everything. We spent a lot of time online looking at cribs and stuff. It was fine. We were happy. We must have bought at least three dozen pregnancy tests."

I rolled my eyes but kept quiet.

"So after a couple of months, she got pregnant. And I don't know, was it the damn hormones, or was it fatigue, or something else? But Diana started sleeping all the time. And when she wasn't sleeping, she was eating. My God. The Dorito people will erect a monument in her honor..."

I couldn't help guffawing. Bryan looked startled, but continued.

"Then she started making lists. All the stuff that WE NEEDED TO BUY. I know babies need a lot of stuff, but a *robotic teddy bear*? And she wanted to redecorate the entire place—because it was too dirty for a baby or something. She started talking about having a full-time housekeeper. Nannies. Beck, the woman lost her mind!"

Not to mention her lovely figure. "Go on."

"We had arguments. I tried to see things her way, but I had to put my foot down on the housekeeper. I tried to point out to her that we don't need a housekeeper when one of us is staying at home all the time."

Oooh. Bad move. I could see the handwriting on that wall in the apartment in Chicago. D had a job. I felt pretty sure the stay-at-home-mom thing was a no-go.

"And I told her she had to send back the jogging stroller. She doesn't jog. Plus, the baby won't need a trampoline until much later. You know, when he knows how to walk."

I hadn't felt this happy in a long time. "So? This still doesn't explain what you're doing here. Cut to the chase, Bryan. It's three in the morning."

"Okay. Okay. So Diana continued to be impossible. And she gained all that weight."

I was in seventh heaven.

"It got to the point where all D did was sit around in front of the TV, watching The Home Shopping Network. All those baby blankets and breast pumps and stuff. She was ordering EVERYTHING. I had no choice, Beck. No choice. I cancelled all but one of the credit cards, and I took that one to the office and locked it in my desk."

Glee.

"Diana was stymied on the shopping. I thought she might come to her senses. But no. She told me that when we came here for the family thing, she would just ask your mom to get her all the stuff that I wouldn't let her have. You know, the deluxe breast pump with the car charger, the jogging stroller with the cup holders, and the Lilly Pulitzer diaper bag.

"It was too much, Beck. I told D that I wasn't coming with her to Ohio. And if she got Claire to buy her all that stuff that she would be in really good shape, wouldn't she? She would have all of that high-tech equipment, and so she obviously wouldn't need *me*."

Grinning ear to ear.

"I thought that would bring her around. But no. She left for Framington in a huff. Without me. The goddamn brunch. Well, you know. You saw her, didn't you?"

"I did. It wasn't pretty."

"Yeah. She told me she wants to stay here for a while. She needs a *break*."

Suddenly, I felt as if I was choking. I struggled to breathe. The blood drained out of my extremities, and I nearly passed out. "WHAT? She told me YOU wanted a break."

Bryan pressed his lips together in a tight line.

"Bryan. We both know Diana. She is the queen of the dramatic gesture. This is all just a way to get you back into line. She can't be serious."

Bryan snorted. "Wrong. She is serious."

The sky was brightening. Time passes quickly during family drama.

"Okay, we need more caffeine. Come on." We shuffled into my tiny kitchen, and Bryan plopped into one of the two chairs at my round glass-top table. I rustled around in the fridge for the coffee grounds, threw some in the pot, and plugged it in. The aroma was heartening. I put two chipped mugs on the table, along with the sugar bowl and two spoons. I sat down opposite the wreck that used to be my boyfriend. "How could you have fallen for D in the first place?" I cast my mind back to those sunlit days in Chicago, when Bryan and I were the center of the universe. "How on earth could you have fallen for that b—"?

He slapped his hand so hard on the tabletop that the spoons jumped. So did I. He spat out the words. "Shut up! She is my wife."

His eyes bulged, and a tiny wad of saliva landed on my hand. I felt as if someone had slapped me. Bryan's eyes rasped my face, and my lungs tightened as if they were collapsing. I thought we were having a meeting of the minds about the bitch that is my sister, but things were suddenly reversed. I couldn't respond.

So Bryan kept right on. "You have conveniently constructed a myth around our relationship. Diana fit so perfectly into the plotline you built around it—the beautiful and evil sister who enters your little kingdom and steals away the prince. Of course, you tend to gloss over the fact that you jilted the prince in the first place."

The coffee pot beeped—coffee was ready—but I had no strength to get up and pour any. My bones had dissolved. I put my hands over my ears, but I could still hear him.

He reached over and pulled one arm away from my ear. I looked into his eyes and dropped my other arm onto the table with a thud. What on earth was going on inside Bryan's head? His face was grizzled and worn.

"Listen." He splayed his hands out on the table. "Let's lay this all out and examine it, okay? You and I: different goals. You wanted . . ." he paused and drummed his fingers on the table. "God knows what you wanted. But it wasn't marriage and a family with me. So you spouted some feminist garbage and left me. Us." He made the "cut your throat" sign across his neck. "So, when your sister entered my life, all beauty, enthusiasm, and an obvious desire for me and for a family, things clicked right into place." His eyes bored into mine, the dark purple smears under them emphasizing their intensity.

Diversion. I needed diversion. I pulled myself up somehow, grabbed the pot, and poured us each some coffee, trying to ignore the fact that my hands were shaking. I set the pot back on its stand and fell back down into my chair, wishing I were anywhere else but here, in my apartment, facing my desolate ex as he spilled all of his guts right out in my direction.

The coffee was scalding, but I slurped some anyway. The burning on my lips and tongue felt appropriate. Bryan kept on pounding away at me.

"Beck, I knew you wanted to write. I felt that you were happy working at the coffee shop and putting in keyboard time whenever you felt inspired. Life was rolling along predictably, and I had no notion of what was going on in your head."

There was some sort of burning starting behind my eyes. It felt like the backs of my eyeballs were drying up. I rubbed my forehead with the heel of my hand.

Bryan went on. "The only clue I had to how you were feeling at the time was the night we had dinner with the Bagleys, and Mimi was so excited about having a baby. You seemed enthusiastic until she mentioned that she was going to quit her job at the law firm and become a stay-at-home mom. You got right in her face about it and told her that she was crazy to give up what she had spent her whole life preparing for, just to sit at home and 'change dirty diapers.' I was embarrassed that you seemed to be unaware of how rude and deflating your remarks were. But I chalked it up to you being a feminist, and I forgot all about it."

Bryan looked thoughtful. Suddenly, he snapped his fingers. "Of course, if I had been really smart, I would have seen this coming. After all, you were gutted when your parents split up. Naturally, after you lost your beloved dad, you would flee any sort of long-term, binding commitment."

This was a jolt I didn't need right then. "Bryan, we don't need to go into all of this, do we? It's history." The ache behind my eyes was spreading. My scalp felt too tight for my skull.

"Yes. We do. Because now that my marriage seems to be exploding in my face, you are the only one who can help me." Bryan pointed a forefinger at me, like shooting me with a gun, for God's sake. "You know D better than anybody, and you certainly know me. So for starters, I need you to help me resolve this misunderstanding with my wife, so I can put my family back together."

I reared back. "Put that gun away, you ass."

Bryan looked down at his finger, then smiled and made as if putting his 'gun' back into his holster. Then he ran a hand through his hair. "Okay. No guns. But Beck, you can't look forward without looking back first." He reached out and tapped me gently on my forearm. "You are right. It is all in the past. And now we both have moved on. And despite her larger-than-life personality, I love your sister. There is more to her than meets the eye. Trust me on this, and give her another chance. Help me, here!"

"I hate to defend my sister, but it sounds sort of like you drove her away."

He rubbed the stubble on his cheeks. "Like I said, the pregnancy hormones made her go nuts."

I burst out laughing. "Oh, *that's* it? Right. So for the entire other portion of D's life, pre-preggers, it was just the *regular* hormones making her bitchy? Of course. The selfishness and the egomania. Just the run-of-the-mill hormones."

He tilted his head back, all of the bristles of his beard glowing white in the milky light coming in through the kitchen window. He looked so *mature*. "Diana is complicated. She feels as if the whole world sees her as nothing more than an animated Barbie doll. So she pushes back. All the time. She makes people mad at her, because then at least they see her as something other than a 'goddess.' She gets back at the world this way. How would you feel if everybody you met wanted to be your friend just because you were beautiful? So they could be seen with you? Wouldn't it make you want to act out all the time?"

Oh, Bryan, *you wonderful, insightful, I shoved you right into my sister's arms* man.

I had to admit to myself that D had a good side.

A Monday night. Basketball game at school. I was rarely put in by Coach Miller, since I suck at all sports, but tonight she had given me a chance. The score was forty to fifty-five. Granted, it looked like a shoe-in for us in the fourth quarter, but STILL. I grabbed a rebound shot after Debbie Pinkley missed, and I lurched forward and tipped it in for a basket. The crowd went WILD. Mom screamed so hard, her voice was hoarse for three days afterwards. I wasn't the hero—we would have won without my score, but it was a huge moment for me.

In the parking lot afterwards, as we passed family after family on the way to their cars, some dads slapping their daughters on their backs, others grinning and holding up their palms to their girls for high-fives, I was empty. Instead of glee, all I felt was numbness—no guts, no brain—just a void. I shook my head at Mom's offer to stop on the way home for ice cream—hell, I just wanted to go home and sneak a stiff drink from the liquor cabinet.

At home, Mom tried her best to make me feel that her pride in my achievement was enough. She stroked my cheek. Told me I was "the star." Then she handed me a fresh bar of Ivory for my shower, hugged me as if she might never see me again, and went downstairs to the TV room to watch Dick Van Dyke *reruns. I nearly boiled myself under the hot water. It didn't help. As I dried off, staring at my miserable face in the steamy mirror, it was Diana who snuck upstairs, a can of Sprite under each arm and a bottle of vodka in her hand, one finger over her lips, whispering, "Ssshhh. Let's get totally drunk and forget we're fatherless!"*

I thought about all the times my sister had let me have half of her Hershey bar. The time that she knew very well that it was me who dropped and shattered Grandma's cut glass water pitcher, but told Mom that she did it because that was the day that Bob Murphy broke up with me in front of everybody in the cafeteria. I also remembered that Diana absolutely loved kids—and spent every sizzling summer weekend helping grade-schoolers make bracelets out of gimp at the community center shelter in the middle of Framington Park while I stayed home in my room, AC blasting, reading books.

"Bryan, you make sense. But you need to understand two things: ONE, old habits die hard, and so not only do I need to reconsider my sister in light of this conversation, but so does dear Diana need to face the fact that she has alienated me for years and years. There is work to be done on both sides. There is no quick fix. And TWO, it is almost sunup, and we both need a little rest. Come on."

I walked into the living room and sank into the sofa. "Sit down. We need to rest our eyes for just a tiny bit, before our heads explode." I leaned my head back onto the cushions as I felt Bryan plop down beside me. It was as if somebody put a black hood over my head, I fell asleep so damn fast.

I was running away from Bryan, who chased me, holding out an empty baby blanket. Even my dreams were second-rate potboilers. He chased me out into the street, where I was almost hit by a garbage truck backing up, beeping, beeping.

We both sat up, bleary eyed. It was my alarm, bleeping away all alone in the bedroom.

"My God." Bryan rubbed his eyes. "I feel like hell. You *look* like hell. What time is it? We need to finish our conversation."

I struggled to stand up. "Bryan. This situation is extremely convoluted. There are many people involved. Well, three people. Maybe four. But one of the most important people in this little drama is your wife and my sister, and I have absolutely no idea right now what to do. Except brush my teeth get dressed, and go to work." I ran a hand through my hair. That would have to do. I brushed past Bryan and stumbled into the bathroom. One look in the mirror was enough—I was the absolute wrath. I did a fast minty scrape of my teeth with Crest, and went back to grab something out of my closet that I could throw on and get out of there.

Bryan followed me into the bedroom like a lost puppy. "Where should I go?"

I had to get ready for work. Hell, this was a man who had seen me naked. No time for modesty. I threw off my sweats and tee shirt. I stumbled into a pair of jeans, stepped into Birkenstocks, and grabbed a white shirt off a hanger. I threw myself into it, buttoning it up incorrectly (I could fix that later), and shook my head at him. "I suggest you go back to Chicago. Or even better, go over to my mom's and talk your stupid, complicated, Barbie doll of a wife out of staying here *on break*. Grab her fat ass and take her back with you!"

I grabbed a silver bracelet out of my jewelry box, shoved it on my wrist, and spritzed some cologne in the vicinity of my armpits, because there was no time to unbutton, go back to the bathroom, and apply deodorant. Plus, I just wanted to GET OUT OF THERE.

As I rushed out the door, car keys in hand, I heard Bryan yell from the bedroom, "She doesn't have a fat ass, for your information! She just sticks out *in front!*"

CHAPTER TWELVE

I managed to pull myself together and serve coffee for about an hour. I gave away two cappuccinos that I had made with whole milk instead of skim, but the customers seemed happy with free, so that was okay. Joe gave me the stink-eye, but I could live with that.

I took an early break and pulled my cell out of my bra and called Gail. I needed some moral support. It went to voice mail, shit. So I texted her:

I am in dire straits over here-u better get in touch-we are talking death and destruction

With Gail, it takes mucho hyperbole to get a call back.

A few seconds later, my cell binged. I did what they do in all the TV suspense shows: I just hit the green button and didn't even say "hello." I didn't need to. Gail was already talking.

"What on earth is going on? Did you throw coffee in somebody's face? Did Robert Downey, Jr. just walk in? This better be good—I am in the middle of a showing, and I left my couple ogling the jetted tub, and I am calling you from the master closet, so make this FAST."

I bashed my forehead with my fist. "Is the fact that *Bryan Dallas* is at my apartment right now good enough for you?"

I heard what sounded like Gail's phone hitting hardwood floor. Scrabbling, then she came back on with a muted screech. "*What the hell?*"

"You want fast, I will give you fast. In a nutshell. Bryan is in town, he showed up at my apartment last night in the wee hours, he looked like something my cat might have dragged in, and he spilled his guts."

Pause. A gasp. "What is he doing here? Are he D are separated? Did he come here for *you? My God, are you getting back together?* WAIT. What about Theo?"

"No, we are not getting back together. Of course not! He is here, looking like a zombie, asking me for help getting his wife back." I paused, to let that sink in at the other end. "Gail, this is all very complicated. Like a Gordian knot. And I am at work. I told him to get out, but who knows if he left. Can you go over there in a bit and see if he's still there?"

Gail has flexibility at work and a company car.

"What the fuck am I supposed to say to him if he is still there?"

I shrugged. "Gail, you're a realtor; you're glib. You will think of something. Just go over there and check. If he is there, get his sorry butt out! Please! I will have my phone on me" (I know; the bra thing and breast cancer—but this was an emergency) "all day, so text me after you find out what's going on. He can't just *hang around* at my apartment!"

She laughed ruefully. "You owe me zillions of dollars and your undying devotion. And every single property listing for the rest of your life."

We ended the call, I put the cell back in my underwire, and I bit my nails for the next hour.

I had just handed a latte and a scone to a lady who did not get the memo that leggings should not be worn if you are more than forty pounds overweight, when my cell pinged. I told Joe I had to go to the restroom. Thank heaven Starbucks has single-occupant facilities. I wrenched the phone out of my bra and immediately wanted to throw up.

I just pulled up in front of your apartment. He is still here. Sitting on the front steps chatting it up with the scooter queen

Hell and damnation. This was *not* what I wanted: My ex-boyfriend hobnobbing with Bob. That would mean I would need to provide a logical, grownup explanation of the mess that was my life just then to a little kid whose own short life so far was also a total disaster. I would have to manufacture some sort of story line that would not end up with Bob thinking I was a sorry excuse for a role model, having an ex spend the night at my house. I groaned.

What I *did* want was this: my cozy apartment with vintage touches, a cat, a secure job that provided me with enough solid income so that I could write a piece of literature instead of sex books. I wanted a fire in the fireplace in chilly weather, challenging recipes with unusual spices. I wanted lazy nights watching British dramas with someone who would rub my feet. I wanted fresh fruit in a fruit bowl on my kitchen counter and an orchid on the windowsill. I wanted to have a blank past and a sunny future.

Instead, I had this: an ex-boyfriend married to my sister who was holing up at my apartment, the potential *scandal* of an ex-boyfriend married to my sister holing up at my apartment, a scarred little kid needing emotional support that I am not sure how to provide, a frail old person depending on me for this kind of help, and a best friend who wanted to make this summer "the one that changes both of our lives."

OMG just get him out of there somehow. I don't care if you say that D is having a miscarriage

This was starting to read like a bad sitcom. My shift was over in fifteen minutes anyway, so I told the "always dependable in a pinch" Joe to cover me (I am going to have to buy him a present), and I made for my car.

So here I was. A woman with a pregnant and extremely unhappy sister who was in town to sort out her selfish feelings about her long-suffering husband, who was right now at my apartment. How would this pan out? Of course, Diana would find out that Bryan came to see me first. She would be furious.

On the way home, I considered my options. One: I could just haul off and sock Bryan in the head with my lug wrench. But then I would have to enlist Bob to help me dispose of the body. Not good to involve minors in murder. Two: I could scream and threaten to kill him. But Bob. Three: I could turn the car around and go over to Mom's and hope that D was home, wallowing in her unhappiness, and drag her over to my house with me to deal with her husband. And maybe he would just be so happy to see her, it would end just like a Lifetime movie, with a passionate kiss and happy ever after. I flipped my left turn signal.

WAIT. Don't get him out of there! Keep him there-I am getting D right now

I know. Texting and driving are a lethal combination. I didn't care. Gail texted back:

Will do my best but hurry

I screeched into the parking lot in front of Mom's, careened into a parking space (or two), and leapt from the car. I ran inside, punching the elevator button at least forty times, because we all know that if you do that, the elevator comes faster. Finally, I loped down the hall to Mom's stylish teal front door. I rang Mom's doorbell, just for appearances. Twenty times. Nothing. I juggled my keychain around like a janitor, located Mom's key, and inserted it in the lock. Just as I was turning it, the door opened. There stood Diana.

Let's just pause for the full effect. She stood, hand on the edge of the door, glaring at me, her eyes puffy from the perpetual crying that was her new most favored activity. Her hair was a mess, greasy at the roots but puffing up in the rear in the glory of bedheaddom. There was a coffee stain on the front of her Ingrid and Isabel maternity top. I swear she was wearing the same damn pink polka-dot leggings she had on the last time I saw her. Her mascara was in disarray. She had a row of pimples across her forehead. In other words, she was a sight for my sore eyes.

"What do you want? I was napping." She rubbed her eyes. Chipped manicure.

"Move your massive ass inside. We have to talk, and talk fast." I shoved D into the hall, noticing that her feet looked dirty. I grabbed her by the wrist and dragged her into the bedroom. "Good God, D. You are a complete wreck. Wash your face, and wipe off your filthy feet. Comb your hair and spray on some perfume, because your sorry excuse for a husband is over at my apartment. You need to go get him. You need to take him and your almost baby home to Chicago, for God's sake."

Diana, to her credit, perked right up. "WHAT?"

"You heard me."

I had no idea a person who weighed over a hundred and seventy pounds could move so fast. She tore off the tee shirt and pulled down the leggings as far as her knees, then sank onto the side of the unmade bed. "Pull these off. Hurry!"

I did as instructed, coming face to face with my nephew through her bulge. I patted her belly. "Hi, little guy! You and your mom and dad are HEADING HOME."

"Shut up." D nearly beaned me. As she lumbered into the bathroom to wash, she pointed to the chair in the corner that was piled with her clothes. "Those are clean; get me an outfit!"

I heard the water running. Thank God. I found a long blue and white striped maternity dress that was not terribly wrinkled from being wadded up. It would do. I handed it in to D who, to her credit, was somehow able to wash up, throw her matted hair into a passable ponytail, and put on lip gloss and blusher within forty seconds. "This? You want me to wear this?"

"Look, D. Bryan was sitting on my front steps twenty minutes ago. Who knows where he is now? If you want to salvage the mess that is your marriage, I suggest you put this dress on, find some flip-flops, and let's get going before he disappears."

As she shuffled into her Havianas, it hit her. "Beck, WHAT THE FUCK IS BRYAN DOING AT YOUR HOUSE?"

"Diana, I don't have a good answer for that right now. No time to lose. I will tell you on the way over."

And I hoped to God that between the closet and the car, I would think of something.

It takes about fifteen minutes to get from Mom's to my apartment—when you drive like a sane person and observe the rules of the road. We got there in seven minutes. I managed to get green lights, and the stop sign I drove through had clear sight lines, so I didn't endanger any lives.

Between gasping for air and yelling "SLOW DOWN," D asked me what was going on.

"Bryan loves you. He is a mess without you. He came to my house last night to ask for advice."

She snorted. "Right. Advice! Naked or clothed?"

Why was this my life right now? I always used to think soap operas were a bunch of crap, but here I was, right in the middle of one. "D. My God. There was no intercourse involved."

Another snort. "Like I believe the author of sex books."

I pressed down on the gas pedal.

Sure enough. As I pulled into the driveway, there they sat, thigh to thigh, looking for all the world like a father and daughter. Bob waved gaily as I stopped the car, blocking my three neighbors from exciting the garage, violating the cardinal rule of apartment living. I could not worry about that right then. No. Gail, looking relieved, blew a kiss to Bob, waved at me and D, and got in her car. She drove off, probably saying a prayer of thanks to be the hell out of there.

We leapt from the car. Well, I did. Diana sort of unfurled herself slowly. I rushed around to the passenger side of the car and helped her unwedge herself. Then we turned to the two chums on the steps.

"What in the hell are YOU doing here?" Diana tends to spew. I put my hand gently (ish) over her mouth.

"What she means is 'Hi, Bryan. Who is your little friend? I am surprised to see you here. Why did you come, if I may ask?'"

Bob hopped up, her sneakers with the blinking lights twinkling red and green. "Hi! Are you Beck's sister? I am so happy to meet you! Can I babysit when the baby comes?"

Bryan stood, looking abashed. Which for Bryan are two red spots on his cheeks and a wrinkled up nose. "Hi."

Thinking fast, as I do, I pulled my sister over to her husband and said in my cheeriest voice, "Here we all are. On this lovely day! Bryan, you and D must really want to talk, I bet. There has been so much going on!"

I sort of shoved D into Bryan's chest. Bob, who was still bouncing, started to giggle. "Oh, Diana, this is my friend Bob. She and I need to go . . . do something . . . so you two just feel free to hang around here for a while," I said brightly.

I took Bob's grubby little hand and turned her toward the street and began pulling her towards the sidewalk. She swung her head back to look at the Dallases, who stood awkwardly in front of the steps. "Bye! Nice to meet you!"

My sincere hope was that while I was entertaining Bob at the park by coming up with some sort of acceptable story line for an eight-year-old as to what the hell was going on, Diana and Bryan would magically disappear from my stoop and from Framington forever.

CHAPTER THIRTEEN

Bob and I plunked ourselves down on a bench. The sun-soaked wood warmed the backs of our legs. This was an idyllic place where moms brought preschoolers to play in the sandbox. There were always boys throwing softballs in the summer afternoons. Leaves swished in the breeze, and all the benches were permanently sticky from juice box residue. Dogs weren't allowed, but they loped around the swing sets anyway, woofing congenially. I loved it there, and so did Bob.

Bob wiped the sweat off her upper lip. "I like Bryan."

I leaned back, letting the breeze ruffle my hair as I wondered where to go with all of this with Bob. "Bryan is very nice. What were you two talking about?"

Bob smiled. "Well. I was across the street, skipping. Because, you know, my scooter is broken. I saw the front door of your apartment open, and a very tall and handsome man came out. For a minute, I hoped it was my dad, but then I knew better."

My heart stung.

"So I waved, because he looked friendly. I know. Stranger Danger. But I thought waving was okay, especially since I was all the way across the street. Do you think Gran will be mad?"

I patted Bob's freckled arm. "No, I'm sure she won't be mad, this time. But you really shouldn't even wave at strangers—men or women. But go on."

"Well. I kept skipping, but in a circle. Then Bryan called over to me and said 'Hi! My name is Bryan Dallas, and I am a good friend of Beck Throckmorton's. I need to get across town.' Then he asked about buses and stuff like cabs."

I wasn't ready to cast Bryan totally into the slimeball category, but I did think approaching little kids for transit advice a bit creepy. But I had to give him credit for knowing when he was in no condition to drive. "Then what happened? How did you two end up on my front steps?"

Bob looked concerned. "I told Bryan I didn't know about that, but that Gran would. I told him that she was over at Mrs. Ellingson's house. She lives just behind us on Flint Street. I told him that Gran has coffee over there, but that she would be home in a few minutes." Bob paused.

Oy. Teachable moment in the midst of my own personal volcano of a life right now. But what could I do? "Bob, you are right. First of all, from now on, you must not wave to strangers. Even when they are across the street. And never, ever tell a stranger that you are all alone and that your gran isn't home. Yes—Stranger Danger! Bob, do you understand?"

"But I knew who he was. You told me about him."

"Bob, honey. It's all right. You're safe and sound. We just need to keep you that way. Okay? You can't just trust a person who says he knows me."

You know how it is when a child displays wisdom way beyond her years? Bob looked at me witheringly. She rolled her denim blue eyes at me like a teenager. "Right. Got it. But anyway, Gran came home, and he saw her. I yelled over and told her that this was your sister's husband, and he wanted to get a ride."

"Okay, kiddo. I see you had the whole situation under control."

Bob grinned to herself and began to pick at a scab on her knee, watching with fascination as it bled a little around the edges. As she picked, I asked her what she and Bryan talked about on the stoop.

"Well. He told me that your sister was mad at him. And that he was scared of her a little."

Oi vey.

She stopped studying her now bloody knee. She looked off into the distance, her eyes narrowing. "So what's the problem? Why is your sister mad?"

Oh boy. "Diana is confused right now. When women are pregnant, sometimes they get moody. And I think that she and Bryan might have had an argument about something silly. So Bryan came here to apologize." I flashed my teeth in an insincere smile.

Bob looked up at the sky. "But he was at YOUR house."

Damn.

Bob peered at me with the wisdom of a baby owl. "You said before that you and your sister don't get along. Because you are furious with her for marrying Bryan. Are you jealous of her all the time, even though you have Theo for your boyfriend?"

I leaned back against the bench so fast I banged my head. Good question. What *about* Theo?

Bob continued, "Because Theo is very nice. He can't fix scooters, but he is very nice. And Bryan is nice, too. I can see why you wanted him for a boyfriend. You said he decided he would rather be married to your sister. Why? Were you mean to him?"

The bench felt hot against my legs. I reached over and mussed Bob's hair a little. "I was mean to him. I didn't realize it at the time, but I was very mean to him."

Bob looked at me with a combination of love and lost innocence. "And it was so bad that you couldn't just say sorry?" I sensed that she was thinking of her own mother.

I needed a spin-doctor, but I was on my own. "I think that I was too young to be serious." Inside my head, a voice was screaming *Trite! Pap! You can come up with something better than this! You are a WRITER, for crap's sake!*

Bob was solemn. "I bet you didn't take drugs."

"Well, no. I didn't take drugs." *For God's sake, don't say you left him because you didn't want kids!* "I was sort of selfish, I guess. I wanted to have a big adventure and write some really important books. I thought that having a boyfriend right then might hold me back. So I broke up with him. I think I hurt him a lot. So I shouldn't be so jealous of him marrying my sister, right?" I nudged Bob in the ribs. She didn't respond. Just stared at nothing.

"Bob. Sometimes adults just can't get along."

I watched as the child next to me morphed from a sweet little kid on a bench in the safety of this pristine Ohio park into a small, forlorn refugee from life, her eyes dull. I watched her body twitch— her bones seeming to clatter together. She drew her chest inward and pulled her arms around her torso, as if trying to cradle herself. Her head dropped to her chest as she asked quietly, "Why do grownups always hurt other people?"

I put my arm around her and rested my head on hers. We sat quietly, listening to the murmurs of conversation, the thrum of traffic, and the beating of our own hearts. I couldn't answer.

▷◁

Thank God, Bryan talked my sister into going back to Chicago with him. According to Mom, they patched things up enough at my house to ride back over to Mom's, where they continued their conversation/argument for a few hours. Then, before she could muster up the courage to kick them out so that she could get her life back, they threw D's things into her bag and trundled her into Bryan's Honda. They left in a cloud of exhaust.

As time passes, things tend to improve. What do they say about time healing all wounds? It certainly helps things, time does. The next few weeks were uneventful, as Gail continued her quest for happiness with Rick, Theo continued being Mr. Almost Right, Ella and Bob started an ongoing Uno tournament that currently Ella was winning, Bob seemed to be on an even keel, and I muddled along, being my usual coffee-stained self.

School had just started, and already Ella was having trouble keeping up with everything Bob-related, so I was helping out as best as I could, what with a job, writing, and looking for my missing cat, who disappeared that day Bryan and Diana made up on my front steps, ignoring the fact that they had left all the doors wide open, so *my* keel was far from even.

Bob sat beside me on the front steps, practicing her whistling and trying her best to cheer me up. It was futile. On this particular Sunday afternoon, I had not washed my hair or brushed my teeth since two days prior. I had been living on coffee. I had managed to meet my manuscript deadline, but my agent wondered why a dead cat figured so prominently in a book about a pole dancer and her surfer boyfriends. I couldn't really come up with an explanation. I had been sleeping poorly, despite the fact that I should have been happy and peaceful since D and Bryan had left town.

Bob stopped her serenade and patted my shoulder. She reached over and took my coffee mug and set it carefully on the steps beside us. "Beck, I know you are so sad about Simpson. I'm sad, too. But you need to cheer up, because school has started, and you promised to start walking with me and Hallie since Gran's knees hurt after the first few times. And you know you have to have faith—cats have nine lives! So can you try to get in a better mood?"

I sighed. "Honey, I will try." I pictured that infamous afternoon. Bryan and Diana, standing in front of my house, working out their stupid differences, holding hands, making up, French kissing. Not noticing one detail around them, such as my darling cat walking out of the apartment, down the stairs, and through the front door, probably passing right in front of them as he padded into God knows what. The path of an oncoming car? The jaws of a neighborhood dog? The arms of a catnapper? I seethed at the thought of the both of them, self-absorbed and clueless.

"Beck? Are you listening?" Bob jabbed me with her forefinger.

I blinked. The image of Bryan and D dissipated. "I'm sorry. I know you're excited about school. I bet you're making tons of friends. You are very busy. I miss having you over so often." I smiled at her, but Bob saw right through me, apparently.

"Beck, you have to get serious about cheering up! Being sad about Simpson is not going to help things. You have to have faith that he is fine somewhere, and he is going to come back. Gran says that to me all the time, whenever I get worried about my dad. She says I should get a picture in my mind of him reading my letters and smiling, and being safe and sound. You can do that, too. Imagine Simpy safe. Like in some other neighborhood. With a nice family taking care of him. Picture them seeing one of your signs at their grocery! They will be so happy to find out that you are looking for him!"

I shut my eyes and tried to picture a soccer mom holding Simpson. Looking at the LOST CAT sign on her street corner. Comparing the cat in her arms to the photo. Listening to Simpson purr. Then shrugging, probably thinking that any idiot who would let a cat like this out of her sight deserved to lose him forever. Then walking back into her neatly landscaped house and shutting the lacquered door behind her and her new cat with finality. A searing pain shot through the back of my head.

Bob sensed the futility of this line of conversation. "I picked out what I'm going to wear on Monday."

I took a breath. "Really? What?"

"It was between the lime green shorts and the sundress with the daisies on it. Gail was over visiting Gran and me, and she had a good point: recess and a dress. So I am wearing the shorts with my new white polo. And I am so excited about my new Toms. Thank you for getting them for me. I think they will be very comfortable and also good for running at recess."

I nodded.

"Hallie and I are going to dress sort of alike. But not twins or anything. She has green shorts with white polka dots. She is wearing them. And all her barrettes will be white. She is wearing a white top, too. So we'll be color coordinated. Hallie doesn't have Toms. So she'll wear her sneakers."

Right at that moment I wished I had the resiliency and bravery of this stalwart little female: her father in mortal danger across the world somewhere, her mother a lost cause in some rehab ward, her grandmother well-intentioned but vigorless. And here I sat beside her, feeling depressed about my lost cat, my dysfunctional family, my boring job, my lackluster writing career, and my kind but mediocre boyfriend.

Ugh. I had to get a grip somehow. "Fake it until you make it" came to mind.

"Bob. What if we went to the shelter this afternoon to look at cats and kittens?" This faking business wasn't going to be easy. I ran my tongue over my grody teeth, but smiled brightly in spite of them. "It might be a good idea to move on." An image of Simpson curled up on the immaculate sofa in the great room over at the soccer mom's house floated into my head.

Bob jumped up and loomed over me, her hands digging into my knees. "No! You can't do that! You can't give up on Simpson! It wouldn't be right! He is going to *come back*." Her eyes burned with an intensity that nearly knocked me over.

She squeezed harder, those chewed-off nails nearly piercing my skin.

This caught my attention. I got it. The situation was bigger than me. I was all grown up—a role model and a very important supporter to this one lonely little person standing in front of me, her fingers digging into my thighs for all she was worth. I put my hands on her cheeks and stroked her freckles with my thumbs. "Bob, you are absolutely right. Simpson is just taking his time getting back to us. I will absolutely not go get any kittens."

Bob beamed, let go of my knees (thankfully), turned herself around, and sat on my lap. I put my arms around her and held on tight. We looked up at the sky.

"Beck, do you see that cloud up there?" She pointed to a fluffy amalgam above the maple tree. "It looks like a duck."

CHAPTER FOURTEEN

It was certainly not what anybody expected. Diana's pregnancy, although filled with her own signature style of drama, lots of whining, and attention-grabbing but inconsequential Braxton-Hicks contractions, had been normal. Healthy.

But delivery was a different story. Things got dicey about seven hours in, when the fetal monitor showed that the baby was in distress. Chaos ensued, as it became clear that the cord was tangled around the baby's neck. Luckily, there were excellent obstetricians involved. The hospital was known for its neonatology department. After an emergency caesarian section, during which Diana began to hemorrhage, Alexander Villiers Dallas was delivered safely, Diana was stabilized. Although it was "touch and go there for a minute," according to the relieved father in his ebullient phone call, all was well. Mother and baby were resting comfortably.

Theo poured us all another glass of wine. He had some sort of sonata playing in the background. Gail ignored Rick's hand on her knee and looked concerned. I polished off this, my third glass, almost instantly, and I held it up to Theo. "Just one more. I need this. It isn't every day that I become an aunt and nearly lose a sister."

Theo looked doubtful, but poured me another half glass. Setting the empty bottle on the mantel, he sat down beside me on the floor. Before I could toss this one back, he gently removed the glass from my hand and set it on the coffee table.

Gail removed Rick's hand and scooted away from him. "Isn't that sort of an exaggeration? Everything turned out all right. It was just a difficult birth. But both she and the baby will be fine won't they?"

Rick, who up until this point had not evinced one iota of interest in anything but Gail's torso, added, "Right. And she is in a good hospital with good doctors, isn't she? And having the cord wrapped around the baby's neck is scary, but they handled it—that happened to my sister. She and the baby were fine. Your sister will be okay. Nothing more to worry about. Caesarians require a slightly longer recovery, but that's all."

Still stunned at Rick's revelation, I looked over at Gail. She raised an eyebrow, as if to say, "God knows where THAT came from."

"Rick, you're right, D is fine, but she lost a lot of blood. It wasn't just the cord thing. The placenta didn't entirely detach, or something like that. I'm not a medical expert, but according to my mother, it was a critical situation there for a time. D had to have a transfusion."

Gail took a sip of wine and held the glass in her lap, gently twirling it with one hand. "Are you going to go to Chicago to help? Or is Claire just going to go over there and camp out for a while?"

"This is problematic. Mom is going for a week, but she has clients. Pressing demands for bathroom makeovers and Italian plaster. She can't stay any longer than a week without one of her design customers having a fit about granite countertops. And to be perfectly honest, I'm afraid if I went to Chicago I would kill either the baby due to lack of any sort of baby care qualifications, or I would kill my sister out of sheer frustration, OR I would murder Bryan for losing my cat. Toss up."

Gail set her glass down. "Well, this is just typical. Beck, you have to look beyond the end of your nose on this one. That family is your family. Can't you learn to just let bygones be bygones, for God's sake?" She frowned, which on Gail looked like a sexy squint.

"But—"

Theo interrupted, but softly. "You know, Beck, it might not be a bad idea to rethink your whole position on all of this. You only have the one sibling. And that baby boy is completely innocent. Think about what you want your life to be like in a few years. Won't you want to have your family all together? Won't you want to know your nephew?"

Whew. This was like some sort of Midwestern intervention reality show. I looked around at the assemblage: one blonde best friend with perfect eyebrows, an all-silk wardrobe and nothing but the best intentions; her devastatingly gorgeous boyfriend who seemed a little bored; me, the sad-sack self-absorbed older sister; and my tall, kind, concerned, and color-coordinated boyfriend. I didn't like being the center of attention.

"By the way—the baby's name is Alexander." I picked my glass back up and had another generous swig of wine.

Theo nodded. "Alexander Dallas. Your nephew. You will want to know him."

I turned and shot him an incredulous look. "You say that like some sort of movie hero. What does this mean? I need to get to know him because he will eventually save my life? I should know him because I will probably not have a child of my own? I should get to know him so that I can be a better babysitter when my sister decides she needs an extended spa vacation? Why, Theo?"

At this point, my negative attitude had created a completely awkward situation. You could cut the uneasiness in the room with a Brie knife. Gail sat up suddenly and looked at her watch— straight out of any number of movie scenes: "Look at the time! I have to check in with a client—I may have a bidding war going on for that house on White Ash Circle. Really, I have to get out of here." She stood, smoothing out the creases in her raspberry douppioni skirt. She finished the last sip of her wine, grabbed Rick, and hauled him off the sofa, his Oakley sunglasses falling from his pocket and disappearing between the suede cushions.

Rick tried to fish them out, but Gail powered him towards the door, his head craning back towards the sectional.

"Honey, Theo will get those and bring them to you. We really have to run."

As they were about to go out the door, Rick still looking pained, Gail turned back for a parting shot. "Beck. The 'Diana steals Bryan' story is old news. I know. It sucked. But adults have to take control of situations. Life isn't always a bowl of cherries, you know! It may be a bitter pill to swallow, but you are the one who may have to swallow it and get this whole family shitshow to end. It's ancient history!"—she fluttered her fingers in my direction—"I know; sort out the metaphors and just get going on this, will you?" And with that, she pulled Rick out the door and shut it firmly behind her.

I hadn't bothered to get up for any of her soliloquy—I was too pooped. It was a combination of stress, my missing cat, boredom with my life, dissatisfaction with my writing career, and just general, all-around malaise. Theo, who had tried to be the perfect host and escort Gail and Rick out, only to have his own door shut in his face, wandered into the kitchen and returned with one bottle of Chardonnay and one of Burgundy.

"We should probably get shit-faced right now, correct? These two ought to do the trick."

I wasn't to be so easily dissuaded. "Theo, no, let's not drink any more, because I really want to know *why* you think I will so 'want to know' my nephew." Theo flinched. "No, seriously. I am not picking a fight—I just really want to know the answer."

Theo poured himself another glass of Chardonnay. I hate Chardonnay, by the way. To me, it tastes like drinking perfume.

Theo sat down on the carpet beside me. He glugged some wine (not in character for him, *at all*), put his glass down, and began:

"Beck, I know you say you don't care for children. I have heard you claim this a number of times. And yet, one of the most important people in your life right now is an adorable little girl who seems to be your, pardon my French, BFF. So your 'I don't like kids' thing does not hold any water. That's first of all."

He paused and looked at me to gauge my reaction. He drew back, screwed up his nose and also squinted at me, covering his face with his hands as if he thought I might haul off and sock him. "Okay, okay, Theo. I am not feeling particularly violent at the moment. Go on."

"Okay." He took another sip of wine. My God, what was he going to say that required such fortification?

"Well. Beck. Here is the second of all. I think you imagine that you are still in love with your ex. But let's face it—that is an illusion you are carrying around with you. The cool guy on campus falling for the slightly off-kilter but charming girl. They make the perfect couple. But Beck, you and Bryan obviously were not the match made in heaven, or you wouldn't have been the one to break up with him, right?"

Yada, yada, yada. I nodded, waving my hands weakly in surrender.

"Third of all. You are not the kind of person who just writes people off. Okay, I actually don't know you well enough to vouch for that, but you certainly seem loyal. This is your family, and the rules of human relationships are not just black and white in families. We are stuck with these imperfect people our entire lives. Whether we hate them or love them. So isn't it easier to hang together with them at a level of at least *cordiality*, if nothing else?"

I was so sick of myself at this point. This was threatening to overtake me in a sea of migraine. "Theo, you speak the wisdom of the Oracles. I will take every single crumb of what you said under advisement. But right now, I feel slightly queasy, and I have an aura."

Theo's eyes popped.

"No, an *aura*, not a *HALO*. I am getting a migraine. I need to go home and sleep it off."

Theo, ever the perfect boyfriend, looked concerned, bent over to help me up, wrapped his arm around my shoulder, walked me to the bathroom for a cold compress to put over my eyes, offered me some Excedrin (which I chewed like candy), and bundled me into to his car, took me home, and tucked me in.

It was so comforting. As I drifted off to sleep, hearing the soft click of Theo latching my front door, I reached out to pet Simpson. The left side of my head lit up with pain as if a firecracker had exploded in there.

I woke up four hours later with a dry mouth, a fragile feeling in the vicinity of my left ear and left upper molars, a very strong desire for a Popsicle, and the horrifying realization that I had to go to

Chicago when Mom got back. Oh, yes. And that other realization: that I should grab Theo and prostrate myself while apologizing to him.

CHAPTER FIFTEEN

Mom came home absolutely *fizzing* with enthusiasm about baby Alexander. She called me at least seven times to tell me that:

1. He was the cutest baby ever born.
2. He had eyes just like mine.
3. Bryan was gaga over him.
4. He had cute, fuzzy hair.
5. He was having a hard time "latching" (whatever the hell that was).
6. He smiled already.
7. Diana was struggling.
8. Therefore, I was needed in Chicago, STAT.

How in God's name having me, her hated older sister, readily at hand was going to help D was a mystery to me. And this whole "latching" business was equally mysterious. Plus, ever since Bryan and I spilled our guts about everything, I quivered with guilt whenever I thought of this baby, or babies in general.

So it was with great trepidation that I stood in my bedroom on a Friday evening, packing my bag for my eight a.m. flight to Chicago (via Columbus; Framington airport flew directly to absolutely nowhere BUT Columbus) the next morning.

Bob sat cross-legged on my bed, directing. Bob began with "Don't forget—you have to pack soft things. Babies like to snuggle, and so you have to be cozy. So don't take that hoodie with the zipper—it will poke Alex."

"Bob, you have never even laid eyes on this baby."

Bob shook her head with eight-year-old vigor. "Have too! You showed me those pictures on your cell that your mom sent you. He is nearly bald and cute."

"Right. Anything else I need to know? Since you seem to be an expert?"

Bob frowned, her freckles compressing into her furrowed brow. "There was a baby who lived next door to us in Iowa. Her name was Lucy, and she liked to snuggle. I held her a bunch of times. Her mom told me that babies like fuzzy things. Are you bringing Alex a present? Like a stuffed animal or something?"

Shit. I hadn't even thought about a present. I wondered if they had baby things for sale at O'Hare. I wouldn't have enough time to go shopping in Columbus. "Right. I will look for something for him at the airport in Chicago before I go over to their house."

Bob looked dubious. "Really, Beck. It should be something special. You know, since this is your nephew. Do you have anything special that you loved when you were little? Something you could take with you and give to Alex? Like a blankie you knitted for him?"

My God. This child was more mature than I was, by far. Of course, I should have been knitting him something. Or crocheting him something. That would entail already knowing how to knit or crochet, however. I rolled my eyes and sighed. "Bob, you make a very good point here. The main problem is that I don't know how to knit, and I am leaving at the crack of dawn. Do you have any other good ideas?"

I have never seen a person leap off a bed so fast. Bob flew over to me and hugged my waist. "I have just the thing! Gran knits! I will go get it! BE RIGHT BACK!"

Bob cantered out of the bedroom, and I heard my front door clap shut behind her. Crisis averted, apparently. I put the zippy hoodie back on the floor of my closet, where it lived, and began rummaging through my things for appropriately soft apparel. I chose four oft-washed tee shirts that were so soft they were nearly falling apart, three pairs of leggings (not particularly soft, but they were like second skin, so I figured that was fine), a jersey night shirt without buttons, and three camisoles. I was considering whether or not I needed a dress when Bob burst back into the apartment and sprinted back into the bedroom, holding the most gorgeous yellow-and-white striped knitted throw I had ever seen.

"Oh, Bob! This is beautiful! But did you just take this? Does your gran know you have it?"

Bob's freckles went neon, I swear. "Oh, YES! I told her that we had an emergency, and that you needed something very special for Alex, and that they don't *have* special baby things at airports, and what should we do?"

She stopped for a quick breath. "And guess what? Gran has a whole trunk full of things that she knits for gifts! She makes them for the church! But she has plenty! So she told me I could choose one for Alex, and I thought this one was the prettiest!"

Bob laid the throw on the bed with great reverence. She ran her small hand over the folds, and then laid her face down against it. "Alexander," she whispered. "This is especially for you from me, Beck, and Gran."

I nearly choked on the lump in my throat. I knelt beside Bob and stroked the softness of the gift. "Oh, Bob. You are brilliant. I will be sure to tell them that this wonderful gift was all your idea. As a matter of fact, do you want to make a card to go with it? You can explain how your gran made this, and how you came up with the idea for giving it to Alex."

Bob nodded. She folded the throw neatly into a square, and I went off to find some paper and a pencil. I set Bob up at the kitchen table, and managed to find a red crayon and a blue crayon in my junk drawer. Biting her lower lip, Bob labored over the card for a good ten minutes.

When it was finished, she folded it in two with a flourish. "Here you go! Do you want me to read it to you? See—this picture on the front is of you, me, and Gran."

She held it up. On the front, bordered in crooked red, stood three blue figures. One, wearing red pants and holding what looked kind of like a blue rectangle with a stick at the end was me, she said. "That blue thing in your hand is a Popsicle."

"Love it!"

The other adult figure was obviously Ella. She had a little red rod in each hand. "Knitting needles," Bob pointed out.

The third figure was a small blue person. She had a round head with a large, red smile. There were blue dots all over her face. "Freckles—I had to draw the truth," Bob said. In her hand, outlined in red, was obviously the knitted throw. "It shouldn't be red. But you didn't have a yellow crayon. Do you think they will understand?" I nodded.

"Okay! Here is what I put inside." She unfolded the card and read

Dear Alex. This blankie is for you to hold when you are sad or scared. It is very soft. My gran made it. But it is from me, Gran, AND Beck. Love, Bob

Bob folded the card closed and held it out to me.

"Oh, Bob, this is wonderful. I don't know what I would do without you."

Bob jumped up and down. "I KNOW. But, Beck, you also have to remember to be nice when you're there. Even if your sister is mean to you—you have to be nice. And don't worry about me walking to school without adult supervision, because Hallie and I are always on the lookout for trouble. Gran says you can stop worrying about us, too, because Framington is safe."

After Bob left, I finished packing, and then sat down in front of my laptop, the screen glaring back at me, nearly empty, but for the title at the top of the otherwise blank screen:

The Summer Child, By Rebecca Throckmorton

CHAPTER SIXTEEN

I had no idea that babies cry so damn much. I mean, when they are conscious, they are crying. Part of this whole shrieking thing had to do with the latching debacle. I now know *all about* latching.

See, the conscientious mother of today knows that the best way to feed a baby is with breast milk. This stuff contains all sorts of antibodies that protect the baby from disease. It is convenient—no bottles to wash, no nipples to sterilize, none of that. All you have to do is pop the kid onto your chest, and he will go to town. And you will feel fulfilled. And the baby will thrive.

I copied this almost verbatim from the brochure on breast-feeding that D brought home from the hospital. It was full of optimistic propaganda, because if what D was going through is typical, breast-feeding is nearly impossible.

Latching is what Alexander is supposed to do whenever he cries. D, who by the way, was even bitchier than ever (more about this later), grabs him away from Bryan (exhausted and also grouchy, see "more about that later," above), who has changed Alex's diaper. She sits propped up by multiple pillows, some sort of nursing pillow thing in her lap. She holds the baby and undoes her nursing bra. Alex, theoretically, just grabs on and drinks the elixir that is life-giving and oh, so perfectly suited to his little baby digestive system.

Here is what actually happens: Alex screams. Bryan, who can barely see, he is so bone-tired, nearly drops Alex while placing him on the changing table. I sit on the chair in the bedroom, helpless. Alex stumbles over to D, who is enthroned in the bed, looking bloated and also completely spent. She takes the baby and attempts to put him to her breast, where he grabs on, tries to take a pull, and then falls backwards, howling.

D, who I am sure, wishes they had a listing for "wet nurses" in the Yellow Pages, begins to whine. "My nipples hurt. My breasts are engorged! I am going to get a breast infection! Where is the breast pump? Bryan, DO SOMETHING!"

That was my first day there.

So, yeah. The place was in chaos. My antipathy towards my sister was not even noticed, because she was so engrossed with her nipples, the fact that Alex might starve to death before he was two months old, her incision, Bryan's inability to respond to her demands fast enough, and the adorableness of Alexander Villiers Dallas—who was even lovable while shrieking.

Bryan, on the other hand, was a great target. I managed to blame him loudly for the disappearance of my cat within the first five minutes that I was in his presence:

"Do you realize that my cat is missing due to your extreme negligence?"

Bleary eyed and half conscious, Bryan took my suitcase out of my hand and began leading me towards the guest room. "Huh?"

I followed him through the diaper-strewn living room. "SIMP-SON. You let him OUT. Remember the night you showed up at my apartment? The night you spewed your soul about how much you *adore your wife*?"

Bryan nearly fell over my suitcase as he twisted around to grab me and nearly stop all the circulation in my arm. "The truth hurts, doesn't it?" Then he let go. "Sorry. I didn't mean to hurt you. Let's not revisit the past, okay? Forget all that." He looked down at the dent he had just put in my arm. "Oh, sorry." He patted the spot, as if hitting the place he just pinched would help. "I shouldn't have even come over to your apartment, I know."

He set my suitcase down in his office, the "guest room." There was a pullout sofa, a stack of clean sheets, and two towels set on the surface. I would need to make up my own bed. Naturally.

"But I am on edge. Diana is on the verge of an emotional break-down with all of this baby stress."

"You mean she hasn't had one? Over the failure to *latch*? You think she is still within the range of emotional normalcy?"

Bryan looked on the verge of tears. "Beck, I swear, if I had the strength, I would slap you. Alexander is a couple of weeks old, and I have had, what, three hours of sleep in that time? I have to hold down a full-time job and live with all of this baby-latching nonsense. You think you can just show up and start hurling accusations? Especially after I just apologized?"

That stung. "Accusations? What? You think my cat might NOT be missing? That I just haven't noticed him, sitting there in the corner of the living room?"

"STOP." It was the loudest whisper I had ever heard.

"Just STOP. You are yammering on about a CAT. A damn cat! I am sorry for letting him out; it was an accident. My life was just a little crapulous at that moment, as you recall. So please accept my apology, get a kitten, and move on. Because right now, I have a starving newborn, a wife with sore breasts, and a massive headache."

"Oh. So things are not blissful at the moment." I smirked a little. It felt great.

"Beck, are you here to help out? Lend a hand? Save the day? Because if not—if you are here to cause trouble—you should just turn around and go back where you came from. I cannot deal with any more shit beyond what is going down between myself, my kid, and my wife right now." He snapped his fingers so close to my face that I flinched.

Whoa. It sank in. As I heard Alexander begin to bawl in the background, I got it. This was an epic shitshow, right here in Lincoln Park. Three people were in the agonies of trying to become a family. Nobody was succeeding at it. For me to stir the pot with my jealousy, my guilt, and my missing cat would just be evil. D had plenty of problems right now. I could revel in her misery without adding to it. Okay, maybe I could grow up and *not* revel in her misery. Yeah. Maybe I could be an adult here. Bob's final advice to me came to mind.

I wrested my suitcase from between Bryan's knees and pointed to the nursery. "Go help D. I can unpack just fine. Then if you give me a grocery list, I can go shopping for you. Or wash dishes. Or something."

Bryan ran a hand under his nose and wiped it on his pant leg. "Okay."

Pitiful.

▷◁

"It says here in the breastfeeding brochure that you shouldn't supplement with formula."

D was frantic, Alex was sobbing, and I had a headache. "It says here that failure to latch might be due to flat nipples. Are yours flat?"

D glared at me with wild eyes. She thrust her right boob in my direction. "Oh, I don't know, Beck! DOES THIS LOOK FLAT TO YOU?" She squeezed it, shooting milk over Alex's bobbing head, right in my direction.

"Okay, okay. Calm down. Have you had a lactation consultation? There is a phone number right here. They come over to your house and analyze the situation."

Diana cupped Alexander's little downy head in her hand, stroking his beet red, screaming little cheeks with her fingers. He would try to nurse, take a couple sips, and then drop off the breast. He looked exhausted and frustrated simultaneously.

"You know what? Screw the breastfeeding! I don't want some hippy woman with flowers in her hair to come over here and comment about my nipples! I don't need anybody to tell me that I am a failure at this!"

D struggled back into her nursing bra, humped off the bed, and carefully placed Alex into his bassinet. She leaned over and kissed him, trying her best, I imagine, to ignore his screams. Then she grabbed me and dragged me into the living room.

"Call the pediatrician." She scrabbled around in the papers that were stuffed inside the diaper bag they gave her at the hospital. "Here is her number: Dr. Stephanie Gordon. Go ON. Call them right now and tell them that I need the name of a formula brand for Alexander." Then call my OB and tell them that I need a home nurse to come over TODAY to give me a shot to dry up my milk. She thrust another scrap of paper at me—this one for Lincoln Park Obstetrics and Gynecology. "DO NOT JUST STAND THERE LOOKING LIKE AN IDIOT. DO IT."

"There are shots to dry up your milk? Really?" I was learning so much new information that would be totally useless to me in the future.

Diana pressed her hands to her breasts, as if that would start stemming the flow. "Yes! Of course! How do you think our mother's entire generation managed not to breastfeed? It's a hormone or something. Beck, make the call! My son is starving to death and my nipples are killing me!"

She scuttled back into the bedroom to comfort her son, clutching her breasts.

I sat down on the sofa, pulled out my cell, and phoned Dr. Gordon's office. After a lengthy conversation with Loretta, the nurse practitioner, I disconnected. My first reaction, I have to admit, was elation. But I tamped that down.

D was in the rocking chair, humming and stroking Alex, who was sighing jaggedly. My heart melted at the dimples in his elbows as he tried to settle himself by stroking the yellow throw that Ella knitted, which D had draped over her shoulder.

"I have bad news," I whispered, sitting on the window seat beside the rocker. "They don't give meds for drying up any more. You are just going to have to gut it out. They say to wear a tight bra, take cold showers, use cabbage leaves as compresses (??), and it should be about a week or two. You can't pump. Oh, and here is a list of formulas—tell me which one to buy, and I will get some right away. They told me not to bother calling the OB, because they would tell me the same thing." I tried my damnedest to suppress a grin.

The shock that registered in D's eyes was epic. I thought she might explode. Alex whimpered and shifted in her lap, his little eyelids fluttering. D put her face on his head and began to cry softly. "Call the fucking lactation consultant."

▷◁

Belinda was very understanding. I guess you have to be empathetic in order to counsel desperate new mothers about how to be successful at what everyone who has never had a baby thinks is the easiest and most natural thing in the world. After all, didn't peasants in the olden days just drop the baby in the wheat fields, deliver the placenta and eat it or something, and then strap the infants on to their chests with a burlap sack, and the babies just sucked away while their mothers harvested?

But that isn't really the way it is, according to Belinda, who was very credible. She did have very large breasts. Belinda told us that she had trouble getting all three of her children to nurse, and that this was very common.

First, to Diana's chagrin, she examined D's nipples. Sure enough, flat as pancakes. The solution was horrifying: D was to grind her nipples between her thumb and forefinger for about two minutes before putting Alexander on the breast. Belinda assured us that it would hurt at first, but not too bad after the first week or so. This procedure would make her nipples stand up and pay attention.

Diana turned a pale shade of green when Belinda demonstrated that. I winced. Bryan gulped.

Secondly, and I wonder why the hell Belinda didn't START with that one, was the *nipple shield*. This made much more sense to me. It is a nipple, like the ones on baby bottles, sort of. The mother places this over her flat nipple, and VOILA! The baby just latches right on and drinks like a champ!

Belinda sort of failed us on this one, because it was apparent that she frowned on the whole nipple shield scenario. When Diana, her eyes moist with relief, asked Belinda to produce one of these gifts from God so that she could nurse Alex right away, Belinda informed us that she didn't have any ON HER.

What good is a lactation consultant without equipment? For heaven's sake.

So we all mumbled assorted thanks to Belinda, and as we gave her the bum's rush out of there, Bryan grabbed the car keys to hustle right over to the CVS for a case of nipple shields.

Meanwhile, D, who was convinced that Alexander was dehydrated, attempted to force water into him with an eyedropper. I had had enough, and so I snuck into the guest room to call Theo.

"How is everything going?" He sounded so *rested*.

"Not well. The nursing is a nightmare. But Bryan just went out for nipple shields, and so that will be the saving grace, we hope."

There was a pause. I forgot that until about forty-five minutes ago, I had no idea what nipple shields were, either. "They are things you put over your nipples so the baby can latch on better."

Another pause.

What did that mean, I wondered. "I'm exhausted. As are we all."

"How long are you staying?"

This wasn't like Theo. Usually he was so interested in all the details. "Are you in a hurry or something?"

"Sort of. I'm with a client."

"Oh, Theo. Sorry to interrupt. Are you in the midst of a bunch of paperwork?"

There was rustling at the other end. "No. I'm at the grocery store, and I nearly dropped my phone on a melon."

"You're at the grocery store? Working with a client? What? Is she *buying* the grocery store?" I had him.

Theo is an honest man. A kind man. A color-coordinated man. He is the last man on earth I would suspect of hiding a second girlfriend. The world was conspiring to convince me that I was destined to be single, evidently. "Theo, what is going on, really?"

He breathed heavily into his phone. I heard the woman in the background whisper something. Ugh.

"Beck, all right. I'm not actually at the grocery store. I am with a client, though. We just finished closing on her new office building. Really, it's nothing. Just having a celebratory drink." Another throat clearing. Really, this was SO telltale.

"Well, Theo, have a wonderful *celebration*. We will talk when I get home."

"Oh, Beck, this isn't what you think!" He sounded convincing, I have to admit.

"Theo, I have to go. They need me to run another load of laundry. Give my best to your *client.*" I hit the "hang up" icon.

I laid back on the bed, against D's Pottery Barn throw pillows. Goose down. I pulled a tiny, needle-like feather out of my neck. This was such a surprise. Theo, perhaps being non-monogamous. I pulled another feather out of the pillow and, disgusted, threw the pillow on the floor. Lying flat, I stared up at the light fixture above the bed, filled with dead insects. D's cleaning woman didn't look up, apparently. I shut my eyes. An argument began inside my head.

What are you so bummed about? My God, you complain about Theo at every available opportunity.

Well, I never expected him to just rush out and have a date with someone the very first time I leave town!

Be honest. Do you really want to have an exclusive relationship with Theo? I mean, the man wears SOCKS that match his polo shirts. And we are talking POLO shirts. All Ralph Lauren, all the time . . .

But Theo is intelligent, kind, exactly what every girl dreams of. And he is good in bed, by the way.

Oh, for God's sake! Sex isn't everything!

This, coming from a writer of erotic fiction. Sense the irony here?

I just like having someone to do things with. A companion. And yes, a sexual partner! What is wrong with that?

I'll tell you what is wrong with that: You are trying to convince yourself to hang on to a guy that you just "like." This isn't Facebook! Liking a guy is no reason to stay with somebody. And it would seem that Theo has picked up on this and is just acting accordingly.

So what am I supposed to do? Just grin and ask Theo to introduce me to the other woman?

I don't know. All I know is that you are not in love with this guy. Face it. You are not. Your feelings of anger at the woman he is either stalking at the grocery store or drinking champagne with from room service come from pride, not love. So you have to admit this. So live and let live.

Shit. Beck, you just told yourself off. You are most likely going crazy.

Just then, Alexander started crying again, and I leapt from the bed and rushed into the living room, hoping like anything that I would see Bryan coming through the door with a crapload of nipple shields.

As soon as Alexander began getting enough to eat, his personality changed completely. He transformed from an angry, red ball of screams into a pacific little fellow with deep blue eyes and a gummy grin. He cooed, for God's sake. And naturally, he turned the three of us into his love slaves.

It was the afternoon before I was scheduled to go back home. We were in the living room, casually draped over the sectional: Bryan and D on one end, Alex propped up on Bryan's knees, drooling happily. I was at the other end, feet up on the coffee table, phone in hand, Googling.

"You guys. You need to get the *What to Expect the First Year* app. It tells you all the stuff you need to know. For instance, did you know that co-sleeping is a thing? It makes the baby feel more confident."

Bryan looked up. "Really? What is co-sleeping?"

Diana flung us both the stink-eye. "It's not going to happen, okay? I love Alexander, but I need my sleep. He is NOT going to share our bed. No way in HELL."

Whoa. I bit my lip and looked at Bryan. He smiled weakly.

"I would probably roll over on him and smother him, anyway."

"No, Bryan. You wouldn't. They have these little bed pods that you put the baby in. They have built-up sides, so you can't roll on him. See?" I held out my phone with the picture of one on it. "On sale on Amazon right now. Only fifty bucks."

Bryan looked mildly interested, but before he could get up and take my phone to examine the sleeping pod, D burst out, "I TOLD you, we are absolutely NOT having him in bed with us! I need my rest! I cannot have you snoring in my ear all night, and Alexander rooting around and making all those baby noises right next to me. My God, are you two crazy?

Bryan laughed, but got up, hoisted his son high up onto his shoulder, and headed towards the "guest room." Diana pointed at his back as he disappeared. "I know you are going to look them up on Amazon! Don't order one, or you may be co-sleeping with Alex all by yourself!"

D leaned back on the sofa cushions. "Do you think I will ever get the hang of this maternal thing?" She rubbed her temples. "It is just one crisis after another. I'm losing confidence by the minute, and I can't have alcohol as long as I'm breast feeding." She let out a ragged sigh.

"They do say that you won't get a full night's sleep for the first twenty years."

Diana shot me a desperate look.

"That was a joke."

She sat there, looking deflated. "This is not at all what I pictured. This isn't the way it looks on TV. This isn't the way it looks in magazines. I should have known that I would end up frustrated, fat, and helpless. My nemesis is just a ten-pound infant!"

I snorted. "D, you have discovered the limits of your powers. Grown men fall under your spell. But males who aren't yet potty trained? They just don't get it. Their hormones haven't kicked in. For the first time in your life, you are up against a guy that isn't putty in your hands. I am so happy."

Diana stuck her tongue out at me.

Neither one of us knew that a tsunami was on its way.

CHAPTER SEVENTEEN

Bob was covered from head to toe with flour and sugar. She looked like a small Yeti, one who was very enthusiastic about tasting the batter in the large blue mixing bowl.

"Keep your fingers to yourself, Bob! Two reasons: one, raw eggs are supposed to give you some sort of food poisoning; and, two, if you keep this up, there won't be enough batter for your gran's cake. So back off, kiddo!"

Bob giggled. "Okay! But can I have one more taste after you put the cocoa in? Just to see if it's chocolatey enough?"

"One. Then we will have to pour it into these two cake pans and bake it. And I have some reservations about this whole project. I have never made a cake in my entire life. This thing may be horrible."

Bob bounced, sending off a cloud of powder, which made her and me cough. Then she laughed even louder. "You SEE, Beck? You need me as a taster! 'Cause if it is awful, then we will have to go to the bakery for Gran's cake!"

Ella was turning eighty-four the following day. Bob had planned this "surprise party" and invited me, Theo, Hallie, Hallie's mom, Gail, and, of course, she had written to her father to tell him all about it. She was wound up tight.

"Bob, although I am not the Ace of Cakes, I think we can pull this off. I got already-made roses at the store, so we won't have to try to make those—they will be pretty. I have this can of white icing—ready to spread. And I have here three tubes of décor frosting: pink, green, and blue." I pulled out my cell phone. "So while the cakes are baking"—I slid them into the oven—"we can watch this YouTube video on how to write on cakes."

We sat down on the linoleum, directly in front of the oven, so that Bob could peer in constantly. We hunkered over my cell and watched the expert write *HAPPY BIRTHDAY* in fancy script on a perfect Martha Stewart confection. It looked so easy-peasy! We smiled at one another smugly.

Two hours later, the layers sat cooling on waxed paper. They looked a little small. We leaned over the kitchen table to inspect them.

"They look dinky." Bob touched an edge.

I agreed, but we had to press forward. "I know. But we have to take this one step at a time. If we by some miracle manage to get this thing iced and decorated, then we can surround it with the flowers I bought. I was going to give them to your gran for the table, but if we need them for the cake, we can use them. Carnations go with everything. It will look okay."

Dubious, Bob picked up the tube of pink gel icing and absently squeezed it. She was unaware that this tube was the one I had opened. Icing squirted out and landed in my hair. Bob gasped.

"Hey! We can't waste this stuff! I only have three tubes! It has to be enough for all of the writing AND the swirls and squiggles!" I squirted some on Bob's nose.

"I know! It's precious!" Bob snorted and squeezed some of it directly into her mouth.

"Stop right now. I have to concentrate. It says here in the recipe that you are to smooth some of this frosting"—I pried open the seal on the buttercream vanilla can—"onto the top of the first layer, but not too much. Because you need to use most of it to ice the cake once the second layer is on."

I used my spatula, the one that I normally scramble eggs with, to spread the icing on the first layer. As I tried to smooth it smoothly, crumbs detached from the cake and mixed with the frosting, also making HOLES in the cake. "OMG, this is a DISASTER!"

Bob grabbed the spatula out of my hand. After taking a generous lick of the mixture covering it and smiling with satisfaction, she said, "Beck, I think this is the wrong tool! Gran uses a skinny metal knife thing to frost cakes. Should I go over and ask her for it?"

I looked at her as if she were a fool. "And just give away everything? Just announce that we are over here making a cake—oh yeah—and she will never make the connection between that and her birthday??" I poked her in the ribs, and she collapsed on the floor in a paroxysm of giggling.

"No, Bob, I am afraid we have to forge ahead on our own. But you may be right about this implement." I put the spatula in the sink. Bob got up, grabbed it out of the sink, and continued to lick it.

I opened my silverware drawer and pulled out a metal cake-cutting thingy that Mom gave me, in hopes I might use it someday on my wedding cake. "Shall we try this one?"

Bob nodded, her mouth still full of icing.

"Okay, here we go." The instructions had directed that I decant the cakes onto waxed paper, cut in circles slightly larger than the cakes. I had somehow managed circles that were ragged, but just barely larger than the cakes. I slid my hand under the waxed paper and very gently lifted the second layer. I placed my free hand on the top. "Wish me luck, kiddo. If this layer crumbles into smithereens, we are bakery bound!"

But it, by some miracle, plopped right on top of layer one. It was even centered.

"SCORE!!!" Bob dropped the spatula and gave me a high-five with a fist bump chaser.

"Okay, Bob. Do you want to do the rest of this frosting, or should I? I believe that neither one of us is in any way qualified to do this, so it's a toss-up."

Bob picked up the cake tool and handed it to me. "I'll do the writing and the roses."

I took a deep breath and started spreading. I was sweating bullets, by God. But after a couple of false starts, confidence kicked in, and I managed to cover the entire cake with a relatively even layer of frosting, and when I set the cake tool down on the counter, I twirled the platter so that Bob and I could view the cake from all sides. Amateurish, but acceptable. I used my finger to smooth out a particularly glaring divot.

"It's not like the bakery, that's for sure," Bob murmured.

I had to nod in agreement. "But maybe with the roses and the writing, it will look good."

Bob bent to her task. She ran out of room on "Birthday," so it read **HAPPY BIRTHDAy**, but with seven awkward looking roses placed strategically, it looked okay. Bob clapped her hands with satisfaction. "It's perfect! But we really need to put the flowers around it."

I had a sudden realization. "Yikes! We should have iced the cake *after* we put it on the cake plate!"

Bob looked at me and moaned. "Oh, no! Are we screwed?"

I decided not to comment on Bob's use of slang, and got out my biggest pancake turner. "I am going to slide this thing under the cake. Get ready to steady it if it starts to fall off. But use your entire hand, not your fingers, so we don't poke holes in the cake. If the frosting gets messed up, we can repair once it's on the cake plate."

I scooted the crystal cake stand that I got at a garage sale for occasions just like this (I had never used it in five years), close to the cake. "Okay, Bob. ON THREE."

It was touch and go, but we got it on the cake stand with just a little crater on one side. There may have been remnants of waxed paper remaining, but that was the least of our worries. I repaired the crater as best I could, and stuck four toothpicks in it to keep the Saran Wrap from destroying our decorations, and covered it for the party. "Whew! It's not worthy of Martha Stewart, but we did it! Bob, you had better go home and act casual. Don't spill the beans about any of this; we want your gran to be surprised."

Bob took a final swipe of frosting when she thought I wasn't looking and sucked it off her finger. "Okay! Hallie is coming over right before. She is pretending that she wants to go to the park. We'll signal to you from the front porch when it's okay to come over!"

I clapped my hands. "PERFECT!"

Bob scuttled out the door.

▷◁

Theo arrived early, as usual. I had been counting on this, as I wanted to broach the subject of the grocery store girlfriend, but had not found the opportunity. I had only been home from Chicago for two days, and we had exchanged a few text messages, but nothing more. Plus, I was not exactly sure what my position on grocery store girlfriends should be. I appreciated Theo as a person. I had fun with him. He was great in bed. Blah, blah. However, I was the one who got the heebie-jeebies just thinking about the gravity of "going steady," followed by eventual marriage and the near impossibility of staying that way.

I opened my door, and there he stood, wearing a crisply ironed white broadcloth shirt, sleeves rolled up to reveal his Tag Heuer watch and tan forearms. His indigo and gold madras slacks were tasteful and also wrinkle-free. In one hand, he held a bouquet that I assumed was for Ella, and in the other, he had two bottles of pinot noir. The man was just too good to be true.

"Are you going to ask me in, or just stand there in awe?" He winked at me.

Okay. The wink. A little icky. "Oh, sorry. Come in. Is the wine for later? Looks delicious."

Theo put the bottles on the mantel, set the bouquet on the coffee table, and glanced at his watch. "We have some time before the party starts. Do you want to have a glass of wine first?"

"Theo, let's just sit down and talk for a bit. You know, we have never really addressed the phone call."

He sat, but on the edge of the sofa, as if he had been expecting something like this. I swear, he looked like a kid in the principal's office. Clasping his hands, he leaned forward, his forehead furrowed. "Beck, I swear it was nothing. Okay. We were not really at the grocery store; I admitted that. I don't know why I said that—you caught me off guard, and I lied. But it was really just a drink."

I raised my eyebrows.

"Okay, okay. She came on to me. I knew she was flirting the whole time this office building deal was coming down, but I am telling you the God's truth here: I did not encourage her!"

"Theo, Theo. Come ON. If you knew she was interested in you, and you met her in a *bar*, then it was a date. You can rationalize all you want, but two single people having a *prearranged* drink together in a bar is a *date*."

Theo sank back into the sofa cushions and put a hand over his forehead. "So what exactly are you saying, here? Are you breaking up with me?"

Good question. I studied the man beside me on the sofa. Tall. Nice looking, in an all-American, totally non-threatening way. Good taste in clothes. Thoughtful. Excellent manners. Soft, genial eyes. The kind of man who would never serve meat to a vegetarian.

I sighed. "Theo, I am not breaking up with you. But I think we need to establish the parameters of our relationship. If we are going to date other people or not. Because it is never fun to think you are in an exclusive situation and have the other person in the relationship think otherwise. We need to be in an open or a closed relationship." The little voice inside my head said *Huh?*

Theo looked understandably confused. "Beck, what are you asking? Do you *want* to have an exclusive relationship, or don't you?"

Good question. I wanted to hit a rewind button and start over. I sat in silence. The little mental voice became a bit more annoyed in there: *Just what the hell are you doing here, Beck?* Theo looked once more at the Tag on his wrist.

"Beck?"

"Ugh, Theo, here's the thing: I am not sure *what* I am asking! But I guess the fact that I was unhappy when I thought you were with another woman means that I was a little jealous."

"Jealous, or possessive? I will be honest here, Beck. I have never gotten the feeling from you that we are headed towards a happily ever after. I don't feel that you are 100% in our relationship. Am I right? So what is this about?"

Theo crossed one impeccable leg over the other. He rested his arms against the back of the sofa and challenged me with a pointed look.

I caved. "Theo, I'm sorry. I am selfish and insecure. After Bryan and I split, followed by his marriage to my sister, I lost all of my perspective on relationships. Can you bear with me on this? I don't want to break up. I want to have trust, is all." As the voice in my head screamed *you are a total chickenshit!* I scooted over to Theo on the sofa and put my hand on his chest. I could hear his all-American heart beating.

Theo's kind eyes darkened. "Let's face facts, here. This relationship isn't going forward; it's stalled out."

He scooted backwards so that there was at least a foot of distance between us. I started to say something, but he waved me off. "As much as I enjoy being with you, I can tell that the feelings I am developing for you aren't mutual. I think the best thing to do here would be to stop trying so hard to be a couple and just remain good friends."

The "good friends" speech. Oh, no. All the saliva in my mouth dried up. "Theo, I am so sorry. I am such a jerk."

He didn't deny it. Instead, he rumpled his hair dejectedly.

I didn't know exactly how to proceed. "I don't know what to do or say. I feel terrible, because I really like you." Pleading look in his direction. "I really do!"

Of course, the logical, objective portion of my brain (very small portion overall) spoke up. *Beck, be honest. You have been grasping at straws here. Theo is absolutely right to feel that you have been stringing him along. Because you have.* I tried to ignore it, but it kept on, doggedly: *You are totally scrambled up right now. Bryan. The past. Your fear of commitment. Your gaping wound from your parents' divorce.* I was reeling. I must have shot Theo a beseeching look.

Theo, bless him forever and ever, slapped his knees with both hands and stood up, an optimistic smile on his face. "I know what to do. Let's just enjoy one another's company, but give up on the whole boyfriend/girlfriend idea. Friends. Not the kind with benefits, though. Just friends. We can still go out, have fun, can't we? Who says men and women can't be just friends?"

I looked up at him. Who was this heroic guy, and what did I do to deserve him in my life? I said a little silent prayer of thanks to the ruler of the universe, God, Buddha, Mohammed, and every other one I could think of. I vowed to them all that I would face up to things. I shut my eyes and sent a *thanks* heavenward. Then I got up and went into the kitchen for the cake.

I brought it out, ceremoniously. "Here is our masterpiece. Bob and I worked very hard on this, despite the fact that it looks as if we dropped it at least once. But we have to put those flowers around it, so it won't look quite so pitiful."

Theo laughed, grabbed the flowers, and took them into the kitchen. "Where are the scissors? We have to cut the stems off."

I followed him in, clanked around in the junk drawer, and handed him the scissors. He made short work of the stems, unwrapped the cake, and bent over, placing the carnations very carefully around the perimeter. "TA-DA!"

"Theo, you are an absolute artist. It looks divine," I lied.

"Okay, then, *friend*. Let's get this show on the road." Theo balanced the cake carefully, and we headed out the door.

On the way across the street, I thought I heard a cat meowing.

CHAPTER EIGHTEEN

Ella feigned complete surprise. When Bob and Hallie carried out the cake from where I had left it on the porch, Ella gasped, hands over her heart. "What is this beautiful thing? A *cake*? Who made this? Certainly you couldn't have made this lovely cake, could you, Bobby?"

Bob beamed. Even her freckles seemed to flash. "Gran, Beck and I made it! From SCRATCH! Well, not the frosting and the carnations. But we did it ourselves! Does it look like it came from a *bakery*?"

Ella leaned over to kiss her great-granddaughter. "It looks like the cakes they make on the cooking shows! It's just perfect!"

Ella reached out and swiped a bit of the frosting off the cake and tasted it. "In all of my eighty-four years, I have never tasted anything as delectable as this. Shall we all share it?"

Theo was already bringing in the plates and a knife. He set them on the glass coffee table and went back to the kitchen for forks. Gail beamed and pulled on her blonde spikes. Hallie and Marva applauded.

"There are nice napkins in the left-hand drawer under the sink!" Ella called out after him.

We all settled down in anticipation of the homemade cake. I hoped against hope that it was edible. Just as Theo returned with forks and linen napkins, the phone rang.

Ella struggled to her feet. "I wonder who that is. Just a minute folks, I'll tell whoever it is that we are very busy at the moment." She toddled out into the hall, where her phone sat in a nook built into the wall, a Windsor chair beside it.

Theo sliced the cake into very generous portions. I decided to start counting carbs the following day. Hallie and Bob passed a piece to me, gave one to Theo, who was surreptitiously licking the cake knife, and then they pushed generous portions towards Gail and Marva. Then the girls each took a piece and sat on the floor to eat. "Shouldn't we wait for Gran?"

I grinned. "I am sure she wouldn't mind if we started in without her. After all, this is just so tempting!" I had my fingers crossed.

It was pretty damn good. Fudgy, and not too dry. We were all chewing away most companionably when we heard a loud thump, a crash, and then some sort of scrabbling sound.

It was Ella. "HELP!"

Startled, Theo and I jumped up. We ran into the hall, where Ella lay, crumpled, the phone still in her hand, the chair on its side beside her. Her face was white, her body trembling. Moans issued from her throat; I thought she sounded like a wounded animal. Before we could get to her, Bob shot into the hall and threw herself down next to her gran. "Gran, what's wrong? What happened? Please be okay! Please!" Bob stroked Ella's head very gently.

Ella suppressed her moaning long enough to grimace at Bob. "Bobby, I will be okay. Don't fret."

But I knew something was terribly wrong. Theo knelt over Ella, and tried to straighten her out, but when he touched her legs, she screamed. "NO! IT'S MY HIP! DON'T TOUCH ME!"

In the meantime, I whipped out my iPhone and punched 9-1-1. Bob knelt by Ella, sobbing and stroking. Gail wisely ran to open the front door, so that when the paramedics arrived, they would have a clear path. Hallie burst outside to wait on the curb for the paramedics. Honestly, children these days have such presence of mind!

Ella rolled her head. I grabbed a pillow off the sofa to prop her up with, but Bob waved me off. "No, Beck! Haven't you watched any TV at all? You can't move her neck or anything, 'cause it might be broken!"

I stood, pillow in hand, feeling totally superfluous. Theo had gone to the kitchen to get a cold cloth to put on Ella's brow. I guess *he* had watched TV. So I just set the pillow on the stairs, righted the Windsor chair, and wrung my hands until the sirens were audible in the distance. Then I ran outside and made a complete fool of myself.

"HERE! HERE! OVER HERE!" Waving my hands wildly and jumping up and down. Of course, all this was totally unnecessary, as all paramedics have GPS. But at least I felt as if I were vital, right at that moment. Hallie joined me in the jumping. We screamed as they drove up.

Two burly paramedics piled out of the ambulance and went around the back to haul out a portable gurney. As they rushed it into the house, they smiled at me grimly. I tried to smile back, failed, and followed them in.

Ella gasped as they put braces around her and lifted her onto the gurney. One of the medics, I think I heard the other one call him Tom, took her blood pressure and pulse. I'm not sure, but in the rush I think I heard him say her pressure was low. As they hustled her into the ambulance, Theo pulled Bob and me across the street and into his car. I got in first and put Bob on my lap. Gail, Hallie, and her mom stayed behind to clean up all the cake mess. They waved until we were out of sight. Bless them.

We headed to the ER. Theo didn't run any red lights, but he certainly drove above the speed limit. Bob strained to keep her eyes on the ambulance, but since it *could* run lights, it got way ahead of us. I wrapped my arms around Bob and held on tight.

"Gran won't die. Gran won't die. Gran won't die."

It was a litany. I put my face next to hers and whispered, "No, she won't die. She just fell down. She is conscious. She will be fine. Bob, do NOT lose faith now. Do NOT LOSE faith."

Bob nodded. "She will come back."

I let out the air in my lungs that I didn't even realize I had been holding. Then I gulped in as much fresh air as I could. I felt as if I might drown. "Bob, I guarantee you that she will come back."

▷◁

Hospitals are grim places. It seems that they all look alike, no matter what city you are in: glossy, speckled linoleum. Tiled walls, usually a minty green. Assorted generic artwork placed at random intervals, always of either waterfalls or pastures with cows and red barns. Supposed to be comforting? Ugh.

The lady at the information desk, Sandi, according to her nametag, looked as if she hated her job. She hardly lifted her eyes from her computer screen as we approached, and merely flicked a glance at me when I asked, "Is Ella Bowers here? We're her family. Well, her neighbors and her granddaughter."

Sandi scrolled. "She's here, but she hasn't been evaluated yet. Do you have her Medicare and insurance information and ID? "Luckily, I had thought about this, and had brought Ella's pocketbook with me. I rummaged around, found her wallet, and searched for her cards. Sandi pulled them from my grasp and got Ella registered. I watched her chipped manicure flying over the keyboard. I felt helpless. Sandi never looked up.

As she slid the cards back across the counter towards me, Sandi threw me a lifeless little smile. "I will call you as soon as there is some information." Then darling Sandi answered the phone. I was dismissed.

It seemed like hours in that waiting room. We sat there, restless, Theo bringing me cups and cups of coffee and taking Bob on walks around the hospital "to look for the gift shop."

I tried to read some *People* magazines, but the status of Brad Pitt and the Kardashians held no fascination. The air-conditioning was set on "arctic." I shivered and managed to shred five napkins and two of the cardboard coffee cups. Finally, after Bob and Theo had put in around five miles in the corridors and purchased a silk rose and a Get Well card in the gift shop, a weary looking doctor in wrinkled green scrubs came out of a swinging door and called, "Bowers family?"

Bob leapt up. "US! IT'S US!"

Dr. Peter Davenport (according to his nametag) held out his arm and shook hands with Theo, and then me. He put his hand on Bob's shoulder. "Are you Ella's grandchildren? Is this your daughter?"

"Not exactly. I'm Rebecca Throckmorton, Ella's neighbor. And this is Theo Blackburn, my friend. This is Roberta (I had no idea why I was being so formal), her great-granddaughter. Ella has no other relatives locally. Her son is stationed in the Middle East." Probably way too much information.

Dr. Davenport nodded. "Shall we go into this consulting room, so we can have some privacy?"

That sounded ominous.

Dr. Davenport motioned for us to sit down on the uncomfortable looking wood-and-pleather chairs. He remained standing. I hate this; it feels like an uneven distribution of power. So I remained standing. Bob sat, twisting the pink silk rose, and somehow managing to thrash around in the chair while sitting in it. Theo sat, hands clasped, looking calmly expectant.

"Mrs. Bowers has a femoral neck fracture." We gasped simultaneously, almost like some sort of horrified choir.

He waved his hands. "No, no. She has not broken her neck. In her fall, Ella's thighbone—called the femoral neck bone—near the top, close to the hip joint, fractured. This will require surgery to repair. We are going to admit her directly into the orthopedic ward, and she will be evaluated by an orthopedic surgeon."

At this point, I thought Bob might explode, so I grabbed her out of her seat and sat down in it, pulling her onto my lap. "Bob, calm down. Things will be okay." Then I looked at Dr. Davenport for confirmation.

He got it. "Roberta—Bob, is it? Bob, your grandmother will be fine. Your grandmother was lucky; her fracture was not as serious as it might have been. The surgery they will do is called hip nailing." I flinched. "She is fortunate that she will not need a total hip replacement. The surgeon will place a nail in the joint to hold it together until it heals."

Bob dropped the rose and covered her eyes, as if to blot out the image of a nail in her gran's hip. I didn't blame her.

"How long will Ella have to be in the hospital?" Good question, Theo.

"It depends on when the surgery takes place. I would guess that due to Ella's age, they will schedule it no later than the next forty-eight hours. After the surgery, she will stay in the hospital for one or two days. She will require some rehabilitation, most likely in a rehab facility"—I flinched again; euphemism for nursing home—"and she will be using a walker for one or two weeks. After that, she will be able to come home and go to outpatient rehab. Probably about six weeks. She may need a cane from then on. But Ella seems like a very strong woman. And she has a very good attitude. I gave her some morphine for the pain. We are in the process of establishing whether or not there is a bed for her in orthopedics, and that will take a while. Would you like to go see her? She's a bit woozy from the pain medication."

Bob jumped up and headed for the door. "Whoa, Bob! Let's have Dr. Davenport take us to your gran!" I grabbed Bob by the hand, and we followed Dr. Davenport into the open vastness of the ER. Theo waved us on—"I will just be in the waiting room. Ella doesn't need a third wheel." Oh, Theo.

Dr. Davenport walked us through the area that was littered with gurneys, rolling equipment of all kinds, bustling nurses, beeping phone lines, and the distinct odor of sickness. We walked past three curtained-off areas, where I could hear coughing, voices murmuring, and the click of machinery.

He swept back the curtains of the fourth staging area, and we saw a tiny, pale Ella, hooked up to an alarming series of tubes. She looked as if she had shrunk. But her eyes lit up when she saw us, and she smiled, reaching out a shaking hand to Bob. In a rubbery voice: "Hi, Bobby. Don't be ssscared. I will be jusss fine!"

Bob didn't look as if she bought that statement. She took her gran's bony hand in both of her little stubby ones, and put her head down on the bed beside Ella's shoulder. "Oh, Gran, please don't die!"

Dr. Davenport got it, *again*. This guy was a prince in scrubs. "Bob, your grandmother will certainly NOT die. She will be just fine after her surgery. And you can trust doctors. We are trained professionals." He grinned and mussed Bob's hair.

Bob heaved a sigh of relief and continued patting Ella's hand.

Just then, a nurse swished in. "Dr. Davenport, we have a bed."

▷◁

The surgery was scheduled for eight the next morning. I got there at seven thirty, so that I might be able to meet a doctor or get some sort of information beforehand.

Thank goodness, they were treating me like next of kin. This was out of the ordinary, I knew, but apparently they were able to get in touch with Charles Bowers' unit, via email. Evidently, Ella carried his information in her purse. He called them back, and they got a cell number where he could be reached directly. The nurses informed me that Charles would make sure that Ella, when she was out of surgery and more lucid, would be signing over an NPA, or notarized power of attorney, to me. They gave me Charles Bowers email address and the cell number. While Ella was in surgery, I was supposed to contact him. Okay. A relief there.

I was surprised to meet the orthopedic surgeon. What I had expected: A tall, distinguished man, late fifties or early sixties, with perhaps graying temples and certainly a firm handshake. Golf tan. No scrubs—a lab coat with broadcloth and a club tie underneath.

What walked in: A young woman, bursting with energy, wearing blindingly enthusiastic yellow scrubs with a sunflower embroidered on the breast pocket. Short, frosted hair. A huge smile. When I attempted to shake her hand, a hug instead. I think I fell in love with her that moment.

"Hi. My name is Dr. Bankson. But you can call me Lauren." She walked over to where Ella lay, looking a little less pale than she had last night in the ER. Ella looked confused. "Are you a nurse?"

Lauren pulled up a chair so that she could be right next to Ella. "Mrs. Bowers?" She reached out and gently shook Ella's recumbent hand. "I am Dr. Bankson. I am the surgeon who will be performing your procedure this afternoon. Would you like for me to explain it to you?"

Ella nodded weakly.

Lauren leaned over. "Ella, I will be glad to answer all of your questions. And I will explain exactly what is going to happen. I will step you through it. But first, I need to examine you. Is that okay?"

Another nod, but I could tell that Lauren was working her magic on Ella as well, because Ella smiled, her eyes bright.

"Would you mind giving us just a little private time?"

"Of course." When I got to the nurses' station, I saw Hallie's mother walking toward me, Bob in tow. What a fantastic neighbor. She had taken Bob for the night, so that I could get some rest and figure out a plan for the future.

We went to the orthopedic family waiting room: more pleather. This time it was gray "sofas" with wooden armrests, assorted plastic ferns, a coffee table with assorted out-of-date magazines, and a coffee and soda machine. We sat.

Marva asked me if I had managed to get ahold of Charles Bowers to tell him about his grandmother. "Not yet. But I have his information, and will get in touch today. The hospital talked to him last night. He's going to instruct Ella to give me some sort of power of attorney to make decisions for her here. I will find out all about that later. I think I may be able to call him."

Bob nearly jumped out of her skin. "Can I talk to him? He will want to talk to me! Can I?"

"Bob, of course you can." Bob's joy was almost palpable.

"When can we go see Gran? Look! I brought the Birthday card I made for her, and the rose, and the Get Well card that Theo and I got. But best of all? *SEE*?" She held out an official looking envelope with a military stamp. "This is the birthday card Dad sent her! She can see it before her operation! Will Gran be able to talk to Dad, too? That will make her so happy!"

Marva stood to go. "I called the school as you asked. Bob is excused for the rest of the week. Let me know if there is anything else we can do for you. If you decide that having Bob stay with you is too much, she can stay with us. Hallie would love that. Oh, and I meant to tell you: I froze the rest of the birthday cake. There was almost a half of it left. I cut it into slices and wrapped them individually, so you can have it when Ella comes home from the hospital."

As Marva Davis walked out, Bob whispered, "People are good. Good."

CHAPTER NINETEEN

Bob and I were taking a much-needed break. The surgery was in process, so there would be no word for at least another hour, I figured. There was a lovely courtyard just outside the main entrance of Framington General, and Bob and I sat amidst hot pink potted geraniums and hanging ferns, drinking lemonade out of yet another vending machine. Bob alternatively sipped her lemonade and gnawed on her thumbnail. I pulled Bob's hand out of her mouth. "If you keep this up, you will have no fingernails LEFT."

My phone beeped. I pulled it out of my pocket. The ID said "unknown number."

"Hello?"

I had seen a few photos of Charles Bowers on Ella's mantel. A high school graduation picture: nobody looks good wearing a mortarboard. A photo of the newly minted marine: A tall, thin young man with piercing dark eyes and a stiff uniform, hat pulled low over his forehead. Fierce expression. No casual photos—no frolicking in the waves, no posing beside a new car. So really, I had no idea of what Charles Bowers *actually* looked like. But he sounded like a radio sports announcer. Smooth and masculine.

"Is this Miss Throckmorton? Hi. This is Charles Bowers. How is my gran?"

So the nurses gave him *my* number. I should have realized that. "Hello, Mr. Bowers. Sgt. Bowers. Charles . . ." (My God, he would think his grandmother was entrusted to an *idiot . . .)*

"Is she still in surgery?" Such a deep, modulated voice. Meanwhile, beside me on the bench, Bob spilled her lemonade all over her front in her excitement. I filled him in as much as I could with

160

a convulsive eight-year-old crowing and trying to grab the phone out of my hand. Finally, I gave up. "Charles, there is somebody here who is absolutely DYING to talk to you. Let me give her the phone, and I will finish about your gran after."

Bob clutched the phone and ran over to a nearby bench. For some privacy, I assumed. However, it was hard not to hear her exuberant exclamations: "Dad! Dad! How are you? When are you coming home? Do you know that Gran is going to be fine?" On and on. I felt like a voyeur, so I went inside and sat on a loveseat by the large window overlooking the courtyard, where I could watch Bob's happiness without impinging on it. She looked as if her heart was pouring directly into the phone as she paced in animated circles. Finally, she seemed to run out of things to say. Looking in my direction, Bob held out the phone. I hustled back outside to finish the conversation with Sgt. Bowers. Bob jumped and clapped her hands the entire time.

I punched the "end call" icon, and turned to the very excited little girl, who by this time had picked some geraniums. "For GRAN!"

"Great. I am not sure that these are here for that reason, but we can take them up to her when she gets out of the recovery room. They will look good with the rose you got her. We had better get back up to the surgery waiting room, in case there's news."

We had a snack. Bob chose Doritos, and I opted for a bag of pretzels. Then we took a walk around the entire lobby floor of Framington General. I had no idea that there was a coffee shop, a McDonalds, a cafeteria-style restaurant, and four more banks of vending machines on that floor alone. Bob said that she wanted to go to the cafeteria for dinner, because the menu posted on the door said that they featured peanut butter milkshakes. That was a perfectly sound reason, as far as I was concerned.

When we returned from our journey around the gustatory hot spots of the main floor, we had just settled down into our seats in the waiting room when Dr. Lauren appeared, her smile saying it all. "The procedure went very well. It was not a large fracture, and I feel confident that your grandmother will do very well." Kudos to Dr. Lauren, who knew exactly who to discuss the surgery with. Bob's freckles glowed.

Molly D. Campbell

"So. Now she'll recover for at least one more day here. I am recommending that she spend a week in rehab at Oakmoor Ambulatory Rehabilitation Center. They do a very good job with people your grandmother's age." Lauren looked over at me. "Our hope is that she will be able to come home after that, and just go to outpatient rehab. But she won't be able to drive for six weeks. Is that a problem?"

Yes, this was all a problem. Although I really didn't need my Starbucks job in the interim, due to royalty income, I selfishly wanted to hold on to my routine. Becoming a surrogate parental figure to an eight-year-old seemed overwhelming. For just a second, I wished that I had never gotten involved with all of this. But then I looked over at Bob, who at that moment was clutching three wilted geraniums, one melon-pink silk rose, and the combination Get Well and birthday cards, covering them liberally with fingermarks and Dorito dust. What was I thinking? I had no choice.

"Dr. Lauren, we will figure out something. I live just across the street. So Bob and I can bounce back and forth until Ella comes home. Ella doesn't drive, so that isn't an issue. I have a car and will be the chauffeur. How ambulatory do you think she will be after just one week of rehab?"

What this world needs? More surgeons like Dr. Lauren. "Oh, with hip fractures—well, with any surgeries, really—these days we get them up and moving within hours. By tomorrow, we will have Ella sitting in a chair. The day after, we will have her using a walker to get from her bed to the restroom. Once at the rehab center, as painful as it might be for her, they will have her walking the equivalent of around the first floor of her house before she is released. Is there a bedroom and bath on the first floor?"

I looked at Bob. I had never been anywhere in Ella's house but the living room, hall, and kitchen.

"Yes. My father's room. I guess you could call it the guest room. And there is a bathroom on the first floor. It has a tub, but if Gran can't get into it, I can give Gran sponge baths, 'cause whenever I'm sick, Gran gives them to me. So I know how to do that."

162

My knees turned to rubber. "Oh, my gosh. I didn't think about stuff like bathing and cooking. And I have no idea of Ella's finances—will we need to hire some sort of nurse or home care provider?"

"NOPE." The answer came from Bob. "Gran has been teaching me things. I can make scrambled eggs and hamburgers. I know how to use a Swiffer and a vacuum. And Gran can teach me anything else I need to learn. See, Gran says that everybody needs to learn how to take care of things. How to take care of themselves. She says it's important for everyone to learn how to be alone. But I already know how to do that."

Dr. Lauren looked as awestruck as I did at this wonder-child standing in front of us, earnestly explaining the meaning of life while twirling her flowers. Lauren put an arm around those tiny, resolute shoulders. "Bob, I have complete faith in your ability. Does that answer your question, Beck?"

"It certainly does. Plus, it sounds as if Bob will be teaching *me* some much-needed skills, and I have lived alone for quite a while."

Lauren handed me some brochures about Oakmoor. "Honestly, by the time Ella comes home, she will be able to supervise quite a bit of what goes on. She will be expected to sit up for at least four hours a day, and she will be able to stand for at least an hour. Do you by any chance have a recliner, Bob?"

Bob scowled. "No. Gran hates those; she says they are for pot-bellied old men. But we have a very comfy easy chair."

"That will do. Bob, would you mind giving me a few moments to talk with Beck? I think they have chocolate chip cookies out at the nurses' station." Bob wandered toward the cookies, shooting me a thumbs-up before she disappeared.

"Beck, Medicare normally covers these kinds of expenses, and most likely, Mrs. Bowers has supplementary insurance coverage as well. But it might be a good idea to have a discussion with her about finances, since you will be acting with her power of attorney. Don't worry, you will get all that sorted. But Beck, there is one thing that I need to warn you about. Many of our patients who have pain with hip surgery can become very resistant to therapy, because, well, it *hurts*. And when patients give up on the therapy, they don't recover: muscles atrophy, pain increases, and it becomes a vicious circle. It will be very important for you to look out for signs of discouragement or depression. If you feel that Ella begins to slip, I want you to call me. I will be able to set you up with a therapist." She read the alarm in my face. "No worries. A certain number of therapy sessions are Medicare approved as well, in cases like this."

"Lauren, I am going to be honest with you: I love these people. But I am in over my head with all of this. I am not a blood relative of Ella's. As you know, her son is deployed and won't be home until after Christmas. I just don't know how I can keep both Ella and Bob afloat all by myself." I must have turned gray, because Lauren led me over to some chairs.

"Sit for a minute. Take a deep breath. I can help you if you need me—just call. But I have another suggestion: Does Ella have a cell phone?"

I almost laughed. "No. She can barely send emails. I think she goes to the library, and they help her use the computer there. But no technology at home."

"I talked with her grandson, Charles, after the surgery. He had called the information line at the hospital, and they took down a number that I could call, if I did so within a half hour. I just barely made the time limit! He said that although making incoming calls to him is nearly impossible, that he does have a certain number of monthly minutes at his end that he can use to call family. He said he hasn't used them, because he has felt in the past that talking to Bob would be detrimental to her emotions. But he wants to call his grandmother and Bob now, in order to keep their spirits up until Ella recovers. I think this would be very beneficial for Ella to know that her grandson is cheering her on from . . ." she paused, "wherever he is over there."

"Right. Wherever he is." I fumbled with the brochures. "Yes. I will get Ella some sort of inexpensive cell phone that she can carry around with her. God knows she won't need a Twitter account."

Lauren laughed. "Hey, not so fast! Perhaps you should get her an iPhone. I am sure there is a Groovy Gran app. Or Bob may get totally into *Minecraft*. And who doesn't love Facebook? I posted a picture of my lunch today!"

I could picture Bob hunched over, checking her status updates. Ugh. "I'll stick with the bare bones. Oops. No pun intended."

Lauren chuckled, and then her pager beeped. "Gotta go. Swing by and have a cookie, and then ask the nurses what room Ella is going to be in. They should be wheeling her out of recovery pretty soon." She reached into her pocket and pulled out a business card. "In case I don't see you before she's released, here is my number. Really—feel free to call if you need me." And with a crisp salute, Lauren left. I was desolate.

CHAPTER TWENTY

The first visit was necessarily brief. Bob and I sat on either side of Ella's bed, watching her sleep, mostly. But her even breathing and pink cheeks reassured us. She woke for short periods, and smiled at us through her drug haze. The nurse informed us that she would be on a pain drip, but that they would be weaning her off the hard stuff and onto IV Tylenol throughout the next twenty-four hours.

At one point, Ella tried to sit up. We both leapt up to prevent it, Bob exclaiming, "Gran! Gran! Don't do that! You have a cool crank-up bed! Here, watch what happens when I push this button!"

We read Ella her cards, and Bob posted them on the bulletin board across from her bed. Ella was cogent enough to tell me that I shouldn't worry—she would write me a check for groceries and incidentals (cell phone!) as soon as she could. Ella pointed to the bedside table, where her pocketbook lay. I handed it over to her.

She rummaged around in its depths, unzipping multiple compartments until she found them. A deck of business cards held together with a rubber band. She held them out to me. "Look in these. You will find a card for Ernest Wallace, my attorney, and August Roseburg, my accountant. Mr. Wallace has a pre-signed document that will give you power of attorney to pay my bills and things. I knew I might need something like this when Charles was out of the country. Call him, and he will take care of it—fill your name in. And I have plenty of money! Mr. Roseburg pays my bills for me; don't even worry about that. If you need any money for anything, just call him; and if he needs some permission, I will give that, too. Rebecca, I thank you so much for helping me with all this!" Her rheumy eyes teared up. So did mine.

I felt overwhelmed, but also flattered that Ella was placing so much trust in me. "Ella, don't worry about a thing! I am going to be right here!" I gulped three times in succession.

All in all, it was a satisfying first day. But Ella, Bob, and I were exhausted, so we left before visiting hours were over to go home and recoup.

"She is going to be okay, right?" Bob asked, looking out the car window at a boy on a scooter racing down a side street.

I nodded as emphatically as I could. "Absolutely. She needs to rest, and then they will get her moving as soon as possible. Dr. Lauren told me that your Gran's rehab will be unpleasant for her—you know, moving around after surgery hurts. But she said it is very important that we encourage Ella to move and to participate fully in her therapy."

Bob winced when I said "hurts." She put a hand to her mouth to bite her thumbnail, but thought better of it. "So we have to be like football coaches? Push, push, push?"

"Exactly. Ella will need tough love. And lots of cheerleading. And guess what? Your father said that he will be part of the team, too." The metaphor galloping away with us, here. "You and I will pick out a cell phone tomorrow that Ella can keep with her—and your dad will call her on a regular basis to check up on both of you."

"You mean I will get to talk to him all the time?" Bob nearly launched out of her seat with excitement. Ok, then—TWO cell phones.

"Not all the time—not every day. He said he has a certain amount of minutes a month that he can use to call with. Maybe once a week or so."

"He got those minutes specially for us? I love the marines!" She held her hands up and high-fived the air.

I did not mention the fact that Charles had had these special minutes ever since he deployed. It would have been cruel.

That evening, after a trip to the Bowers' for Bob's clothes, a few of her stuffed animals, and a trip around the house to make sure everything was secure, we returned to my apartment. I thought pizza delivery and TV would be appropriate.

We were just finishing up our Cheeselovers' Delite—deep dish. Bob had crammed down three slices. I had managed two and a half. Our doorbell rang.

Bob jumped up and ran to answer. It was a gift from above. There stood Gail and my mother. Not usually a pair. Gail held a bottle of wine and a bouquet of daisies. Mom had a grocery sack. Mom leaned towards me and whispered, "We want to help."

"Hello! Are you Bob? We have heard so much about you!" Bob stepped aside with a tentative smile. "I'm Claire, Beck's mother, and of course, you know Gail. We're bringing some supplies." She smiled her lovely movie-star smile.

My mom bustled into the kitchen. "I heard that Bob likes Popsicles, so I got two boxes. That should last you for a while, right, Bob?" Bob's smile grew more expansive.

Gail followed, putting the Chardonnay in the fridge, and artfully arranging the daisies in a water glass. She had some major staging skills—between them, Mom and Gail could make any old dump look like something out of *Architectural Digest*. Mom unloaded a box of Cheerios, a half-gallon of milk, a bunch of bananas, a loaf of bread, and a jar of Nutella. "This ought to tide you over for breakfast and lunch."

I heaved a sigh of relief and hugged them both.

Gail turned to Bob. "I see you've had dinner. But I could use some dessert. How about a round of Popsicles for everybody?"

"Yay!" Bob pranced around the kitchen.

We took our Popsicles onto the back stoop, where the air was just cooling, and a breeze rustled the leaves in the honeysuckle.

The Popsicles were particularly drippy, but we didn't care. Bob skipped around the yard, licking her pop and running her hand along the fence.

"Have you taken some time off work? Are you going to be in charge of things across the street?" Loaded question. Mom, I am sure, thought that this was not totally my responsibility. Well, I didn't either, but of course, there *was* nobody else.

"I have no choice." I looked around and put my finger over my lips. "Little pitchers and big ears.." I moved closer to them and continued softly, "Ella and Bob need me. And we all know that I can make it just fine on my royalty money. I can easily afford to take a Starbucks sabbatical."

Gail put her Popsicle stick on the step and licked her fingers. This was out of character for one so pristine. "I get it. This is a very humanitarian thing you're doing. But you need some help—first off, you are a horrible cook."

"I take umbrage at that remark!" I wanted to punch her arm, but my hands were also sticky, and Gail was wearing something flowy and of course, silky.

Mom chimed in, "Gail and I were discussing this on the way over. Tomorrow, we are going to canvas the neighbors with a meal rotation sign-up sheet. I know all the neighbors must love Ella and Bob. I am sure they would be happy to help out. This will save you a lot of headaches."

"AND STOMACHACHES!" Bob flourished her Popsicle stick.

Mom wasn't finished. "What about the yard? Who will take care of that?"

Bob answered that one. "Gran has a yard man who mows and stuff. I know how to set up the sprinkler."

"Well, if you think of anything else, we can help out. She won't need a home nurse?"

"The doctor said no. Ella will be ambulatory. I will be taking her to rehab every week; I'm not sure if it's more than once. The Dr. said she will be in rehab for six weeks. Guys, this is a good thing. I have started a new book, and this will give me time to work on it."

Gail smirked. "*Frannie Does Framington?*"

"Nope. This isn't my usual. I'm writing a novel. About friendship. That is all I will say. So this time-out will be perfect for me, for Bob, and for Ella." I sounded much more confident of this than I felt.

"It's getting late. I'm sure it is past Bob's bedtime! What time do you normally go to bed, now that school has started?" Mom ran a hand through Bob's curls.

"I stayed up until ten during the summer, but Gran said I have to go to bed by nine now. I am awful tired tonight."

169

We stood to go up. Gail picked up all the Popsicle sticks and walked over to the trashcan by the garage, lifted the lid, and dropped them in. Then she cocked her head.

"I could swear I just heard a cat meow."

We looked all around the yard, but found nothing.

▷◁

Dr. Lauren hit the nail directly on the head. Ella wasn't doing well with rehab. The transitions went well, and she seemed happy to be at Oakmoor, but by the second day, she had lost her appetite. Despite the cookies that Marva Davis sent, along with a card that Hallie drew, covered with polka dots. Despite a phone call from Charles. Despite the flowers and the classical music station playing softly in the background. Ella was resolutely miserable. The therapists recommended that her stay be extended for at least two more weeks. After that, it would get dicey.

"Ella, the physical therapist told the nurses that you wouldn't get up out of your wheelchair in your afternoon therapy session. You know how important this is. If you don't cooperate, you may never be able to walk again. This therapy is critical."

Ella grimaced. "This cookie tastes bitter. Everything tastes bitter." She dropped the cookie on her tray and closed her eyes. "I am very tired. I just need to rest, right now, Rebecca. Can you come back later?" I put the cookie back in the tin on Ella's tray along with the others. The card on the lid said TO ELLA WITH GET WELL WISHES FROM THE DAVISES.

"What do you want me to tell Bob when she comes home from school? That you have just given up?"

Ella's fingers waved me away. She didn't answer. "Ella, the longer you refuse to cooperate, the longer you will have to stay here."

I wasn't sure if she heard me. "Ella."

She groaned and slowly turned her face away from me. Her hair was mussed, exposing large patches of pale, waxy scalp. This despondent, unkempt and defiant wraith was not the Ella I knew. "It doesn't matter to me where I am. Leave me be for now. Just leave me."

They smiled encouragingly at the nurses' station as I passed, but somehow, those smiles seemed rote. They probably smiled like that at all the families. I felt like screaming in the elevator, but I figured that it might alarm the little lady with her hospital gown on backwards, who patted me on the arm and wished me a "happy birthday."

When I got back to Ella's (I had decided that it made much more sense to spend most of my time at Ella's with Bob until Ella came home), I took the little yellow business card that Lauren had given me out of my pocket and studied it. I didn't want to send Ella to yet another doctor, not just yet. I wanted to give her a chance to rally on her own. I wondered how I would react if I had eighty-four-year-old bones, and one with a pin in it. Old people ache all the time in good circumstances, so I felt that Ella was probably justified in her despondency. She would perk up, wouldn't she?

I turned the card over in my hand, thinking about how just a few months before, I had been all by myself over there across the way, thinking I was very content, thank you, with my cat and my keyboard. But right now, despite being exhausted with responsibility for both Ella and Bob, I felt very good about being able to help them. Plus, I had the beginnings of a new novel that I knew I would be proud of. A book about friendship and faith, and how one small child changed everything for all the people she encountered. All because of one funny little kiddo. Huh.

My cell beeped me out of my reverie. I hoped it wasn't Oakmoor calling me back in.

"Hello?"

"Hi, honey. Are you in the middle of something?" Her voice was just a slight bit off.

"Hi, Mom. Not at all. Just waiting for Bob to get home from school. What's up?"

There was a long pause, during which I heard her sigh. Twice. Never a good sign.

"Mom?"

"Your sister is a mess. She needs help. Alexander has developed colic, and he cries all night long, every single night. Diana says you can set your watch by it."

I felt sorry for the little guy, but I didn't get the reason for Mom's dejection. "Isn't colic sort of normal? He'll get over it. Doesn't colic go away on its own?"

Another huge sigh at her end. "Beck. Diana needs help. Bryan has to sleep at night in order to go to work. He can't, with all the screaming. So Diana is coming home."

My God. The enormity of this sank in. "Wait. What do you mean, coming HOME? She lives in Chicago!" My heart was pounding and my tongue suddenly dehydrated and stuck to the insides of my cheeks.

"She is coming here to stay until either Alexander gets over this or Diana gets stronger. I told her we would be willing to help her with him. But honey, I work, too. I have to get a good night's sleep. So I told her that maybe she could stay at your apartment, since you are mainly across the street now. I said you could pop over there in the evenings to give her a break. You know, you could stay with the baby for a while, and Diana could stay with Bob, so that she could get some sleep. You could spell each other off. And I would come over some nights to stay with him, too. And of course, Bryan will come on weekends."

I put my hand over my heart. Yup. It was thumping as if trying to escape out of my chest. "Let me get this straight, Mom. You want the three of us to become some sort of nomads, cycling in and out of my apartment? For weeks? My sister and my ex and their baby will be using my apartment as a home base?" This was incredible.

To her credit, Mom sounded unsure. "I know this isn't the greatest solution in the world, but Diana needs me. Us. She is at the breaking point, Rebecca. And we have to think of what's best for Alexander. I just can't think of any other way around all of this. We are a family, and who else can your sister turn to?"

Bryan came to mind. "Don't other couples who have babies with colic somehow manage to handle the situation by themselves?" She didn't say anything. "Mom?" Perhaps she was formulating a retort.

"Mom. Here is my situation. I have taken on both Bob and her gran. As you mentioned, I have basically moved across the street, I have temporarily quit my job, and now you need me to also become a colic-sitter? Mom! I love you, but have you lost your mind?"

She tutted at her end. "Rebecca. Of all people, you should understand. After all, you didn't hesitate to jump into the breach to help Ella Bowers and her granddaughter. You are a Good Samaritan! That is what humans do for one another. And so now your sister needs us, because she is at the end of her tether. If you don't believe me, just call her. You will see what I mean. We don't have a choice. This is for the good of our family. My daughter. Your sister. And our adorable Alexander." Another long pause.

"Ugh, this is just unbelievable." The wind was just *rushing* out of my sails.

Funny thing—I heard my mother snort. "Honey, she is coming, whether we like it or not. You know your sister; she's made up her mind about this."

"Mom. Oh, my God." Now I was in a cold sweat.

"Call your sister. You will see what I'm talking about. There is no alternative. I mean it."

I set my cell phone down and laid flat on the living room floor, gazing up at Ella's elegant crown molding. I pondered this predicament. Pondering time was limited, as my cell phone vibrated. Caller ID: my maniacal sister—I wouldn't have to call her, after all.

"Oh, my God. Beck. In addition to the colic, Alexander has an ear infection! SO NOW HE CRIES TWENTY-FOUR HOURS A DAY. It seems like he's dying! There is nothing we can do about it, because the pediatrician doesn't want to start him on antibiotics because the infection is *mild*. I can't give him Tylenol because he is too young, he spits up all over me, Bryan is worthless in a crisis, and I think my milk is drying up! I cannot stand ONE MORE MINUTE OF THIS!"

"Hi, to you, too, D. Feel better, now that you have spilled guts over cell towers from Illinois to Ohio?"

She seemed to calm down a little. "I have to get *out* of here."

I have to admit, I heard the baby howling in the background.

"I know. Mom told me you want to come back to Framington."

Diana gave a rueful laugh. "Yeah, but I have to bring the baby *with* me." The howling was becoming louder.

I wanted to stab her. Yup. "You want to come over here for some *back up*. From me and Mom. Oh, this isn't too much of a problem. I am not that busy, heck NO! I am just OCCUPIED. OCCUPADO. Twenty-four/seven. I am taking care of an eighty-four-year-old with a broken bone; I am a surrogate gran to her great-granddaughter who is afraid she will lose the only parental unit she has at the moment. I have quit my job in order to do this!" Saying I quit my job to do this made me feel so gratifyingly martyr-y.

To her credit, D sighed and said, "Oh. I see." Now Alex was screaming.

But Diana is a Pit Bull; she doesn't like to let go. "If I don't get some help, I don't know what I am liable to do. I think I have post-partum depression. I have to get a break here, before I do something desperate, do you *understand*, Beck?"

By this time, it sounded as if Alex might be breaking his own eardrums with the noise he was producing. Despite myself, I felt a stab of sympathy for this hysterical duo. What can I say—I caved. "Go ahead, get your hopeless ass in the car, or on a plane or something, and come home. Mom already offered up my apartment—I have moved temporarily across the street. All I can say is, it's a good thing my neighbors are all elderly and hard of hearing, because all that screaming won't be any picnic."

This apparently took my sister aback. "Wait. You are living at that old lady's with the little girl?" A pause. She had to raise her voice to be heard over her son's bellowing. "And you quit your job?" Another pause. "My God."

Apparently, Diana had a eureka moment. "First, you have a fake feminist epiphany and decide that you can't be in a permanent relationship with Bryan. Then you use me, the boyfriend robber, as a scapegoat to explain away your own irrational fears about marriage—so scared that if you got married it would be a repeat of Dad and Mom." She paused to let *that* sink in. "So now you're compensating by saving this little girl? Whoa."

There it was, in a nutshell. I put my head on my knees. "So, Dr. Freud, are you coming, or not?" I felt a huge headache coming on. Alex's roaring was getting to me.

"Of course I'm coming. I already went online and got plane tickets. I will text you my itinerary. I have to go; he's beside himself!" And she hung up.

I tried to imagine what it would be like to have my sister living in my apartment, with all the equipment that it would entail and that I would most likely have to scrounge up for her: bouncy seats, diaper genies, some sort of crib arrangement, educational toys, and stuffed animals. I pictured her stomping across the street with Alex yowling—and thrusting him into my arms as I tried to cook dinner and help Bob with her homework. I pictured having to see Bryan over there. Living with his little family in my apartment. Shitballs. Then I added Ella into the mix, home from Oakmoor, but not recovering the way she should. I pictured Ella holding Alex and dropping him, me helplessly looking on. Bob weaving in and out of the image, offering everybody Popsicles. It was a depressing daydream. I banged my head against Ella's polished hardwood floor, hoping to put myself out of my misery.

CHAPTER TWENTY-ONE

It was an uncharacteristically gloomy day for the beginning of fall in Framington. The glorious foliage was dimmed by the cloudy day, and leaves clattered in the breeze. It felt humid, and my mood matched the weather. Mom and I sat on her sofa, drinking green tea. Mom looked as put together as ever, but there were worry circles under her eyes.

"I know that this is going to be a challenge for all of us. You have so much on your plate already. I can barely remember what taking care of a tiny baby entails. Neither of us is looking forward to walking the floor with a screaming infant, I know. And they say that colic can last until the baby is three months old." Mom shook her head slowly, set her tea down, and got up to look out the window of my apartment toward Ella's house. Currently empty—Bob was at school and Ella still at Oakmoor. We weren't exactly sure when Ella would be released. Her being in the convalescent center and Diana's arrival were synched perfectly. For D. "Have you cleared out a space for her and Alex in your room?"

Ugh. I motioned for Mom to follow me into my bedroom, where I had spent the better part of an afternoon clearing out. "What do you think?"

Mom looked around. I had removed all the stacks of books that filled the corners of the room. That immediately made things look more spacious. Because babies need to breathe clean air, especially ones that had sensitive systems already tainted by colic, I had actually Swiffered the blades of my Venetian blinds free of the thick layer of dust that typically adorned them, and washed the nubby linen curtains. They shrank about two inches, and I am sure that Mom noticed, but she said nothing. She ran her palm over the top of my bureau (I had emptied two big drawers—one for D, and one for Alex). "Beck, this is immaculate. I am proud of you."

I opened my closet door. "Look at this. You won't believe it, either."

The floor of my closet, usually strewn with mismatched pairs of shoes, dirty clothes, dust balls, and Simpson's litter box, was clear. The hardwood floor didn't gleam, but it was clean. I had washed it out with vinegar water. When I dumped out Simpson's litter and soaked the box with bleach water, I cried a little. But afterwards, I propped the box against the back of the closet, because I had not totally given up hope. My clothes were shoved over to make room on the hanging bar for D's stuff.

"Oh, honey. This is so nice. And I know you didn't want to do any of this."

I shut the closet door, and Mom and I sat on my bed, both of us lost in thought. "Does colic *really* last for three months?"

Mom slowly lowered herself onto her elbows and gazed up at the cracks in my ceiling. And the cobwebs that I never noticed until right that second, as I leaned against my headboard. "It can. Usually it comes without any warning and disappears just as suddenly as it comes. They still have no idea what causes it, but perhaps it's a developmental sort of thing that they just grow out of. It can be a lot worse than what Alex has—he cries just a couple of hours a night. Some babies are colicky all day and night."

I looked heavenward with gratefulness.

Mom sighed and looked over at me. "We just have to gird our loins for this. I think it will be easier for us to deal with all the crying, because we aren't Alex's parents. It's much harder for them. You had colic, did you know that? It was no fun. I walked the floor with you for what seemed like months, but you only had it for six weeks. It nearly killed me."

I bounced my head against the headboard. "Well, I can't imagine that listening to my nephew cry as if someone is stabbing him in the gut every night for hours will be a breeze. And they don't have any medicine for this? We put a man on the moon, but we don't have medicine for colic?"

Mom bounced her head a couple of times, but I guess she didn't like the sensation. She stopped and looked over at me. So I stopped, too, and smiled at her. She laid a hand on my stomach. "No. No medicine. There was something we used to use back when you two were babies, but it had belladonna or something in it. We will just have to get used to it. And maybe get some earplugs. And remember, it won't be every night. We will take turns minding him. At least Diana will get some rest." A bright look crossed her face, but I leaned over and squelched that one fast.

"Mom. Don't. I know what you're thinking. You have put your usual optimistic spin on this situation, haven't you? This will NOT be a great chance for the three of us to *bond*. There isn't necessarily a silver lining here."

Mom only smiled a bit more brightly. "You don't know that, Rebecca." She bounced her head a couple of times for good measure. "Well, you DON'T."

⊳⊲

So, Friday after school, Bob and I got into the car to go to the airport to pick up my self-centered sibling. Bob had a few questions.

"Is Alexander cute? Do you call him Alex, or Alexander?"

"Both."

"Does he have hair?"

"A little."

"Are you still mad at your sister for stealing Bryan?"

"Sort of." (Note to self: come to grips with this, *you idiot*.)

"But don't you love Theo now?"

"I like Theo a lot. But to be honest, Bob, he hasn't called me since your gran went into the hospital."

"Really?"

"Yes."

"Is that why you aren't really talking to me, but just answering my questions like a robot?"

I looked over at Bob, who was chewing on her cuticles now, having run out of actual fingernails. "Bob, I have a lot on my mind."

Bob continued chewing. "So can I babysit for Alex sometimes while your sister is here?"

"Maybe."

I think Bob realized that conversation was futile. She was silent until we entered the terminal.

We stood at the end of the corridor, waiting for the Chicago arrivals to trickle down the entrance to the luggage claim area. One old man in a frayed windbreaker, leaning heavily on a cane. A heavyset woman wearing hearing aids and carrying a gigantic Macy's shopping bag. A harried mother with frizzy pigtails, pushing a stroller containing a frustrated looking child, dragging her feet against the floor. There was a lull.

And then we saw her. A tall, leggy blonde, hair swept up in some sort of messy French starlet bun, held up with a red chopstick. Dark red jeggings. Probably Jimmy Choo sandals. Aaah. She was obviously getting her shit back together—she was wearing false eyelashes at least a half-inch long. A crimson-and-black geometric tunic. And strapped to the front of it, Alex—his tiny, baldish head barely visible.

Bob gasped. "Is *that* your sister?"

Still monosyllabic. "Yes."

"But she didn't look like that when she was here before! She looks like a Disney princess!"

I threw up a little in my mouth. "Looks can be deceiving."

Diana glided up to us and put out her cheek for a kiss. "I am exhausted."

"We are fine, thank you. Oh, and you might recall this person standing beside me? D, this is my best friend Bob."

Bob shot me a look of sheer happiness at the "best friend" part. Then she recovered and stuck out her small hand to my sister. "Hi! I remember you from before, but you look a lot better now. May I hold the baby?"

Diana immediately unbuckled the Baby Bjorn, or whatever the hell the contraption was called, and untangled Alex. She plopped him unceremoniously into Bob's arms. I nearly had a coronary and jumped with both hands to catch him in case Bob dropped him.

But Bob was a pro, and she cradled him in her arms, cooing. He smiled at her.

"I have a bag and a stroller. Come on." Bob, who looked as if she was struggling, relinquished Alex to me with a look of relief. Diana strode off to the carousels, her Michael Kors diaper bag slung over her shoulder, leaving us to follow in her wake.

Before we left baggage claim, Diana handed off the Bjorn thing, the car seat, and the collapsed stroller. "Carry Alexander, it's too much trouble to unfold this damn thing."

She also stopped at the Starbucks kiosk for a large skim-milk latte. We trooped to the car—me pulling the stroller behind me and gripping Alex with my free arm, Bob struggling to heft the car seat, the Bjorn strap draped over her forehead like a tumpline— she looked like a mini Sherpa. D strolled beside us, pulling her roller bag and sipping her coffee.

At the car, we set all of D's paraphernalia on the pavement and turned our attention to getting Alex legally installed as a passenger in the backseat of my car.

It took me ten minutes to figure out how to affix the car seat to the clamps built into the car for that very purpose. (Who knew? D informed me between sips that all cars have them.) I looked at her for help. "Bryan always does that." Sip, sip.

"DIANA. You are here because you need me and Mom to help you. *Help* is the operative word—we are not your minions."

To her credit, that sort of shook her up. She came to her senses, sweeping the perfectly platinum bangs out of her eyes and focusing on us as if she hadn't noticed us before. "Sorry. Old habits." She smiled, most likely putting Bob under her spell forever, and handed me her coffee. "You can finish this." She grabbed the stroller, took back the baby carrier, and loaded all of her stuff into the trunk. Slamming it shut with a bang, she pushed me aside and deftly clamped and snapped Alex into the car seat, like a total professional mother. Wow.

Bob clambered into the backseat and beamed at the baby facing backwards, who by this time was absently sucking his thumb and looking as if he were in a trance. She made duck faces at him as Diana descended gracefully into the front seat beside me.

"Hey, you two. Alex is just about out cold. The ear infection is nearly cleared up; he should sleep for a while. So do you want to stop at the Dairy Queen drive-thru on the way to Beck's? I would *kill* for a dipped cone." The fun was about to begin.

▷◁

Mom took the first night shift. "I have the most experience with this. Diana needs to get settled in and rest. You need to go over to Mrs. Bowers' and get organized there. She's coming home, and you must have a lot to do to get things ready for her."

That was fine with me. It only took me two trips to carry over my suitcase, my laptop, the four books I was reading, and my toiletries across the street. I had been bouncing back and forth, but now I had to make the more permanent shift. Ella had agreed that when she returned, she would stay in Charles' room (now a guest room) downstairs, and I would move into her room upstairs, across the hall from Bob. Ella would not be doing stairs any time soon. As I unzipped my suitcase on the floor of Ella's closet and stared down at my clothes, I wondered how long I would be living out of my suitcase over here. I felt a stab of uneasiness. What on earth was I getting into? Old ladies, little kids, and an infant who screamed all night? What happened to my spinsterish existence, and the only excitement being the orgasms I typed into my manuscripts?

CHAPTER TWENTY-TWO

We sat my sofa, drinking tea. Mom reported that the first night wasn't too bad. Alex only cried for two-ish hours, and Mom said the earplugs she got helped a lot. Also, she played Baroque music on the public radio station, which she thought helped.

"Frankly, you guys, I am scared to death of my first shift. Baroque music notwithstanding. And he doesn't even *know* me that well—how am I supposed to soothe a baby to whom I am a complete stranger?"

Diana, holding the infant in question in her lap, gazed down at him, sleeping soundly as if nothing in the world could possibly bother him. "Well, I have him tonight. Go to the CVS and get some earplugs before tomorrow. And you do have an iPod, you know. He might like your playlist even better than classical music. Knowing you, you have Michael Bublé on it. He's soothing."

Mom, who had finished her tea and looked as if she wanted a nap more than anything in the whole world, ran a hand through her hair and stood to leave. "You two have a nice chat. I have to get going. I have to rest my eyes for a bit, and then I have a client meeting—we are looking at fabric samples for her new sofas. Ta!"

As she swished out, she dropped a kiss on D's head, stroked little Alex's peach fuzz hair, and blew me a kiss.

We watched her leave. Diana looked completely serene, probably because she had had her first full night of sleep since Alex was born. I felt panicky and anxious. It occurred to me to get some Saint John's Wort along with the earplugs, because I was as far from serenity as I could get.

It started out fine. Alex was fresh from his bath, slick with baby lotion, sweet-smelling, and adorable. Nothing seemed to be bothering him at the moment. His little fluffs of hair felt so soft against my palms. I tried to give myself a confidence boost: *Maybe he doesn't actually have colic. Maybe the water in Chicago affected D's breast milk. Maybe he's fine now that he's been here on Ohio-water breastmilk for a couple of days.*

Of course, as soon as he drew up his little legs as if something was poking him, then commenced screaming on the dot of ten p.m., I remembered that Mom had said that "you could set your clock" by his colic. It apparently started up very suddenly, kept up until just past midnight, and then quit. Writhing in my arms, Alex seemed in agony. I had a hard time holding onto him, his little knees knocking against my abdomen. His cries were ear-splitting. Just looking at those little legs writhing in pain made me want to trade places with him, the poor little mite.

I set him down on Ella's yellow blanket on the floor. On his back. He continued to pull up and shriek. His tummy. Okay, maybe being on his stomach would put some healing pressure on his guts and calm him. I turned him over. This just caused him to propel himself forward by the motion of his knees as they pumped up and down—it looked for all the world as if at six weeks old, he was crawling. Accompanied by blood curdling wails. The colic came in waves. Just as it seemed like it was all over, and he would be all right, and I started to relax, another cramp would hit him, and he would start contorting in pain once more.

My God. Will he puke? Diana didn't say if colic makes them vomit. Beck, do something! The poor kid is in agony! Pick him UP.

He didn't seem to like being hoisted onto my lap, where I tried to rock him back and forth calmly on the sofa. As a matter of fact, with one of the colic "contractions," he writhed so hard that his little skull smacked into my face with such force that I thought my nose might be broken. Of course, hitting his forehead on my nose hurt Alex's face, and so now he screamed at the pain there as well as in his tummy. Thank God my neighbors were nearly deaf.

How much longer will this go ON? He has been screaming forever!

I glanced down at my watch. Sweat cascaded from my armpits down into the waistband of my underwear. It was ten fifteen. I stood and started walking back and forth with him, trying to sing something soothing, but all I could think of was "Happy Birthday." I went with it. We walked around, wishing the world many happy returns for about five minutes, until my arms got tired of trying to keep him from throwing himself out of them in his torment. We sat down for a break, but as soon as another pain hit him, we got up to pace around once more.

On one of the laps through the apartment, I switched on the TV. *American Idol* rerun. Good, maybe Alex and I could commiserate about which singer was the most talented. I turned him around and aimed him at the screen. "See, honey? That guy is trying to sing just like John Legend. What do you think? Is he any good?" I jiggled Alex in time to the music. Nada. The yowls continued.

For the next two hours, I alternated between jostling Alex, putting him on the floor to cry it out, changing my mind about that and picking him back up and jostling him some more, dancing for Alex (he seemed to hate that more than the singing), offering Alex a bottle of breast milk (he knocked that right out of my hand), rubbing Alex on the back, and finally bursting into tears myself.

At twenty after twelve, Alex laid his head down on my shoulder, heaved a jagged baby sigh, and stopped crying. It was a miracle. I carried the now placid little person into the kitchen where, as instructed, I warmed a bottle of breast milk and offered it to him. As he leaned back in my arms, sucking madly and reaching up to stroke my cheek with his sweet little fingers, my heart nearly burst out through my bra.

We strolled back into the living room, where Alex finished his bottle and farted. Oh. I set him down, changed his diaper (breast-fed babies don't have stinky poop, thank goodness), and laid him down on his blankie. I lay beside him, just to rest for a second.

The next thing we knew, it was six thirty in the morning, and D was bursting through the door, lifting her shirt, and unfastening her nursing bra. "Hand me up one of my nipple shields and that baby—my boobs are killing me!" I looked at Alex, who blinked his little sea blue eyes and smiled at the sound of his mommy's voice.

I stretched my arms, heard my spine crack, and flexed my toes. I blinked three times as I watched my sister scoop up her son, enthrone herself on my sofa, and begin to nurse. They looked like a Madonna and child. I couldn't help but smile. Then I realized that I had slept for six hours, uninterrupted. *What the hell?*

"Hey, D!" I sat up. "How exactly again is this colic situation," here I used finger quotes, "*killing you and Bryan?*" Diana lifted her eyebrows. "I got six good hours in."

Diana remained silent as Alex sucked blissfully on the nipple shield. One lock of bleached blonde hair fell over her forehead, and she flicked it away.

"D, why are you really here?"

My sister stared at me over the downy head of her infant. Her lips trembled. Mascara tears ran down her cheeks, washing little ruts into the rouge on her cheeks.

"D. Speak!"

Instead, she blurted. "Everything sucks right now. I am a shitty mother. Bryan is completely helpless with babies. Alex may not seem like a handful to *you,* but I am completely overwhelmed. I am still totally fat. I have no energy. We eat microwave dinners. Bryan farts and guzzles beer. We have nothing to say to one another, except for arguing about how to deal with the colic. And I am not sure if we are going to stay married."

Hell and damnation.

I lay back down on the carpet and shut my eyes. My brain hit the "rewind" button.

It was a tough semester. I had bitten off more than I could chew and registered for twenty credit hours. One of the courses was Psycho Linguistics, and Noam Chomsky was a pain in my ass. I had gained weight eating too many brownie delights in the dining hall. My room-mate Freda had blonde dreadlocks, inflamed gums, armpit hair, BO, and lesbian tendencies. Mom sent high-calorie care packages, which I tried not to eat, because my flabbiness was getting out of control.

I was depressed as well, because the very few letters I got from Dad kept mentioning someone named Melanie. And just when I was about to self-combust, my little sister came to visit for the weekend. She dragged a duffel up the dorm stairs that seemed like it was full of anvils, but it turned out to be beer, diet pop, rice cakes, and enough marijuana for the entire third floor.

She knocked on my door, and when I opened it, there she stood on the threshold, her slim profile outlined by the lights in the cellblock that was our hallway, an electric smile on her face. "Mom says you are fat and depressed. So I brought low-calorie stuff and plenty of joints. Let's get happy."

We did. D told me with great detail about her new boyfriend, Jack, who was extremely proud of his penis, even though, as D noted, "There is absolutely NOTHING exceptional about it." She gave Freda a deep kiss that I am fairly certain old Freda, wherever she is these days, still dreams about.

We got high, laughed ourselves silly, and ate every single rice cake, but we slathered them with peanut butter we stole out of Freda's stash. D cranked the music in our room up so loud that it started a dance party out in the study lounge. The smell of pot wafted through the air, Freda got so sweaty that she actually took a shower, and not only was I cheered up, but the entire third floor wanted to adopt D as their little sister. When she left Sunday, I nearly sobbed. Nearly.

"My God, D. You have to go home. Right now!"

My sister broke the suction between Alex and her left nipple with a moist *pop* and shifted him over to her right breast. "Huh?"

"Diana. If things are that bad between you, you have to do something! This is just a rough patch. Babies are stressful. Who knew that you wouldn't be an earth mother? So your actual baby isn't exactly the dream baby you imagined. So he has a little colic. So Bryan doesn't change diapers or hover, or whatever he doesn't do. But you can't just give in to this. You cannot split UP." By this time, I was sitting cross-legged, sweating profusely, my stomach clenched so hard that I felt sick.

Diana paled. "Going home won't change anything. It sucked at home. THAT IS WHY I CAME HERE, YOU MORON."

I slapped my knees so hard, it left red marks on my inner thighs. Then I spoke, and it was as if I had stepped outside of myself. It was as if the "soul" me was floating on the ceiling, watching the "real" me speak. "So leave Alex here with me. I can handle him. You know, pump a ton of breast milk. Get on a plane. Go home and get some emergency marriage counseling. Have a bunch of sex. Or couples massage. Or, I don't know, call a doctor and get a double prescription for Zoloft. But for God's sake, don't get divorced!" The floating me was flabbergasted at what the real me was proclaiming.

Diana looked skeptical at first, then, as I could almost see the wheels turning around in her brain, she perked up a bit. "You're right. If I leave in a couple of days, that will give me time to pump you a supply of breast milk. Plus, you can supplement with formula if you have to. It doesn't seem to affect the colic, because we tried it to see. So that won't change . . ." she joggled Alex as she warmed to the subject. "And I can pump and dump while I am there."

"Enough with the breasts. Think about saving your marriage. Call for some reservations at a five-star restaurant. Make a waxing appointment for tomorrow. Get a mani-pedi. Honestly, Mom and I can handle Alex for a few days."

D drew her eyebrows together. "Have you forgotten? Mom is leaving tomorrow for Atlanta. The design conference where all the HGTV stars are keynoting. If I go, you will be on your own. Well, you and Bob. When is Ella coming home?"

The soul me re-entered my body and slapped me upside the face. "Shit. I don't know. It will be at least a couple of weeks. And Gail is tied up all day with work and all night with Rick." I fell back on the carpet. "But never fear. Because I can handle this."

My soul didn't buy it.

CHAPTER TWENTY-THREE

Diana made me a list as long as my arm of things I needed to know for Alex. Don't use Tide to wash his clothes, use Ivory Flakes. Don't give him tap water—only distilled. At the slightest sign of a rash, use A&D ointment. Never turn your back on him while bathing him. Support his head. Pediatrician phone number. Emergency babysitter number (Did D think I might want to go on a few *dates* while she was gone?), and ON AND ON. I posted it on the fridge while rolling my eyes.

I made sure she visited the waxing salon, although she balked. I did her nails myself, and urged her to make an emergency stop at Victoria's Secret at the mall. By the time she was sobbing while hugging Alex at the airport, I was sort of relieved to see her go. I made her put her hand over her heart and promise me that she would only text me three times a day.

Alex and I got back from the airport, and I set him in his bouncy chair while I loaded the dishwasher. We had an interesting conversation, as we waited for Bob to come home from school.

"Well, guy, do you think you will miss your Mom?" Alex gurgled. "Don't answer that. It will hurt my feelings." I studied the spots covering my glassware and decided I needed to try another dishwasher powder. Maybe those pod things.

As Alex shook his dinosaur, I wiped down the counters. There was a knock on the door. I hoisted Alex out of the bouncy chair, and he punched me in the eye with the Tyrannosaurus. *Maybe I should put that one away for when he's older.*

Bob stood on the porch, knocking on the door with her shoe. Her arms were full of bags. "Oh, thanks, Beck! I couldn't open the door. These are things for Alex and for us, too. From Hallie's mom."

Not wanting to hurt her feelings by pointing out that she could have *set the bags down* to open the door, I smiled instead. "What on earth did she send over?"

I followed Bob into the kitchen, where she set the bags down to unload. "One tin of chocolate chip cookies, for energy. Mrs. Davis said we would need lots of energy for taking care of Alex full time." Bob opened the tin and helped herself. She held one out to me, but I decided to hold off to see what else Marva sent.

Bob rustled around and pulled out a stuffed rabbit. He was nubbly white, with pink embroidered eyes, and a puff of a tail. "He doesn't have any loose parts. So he's safe for Alex. Mrs. Davis *crocheted* him! Can you believe it?" I was amazed, to be honest.

Next, Bob opened the second bag and extracted a book. "For you. Just in case, Mrs. Davis said to tell you." It was called *The Happiest Baby on the Block*. "She says she gives this to all her friends who are expecting, and she had a spare one that you could have. It has advice in it." Okay, then. Backup.

Finally, Bob pulled out a box containing two dozen popsicles, and two quart-sized containers of Graeter's coffee ice cream. My favorite. I made a mental note to kiss Marva the next time I saw her. I opened the freezer door for Bob, who deposited the treats inside. Then she sniffed. Sniffed again.

"Beck. I think Alex is poopy."

I groaned. "Now it begins, kiddo. I guess I have to take him up and change him. Want to help?"

Bob held her nose, squinted, laughed, and ran out of the room calling "NO! NO! ANYTHING BUT POOP!"

I heard the front screen door slam after her as she thundered outside. "I will be playing in the front, okay?"

I called back my assent as I carried Alex upstairs. D had provided a changing pad, which I had unfolded on my bed as a diaper station. D had included wipes and the inevitable A&D. Those were beside the pad. I stretched Alex out, and noted with alarm that the poop had oozed out of his diaper and saturated the front of his onesie. Ugh.

I peeled off the onesie, threw it on the floor to address later, and undid the tabs of his Pamper. My God. The kid had a poop extravaganza going on in there! Poop in the crotch. Poop on the buttocks. IN the buttocks. On his chest and up his back.

About fifteen wipes later, he was finally clean. The changing pad was besmirched, so I would need to do a load of laundry. I threw the changing pad on the floor with the onesie. Alex seemed to like the feel of Ella's chenille bedspread under his skin. He smiled. I put a fresh Pamper on him, first backwards. Then I saw that thankfully, the diapers were marked FRONT AND BACK for idiots like me. I switched it around and did the tabs.

Shoot. He needed a clean outfit. I pushed him onto the center of the bed, where he would be safe, and turned to grab a clean one-sie out of the drawer. I swear to you, God, and the angels in heaven that my back was turned for less than one second.

All his onesies were inside out. As I turned the fresh one right side, marveling at how *small* these outfits were, and how *tiny* humans could be, I heard a thump. I pivoted just in time to see Alex roll off the edge of the bed and face plant on Ella's Persian rug. There was an eerie silence, and then a strangled cry.

I dropped the onesie, leapt over, and grabbed Alex, who by this time was beet red, gasping, shrieking, and heaving for air. "Baby, baby, baby, are you okay?" I ran my hand all over his head, looking for bumps. It seemed okay. I put him on the bed, and checked his legs and back. Everything seemed to look normal.

But Alex kept crying. And doing the gaspy breathing.

I started to sob myself, and I grabbed Alex, the onesie, the dia-per bag, and stumbled down the stairs, screaming. "BOB! BOB!"

I ran out onto the porch. Bob had stopped dead in the mid-dle of a hopscotch. Both hands over her heart, she called, "OH NO! WHAT HAPPENED?"

I sat down on Ella's front step, rocking Alex back and forth in my arms. Bob rushed over and flung herself down beside us and peered into my arms. "Oh, Bob, he fell off the bed! I swear I turned my back on him for less than a second! What if he's really injured? Do babies get concussions?"

By this time, Alex had quieted down. He nestled against my shoulder, his tiny face streaked with tears, his whole body limp. Bob stroked his head. Now Alex was quiet, but Bob and I were crying.

"Bob. We have to take him to a doctor. What if something is broken? What if he's really hurt?" I pointed inside. "Hurry in and grab the list off the fridge that Diana gave me. And get my car keys. They're on the hall table. And my cell! It's should be beside the keys. HURRY!"

Bob and I managed to stop crying, buckle Alex into his car seat, and back out of Ella's driveway without incident. I steered with one hand and held the list with my other.

I read out the phone number of the pediatrician to Bob and told her to punch it in on the cell. "Tell them that we have an emergency, that this is Alex Dallas coming in. He is Claire Throckmorton's grandson. They know who that is."

Bob handled the call admirably, ad-libbing that it probably wasn't an emergency, but that we just wanted to make sure he was okay. After she hung up, she looked at me with a pale face. "I said the part about it us wanting to make sure he was okay so they won't think we are child abusers."

I didn't have time right then to process that entirely shocking statement from Bob, but it lodged itself in the forefront of my brain for later.

We didn't have to wait long at Dr. Walker's office. The receptionist was kind, the waiting room wasn't full, thank heaven, and by the time we got into the exam room, Alex was asleep.

Dr. Walker, a tall, slender woman with a monkey clipped to her stethoscope, looked Alex over. She listened to his heart, but had to hold a hand up to shush me while she listened. I blabbered on about how I had only turned my back for a second, was he going to be all right, could there be brain damage, etc.

Dr. Walker finished her exam and smoothed her hand over Alex's little forehead. She looked up at me and smiled reassuringly. "He is just fine. You know, babies have a way of bouncing. As I tell all my new mothers, it is pretty hard to kill a baby. But you were wise to bring him right in. So you and your kids"—she tilted a head in Bob's direction—"are in town visiting? You're Claire's daughter from Chicago, is it? Claire talks about you in book club."

Still shocky, I let her words slide right over my head. All I really heard was the "he's just fine" part. I nodded, dumbly.

Dr. Walker put her stethoscope back around her neck and opened a drawer. "Would you like a sticker, big sister?" She fanned out a deck of assorted stickers, and Bob chose a sheet of ladybugs.

I must have smiled and said thank you, because Dr. Walker said, "You're welcome. Any time. And you might want to consider changing his diaper on the floor from now on." With a flip of her lab coat, she left the exam room.

Relief didn't wash over me until we were halfway home. I heaved a huge sigh, wiped my damp hair back from my forehead, and remembered that it was past lunchtime. "Bob, when we get home, we can have grilled cheese sandwiches and eat a whole bunch of Marva Davises' cookies, okay?"

"Beck, Dr. Walker thought you were our mom. Me and Alex." I looked in the rearview mirror to see Bob flashing a huge grin, her freckles gleaming. She had one arm flung protectively over Alex in the car seat, and with her other hand, she popped me a thumbs-up.

Every single nerve in my body sang a happy song.

▷◁

We each had four cookies. Alex had two bottles. He was exhausted. I put him down for a nap, so that he would be nice and fresh for his late night colic session. Bob and I played a few rounds of Uno, and after a healthy late lunch/early dinner of grilled cheese and apple slices for fiber, we put my favorite old movie on the DVD player. I am a sucker for old Hollywood. *Breakfast at Tiffany's.*

About halfway in, after Alex woke up and we brought him down to *lie on his tummy on the floor* to watch with us, I realized that perhaps this wasn't the best choice of entertainment for an eight-year-old.

"Why does she wear an evening gown in the street in the mornings?"

"How come everybody smokes?"

"What's a martini?"

My explanation was long winded, and involved how "glamorous" Holly Golightly was. So glamorous that she wore evening gowns a lot. Even in the morning. The smoking and martinis were what people did to be sophisticated. Of course, then I had to explain what sophisticated meant. That involved Googling the oldies but goodies: Cary Grant, both Hepburns, and Marilyn Monroe on my phone. Bob and I spent a good half hour looking at Hollywood's heyday while Alex gurgled.

"I have an idea. Do you want to be glamorous?"

Bob jumped up, clapping her hands. "Yes! How can we do it? We don't have any evening gowns."

"No. But we can smoke and have martinis. Watch the baby."

In Ella's kitchen, I opened the cupboard over the sink. Ella, like all good hostesses, had martini and wine glasses in there. I got out a couple of martini glasses and filled them with orange Kool-Aid. Then I pulled open Ella's junk drawer. Jumbled among the twist ties, two corkscrews, a melon baller, a roll of twine, skewers, notepads, and masking tape, were some pencils. I removed two shortish ones.

Setting the martinis and the pencils on Ella's tole tray, I looked around. Cocktail napkins. We needed cocktail napkins. Of course. Ella would have those. Sure enough, in the top drawer of Ella's burled oak buffet in the dining room, I chose two small squares, embroidered with the word CHEERS.

I set the tray down on the coffee table, and handed Bob a martini and a pencil. "Here are the rules. We have to lean back like *this*," I tilted elegantly backwards as I imagined Audrey Hepburn would, "and call each other *dahling*."

Bob stood, giggling, and flipped back some imaginary long hair. She took a tiny sip of her martini. "Divine, dahling!" Bob picked up a pencil. "What's this?"

I took a drag on my pencil and blew out some pretend smoke. "Cigarettes, dahling. All the elegant people smoked back then." I stepped out of character for just a moment. "Back THEN. Nobody elegant smokes now, because it gives you cancer. Got that, Bobbo?"

Bob took a puff. "Of course, dahling. Gran told me that smoking makes you stinky and turns your teeth brown."

We both laughed. Elegantly.

▷◁

Bob was exhausted, too. Even though it was Friday, she went to bed early. I was tired, too, but of course the colic was imminent. So I plopped down on the sofa, turned the baby monitor to face me, and called Gail.

"My God. Today was the worst. I nearly killed the baby."

Gail murmured encouragingly at her end.

"No, really. He fell off the bed. I only turned my back—"

"For ONE SECOND." Gail laughed. "All babysitters say that. Was he okay?"

I told her the whole story, and she laughed. A lot. "You will be fine. This was just a head's up. You are a very responsible woman."

"Ha! You know what Bob and I did while Alex was napping? WE SMOKED CIGARETTES AND DRANK MARTINIS." I explained about *Breakfast at Tiffany's* and our cocktail party. "Yup. Day one of being the surrogate mother, and I nearly kill the baby and then turn Bob into a chain smoker and an alcoholic!"

"Oh, stop it. You are a very creative and interesting person, and you know how to have fun. It was totally an accident that I am sure happens to a lot of people—you're exaggerating for effect. My God, I'm sure Bob loved it. It's not like you're some kind of child abuser, for heaven's sake!"

Then I remembered what Bob told me in the car. "Gail, I have to go. I think Alex is waking."

I set my cell phone down. I shut my eyes. In the blackness behind my eyelids, I thought I could hear a little girl crying somewhere in Iowa. I heard a door slam. The crying subsided. But I knew the child was hurt, and she was all alone.

Damn Rowena.

Just as Alex began to pull his legs up and wail, I picked him up and began to walk him back and forth, whispering in his ear, "I'm sorry, little guy." It seemed to soothe him more if I jostled him and whispered. So I whispered the tunes of "Happy Birthday," "Frere Jacques," and "Twinkle Twinkle." I was on about my fifteen lap around the bedroom and the tenth version of "Row Your Boat" when Bob stumbled in, her hair in her eyes, her lids swollen with slumber. She crept up to us and reached for Alex. "We need to stay up with him tonight, to make sure he's okay," she rasped in her sleepy voice.

"Are you sure?" I had to admit to myself that I was so relieved to see her moon white face just then. "Here. I will make us a nest."

I pulled the chenille bedspread down, placed all of Ella's extra pillows from the closet to make an Alex tunnel in the center. "Okay, you lie on one side, and I will lie on the other. That will keep him from falling off. But he won't do that again, because *we will be watching him.*"

Bob tumbled into the bed, and I laid the agitated baby on his back between the pillows. I got in on the other side. Bob and I leaned over the little guy like he was the baby Jesus in the manger.

I will be damned if he didn't settle down some. His legs stopped churning, and his fists unwound into little pink five-petaled flowers. Bob gently stroked his tummy. Instead of shrieking, he descended into a low hum.

"Don't worry, Bob. You can close your eyes. I'll keep watch."

I awoke the next morning with one arm flung over Bob's arm, which was flung around Alex's midsection. They were both snoring. Alex's tiny fingers tightly clasped Bob's thumb. I let the sweetness wash over me.

CHAPTER TWENTY-FOUR

Things calmed down. Thank God. D really did limit her texts to three a day. However, she phoned every night, timing it so I would stay awake until Alex began to scream. She had advised earplugs for Bob, which really helped. Bob slept like a log from then on.

I mustered up the courage to tell her about Alex the day after it happened. The conversation started out inconsequentially, but then I spilled it. She hardly seemed to hear me when I admitted things.

"D, did you hear me? I said that Alex rolled off the bed. On the freaking first day of my watch. Jesus, he could have been seriously injured, and I am telling you that it's my fault and I am so very sorry, but he is okay, and the doctor Mom recommended was really nice, and even though she didn't tell me to, I woke him up at four in the morning just to make sure he is okay . . . Bob and I kept watch all night . . ."

D sniffed. "Yeah, I heard you. It's fine. He rolled off the sofa once here."

Bland. Not at all characteristic of my sister. "Diana. What the hell is going on? Normally you would rake me over the coals and never let me live something like this down." I heard her breathing, so I knew she hadn't hung up.

"D?"

"It sucks here. Bryan has not taken any time off work."

Oh, no. I gripped my cell with white knuckles. "Not a tragedy. Gives you time to think."

"NOT. It gives me time to work up a head of STEAM."

I moaned into the phone. "And then, when Bryan gets home..."
"We fight all evening. I am not joking."

Instant anxiety attack. Time spun backwards. *I stood in our driveway, Mom's arm around my shoulders and D's as Dad drove off. The sourness in my throat. The dread. As we watched his black Mercedes disappear around the corner, Mom's knees buckled. D and I managed to get her into the house, where she sank into a chair in the kitchen, laid her head down on the table, and cried for what seemed like a week.* A huge and happy corner of my life had been ripped off that day.

I tried to be wise. "Can't you calm down and make a real effort to resolve things? Come back here and get Alex, then start marriage counseling?" I paused, then decided to just go for broke. "You know, avoid divorce, so that your son won't be scarred for life for want of a traditional family? Like, you know, YOU AND ME?"

Diana began to sob at her end. Not a good sign. "Shit, Beck! Last night things got so bad that I threatened to divorce him. So he sneered at me and suggested we split for a while!" More sobbing, some nose blowing, and then a sort of wail.

My sister was dissolving completely in Chicago. I wasn't holding up so well in Framington, either. "D. Diana! Are you sure? Did you hear him right? Maybe he said you should, I don't know—spit? Sit? Sweat? Are you *sure* you heard him right?" I bit the inside of my cheek, and it started to bleed.

"Separate! He wants a trial *separation*! So yeah, here I come, just like Mom—single motherhood." Profuse wailing.

Cleansing breaths. I tasted the blood in my mouth. I nearly dropped my cell. "Well, this is good news and bad news. The good news is that even though you were the idiot to bring up divorce, he just used the word *separation*. So there is some wiggle room."

D spluttered at her end. "And the bad news?"

I stood up, the phone plastered to my ear, making my eardrum sweaty, I swear. I paced back and forth on Ella's rug, noting that there were little bare areas where generations of folks had worn through it, pacing. Walking back and forth with babies. Decorating Christmas trees. Worrying about dying. Maybe dancing, for all I knew. Good God, if the walls had ears...

"Beck! What is the bad news? Not that I need any!"

I snapped back into the present. "Isn't that obvious? We will be living nearly in one another's pockets! So not only will you have family troubles in Chicago, but most likely there will be trouble right here in River City, if you catch my drift. I am not exactly stress-free myself at the moment. And we are SO not soulmates."

Diana laughed, her voice, as I would say in a novel, *dripping with sarcasm*. "Isn't that just too bad for you. I am sorry that my disaster might make your life run a bit less smooth."

"Smoothly."

She hung up on me. I went into the bathroom, splashed water on my face, looked at my sorry, wet, grim face in the mirror, and felt remorse. I swabbed my face with an embroidered hand towel that I am sure nobody had ever used before, counted to ten, strode to the top of the stairs, sat down, and dialed my sister back.

"Okay, I am an asshole. When are you coming back?"

So my sister was going to have a *trial separation*. My God. This meant that I would stay at Ella's longer than I wanted to, but probably that was better for Ella anyway. Diana and Alex would become temporary residents of my place, and she even offered to pay rent. Diana was coming home in a week "or so." She had to stay in Chicago to "tie up some loose ends," which I took to mean quit her job, haggle with Bryan about what stuff in the apartment would be hers if they broke up permanently, buy a car, and pack up way too many suitcases full of stuff than would ever fit in my apartment. Ella was due to return in a few days, but Oakmoor was still not sure when. This would mean that before D came back, Bob, Ella, me, and scream-at-night Alex would be living under the same roof. My God. I would have to get Ella some earplugs, too.

That night, as I cleaned up the kitchen and Bob kept me company at the table doing math homework, I asked her if she was looking forward to having her gran return. Bent over the table with her lip tucked beneath her top teeth, Bob held up a hand. "Just a minute. I have to subtract." She erased something carefully, entered in another digit, then looked up at me with shining eyes. "Of course I am! We're a family!"

I dropped the sponge and it fell inside my shirt. By the time I wrested it out and blotted my chest, the moment had passed.

▷◁

Ella was coming home with a walker that she almost refused to use. Her hip was healing "not as well as I would like," according to Dr. Lauren. The physical therapist at Oakmoor was turning her over to the outpatient PT department at Framington General, where I hoped there would be just the right therapist for her. Ella needed a combination of drill sergeant and Mr. Rogers—someone to kick her in the ass and fluff her up at the same time. I wasn't optimistic.

Meanwhile, had I spent the few quiet mornings I had left working on my new novel, *Summer Child*, which made me very happy. I had already written the dedication: *To Bob, with thanks and Popsicles*. It's a book about a tired-out, dishrag of a woman, who spends her days locked up in her apartment in New York, writing poems that no one could possibly ever want to read. Her life, after losing her son in a car accident in which both son and husband died, has left her an empty shell. The book centers on her relationship with her ten-year-old niece, who is sent to spend the summer with her. The chapters seemed to pour out of me, fully formed.

On normal afternoons, I did a little housekeeping while the baby napped. But today, with Ella's return looming, I pledged to myself that the book needed a rest, and I needed to get the environment at Ella's whipped into shape. I had to do a deep cleaning, get the "guest room" on the first floor ready (it looked like Charles still lived there—I had to get rid of all sorts of model airplanes, books, games, and sporting equipment), and ask Mom what sorts of things I should get for Ella to eat. Pudding?

I vacuumed. Dusted. Put footstools and a few baskets of magazines in the basement—tripping hazards. Ugh. The kitchen wasn't too bad, until I got out the mop and started washing the floor. With the first swipe, the mop turned black. I realized that Ella's linoleum hid a multitude of sins. I added a capful of Clorox to the water. When I finished—it took me two buckets' worth before the water was clean—the floor didn't exactly *gleam*, but it looked the way it did when Ella was in residence: unpolluted.

The bathroom downstairs needed to be sanitized. I used Comet in the sink and shower, and squirted Tidy Bowl into the toilet. Swish. Looking good. I folded some clean towels onto the bar, spritzed some Glade into the air. Nice.

I put away the clutter in the living room. Not too bad. Bob's and "my" rooms were upstairs. I hiked up there to straighten up a bit, even though Ella wouldn't be going upstairs any time soon. It wouldn't be right to have Ella back, worrying about things upstairs going to wrack and ruin.

The bathroom. Okay. We had been keeping that pretty clean. I applied Comet liberally to everything.

Then I moved on to Ella's/my room, just for a quick once-over. I had to be quiet. Alex was napping.

Let me pause to describe what it is like to sleep in the bedroom of an eighty-four-year-old widow. The walls in the master bedroom were covered with faded, moss green wallpaper. I loved that wallpaper. It had a tiny repeating pattern of what once were probably red birds, now mellowed to a rusty orange. They sat on Pussy Willow branches. When I got into bed, I imagined them singing, all at once, my own avian lullaby. Ella's windows faced the street, and I pulled up the new blinds to look over at my apartment building. I wondered what I would be doing over there if I hadn't met Bob. Probably writing sexy drivel and being miserable.

Ella's bed had the softest, whitest chenille bedspread—the one Alex enjoyed before he dove right off. Alex's porta-crib stood in the corner. Alex snored deeply inside, his hands curled up like tiny seashells. Over his crib hung an antique sampler that said *ALL'S WELL THAT ENDS WELL*. Ella had an antique dresser, naturally. On top was a china tray with a Havilland "dresser group," as she called it: a delicate china set with a box for jewelry, a little vase, and something that looked to me like a saltshaker, for powder. All covered with scarlet roses. There was a floor lamp by Ella's bed that cast a soft glow on my laptop as I typed late at night. I looked around for dust balls. The glossy hardwood floor was covered with an old, nearly threadbare Persian carpet, a beautiful, geometric design of maroons and creams. Thank God it broke Alex's fall. Ella's rocker angled out of another corner of the room, where I back-and-forthed, comforting Alex, trying to imagine what I would be like when in my eighties. The room had the aroma of gardenias and BenGay. I absolutely loved it. I wiped off the dust on the dresser with my sleeve, lined up my flip-flops, running shoes, and bedroom slippers just under the bed, and shut the closet door on the mess of my dirty clothes on the floor. Done in there.

Bob's room took a little time. She liked to discard *her* dirty clothing randomly all over the floor. I stuffed the hamper with all of that. One spotty black banana peel on the dresser. Ugh. Other than that, things weren't too bad. Bob had started the Harry Potter series, and I put two of them back in her bookcase, pausing only briefly to read the first chapter of *The Chamber of Secrets* before catching myself and putting it back with the others. I straightened the antique quilt on Bob's bed. It was one out of Ella's hope chest in the attic. Yellow, orange, and blue log cabin pattern. A bit faded from many washings. Sitting on her pillow was the worn teddy bear that had passed down from Robert Bowers to his son Charles, and on to Bob. I picked him up by one grayish ear and gave him a little kiss, rubbed his nose, and put him back on the bed. "Take care of Bob, okay?" I whispered. "You know, when Ella and I aren't around?" Then I picked up the framed picture of Charles as a stoic young marine recruit. The same one that Ella had downstairs. The tightly drawn mouth, the macho stare, the piercing eyes. The same face that stared out of every single portrait of every single recruit the world over. Fear masked as toughness. I told him, "Look. Since you, Teddy, and I are having heart-to-hearts, let me just say this to you, Charles: Be safe. Come home. They need you to return. Hell, *I need you to come back here. I can't keep this up forever, you know.*"

When Alex woke, we trekked to the Kroger for provisions. We were both dazzled by the health food aisle. I wondered if I should get a "Healthy Senior" supplement, but I put that one back on the shelf. I got yogurt for the probiotics, applesauce—because all old ladies like that, right? Alex talked me into getting Jell-O, and I also chose things that I thought convalescents would love: Yup, some pudding. Chicken soup, oyster crackers, and, of course, Velveeta. On the way home, I sang a lusty version of "We Are Family" to Alex, who drooled with enthusiasm. I looked at him in the rear view. D had rigged a mirror system that allowed the driver to see the baby—so clever. "Alex, honey. That was meant to be TOTALLY ironic!" Alex ignored me and gurgled.

By the time we got home, everything was shipshape. My back hurt. Alex's almond eyes were closed. I trundled him up to his crib, set the monitor, and carted my weary bones downstairs. I dropped down on the sofa for just a sec, to rest my eyes.

Bob raced into the house at 3:40, calling "BECK! ARE YOU READY? LET'S GO FOR GRAN!" She stood in the hall, looking at me, crumpled up on the sofa. "Beck? Beck—WAKE UP!"

Staggering into the kitchen, I reached into the cupboard, got out the Bayer, and popped a couple of aspirin, washing them down with a glug of water. I carefully rinsed out the cut glass tumbler. Ella had nothing that wasn't just gorgeous, antique, and breakable. However, Bob drank out of the two Tupperware cups that Ella provided, early on. I preferred the antiques. Bob pounded into the kitchen after me.

"I need a very fast snack." She pulled open the refrigerator, leaning in to enjoy the cool. "Okay! I'll have this apple half." Crunching, she twirled on me. "Are you excited?"

I took the plastic wrap out of her hand and dropped it into the trash basket under the sink. "Bob. Calm down a bit. Remember, your gran is still far from her old self. She is depressed."

"But I bet just being back home will make her feel much better. Plus, having Alex here will make her feel better, right?"

I nodded. "But we have to be prepared, in case it isn't. We may have to really nag her about doing her exercises and walking. They told me that she is supposed to do at least four laps around the house in the morning, and four in the afternoon. We are supposed to get her walking up and down the block by next week. They say she isn't interested in doing that. Setting goals for herself. I have to admit, I am worried."

Bob finished the apple and set the core on the counter, frowning. "Does Dad know about this?"

"I'm not sure. I haven't spoken with him. He is saving all of his minutes for your gran. But when she comes home, you will be able to talk with him when he calls, and maybe the two of you will be able to come up with a plan to get your gran back on track. And I bet he will call YOU on your new cell, too, once your gran gets settled."

Bob's eyes lit up, her grin wrinkling the freckles on her nose. "I can't wait to talk to Dad!" She thumped her heart with her hand. "That is a great idea! I will start thinking up some things! Let's go get the baby!"

Alex woke up graciously. I changed his diaper *on the floor.* Bob chose a bright blue tee shirt with a sailboat on it and a pair of tiny yellow footed pants. He looked adorable. Bob smooched Alex's head. "Let's GO!"

As we approached my car, Bob, skipping happily, tripped over an uneven slab of pavement, hurtled forward and nearly fell down. I managed to hold onto the baby and grab Bob by the arm before her knees crashed into the concrete. She scrabbled to regain her balance, giggling loudly. "Oh, THANK GOODNESS. If I broke my leg, you would have to nurse BOTH OF US!"

Bob thought that was hilarious. I thought it was horrifying.

▷◁

We were greeted in the lobby of Oakmoor by the resident manager, April Lever, and the physical therapist, Mandy somebody—sounded like Ritzcracker, but I couldn't be sure. They sat us down for a chat. Inauspicious.

April, who looked bloated, but it might just have been her watermelon-bedecked scrubs, began. "Mrs. Bowers is not doing very well. She has lost five pounds since arriving at Oakmoor." Could it be the pablum and other pureed crap they called food here, I wondered? "She also seems disinterested in her therapy, socializing, or even watching television."

Mandy Ritzcracker, who had a kind smile, dazzlingly white teeth, and a perm right out of the fifties, tried a more subtle approach—she patted Bob's shoulders and cooed at Alex. "Ella is probably just unhappy being first in the hospital, then here—although we try for a homey atmosphere, I am sure Ella is very anxious to be home. I feel very hopeful that things will go better for her once she settles back in her own environment." She handed me a sheet, which contained the instructions for care—no baths or showers (Bob had that one covered) for at least two more weeks, no stairs for six weeks, no driving, etc. A second sheet had a list of directions for Ella's home rehab—the escalating laps around the house with the walker, practice getting in and out of a chair, how to help her into bed, etc. It looked challenging, due to what they were telling us about Ella's state of mind. I handed them over to Bob, who looked them over a little dispiritedly as well.

April stood, her watermelons billowing. "Shall we go and get your aunt?"

"You mean Bob's great-grandmother? Certainly." I couldn't get Ella out of that place fast enough.

When we got to her room, Ella sat stiffly in a chair, her walker in front of her. As soon as she saw Bob and the baby on my chest, she smiled anemically. "Hello, sweetie. Bobby, I am so glad to see you! Hello, little one." She glanced wanly in my direction. "I wish you didn't have to see me like this. I am so sorry for putting you through all of this."

Her voice was barely above a whisper. Jesus. This woman needed to be at home with us, pronto. We needed to eat steak, spinach, and lots and lots of ice cream. I made a mental note to stock up on high-calorie, nutrition-dense foods. The stuff I had purchased was just not going to cut it. Of course, first I would have to Google "nutrition-dense foods."

April had pushed the bedside call button, and a very buxom nurse's aide materialized. Her name, she informed us with a broad smile, was Honey. "Cause that's what all they patients calls me, anyway." I liked her immediately.

"Miz Bowers, let's get you outta here, right?" And with two capable arms, she hoisted Ella to her feet. I tried to memorize her technique. Put walker on the side. Plant legs about two feet apart, for good stability. Hands not quite in Ella's armpits, but nearly. Tell her to get ready, on the count of three. Count, and then HOIST. SMILE the whole time. As soon as Ella is upright, grab walker. Slide it in front of Ella while stepping away. Okay. This was a procedure that would become second nature, but right then it looked nearly impossible.

Ella stood, gripping the walker for dear life. Bob clapped. "Gran! You did it! Yay! I am so proud of you! And guess what? We have the house all ready for you, and Beck bought pudding!"

It seemed to be agony for Ella to walk. Despite her grimaces, Honey kept urging her on. "You can do it, Miz Bowers. Just one foot in front of the other. The more you practice, the easier! The feet need to keep movin'!"

We shuffled out to the lobby, and moved painfully out to my car, which I had left directly in front of the sliding glass doors under the Oakmoor portico. Honey looked at me and said, "She got to back into the car. Then twist her legs around. You help her with that. Getting out is easier. Twist them legs around and then help her out, just like the chair." Honey demonstrated. First, she opened the passenger door. "Ella, just walk up like you know how to get in." Ella minced to the open door. Honey slid the walker to the side, supporting Ella with an arm around her shoulders. "Now turn around, sweetie, and aim you's ass at the seat."

Ella cried out in pain as she jackknifed into the seat, but she made it. Honey lifted her legs and swung them into the car. A moan from Ella. Then Honey bent to fasten Ella's seatbelt. "See, sweetie? You can do this! Just keep up the practicin'! I'm gonna miss you!" She bent and kissed Ella's cheek. "You gotta have faith. You gotta get better for this little granchile here. Now scoot!" She deposited the walker in the trunk and slammed it shut. She opened her arms and enveloped me and Alex in a hug. I didn't want to let go. Then she bussed the top of Alex's head, pinched Bob's cheek and patted her wiry curls, and turned to go.

"Don't you come back here!" As she disappeared through the sliding doors, I wanted to run after her.

On the way home, I said a prayer of thanks for the fact that Ella's side entrance had no steps. We could get her in and out of the house through the kitchen. Bob provided the cheerful chatter from the backseat. Alex was thankfully silent. Ella kept her eyes closed the entire way home.

When we landed in the driveway, I girded my loins for the disembarking. Bob went ahead and held the side door open. I hoisted Alex out of the car seat and buckled him into the Baby Bjorn. Then I popped the trunk and wrestled the walker out and pushed it to the passenger side. Ella opened the door, and I swung it wide. Planted in front of the open passenger door, I said a little prayer to the gods, and took Ella's legs. "Now we have to pivot. Ready?"

Ella pursed her lips and dipped her head slightly. She put her left hand on the dash and her right on my shoulder and began to twist sideways as I pulled her legs. She groaned softly. First maneuver, completed. Her legs were outside the car. We both breathed heavily. Alex burped.

Bob cheered us on. "Come on, Gran! You can do it!" Bob managed to hold the door open and bounce simultaneously.

"Now for the lift." I braced my legs. "On the count of three, Ella. Ready? ONE, TWO, THREE!" I lifted from underneath her arms, Ella grunted with effort, nearly pierced my shoulder blades with her grip, but HOT DAMN, she stood!

My walker maneuver was not nearly as smooth as Honey's, but I managed to get myself out of the way and the walker in front of Ella. I thought the rest would be a piece of cake. Not that there was any inside—only pudding.

It took what seemed like an hour. It must have actually been about five minutes. Ella just couldn't establish any sort of pace with that walker. She had to take two steps and then rest. Sweat (I hoped it wasn't tears) dripped down her cheeks. She puffed. She cried out twice. But she got inside. Bob and I gave her a round of applause.

"I need to sit."

"Okay, Gran! We cleared out all the space in the living room! We pulled the comfy chair around so that you can sit and watch TV, and if you want to, you can read! Beck moved a lamp and a little table right beside your chair!"

"No. I need to sit NOW." Her face drained of color, Ella looked faint. She looked around for a chair. I pulled one out from the kitchen table and helped her lower herself into it.

Bob rushed to get her a glass of water, but Ella waved it away. "I am not thirsty. I just need you two to leave me alone for a minute!" She pushed the walker away roughly, and it toppled onto the linoleum. Ella's spindly shoulders shook, and she began to weep.

"Bob, let's give your gran a minute." We left Ella alone and went into the living room. I unbuckled Alex and set him on the floor with a few toys. Bob sat cross-legged on the floor and put trembly little hands on her forehead.

This little girl, who had worked so hard and hoped so high, was bewildered. She lifted her hands away from her eyes. "Why is Gran crying? Isn't she happy to be home? Doesn't she want to be with us?"

"Oh, kiddo. Your gran is in pain, first of all. And she is very demoralized. We have to give her time, and we also can't let her get *us* down. Remember what Dr. Lauren and all the folks at Oakmoor told us? That your gran is down in the dumps, but that this is understandable. We have to be the chipper ones. We can't let her think that we're as discouraged as she is. Even if we have to fake it. Understand?"

Although I am pretty sure that she didn't understand, Bob brightened. She drew herself to her feet and bestowed me with a high-five. Her flint blue eyes flashed with determination. "Gran! I bet you just need a snack!" And with that, she bounded back into the kitchen to load Ella up with pudding.

A surge of relief washed over me, but of course then I remembered that I was temporarily responsible for one baby with very loud colic, one small girl with a past chock-full of things I didn't even want to imagine, and one very frail—and at the moment very miserable—old lady. My soul, the one that floated around the room in times of severe stress, left my body once more. It looked down at me, cringing with apprehension on the chintz sofa. My soul got a migraine.

CHAPTER TWENTY-FIVE

We established a routine. Ella and I spent the mornings at logger-heads. Polite ones, but still a clash of wills. The first morning, after Bob left for school and Alex had his bottle, new diapers, and a clean adorable outfit, I plunked him into his stroller and began pressuring Ella to walk around the block with us—for "some air."

Ella reluctantly stood, gripped her walker, and followed me onto the porch. I told Ella to stay on the porch with her walker until I got the stroller down the steps and put on the brake. I turned to start up the stairs to help Ella descend, but she was halfway back into the house, her progress slowed by the fact that maneuvering herself and her walker through the open screen door was problematic. I sprinted up the stairs, gently took her by her bony but determined shoulders, extracted her and the walker from the doorframe, turned her around, and pushed her gently to the top of the steps. This was a bold move on my part. They told Ella no stairs. But I felt that she had to learn how to go up and down the three wide steps of her front porch, or she might refuse to ever go outside. It was a gamble.

It took me one second to realize that Ella, a walker, and steps were a no-go. I wasn't ready to give up. "Wait just a sec." Ella gazed witheringly at me and sighed. "Just stand here for one minute!" I sprinted down and pulled Alex out of the stroller, rushed inside to get the Baby Bjorn off the stairs where I had dropped it. I by this time was a Bjorn expert. I threw it on, fastened in the baby, who thought this was a fun game, and shot back onto the porch.

"Can't we just sit here and enjoy the morning?" Ella clicked towards a chair.

"NO. You need to walk. They said you have to do this." I took Ella's hands off the walker and put them on the back of the wicker chair. "Don't sit. Just wait here."

With the walker ready at the bottom of the steps, I took Ella by the elbow and we proceeded. "I am going to go down two steps. Hold onto both of my shoulders and step down." That took about a minute for Ella to accomplish. "Okay, now down the next." After what seemed like a year, Ella was on her front walk.

I could tell that this had exhausted her, but I was determined. "Let's walk a half block, then turn back. I think we will go in the side door; it will be easier."

She did it. She grimaced the whole way, but she did it. When we finally made it back into the kitchen, she sank into a chair, pushed her walker aside, and proclaimed, "That was just horrible." I gave her some Kool-Aid, for energy renewal. Ella tossed it back like a barfly. The rehab had begun.

▷◁

I never thought I would say this, but having my newly separated sister back in town and ensconced across the street was not that bad. Before I knew it, a month had flown by. There was a tiny hitch: one month of absolutely no progress on the marriage front.

Diana and Alex liked the park. There was a flock of sparrows there that Diana threw crumbs to. Alex absolutely chortled at that. We sat there one afternoon about five weeks after D's arrival. The sparrows cheeped greedily, and we sat there, soaking in the sun.

"I like being single. No compromises or negotiations."

I felt as if an anvil had just hit me. "Diana. You can't be serious." I felt like slapping her. That old, familiar feeling.

"Bryan is not the easiest man to live with. He wants everything to be so neat and tidy, with no loose ends. You certainly know this, as you lived with him, for God's sake." She narrowed her eyes at me in that snotty way she has.

"Jesus, D. You sound so damn selfish. Have you talked about this with Mom? Shot this arrow through *her* heart?"

Diana gently pushed Alex back and forth in his stroller. A but-
terfly fluttered toward his face, and she swished it away. "Mom and
I have had conversations. She sort of knows what's going on. Sort
of."

I looked at my sister, sitting on the bench, her expertly
bleached hair wafting around her heart-shaped face, her lips full
and pink, but the creases on either side etched sharply into frown
lines. Beautiful but aggressively forceful features. Diana, the ruler
of the universe.

Diana tucked a strand of hair behind her ear, revealing a one-
carat diamond stud. "Look. I don't know what's going to happen.
I'm leaving the door open for discussion. But right now, I am happy
being here with Alex."

I thought backwards to our years after Mom and Dad divorced.
I spent so many days feeling as if my heart had been gouged by
knives. Walking wounded. My sister seemed to reinforce herself
with thick skin and a heavy-duty *attitude*. The fact that we both
ended up with the same man is the irony of ironies.

"Promise me you will try to make things work." I grabbed D by
the arm and pinched.

"You are hurting me!" She peeled my fingers away. "Beck, I
can't help it that you were so totally devastated by Mom and Dad's
divorce that you can't deal with life. I can deal with it. I *am* dealing with it. You need to stop hoping that somehow I will end up
living the happily ever after that you and Mom didn't have. I can't
repair all the things that happened to our family back then by living the *right way*." She rubbed the red mark on her arm where I had
grabbed her.

Alex gabbled at the sparrows that pecked at the crumbs
around the stroller. Diana cooed, "Birdies, birdies! Look at all
the birdies who love Alex!" The smile she beamed at her son was
Madonna-like.

We stood up, the birds flew off, and we started for home. There
wasn't much conversation as we wheeled the baby down the street.
A few horns honked, and a soft breeze dried the cold sweat that
had broken out on the back of my neck. We turned a corner, and

Diana reached out and took me by the hand. Startled, I squeezed her fingers. She rubbed my palm with her thumb. Something inside me eased a bit. We walked the rest of the way home that way.

I had no idea that D could actually be charming to other people, but Ella seemed thrilled to see D and Alexander whenever they stopped in, which was at least every other day for an hour or so, plus her nighttime stints. I could have time to myself for errands, writing, or just resting, for God's sake. Being a caregiver was using me up.

Diana made good, strong tea, and while she puttered around in Ella's kitchen, Alex entertained Ella with his gurgles. Luckily, he wasn't mobile, so D could just plunk him on the floor and leave the two of them alone. That was the only time that Ella perked up. Even Bob wasn't able to jounce Ella out of the dumps, it seemed.

Dr. Lauren wasn't giving up on Ella, though. After two weeks of unremarkable progress with the outpatient therapy, and after Ella refused to do her at-home exercise walking "for good, I cannot stand it," Lauren prescribed an anti-depressant. "This will take about a month or longer to kick in fully," she said. OMG. "So it's not a quick fix. You just have to steel yourself to her attitude and just push her, push her hard. Believe me, this is the only thing that you can do. You just can't let her convince you that she can't improve. She can."

Bob didn't waver. She drew pictures, inveigled Ella to play cards. She sang songs, acted out playlets, and when all else failed, she made slice-and-bake cookies, all by herself. Gail came over as often as she could, bringing treats and town gossip. Theo, of course, was out of the picture for me, but Gail kept in touch with him, and he sent his regards to Ella, along with a very nice card that I am sure Theo picked out carefully. Funny thing. Although the envelope said *To Ella* in Theo's handwriting, both Theo and Gail signed the card.

Charles' phone calls became more frequent. He must have gotten more minutes, somehow, because he called Bob once a week, too. Bob loved those calls, and Ella perked up whenever she heard her grandson's voice. So we chugged along, but I was beginning to lose *my* positive attitude.

One evening, when Ella and Bob were watching *America's Got Talent* (Bob was watching; Ella was staring), I left them to go over to Diana's. Wait. To MY apartment. Diana had brought Mom over to have a gab session. Diana picked up some New York style cheesecake from the bakery, and she knew that there was always great coffee to be made, thanks to my Starbucks perks. Well, former Starbucks perks. I had stocked up before I left my job.

Alex was getting some more caramel-colored hair. He was more adorable by the minute. Other than the scream-sessions at night, he was happy-go-lucky. It was entertaining just to watch him wriggle. With cheesecake, it was an event.

Mom looked great. She wore a flowing, slate gray chiffony tunic top with tiny white flowers. D looked spectacular in black leggings and a tight fuchsia tank top. She gurgled back at Alex, who turned on a lopsided grin that melted all three of us.

Diana, sipping her latte, broke the spell, pronto. "Well, now that all seems to be on an even keel, I think I need to start thinking about getting my own apartment. I'm going to call Gail."

Mom and I spit coffee simultaneously. Then we both said "WHAT?" also at the same time. D squinched her eyes at us, and pulled a stray eyelash off her cheek. "If I am going to have to end up a single mom, I need to be *here*. I need support."

The look that crossed our mother's face was an amazing combination of joy and consternation. She smiled, then covered her mouth with one graceful hand while drawing her eyebrows together as if someone had just pinched her. "Oh, honey. It's *that* bad?"

I, on the other hand, didn't know how to sort out the maelstrom of emotions rocketing through me, despite the fact that I had ample warning from D. Nausea at the thought of another divorce to get through with my sister. Anxiety at the prospect of having to "support" Diana while somehow propping up Ella and Bob. Dread at the idea that little Alex would have to be "that kid with no dad" at school functions, Little League, and Boy Scouts. And finally, joy at the realization that I would have Alex handy—maybe forever.

Mom set her cheesecake down on the coffee table and stood up. She leaned over D and hugged her. D wrapped her arms around

Mom and whispered, "I am so sorry I couldn't make marriage work, either. I guess I screwed up."

I yelped, "Not just you! I fucked up my life, too! My God, I was the first one to leave Bryan!"

With that, Mom pulled herself upright to face us both, clenching her fists and stomping a foot. "Diana and Rebecca. You are MY girls. I am so proud of you. Neither one of you screwed up, or anything near that! My guess is that Bryan is a difficult man. He has his good points, of course. I am sure he adores his son, what little time he has had with him." Mom's hazel eyes softened, and she dabbed away a tear before it could run down her cheek. She tossed her head. "Your father was also a difficult man. He was charming. He loved me as well as he could, and he adored you both. He couldn't help the fact that other women found him so magnetic."

D put out her hand to stop Mom. "Don't. It's okay."

Right at that moment, it was like my soul had just *had* it. Instead of leaving my body like a coward, to float around the room, it erupted. I heard myself shout, "NOPE. DON'T STOP. WE HAVE TO FACE THE FACT THAT ALL THREE OF US FUCKED UP."

Mom, shocked, sat right back down next to D, and they clutched each other.

I took a breath. "Mom. As wonderful and beautiful as you are, there must have been something simmering under the surface. Dad might not have left if you were both happy in the marriage. And we all three know that I walked away from Bryan because I felt hemmed in; it was way too soon for me to be in that sort of committed relationship Oh, hell; I was totally selfish. And for God's sake, D. You can be a royal bitch."

With that, I put my head down in my lap and covered it with my arms, waiting for the explosion. Silence. Nothing, just jagged breathing from me.

I heard a fork clinking against a plate. I looked up to see my mother pick up her dessert, take a generous bite of the cheesecake, and for the first time in her life, probably, speak with her mouth full. "D, your sishta maksh a lot of sensh."

I looked at my sister. Diana had stopped in the midst of taking a sip of her coffee to stare at Mom, dumbfounded. Slowly, she lowered her coffee and set it back on the table. She raked her hot pink nails through her hair, scraping it away from her forehead. She turned her hands up in a gesture of helplessness. "They say the truth hurts. Damn right." D framed her face with her palms and smiled. "And I am the best looking royal bitch you two will ever meet!" With that, she threw her head back and cracked up.

Mom and I joined in, and the three of us laughed so loud that we alarmed Alex.

CHAPTER TWENTY-SIX

Ella sat on the wicker chair on her porch. The early fall breezes ruffled the fine strands of her hair, sending wisps into her eyes, which she batted away like flies. We had spent a somewhat successful morning doing stretches; and although she still seemed to dislike walking, either I was getting more persuasive, or she was just worn down by all my pushing and prodding. Perhaps the anti-depressants were kicking in sooner than expected. Just now, we had made it around the block once. Of course, by this time, Ella should have been cruising around town wielding her walker like a pro, but it was what it was.

Resting on the porch afterwards, I told her about Diana's apartment hunt, and that she had found a couple of cute places within walking distance. I exclaimed how great it would be to have Alex so nearby, and made a smart remark about how maybe it wasn't so great to have D so close, though. Ella didn't seem to hear that. She shifted around restlessly in her chair.

"Ella, is something bothering you? Does your hip ache?"

Ella dug around in the pocket of her housedress and brought out an envelope. "Rebecca, I don't know what to do about this."

She held it out to me. It was postmarked Des Moines, Iowa, and it was addressed to Bob. "A letter from her Iowa grandparents?"

Ella shook the letter at me, so I took it.

"Rebecca, it isn't from her grandparents. It is from Rowena. I know that handwriting."

I looked down at the rectangle in my hands. Pale, sickly green stationery—probably from the Dollar Store or the like. Dirty around the edges, as if it had been in Rowena's possession for a long time. It was addressed in barely legible red ink to *Roberta Bowers, c/o Ella Bowers*, etc. No return address. I smoothed out some of the wrinkles in the envelope. I turned it over. The flap was sealed with a piece of Scotch Tape, what looked like a black dog hair (or maybe Rowena's) stuck underneath it, along with several dirt particles. I wondered how long ago it had been written.

"I don't want to give this to Bobby."

Ella looked at me. Despite the wispy hair, the cataracts clouding her gray eyes, and the age spots on her cheeks, I could see the fierce protectiveness behind it all. She must have been a real warrior back in the day.

"But, Ella, Rowena—no matter how damaged—is Bob's mother. And this is addressed to Bob, so I don't see how you can keep it from her." I set the envelope on Ella's lap.

"What if it has something in it that will devastate Bobby?" She stared at the letter as if it were contaminated.

"I know what you mean. But I just don't see how you can hide something like this from her." Ella looked so stricken, I wondered if maybe we *should* destroy the damn thing. "Do you think it would be easier if you gave it to her when I'm here? So we both can support her if it's something upsetting?"

Ella folded the envelope in half and slid it back into her pocket and pointed to the end of the block. "She is heading home from school right now. Oh, Rebecca, what should I do?"

Bob waved at us gaily and began skipping towards us, her lunchbox banging against her knees. She looked carefree. I felt a pang. "Ella, it is your decision, but the letter is for Bob. Do you want me to stay here or to go?" I wanted to bolt.

"Don't you go. No."

So I stayed put, clapped my hands as Bob hopped up the front steps, and I asked, "Hey, kiddo, how was school? Did you flunk anything today?"

Bob dropped her lunchbox on the concrete and flopped down in the chair next to me, waving her hands in front of her face to cool off. "Of course not! Gran, do we have any Popsicles?"

Ella smiled. "Bobby, you know Rebecca keeps us stocked up. Why don't you bring us all one? We need something cool."

Bob jumped up and went into the house, letting the screen door bang behind her. A small reprieve. I looked at Ella. "You might as well get it over with. You don't need to have one more thing to worry about right now. You need to trust Bob's ability to handle her own life. Bob is a very strong kid. You need to focus on *your* recovery, Ella. You owe that to Charles and to Bob."

Ella didn't respond. She seemed to be lost in her own head. I leaned back against the wicker headrest and waited.

Bob opened the screen with her rear end. "Here's an orange half for you." I took it. The wooden stick was tacky.

"Gran, you get the last cherry one. Just a half, the way you like it."

Bob broke the red Popsicle in two. Ella took the proffered Popsicle half in both her hands and stared down at it. Bob slurped vigorously at the other half, hopping on one foot while balancing with her free hand on the back of Ella's chair.

Ella set the treat on the table beside her, untouched. She reached into her pocket. "Bobby, honey. How fast can you finish your Popsicle? I have something for you."

Bob smiled and took an icy bite. "I can eat this in about ten seconds." She grimaced as the Popsicle melted against her teeth. "I might get a headache, though!"

I licked my half without really tasting it. We sat awkwardly, Ella and I, as Ella's Popsicle melted on the table and I tried to finish mine without choking on it.

Bob took one final bite and set the stick on the table. She turned to us. "Okay, guys!"

Ella smiled half-heartedly as she pulled the letter from her pocket and handed it to Bob. "Honey. It's a letter from your mother."

Bob backed up, nearly tripping over her lunchbox in the process. She threw out her hands as if warding off blows. "I DON'T WANT IT! RIP IT UP! I DON'T WANT IT, GRAN!"

I watched Bob's expression go from anger to hurt to terror, all in a nanosecond. I tried to grab her arm, but she flung herself away from me and turned to run into the house. As she swung the screen door open and hurtled inside, she began to cry. Her sneakers scudded against the stairs as she ran up to her room. The door didn't slam, however. We both waited for that, but it didn't happen.

I was surprised at Bob's explosive reaction. I turned back to look at Ella, who sat, still holding out the letter as if she expected Bob to magically reappear and take it. "Ella, is Rowena some sort of monster?"

Ella dropped her hands and the letter into her lap. "No. Not a monster. Rowena is just a very sick, weak person. Angry. And she shouldn't have ever had a baby in the first place. Rowena wasn't cut out to be a mother. She was too young, too troubled. Bob was just a victim of all of that."

"Do you want me to go up there and take it to her? Get it over with?"

Ella pushed the letter off her lap onto the concrete. "Yes. We have to know what we are dealing with."

I picked up the soiled rectangle and leaned down to squeeze Ella's bony fingers. "Let's hope for the best, here."

I walked as slowly as I could up the stairs. I knocked on Bob's door.

"It's okay. Come in, Beck."

She sat on her bed, legs crossed, her father's teddy bear in her arms, her face flushed. I sat on the bed and held out the letter. "Shall I stay while you look at it?"

Bob buried her face in Teddy's. Her voice was muffled. "No. I need to be by myself."

I left her with her father's bear and her mother's envelope. Before I shut the door, I turned and whispered, "Bobby, we love you, your gran and I."

Dinner that night was very quiet. The subject of the letter didn't come up, but the letter might as well have been taped on Bob's forehead. Ella tried to talk about what we should watch on TV later. I asked Bob if she had any homework. We all poked at our spaghetti. Bob answered in monosyllables.

After I cleared up and loaded the dishwasher, I joined the two of them in the living room. Ella stared at the television. Bob lay on her stomach on the floor, her forehead on the carpet.

When the doorbell rang, Bob sprang to her feet and raced upstairs, this time slamming her door behind her.

Gail stood on the porch, a bouquet of bright orange chrysanthemums in her hand. As soon as she saw my face, she said, "Oh, no. Some sort of shit just came down, am I right?"

"Come on in. You and I need beer. Ella needs sherry. We have to make a plan."

By the end of that evening, Gail and I had a buzz on, Ella had finished two glasses of sherry and seemed a bit more relaxed, and the three of us decided to leave Bob alone for a while. Gail convinced us that to try to force Bob to talk about the letter, or even to tell us what was in it, would be an invasion of her privacy at the moment.

My stomach excreted what felt like a gallon of acid. "I hate to think of her up there all alone, coming to grips with whatever poison might be in that letter."

Gail shrugged. "She's pretty tough. And she knows she can depend on you two. And me and Diana, even. I am not saying to pretend there's nothing going on. But just give Bob a bit of time to process. She'll ask for help when she needs it. And if she doesn't, then you can step in. Give her a day or so."

Ella agreed with Gail. "I will tell Charles about this when he calls. He can help her, too. And we don't even know what's in the letter."

After Gail left and I got Ella settled, I went upstairs to check on Bob. Her door was cracked. I peeped in. Bob lay across her bed, still clothed. The quilt was tangled around her as if there had been a tornado. Bob lay in the center, Teddy clutched in her arms, her knees pulled up into her chest. Her eyes were screwed shut, lines etched into her forehead. There was an aura of such vast sadness surrounding her that I wanted to snatch her up and tell her that nothing in the world would threaten her ever again. But I didn't have that power. So I tiptoed over to her and stroked her forehead lightly until the lines in it smoothed. Then I kissed my finger and touched it to Bob's cheek.

I couldn't get to sleep that night. I stood at the window, looking across at the light in my bedroom across the street, where Alex and D were most likely screaming and pacing. I wished like hell I was over there.

Two days passed. I was tense. Ella was distracted and taking more Tylenol than usual. Today, Bob was supposed to be playing after school at Hallie's, but as I stood in front of the open refrigerator, wondering if I should try to make oven-baked chicken for dinner, Bob wandered in.

"Hi, kid! Weren't you supposed to be playing with Hallie this afternoon?"

Bob dropped into a chair. "Too tired." She did look pale, and there were purple smudges under her eyes.

"How about a Popsicle?" Bob shook her head. "I just want some water."

I loaded her cup with lots of ice, and filled it up from the tap. She took it from me and drained it. Instead of setting it upright on the table, she tipped the glass on its side and rolled it across the tabletop, ice cubes clattering out.

"Honey, maybe you should go up and lie down for a while. D and Alex are coming over later, and you could rest until then." I scooped up the loose ice cubes in a tea towel and dumped them in the sink.

"Beck, I need you to come up with me. I want you to see the letter."

I gulped. "Are you sure?"

Bob held out her hand. As we climbed the stairs, I stroked her cold little fingers and tried to stop my heart from rupturing.

By this time, Rowena's letter was gray with soil, fraught with wrinkles, and nearly torn in half. The envelope looked as if it had gone through the wash cycle. Bob held it out to me with two fingers, as if it were poisonous, despite the fact that it looked as if she had read it many times over.

"Are you sure you want me to read this, Bob? It's private."

Bob sat on the bedroom floor, cross-legged, Teddy in her lap. I took the letter and sat on the edge of Bob's bed.

Bob looked up at me with sad eyes. "I want you to."

I opened the envelope. Inside the letter was a photo. I looked at that first. In it was a young girl standing in front of a brick wall.

She looked to be in her late teens, I figured—mostly because of the short, short denim cutoffs, the yellow tank top, and the large hoop earrings. Her face, however, reminded me of the haunting shots of sharecroppers in history books. It was sucked in, gaunt. Her smile was flat, no teeth showing. Her hair was dark and thin, uneven bangs hanging over expressionless eyes. Despite all that, there was a blunt beauty about her. A purity in her stark stare at the photographer. She was holding a fat, bald baby awkwardly, as if someone had just thrust it into her arms.

"Is this your mom?" I knew the answer.

"Yes. When she was young. I don't really remember her looking that way. She is a lot older now. But I remember she has a tattoo of a heart on her back. She was always skinny. That's me in the picture."

My breath was ragged. I put the photo face down on the table beside me and unfolded Rowena's letter.

Dear Roberta,

I want you to know that I am sorry for hurting you. I never wanted to hurt you. You are a good girl. I should have told you that. I am the one who failed.

I am sending you the only picture I have any more of the two of us. I thought you might want to look at it someday and remember that you had a mother who loved you. I will always love you, even though I don't deserve to have you love me back.

I am very sorry. I guess I said that. My hope is that you will know I tried.

Your mother, Rowena

I had no words. I handed everything back to Bob. She stared at the photo. "I don't want to have this." She dropped them onto the floor.

I wondered why things of such magnitude seemed to happen with such crappy timing. How was this little girl going to deal with an absent father, her convalescing and frail gran, and her ultra-lost mother right this minute, and then mosey on to school and play at recess? What on earth could I do to help her?

I mustered up all of the fragments of good sense that were swirling around in the shambles of my own head. I sorted through my own thoughts about children, motherhood, and mistakes. I put my palm on Bob's hot, crinkled head and made an attempt at consolation.

"Bob, I think you will want to keep this. You don't have to look at the picture or read the letter for a long time if you don't want to. You can give the envelope to your gran to put away somewhere safe for you. Then when you are ready—maybe not even until you are a grown-up yourself—you can look at your mom and read her letter again."

Bob shoved the letter and photo away with her sneaker. "No. She is bad. She is an addict."

I nodded. "I know. You have good reasons to feel horrible about that. But your mom is hurting because she knows it. And she wrote this to tell you that she knows it. She isn't asking you for anything right now. She just wants to tell you how sorry she is. Can you at least see that from the letter?"

The words came out in a torrent. "I get it that she's sorry. But let her be sorry. I want a mom! And I won't *ever* have one. Everybody I know has a mom! You know what the thing is about *my* mother? She wanted drugs more than a kid. She has that stupid tattoo of a heart on her back. But it didn't mean she loved *me*. It was for the drugs. She loves those more than anything!"

There were no tears. Bob's eyes were hot, red, and dry.

I pulled her up and wrapped my arms around her. "Bob, believe me, your mom loves you. You don't have to believe that she is good, or smart. You are probably right if you think she is selfish, or weak, or sick. But all you need to hang on to is that she loves you and she always has."

Bob's question was muffled. "Do I have to forgive her?"

I hugged this child very hard. "I hope that you can. Do you know what forgiveness is? It is nothing more than just *understanding*. Maybe you can just try to understand your mom. Understand that she is a broken person. But despite that, she loves you. That's all."

Bob pulled away from me. She took a breath, pulled her shirt into place, and leaned down to grab Teddy. She rubbed her eyes hard with her free hand. "I don't have to love her back, right?"

"No. I don't think that anybody would expect you to love her back. Not right now."

Bob lifted her head. "All right. But I don't want the letter." She kicked at it again with her foot.

"Bob, I will give it to your gran, and she'll keep it for you. Okay?"

"Okay. I have to go now. I'm not that tired. Hallie will be waiting for me." Bob straightened her back—thrust her chest out like a prizefighter. She kissed Teddy twice and set him on her bureau. And with a final poke at the letter with her sneaker, she was gone.

I carefully put the photo inside the note, slid them into the envelope, and walked like a zombie down the hall. I pulled open the bottom drawer of Ella's bureau, and tucked the letter under some of Ella's sweaters.

Then I sank onto the bed and listened to my heart pound.

CHAPTER TWENTY-SEVEN

I loved D's new place. It was one-half of a Tudor double. She had hardwood floors, two small but charming bedrooms, one with an actual window seat, a darling eat-in kitchen with scalloped open shelving and blue-and-white checked linoleum, a bathroom with a claw-foot tub perfect for bathing Alex, and a working fireplace. It was absolutely the last place on earth I would picture my sleek and modern sister living. But it was immediately available, the landlord probably had a crush on D, and the rent was reasonable (see landlord, above).

Diana was packing things up at my place before Two Men and a Truck showed up. It is amazing how much paraphernalia is involved with babies. Some of it would have to be left behind, because Mom and I insisted on keeping certain things for Alex. I talked D into letting me keep the Bumbo chair, because Alex was still too little for it, and I would need a place to stow him when he came over to visit in the future. A Bumbo chair, if you don't know, is the absolutely funniest pot-like seat made out of some sort of gel material. When you plop a baby in it, he sits there like a tiny Buddha, gravely surveying all the activity around him. Mom convinced Diana to let her buy Alex a crib for the new place so that she could keep the porta-crib. I had already decided that whenever the baby slept with me anywhere at all, it would be on the *floor.*

We were in the chaos that was the bedroom, now looking more like the aftermath of an infantile explosion than ever. There was a baby monitor on the bureau. A bag of nipple shields on the bed. The Diaper Genie, assorted rattles and soft blocks, baby bottles, and educational, age-appropriate toys strewn all over the place. As

D stuffed little outfits, tiny socks, and burp cloths into a box, she asked me when I was moving back here.

"I don't know. Ella still has a hard time getting around, and she still has to go to physical therapy once a week. I don't see how I can leave and come back here. But I am so sick of not being in my own place."

D bent down to turn Alex from his back onto his stomach. "Pretty soon, he's going to be crawling all over the place, and I won't be able to turn my back on him for one second." She pretended to smack him on the head. "Beck, have you considered hiring a caregiver? They have agencies for just this kind of thing. And you can interview the candidates. I am sure that Ella can pay for this. You told me she's financially secure."

I opened a drawer and handed D three pairs of her leggings (a size way too small for me; dang, I would have liked to keep them) and a couple of her filmy tops. "Ella and Bob would hate that."

"I know. But they will have to adjust. And you said that Bob is really coming into her own over there. She knows how to do laundry, she can certainly do basic cleaning, and the caregiver would do the rest. You could still go over there for dinner and things. Hell, I'm sure you would be over there a lot, seeing as how you are so attached to them. It would work. You have to get on with your own life."

It made sense. I missed my job at Starbucks. I missed the socialization, the chatter, and frankly, the muffins. I had sent *Bad Boys on the Beach* to my agent, and told her it might be the last one for a while. I felt sure that it would go under contract. I was making a decent income from royalties—nothing to shout about, but my rent was small, my needs few, and I was very excited about devoting my full attention to *Summer Child*. Of course, I had never even discussed literary fiction with my agent, but she was a go-getter, and so I figured that if I managed to write a good novel, she could sell it to somebody.

"How would I even broach the subject of a caregiver to them?"

Diana laughed ruefully. "Of course, you are asking the queen of selfishness this question. If it were me, I would just hire somebody and march over there and tell them that the party was over." She sat down on the bed, a burp cloth in her hand. "I suppose that you should discuss it with them. Appeal to Ella's sense of fair play. Tell her that she really has to step up to the plate and recognize that she needs help on a permanent basis. Or at least until her son comes back—when is it, in the winter?"

I nodded bleakly. "He's over there in the midst of that never-ending shitstorm. They won't even tell anybody over here where he is. And since things keep escalating, who knows when he'll be back. But yeah. Supposedly he will come back in February, something like that. I never talk to him. He talks to both of them on the phone, and I get an email from him if he has some kind of question about how things are going. He does seem like a very nice man. But he can't do anything for them. He's too busy staying alive."

Diana got up and resumed gathering up the accouterments of motherhood. "Make a call to an agency. Stat. Get someone started over there ASAP."

The handwriting was on the wall; I knew that.

▷◁

"Gran! Have you ever heard of a FLUFFERNUTTER?" Bob had a piece of bread in one hand and a table knife in the other.

Ella took a sip of tea and set her cup on the saucer. I wanted a set of dishes like the ones Ella used every day. Havilland china from the 30s, pale cream with a border of violets around the edge. "I have, but I can't remember. Is it peanut butter and honey?"

Bob brandished her knife like a baton, conducting the luncheon operations like a maestro. "No! But that sounds pretty good. It's peanut butter and *marshmallow fluff*. Diana learned how to make them in Girl Scouts. Her Mom was the scout mistress, and they made these to take on a hike one time. Don't they sound totally *delish*?"

"Oh, Bobby, the thought of them makes my teeth ache! So, so sweet!"

I took the peanut butter sandwich that Bob had made. She had been very generous with the grape jelly. "I know, Ella. They were. But D and I loved them, especially with a big glass of very cold milk. I think it was a Midwestern delicacy. But I promised to get some fluff so Bob could try one."

Bob beamed as she buttered toast for Ella. She had pulled the orange marmalade out of the cupboard and set it on the table next to her gran's cup. Peanut butter was a bit overwhelming for Ella. "I also want to try a fried peanut butter and banana sandwich. Beck says that Elvis loved them."

Ella chuckled. "At this rate, Bobby, you will need to go to the dentist and maybe start going to Weight Watchers!" We all three burst out laughing; Ella could be a real card.

Between bites of my sandwich, I decided to go for broke. "Diana is moving into her own apartment, you know. Ella nodded. "I hear it is very cozy."

I dove in. "But you know, once Diana has left, I really need to go back to my own home."

Ella's powdery face crumpled. Then she seemed to catch herself. She straightened up in her chair and clapped her hands. "Of course you have to go back home! Bob and I will be all right. We will."

Bob stopped chewing her sandwich. Her mouth dropped open, revealing a mash up of peanutty grape. She tried to say something, but it came out garbled. "Budickifwecnadatnigh . . ."

I held out my hand to stop both of them. "Ella, you and Bob can't be alone. It isn't safe, it's too much for Bob, and if anything happened, the two of you would be helpless. I called Home Helpers today, and they are sending over some women that we can interview who will be able to live here temporarily, to help. Just the way I have been. They are trained. And we can choose the one we want."

Ella rubbed the surface of the tabletop with shaky hands. "A nurse's aid? I have heard horror stories about those people."

Bob nearly choked. I slapped her on the back, and then hugged her. "No. It won't be like that. First of all, these are NOT the kind of people you see on *60 Minutes* exposés. And Ella, I will be coming over *all the time* to check on you." I pointed to Bob's horrified face. "And do you think BOB would let anything sinister happen around here? She will be your bodyguard!"

Bob managed to swallow her peanut butter, and she took a sip of milk to wash it down properly. Then her face lit up. "Gran! Right! I will make sure nothing terrible happens! And we can teach her how to make fluffernutters!"

Leave it to an eight-year-old to put things into perspective. I turned to Ella. "I consulted Mr. Roseburg. He says that their prices are high, but that is understandable. You can afford this, don't worry."

A look of resignation. "Of course. You are so good to us, Rebecca. I am sure Bobby and I will be just fine." A wavery smile. "Just fine. So go ahead and send them over. Bobby and I will choose a good one, won't we, honey?"

Bob nodded trustingly. "And Beck. Tell them she has to like cooking and playing cards. Gran can teach her how to play pinochle. I just don't get that game."

Why did I not feel relieved?

▷◁

It only took one day. The second woman that we interviewed seemed to be the caregiver for us. We chose a plump, capable-looking woman named Janey. Janey was forty-seven, divorced, and her son Chip was in high school, had an after school job, and drove his own truck. "He's a good boy, just fine on his own. He has never touched drugs. He don't even like beer very much. So I kin be here; ain't no worries."

Janey started that Wednesday, the week before D's move was final. I felt that a few days of trial would be enough time to ascertain whether or not Janey was really the solution, but the way Bob took to her, there didn't seem to be any doubt.

Janey was a miracle, really. Her hair was the color of pencil lead. She had freckles dappled all over her face and arms, and although her teeth were stained from years of smoking ("I quit cold turkey," she informed us), she had a dazzling smile. She wore camo pants and white tee shirts, Nike sneakers, and three earrings in her left ear. Bob was enchanted. The first day she was in residence, Janey taught Bob how to make popcorn balls with blue and red food coloring. She could lift Ella as easily as a feather, if need be. Ella was quick to assure her that need would NEVER be.

Janey could drive, cook, she loved to vacuum, and she was a whiz with tools. One day, when Bob came home from school, there was her scooter on the front porch—the back wheel as straight as a die, the chrome polished bright. The dents were gone. Bob hugged Janey and kissed her on both cheeks before grabbing the scooter and shooting down the sidewalk shouting, "WAIT TILL HALLIE SEES THIS; SHE WON'T BELIEVE IT!" Yes, Janey Donohue was a find.

▷◁

Mom insisted on the three of us having a "happy moving day" luncheon. She was too busy to cook, and so she ordered a carryout from Beth's Bistro, which D picked up on the way over to get Mom. I was in charge of watching over my sleeping nephew. I found it very difficult to keep my hands off him as he twitched in his sleep. It was even harder to stop myself from kissing him until he woke up, but I thought better of it.

They arrived carrying a bag filled with turkey sandwiches on flaky croissants, spicy pickle chips, seltzers, and cherry pie. Melt-in-your-mouth, crust-made-with-lard, you-don't-want-to-know-how-many-calories-in-one-slice cherry pie.

I finished my croissant. D had just picked at hers. Mom had successfully shredded hers into bits. What a waste. I reached for the pie. "Now come ON. This stuff is manna from heaven. I don't care how fattening it is, we have to consume this entire half-pie this afternoon. It is soul satisfying. Almost better than sex."

I divided it into three pieces. D and Mom eyed it with suspicion, despite the fact that neither of them had thighs larger than a teenager's (I won't discuss the size of my thighs at that moment). But after one bite, they both moaned with pleasure.

We were licking our fingers and dabbing at the final crumbs when Diana hit us with the bombshell. "I think it's really over between me and Bryan."

Mom blanched. My lungs stopped working for what seemed like an eternity. I had to hit my chest in a sort of self-inflicted CPR maneuver. "WHAT? You said that you were having a *trial* separation. TRIAL."

D rubbed her nose with her index finger, and her eyes got suspiciously watery. "Being a family takes more than the two of us can handle. Mom, you must know what I am talking about."

Mom stared at Diana. I have never seen my mother look so defeated. She massaged her thighs with her fingers, her knuckles white. It was as if all the air in the room became suddenly so heavy that breathing was an effort. Mom could hardly speak; she gasped out her words. "My fault." She put a hand to her chest, as if to help herself breathe. "I set a bad example."

Diana thrust out her hands, as if to ward off a blow. "You did *not*. That is absolute nonsense!"

"Damn it to hell! Why did you and I get mixed up with Bryan in the first place?" I wanted to get on the next plane to Chicago and do some serious ass whooping. Maybe with a handgun thrown in for good measure.

Mom, by this time, had her head in her hands. She was listing to the side. I went to sit beside her and prop her up as Diana continued.

"Let's just put all this blaming and hating to rest. One: Mom, I am sure that you are not responsible for the fact that although we all adored Dexter Throckmorton, he had a wandering eye. I know. I said that there must have been something not right about your relationship. I wish I hadn't said that, because, the fact is, Dad couldn't always keep his fly zipped. He was an absolutely great dad, while things lasted. But, Mom. *He chose to walk off. He didn't look back much, did he?*"

Mom looked up with blank eyes. "I should have done something."

I put an arm around her. "What could you have done? Taken some lovers on the side yourself?" I was shaking.

Diana continued. "Mom, she is right! Don't bash yourself one minute longer. And by the way, Beck, it wasn't all a bed of roses with

Bryan. I should have taken it as a head's up that *you* left him. But no—I thought that you were just an immature blockhead that was afraid of commitment. That I would be the one to show everybody how to be the relationship queen. Hah!" Diana actually blew her nose on the hem of her silk tank top. "Marriage and motherhood can suck, big time. All that *maintenance*. He wants dinners and clean sheets. Sex on demand. The baby wants to be held all the time. All that crying. All that laundry. All those goddamn nipple shields! Jesus. And then Bryan whines about everything being different than it was *before*. He doesn't like getting up at night to change diapers; they are 'disgusting.' *So? I think they are disgusting, too!*" Diana looked down at the mess on her tank top and tried to wipe it off with her palm. Futile. She snorted. "Mom. Beck. I have come to the conclusion that marriage simply sucks. I have room in my life for the adoration and coddling of only one man, and that is Alex." She snapped her fingers.

We sat in silence. I felt as if everything was swirling around, tumbling and turning, my life a kaleidoscope. My mother, my father, my sister, Bryan. Bob. Ella. Gail. My books. All that I had done, just a great big jumble. But then Diana leaned over and touched her baby on his head.

"Mom. Beck. I swear on Alex's little noggin that this whole marriage breakup has been a long time coming. And you two should not blame yourselves for anything. I have made the right decision for myself. You two made the right ones for you." She looked down at Alex and bit her lip. Then she nodded at us both.

Mom's face regained a little color. Two circles of pink appeared on her cheeks, and her eyes brightened. "Your father was good to you girls, wasn't he? He was a loving man." She laughed, but it sounded more like strangling. "He was just too loving. He loved himself right out of a family." A drop of something formed on the end of her nose. She ignored it. "It wasn't my fault that he was so Goddamned *loving*."

We three sat, letting the weight of our realities envelop us. I hiccupped. Diana reached for a napkin and handed it to Mom, indicating that she needed to blow her nose. Mom complied, and then we looked at one another. Then we all smiled. Hell, we three began to *double over* laughing. That woke up Alex, and we grabbed him and passed him around, covering him with kisses. He hated it.

▷◁

As we cleaned up after our soul-baring lunch session, each of us looking as if weights had been wrested from our spines, Diana hit us with yet another incendiary.

"Oh, by the way. I've been meaning to tell you. You might want to go down to the Humane Society and get one of those Have-a-Heart traps, because there is a really mangy-looking feral cat living under your neighbor's back porch. I've been feeding him scraps, but he won't come out."

I screamed. "SIMPSON!"

I nearly broke my neck in my rush to get outside. D and Mom got there a minute or two later—D had to put on some flip-flops, and Mom had to carry Alex.

"Simpy? Simpson? Here Simpy!" I didn't hear anything at first.

"He may be way in the back. I heard him meowing the first few nights I was here. Late. He woke me up. I went out and called 'kitty, kitty,' and he answered. He seemed to be way under there. I went up and got some bologna and set it by the hole in the lattice, here." She pointed to a small opening in the rotting grid under Mr. Warden's back stoop. "After a few days, he would come towards the front, and I could just catch a glimpse of him, and he ate the food I put there for him. But he wouldn't come out. So you have to crawl under there."

D pulled at the lattice, breaking it. Now there was a hole big enough for somebody to fit through. Me, obviously. "But what if this is some sort of wild animal? Not even a cat? What if it's a raccoon? They look kind of like cats."

I was down on all fours, peering through the hole. D kicked me in the rear. "Do raccoons *MEOW?*"

Good point. I squinted, but it was so dark in there. I shimmied part way in, catching my shirt on God knows what, probably rusty nails. I cursed at the fact that Bob, skinny little Bob, was in school right then.

It smelled like rotting corpses under there. As my eyes adjusted to the darkness, I saw him. Dirty. Matted. Skeletal. Afraid. *Simpson.*

"Come here, Simpy! Oh, Simpy, you're home! Come here, buddy! Are you sick?"

His ears pricked up. I think a light came into his golden eyes, but I may be over-dramatizing it. He knew me, though! As I called to him softly, he crept towards me. He began to purr as he dragged himself towards my face. I reached out to touch him, and he butted his filthy head into my palm. I could feel the sharp ridge of his skull. My darling boy. I didn't want to spook him, so I just petted him gently, and we had a small conversation.

"What happened to you, boy? Where have you been? Are you hurting?"

He rubbed against my knuckles.

"What you need is a good meal and a veterinarian, don't you think?"

He purred a bit louder and began to knead the dirt underneath us.

"You have been gone for weeks! Have you been under here the whole time?"

He licked my hand.

I scootched a bit closer to him, and stroked him from his head, down his backbone, towards his tail. When my hand grazed his flank, he flinched, but didn't retreat. I touched him on the side, very gently. His right leg was distorted somehow. It felt warped. Oh, my God—it was broken!

"Simpy, we have to get you out of here. Now just trust me. I am going to pull you out. I will be as gentle as I can, so don't panic, and don't bite me, okay?"

D kicked me again, this time on the sole of my sneaker. "What is going on? Do you KNOW this cat?"

Mom cheered. "Oh, honey! It's Simpson, isn't it? Is he okay?"

"Oh, my God! Bryan and I let him out! I thought he had been hit by a car!" Poor D.

I grasped him by the scruff, very carefully. No protest, only purring. This was an awkward maneuver—I snaked my way out, trying to keep my grip on Simpy's neck while extricating myself from the crawl space. On the way, I ripped a hole in my shirt and would certainly need a tetanus shot for all the stuff piercing my midsection. A tetanus shot and antibiotics, certainly.

We emerged into the sunlight. I cradled my cat in my arms. He looked pitiful—so thin, he seemed almost weightless. That mangled leg. Fleas. His paw pads were abraded. His fur was missing in spots all along his spine. But he was alive.

"This looks nothing like your cat. And he stinks." D was right. He smelled like infection. But I couldn't stop kissing his head, and he couldn't stop purring. It was Simpy, gone but never forgotten. I would recognize him anywhere. He was my little marble-eyed soul mate.

Mom, always thinking, said, "Let's not just stand here. You have to take him upstairs and give him some food. He looks like he is starving to death. And then, you have to get him right to the vet. I mean RIGHT OVER THERE."

We trooped upstairs. I held him, afraid to put him down. I told D to scramble him an egg with Muenster cheese. His all-time favorite. I set him down very gently on the kitchen floor. D handed me the dish full of eggs. I blew on it to cool it down.

"Don't give it all to him; he will just barf it all back up. Just give him a bite." Since when was Diana the cat expert?

"How do you know this?" I dumped the majority of the egg out of his bowl and placed the one bite on the floor in front of him. He scarfed it and looked up at me for more.

"Everyone knows that when you are starving, if you eat too much, it will just come right back up. I watch *Survivor*."

Mom agreed. "Haven't you seen all those documentaries about the Holocaust? It took weeks before those people rescued from the camps could eat. Many of them died of starvation even after they were liberated. It takes time to get the digestive system working again."

D handed me a custard cup full of water. I put that down, too.

"Okay, gang. This has been a superb teachable moment. Thank you both for your wisdom. But right now, after Simpy finishes his drink of water"—he was lapping to beat the band; I figured all that liquid would come up in the car on the way to the vet—"I need to put him in the car and take him to the vet. Are either of you coming?"

Mom backed out gracefully, citing the need for a rest. D, however, surprised the hell out of me.

"Of course, I'm coming. I found him, remember. I want to see this through. Mom will stay here with Alex. They can both nap."

Mom nodded assent, because when the queen gives an order, her minions obey. I got the cat carrier out of the closet, put in a fresh towel ("Good grief, you spoil that animal," D observed), and gently pushed him in and shut the door. Simpy howled, but it was a weak attempt at best.

Mom waved us off. "Call me and tell me what happens!"

D honked the horn as we pulled out—I unrolled my window and yelled over to Ella and Janey, playing cards on her porch: "WE FOUND MY CAT! GOING TO THE VET! I MAY BE AWHILE!"

Janey, who didn't know I had lost a cat, but was prepared for any eventuality, bless her, yelled, "DON'T YOU EVER WORRY, I GOT THINGS COVERED OVER HERE!"

I heaved a sigh of relief. As I rolled my window back up, Ella lifted her hand and waved. Her smile seemed genuine. Bona fide. Authentic. She looked like her old self. But as we passed, Ella's hand dropped, and her face fell once again. Dammit.

▷◁

Simpy usually hated going to the vet, but this time he was just so depleted, he drooped in the carrier, barely moving, as D checked us in. I had to hand it to my pushy sister, who made it very clear to the receptionist that "not having an appointment" was of absolutely no significance.

"This cat is EXTREMELY SICK AND DEHYDRATED. HIS LEG IS OBVIOUSLY BROKEN. I am sure that your doctors would agree that DYING ANIMALS do not need appointments!"

The receptionist—probably afraid that if she didn't do as Diana said, D would beat her up—agreed to inform the doctors that there was an emergency in the waiting area.

It took about ten minutes for a vet tech to appear and escort us into an exam room. I put Simpy on the exam table, where he trembled and shed hair all over the place. D was waiting outside, which was a good thing, because it would have been too crowded—the room was tiny. I studied the heartworm prevention posters and blew my nose with one of the Kleenexes provided. Probably for sobbing owners during euthanasias. I shuddered, hoping that wouldn't be me in a few minutes.

Dr. Demarco was my favorite vet. He knocked softly before entering the room. I liked his petside manner. I think he might have been a football player in a former career—scrubs could not conceal his broad shoulders and bulging biceps. Despite all the muscles, he moved as gracefully as a ballet dancer. I also liked his eyes, which were very kind.

He gasped a bit when he put his hands on Simpy. "You've been through the wringer, haven't you, guy?" He palpated Simpy's abdomen and ran his hands all over Simpy's body. "No internal injuries that I can detect." He placed his stethoscope in various spots and listened. "Sounds good. No pneumonia."

I wondered how long it would take for Dr. Demarco to comment on the leg. The leg. The leg. He looked into Simpy's eyes, pried his mouth open to study his teeth and gums, and used that little cone thing to examine his ears. "Ears dirty; mites. Easy fix."

He ran his hand the wrong way from tail to neck. "Fleas and flea dirt. No ticks. Some scabs, but not too bad." He stopped and palpated a spot on Simpy's neck, then squeezed it. Pus gushed out. I nearly fainted. Simpy merely growled.

"An abscess. That is what smells. I will take him to the back and shave this down—then we'll clean it well. I will give him an antibiotic shot, called Convenia. It will take care of this and any other indolent infections. It lasts two weeks systemically."

The leg. The leg.

"It looks to me as if he was hit by a car. This leg was completely fractured, but as you can see, there is no bone protruding, which is a good thing. There is nothing I can do about the fracture now, because it has already healed. It healed badly, and he will probably not be able to walk without some trouble from now on, but I think he will be fine. Let's see how he does on the floor."

Simpy stood for a moment, and then sensed his chance to escape. He ran crookedly to the exam room door, and when it didn't open, he reared up and jiggled the handle with a paw.

"He will be fine. If you want to leave him with us for the afternoon, we can give him a flea bath and get him cleaned up."

"Oh, no! I just got him back! He needs to go home with me and rest. Can you just give me the shampoo and stuff? I can bathe him myself."

Dr. Demarco smiled. My God, pearly white teeth. This man's wife was very lucky. "It may be a struggle. He is weak, but cats hate baths. Even this guy will be able to put up a fight. Are you sure?"

"Completely." I picked up my skeletal cat and hugged him, trying to avoid getting any pus on my top.

Dr. Demarco flashed me another one of his blinding smiles, and opened the door to the surgery area. "We'll be back in a second."

A technician came and reached for my cat. She must have sensed my anxiety. "No worries. We are just going to get a weight on him, then take care of that abscess. It won't take long.

It seemed like an eternity. I paced back and forth in the tiny room, sneezing a few times from the filthy cat hair floating in the atmosphere. I thought I heard Simpy yowl, but really, it could have been any cat, I told myself.

The technician brought him back in. It looked like they had shaved his entire upper body. Pitiful. "He had a couple more abscesses on his neck, see, right here, under his chin. We think he's been fighting." We gave him a tablet to kill any live fleas on him right now." She handed me a sleeve with four pills embedded in it. "The pills don't kill eggs. So you will need to give him one every other day for the next week. That will take care of any eggs that hatch. A bath will get rid of the dirt, but not the flea eggs. We also cleaned out his ears."

She set a bottle of shampoo on the exam table, along with a bag of what looked like tuna cans. "Use this. Soap him up well, and let it sit on his skin for at least a couple of minutes. It's medicated.

It will help clear up all the skin irritation." Oh, boy. "And we are sending home special wet food. He should be on this for about a week or so. It stimulates the appetite, plus it is very high in protein, which he needs right now. One tablespoon at a time, three times today. Then increase to four times tomorrow. We have to get him back to food gradually. After tomorrow, you can add a bit of dry food. When the cans are gone, back to the usual diet."

She smiled. "Are you sure you can do all this?"

I nodded emphatically. Then I made a mental note to get Bob involved. Yes. Bob was just the ticket.

On the way home, D steered with one hand, and held her nose with the other. She was such a pain in the ass.

CHAPTER TWENTY-EIGHT

We were jogging on the track at the gym. Since Alex and D had moved into their own place, there was a hole in my routine, so Gail suggested I start working out. "The thighs aren't getting any smaller," as she put it. I hate exercising indoors, but it was way too hot outside—Indian summer in Ohio—to run in the park. Humidity in the heartland is lethal, let me tell you.

We were discussing the end of me and Theo. "Gail, it was probably the best thing. I had so much going on in my life this summer. There wasn't really time for a relationship. Don't give me that aggravated look!"

Gail pumped her arms and panted. I was having trouble keeping up with her. All my caregiving had left me with strong shoulders but weak legs. "Beck, at this rate, you will be single forever!"

"Don't worry about it. Theo and I were not a match made in heaven, anyway."

Gail brushed a bead of sweat from her eye. "Yeah, but as far as I'm concerned, there is no such thing. You didn't appreciate Theo enough."

Although exploring my philosophy of life while puffing and dripping my way around a gym balcony in the middle of a sweltering late October in Framington, Ohio, was not my idea of the right time and place, I felt I had to expound. "Gail. He is a wonderful man. Husband material for somebody. But just not for me. He knew I wasn't in love with him, and he deserved better. He was right to call it quits. I don't think I'm destined to be part of a twosome."

Gail slapped me on my arm. "That is bullshit."

I chugged a sip of water from my Nalgene. "No, really. Gail, I don't think I ever want to get married. I really enjoy my freedom."

Gail grunted with disgust. And picked up the pace. Damn, I was out of shape. "You are lying to yourself. But fine. If that's what you want to tell yourself, it's none of my business."

I concentrated on keeping my pace in sync with hers. "I do fine. I like my life the way it is. And frankly, Theo was as boring as a blank sheet of paper." My knees ached.

"Hah! What exactly are you looking for? A pirate? A mobster? They aren't boring. But, honey," Gail poked me in the ribs, "Johnny Depp is taken."

"Gail. Can we slow down a little? You are killing me, here. And no, I am not looking for a pirate, for God's sake. Just someone with a little flair, and not necessarily one with an all-Ralph-Lauren-all-the-time wardrobe."

"That sounds like defensiveness to me."

I straightened up and looked her in the eye. Gail's mascara never ran, even in the midst of a workout. "Gail, I love you, too. I know you have my best interests at heart. I know that having a man in my life is a good thing. But it has to be the right man." I grabbed Gail's arm. "We have to walk for a while."

Gail slowed down and matched her pace to my pitiful, out-of-shape shuffle. "Actually, I'm glad we're having this discussion." She stopped suddenly. "How would you feel if Theo and I went out on a date?"

I blinked the sweat out of my eyes. "Huh? What about Rick?"

Gail pulled me against the rail so that other joggers could pass us. "Rick and I were never serious. He was luscious and all, but it was a fling. And I am so damn sick of flings. And then you and Theo didn't jell. He has called me a few times, just to talk. We've had dinner a couple of times. Beck, I really like him. He's such a terrific guy. But if this bothers you, I won't pursue it." She looked so serious.

I punched her on the arm. "Gail, I have so much going on in my life right now. A new book, maybe a new career. I spent the summer with an eight-year-old girl and her great-grandmother, learning how to give sponge baths and make nourishing meals. My sister came here to stay, and I realized that she isn't always Queen of the Bitches. I quit my job. My cat ran away and nearly died. So no. Of course I am not upset about you dating Theo. I am sort of envious that I wasn't able to fall head-over-heels in love with him, but that's about it."

Gail laughed. "You just said he was as boring as a blank sheet of paper."

"I know. But that's me. We both know there's something wrong with *my* head. What about you, though?"

She hugged herself. "No, I think he's almost *perfect.*" Gail absolutely beamed.

Enough said.

▷◁

It was Janey's afternoon off. She needed some time for herself and her son. I spent Tuesday and Thursday afternoons across the street at Ella's until Bob came home from school, often with Hallie. They entertained Ella and each other until bedtime, when Janey came back, much restored. On those days, Ella and I made dinner together in the kitchen. I cooked, and Ella instructed me. Today, it was just the two of us, and I was making creamed tuna, to be served on toast later. It sounds horrible, what with the canned peas and condensed milk—straight out of a WWII cookbook, but it was actually a favorite at the Bowers' house. I had been known to have two helpings, myself.

"Rebecca, something is going on with Bobby. She seems worried."

I looked up from the pot, but kept stirring, so the cream sauce wouldn't separate. "What do you mean, exactly?"

Ella shook her head. "I've asked her if something is bothering her, but she just clams up. And Janey said that Bob had a nightmare last night. She asked me this morning if she could stay home from school today."

I turned the heat off under the sauce. I turned to look at Ella, whose face contorted, her lips drawn into a thin line. She looked even paler than usual.

"She's due home soon. Let's see if we can draw her out. Maybe it's just some sort of issue at school. Maybe one of the girls snubbed her or something. You know how awful girls can be to one another." Ella didn't look convinced.

As I finished making the tuna, I tried to change the subject. I mentioned that Theo and Gail were dating. I don't think that even registered with Ella, despite the fact that she had been very sad when I told her that Theo and I were no longer an item. I asked Ella if she knew how to make Floating Island, because it was mentioned in a book I had read recently and sounded delicious. Nothing.

A few minutes later, after we had moved into the living room, and Ella fanned herself nervously with a magazine and I fidgeted in my seat, we heard Bob pounding up the front steps. She slammed the screen door and started to go upstairs, but I stopped her.

"Bob! Come in here for a minute. We want to ask you something."

Bob dropped her backpack on the hall table, trudged into the living room, and stood there, biting the inside of her bottom lip and looking down at her feet.

"Bobby, honey. Something is wrong. We can tell. Come in and sit down and tell us about it, so that we can help you." Ella patted the cushion beside her on the sofa. Bob seemed reluctant, but she shuffled in and sat down. She still wouldn't look at either of us.

"Bob, has something happened at school? Did you get in trouble?"

She shook her head, then began gnawing on her thumbnail.

"Are you worried about your dad?" I was casting around for something, anything. But Bob was just not herself. Ella wasn't kidding.

Ella reached over and touched Bob on the cheek. Bob looked at her gran and it all came tumbling out. "There was a lady on the other side of the fence at recess yesterday and today. She was staring at us. And today, she waved at me."

This was alarming. But women aren't usually child stalkers. I started to say something.

Bob continued, her voice almost a whisper. "It was my mother."

Ella gasped, "ROWENA IS HERE?"

We sat in stunned silence for what seemed like minutes, but it was probably a split second before Ella scrabbled to get up off the sofa and fell backwards. I jumped up and ran to the front door, expecting to see Rowena standing on the front porch waiting to be invited in. Of course, the porch was empty, and there was nobody coming down the block, either. A relief. I turned back to see Ella still struggling to get up.

"We have to call the police! Bobby isn't safe! What if Rowena is here to abduct Bobby?" Her voice cracked. "Rebecca! Help me UP!"

Bob jumped off the sofa and turned on us. "I hate her! Why is she here? I won't go with her anywhere! Make her go away!" With that, Bob hurtled up the stairs and slammed her bedroom door.

Ella reached out for me, her arms trembling, her legs scrambling beneath her. I took her hands and sat beside her, trying to hold her down. "Ella. We have to collect ourselves. We need to take a deep breath here and think for a minute."

Ella pulled her hands away and began wringing them. Her eyes filled. "I can't bear this!" She shut her eyes and sat, the tears catching in the creases of her cheeks. "She wants to take Bobby."

"Ella, we don't know for sure that the woman is Rowena. Bob hasn't seen her for a long time. It might just have been someone who looks like Rowena."

Ella's eyes shot open. She reached over and gripped my forearm and dug her nails into my skin. "Go out there. Find her. She knows our address. Please find her before she comes here for Bobby!" Ella let go of my arm and waved toward the door. "She is out there. You have to stop her!"

All I knew of Rowena's appearance was that one old photo that was folded into the letter she sent Bob. I didn't have a lot to go on. But at this point, with Bob barricaded in her room and Ella quivering in terror, I didn't feel I had a choice. I got up and headed for the door.

"I am going to lock the door behind me. Don't answer the doorbell. Tell Bob not to, either." With Ella nodding and gesturing wildly for me to get out of there, I did.

I was drenched in sweat, but not from the heat. I started off in the direction of the school, thinking that maybe this woman was hanging around somewhere in the vicinity of the playground. I held my cell phone in a death grip. If she jumped me or something, I could dial 9-1-1. My thoughts twisted inside my head.

What if you walk right past her and don't recognize her?

I know. But so far, I haven't seen anybody.

What does a drug addict look like? Are they really thin? Do they have obvious track marks on their arms and stuff?

Don't be stupid. I can't just walk up to a woman on the street and ask to see her arms! And there are other places to put needles. No. I have to focus on that face in the photo. Dark hair. Haunting eyes. Yes, THIN.

What will you do if you see her? GRAB her?

Shut up, Beck. I don't know.

OH MY FREAKING GOD.

Because there she was. Sitting on a bench in the little park where Bob and Hallie often played. Sitting there with her hollow eyes and bony knees on the bench where Bob and I sometimes sat slurping Popsicles. Her hair was lank, the color of used tea bags. It hung in front of one eye, greasy and dull. She looked sunburned and scarred, baked by the elements. She wore blue-and-black striped leggings with a hole in each knee. Smoking as if her life depended on it. I hesitated to approach her, but she looked up at me and stood immediately, throwing her cigarette to the ground, as if she had been waiting for this.

I stopped so abruptly on the pavement, I nearly tripped and fell. "Hello. Are you by any chance named Rowena?"

She nodded. She was so thin that her leggings hung in folds below her waist. This was a woman far beyond anorexia—she was skeletal. Her forearms were riddled with scabs. I was reminded of the stray dogs with mange that appear in all of the rescue videos on Facebook.

My throat was dry. "My name is Rebecca Throckmorton." I regained my balance and forced a smile. "I am a good friend of Bob and Ella Bowers."

Rowena stuck out her hand. It wasn't exactly clean. Her fingertips were nicotine stained. But I reached out and shook it. I was surprised at the strength of her grip. She motioned for me to sit down on the bench beside her.

"I knew Roberta recognized me today. And I figured somebody would come looking for me."

I didn't waste any time. "Why are you here? Aren't you supposed to be in rehab? What do you want with Bob—Roberta? You don't have any claim on her." I puffed up like a tomcat.

"She put her hands together as if praying. "Peace. I come in peace."

Her eyes were clear. She didn't look high to me. But then again, I have no experience with drug users, and so I didn't really have much to go on. But her expression blasted me with such sincerity, so I relaxed just a bit. "What do you want?"

She sat back. She wore a tank top, her collarbone slicing her neckline. This woman sorely needed a few thousand calories. I wondered when she had eaten last. "Well?"

"I am clean and sober. I got out of rehab four days ago. Sober now for sixty days. That is a record for me."

Whoa. Not much of a record. "Go on."

She reached into her filthy backpack, rooted around, and brought out a package of cigarettes and a Bic. She pulled out a cigarette that had already been half-smoked, clicked her lighter until the end of the stub glowed, and inhaled deeply. "I just want to see my daughter. Who are you—the go-between?" Rowena's grin flared ruefully.

"Sort of. Yes. I'm Roberta's neighbor—her good friend."

"The guard? The sentinel? What is your name, 'good friend'?"

"As I said, my name is Rebecca Throckmorton. I have been taking care of Bob—she doesn't like to be called Roberta—and Ella since Ella fell and broke her hip. And they are both very upset that you just blew into town. They are scared."

She raised an eyebrow. "Scared? Why?"

"Isn't it obvious? Your history of addiction is no secret. And you hit Bob, didn't you? Punched her? You have failed your family and your daughter. You gave up custody. Bob hasn't heard anything from you, for what, years? And then suddenly you send her a letter begging for forgiveness, and now you just show up and lurk around the playground. This is like the plot from some *CSI* episode in which people are kidnapped or worse." I wanted to kick her.

I have to give her credit. She slumped and sighed. "I know. I know."

Here we were, in the midst of small-town America, with leafy trees, chirping birds, and traffic humming all around us. Kids playing on the swings. Dogs barking in backyards. This was some kind of seismic event in the lives of the Bowers family, and it was playing out on a park bench on a breezy afternoon.

Rowena. Stringy, pale. She sagged with exhaustion. But there was something about her. There was a strength.

"How did you get here? And why now?"

"I took buses."

This would be a long story. Too long for this bench. "You look hungry and tired. Do you want something to eat?"

She smiled. Her teeth were very white. She must have been beautiful once. I could see why Charles Bowers had been smitten back then. "I *am* hungry."

I still clutched my cell phone. I tipped it up and called Ella. She answered on the first ring. "I found her. Don't worry. We are getting something to eat. Sit tight. There is no need to call the police, Ella. Ella?"

I heard her take a deep breath at her end. "Rebecca. I am so worried."

I told Ella not to be scared. But I was panicked.

▷◁

Rowena inhaled two hamburgers and an order of fries. I could see the lumps of food as they made their way down her stalk of a throat. I guess she *wasn't* anorexic. As she ate, she tried to talk, but I told her to wait until she could speak without chewing. After she finished her food, she pounded back her large Coke, wiped her mouth with her napkin, and started her story.

"Do you know anything about addiction? How it starts?"

"Not really."

Rowena smiled. "Drugs are magical. Especially to certain sorts of people. People who have big holes in their lives. Like me."

"Okay. Go on."

"I grew up in Oceanside, Cali. My parents were losers. My dad was a marine—saw a lot of action, but when he got out, he had what he said was PTSD. But that was just an excuse for him to drink. He stayed near Camp Pendleton and did odd jobs. My mom had bipolar disorder. Around our house, it was like a shitstorm all the time. My mom committed suicide, and then my dad just disappeared. This was when I was fifteen, and so I went into the system. I had a crappy set of foster parents who basically ignored me; they just liked the stipend they got for having me. So guess what? I started smoking pot. It was okay. But then, one of the girls at school gave me a Vic."

I had no idea what she was talking about. "A what?"

"A Vic. VICODIN. You know? The painkiller. It was so, so smooth. It felt sort of like I had swallowed velvet. You know?"

I didn't. But I nodded, anyway.

"Yeah. It was heaven. And she had a bunch of them. She stole them from her mom. She charged us a buck a pill. That was sweet."

Jesus.

"Then she ran out of pills, but it wasn't a problem, because there was this guy, Tommy, who sold them out of his locker. He charged five dollars for three pills. Cheap. I took them all through high school."

She went on. "So I was hooked. I graduated, and got a job waitressing at Lu's Diner. Lots of marines from Pendleton came in all the time, because we had good food, and all of us waitresses were cute. And I was on pills, but I was a nice girl. I had dreams. I had flair. Anyway, that's where I first met Charlie."

"He knew you took pills?"

"Yeah, after a while. But he was so good to me. He told me I was smart and beautiful. I loved him. And then I got pregnant. So I quit the pills. It was like going to hell. I quit cold turkey. It made me so sick. It was like having a fire under my skin all the time, and I couldn't even sleep. But I did it. Charlie was so proud of me. He loved me then. He thought I was a good person. I loved to draw. He said I was an artist. He and I loved to talk about things. We loved movies. We laughed so much. Charlie was such an optimist. He was convinced that I would just put all of the shit behind me and be a good partner. A great Mom." She raised her thumb to her mouth and bit the ragged nail. "I had every intention of doing that, too. But what a pipe dream *that* was."

I ordered two more Cokes. We needed the table for a lot longer; this story wasn't going to be quick.

She sipped at the Coke. "So we had Roberta. She was such a good baby. We were happy for the time being. Then Charlie was deployed, and I was alone. I was stuck with this kid, I didn't know how to be a housewife or anything, and I got bored. I started having a few beers after she went to bed. That only took a tiny bit of the edge off. But the walls started closing in." She sniffed and looked down at her drink. "Do you know how much kids cry? How much they whine? They won't sleep good. They never shut up. So I had to do something to make her behave. When I hit her, she got quiet." Rowena pulled at her eyelid, extracting a couple of lashes. She stared at them between her fingers. "I hit my own child."

I wanted to believe she was a monster. I wanted to revile her. But she was so small, thin, and sick. Her veins showed blue and pulsed at her wrists and temples. This woman was clearly shattered. "Go on."

"Yeah. I felt like I was living in a cage. So I looked around for some pills. They weren't hard to come by. So yeah. I got high." She looked at me and bit at a piece of dry skin on her bottom lip. She couldn't seem to sit still. She pulled her backpack into her lap and pulled out a dingy pack of cigarettes, then put it back in and shrugged. "Why don't they let people smoke in public any more? Total shit."

"Is that when you and Charles broke up?"

"Oh, you want me to bottom-line all this? Yeah—this is a long story." She took another pull of her Coke. "No. Not then. He stuck by me. Well, really, he stuck by Roberta, because he loved her and wanted to protect her from me. Because I graduated from pills to heroin. But you know that."

"I know that."

"Okay, okay. Yeah, he stayed around as long as he could, but then I was just another sicko, drunk, kid-abusing junkie, and pretty soon, he couldn't stand me. Right? Who could? I am a loser. No mystery there. So he took Roberta and I signed her away. Put my name on some document he got from a lawyer that said I had no rights to her, and didn't want any. I didn't even care at the time. I just wanted my next needle, you know?" She stopped and tried to swallow, looking out the window.

I shredded my napkin and waited.

"Rebecca, what is the best you have ever felt? Was it when you picked out your prom dress? Ate your first lobster? Found a new bike under the Christmas tree? Well, that is nothing. Nothing compared to the glorious way you feel when the H hits your veins. It's better than an orgasm, better than the happiest happiness. It is like nothing else in the world. So giving up your kid? Nothing. Giving up your guy? Phfft. I gave up everything for smack."

"But you're clean. You said you're clean."

She shoved her glass across the table. "I always wanted to get clean. Even while I was shooting up, I wanted for this high to be my *last* high. I tried rehab. More than once. But I always went back. But then I got on Methadone. It worked for a while, but you have to go to a Methadone clinic every day to get your dose. My place was three bus rides away. Then it closed. So I relapsed. But then I scored some Suboxone from a friend who was selling it. It's a new drug to help people get off heroin. It works. You can get it by prescription, but only from a few doctors. And they can only give it to a few patients a year." She snorted. "Go figure. A drug that stops heroin addiction—but only a handful of addicts have access to it. So we have to stick with heroin or get Suboxone on the street, like I do. And pretty soon, they'll start cutting it with smack or other crap. So I don't know how long I can stay clean."

"So you have substituted one drug for another one?"

She cocked her head and shot me a snotty look. "That's *right*, Miss holier-than-thou. But this drug blocks the need for heroin. I am not getting high on it."

"Rowena. Okay. But I don't need your life history. I want to know why you are HERE."

Rowena rolled her eyes at me. As if I were an idiot. "I am here because I am straight. I love my daughter. I want to see her and talk to her while I am straight. I want her to know I love her. *Because I know that I won't stay straight.* Understand? I know that I will not be straight forever. That is not the way my story is going to end, and I want Roberta to remember me *this way.* Can you understand? I love Roberta. But I love drugs more than any other human. Addicts love drugs, period."

She slammed her hands on the table. The conversation was obviously over, and I was both relieved and unsettled. "Well, you can't just go over there with me right now. I have to prepare them. And you know Bob does *not* want to see you. She has made that very clear."

"I know. But I can wait a bit. I'm staying at the YMCA. I have money. I can be here for a few days. Long enough for you to talk her and Ella into giving me this one chance. You can do that. They will listen to you. And all I want is a little time. Five minutes. That's all I want."

It was a very tall order. "I am not at all sure that I can." But this woman sitting across from me was resolute. She radiated a desperate confidence.

Rowena pulled out a cell phone. "What's your number? I'll program it into my phone. And here's mine. Please. Get back to me. Please."

We exchanged information, and when we stood to leave the restaurant, Rowena threw her arms around me in a crushing hug. I stood like a statue. She dropped her arms. I watched her march away, her shoulders pulled up close to her ears, her head thrown back like a soldier's.

▷◁

By the time I got back to Ella's, the dear woman was in a state. Her hair, what there was of it, stuck up all over her head. She had gotten up with her walker and managed to make herself some tea, but it stood on the coffee table, the cup almost full. Ella's walker was knocked over where she'd apparently kicked it as she got into her "easy" chair. She sat, her dress bunched up in her lap, her knee-high panty hose showing. She didn't even look up from rubbing her forehead and twitching in her chair.

"Ella. No worries. I can pretty much guarantee that Rowena is not here to kidnap Bob. I sat with her for a long time, as you know, and she told me her story. She is pitiful."

Ella looked incredulous. "What kind of bill of goods did she sell you? This girl is unstable!"

"I know she is. But Ella, the important thing is that *she* knows she is. She has no illusions about herself. She is currently taking some kind of drug that helps people stay off heroin, and while she is"—I used air quotes—"clean, she wants to see Bob."

Ella wrung her hands. "Why?"

"She wants to see Bob to reconnect with her. She wants Bob to remember her as a sober person. She wants to tell Bob she loves her. I guess. She says she'll settle for just five minutes with her." Now that I was saying it, it did sound a little farfetched. A cross-country trip for a mere five minutes. "Did you tell her she could?"

I shook my head. "No. I told her that all of this was up to Bob. And to you."

Ella seemed more agitated than ever. Her head trembled on her neck, she twisted in her seat, bunching her skirt even farther up into her lap. "I feel sick. Just sick about this."

"Shall I call Dr. Bankson?"

"No. No. I don't need a doctor." And with that, Ella fainted in her chair.

CHAPTER TWENTY-NINE

Bob and I sat beside Ella's gurney in the ER. Luckily, Dr. Bankson was on call; a nurse told me she was on the way. They had hooked Ella up to an IV, and though she seemed fine, nobody wanted to take any chances. The nurse said her vitals were "in the satisfactory range," but we had no idea what that meant. Bob, in the meantime, chafed her gran's hand and apologized over and over.

"Oh, Gran, I am so sorry! I shouldn't have run upstairs and left you all alone! It's all my fault. No it's HER fault!"

"Let's take things one step at a time, okay, Bob? We need to wait for Dr. Lauren, and in the meantime, we need to keep calm. Let's not think about all the other stuff right now." I gave her a warning look.

"Oh, right, Gran. We need you to get better! Oh, Gran!" And Bob leaned her head down onto the gurney next to Ella's. With their eyes closed, they looked like two angels right then. A bright one and a faded one.

Dr. Bankson bustled in, holding Ella's chart. "It says here that you got very stressed. How are you doing now?" She moved to the other side of the bed, where she could stroke Ella's wrist and look at the monitors. "You seem to be settling down. But I think we might want to put you on an anti-anxiety medication, just temporarily. It won't conflict with your other meds."

Ella's eyes popped open. "It's a terrible thing."

Dr. Lauren pulled up a chair and sat by the bed. "What is?"

Bob stood and blurted, "My mom is here. She just showed up. We don't like her. No. I *hate* her! She wants to see us. And it upset Gran!"

Lauren nodded to the nurse, who pumped something into Ella's IV. Ella's eyes immediately drooped. "Here is what we are going to do. We have just given your gran some medication to make her rest calmly. I am going to admit her into the hospital here for just one night, so that I can make sure she's okay. So right now, the best thing we can do is let her get a nap, okay?"

Bob looked down at Ella, who by this time was snoring gently. "Okay. You promise she will be better tomorrow?"

Dr. Lauren beamed at Bob. "I promise. And, Bob, you look tired, too. I think you need to go home and rest also. Can you just stay here for a few minutes and look after your gran while we wait to transfer her to her room? I want to chat with Rebecca."

Bob laid her head down again next to Ella's and again shut her eyes. Lauren motioned me out into the hall.

"I would like to shoot Rowena right now! For all we know, Ella might have had a stroke and died! This is just too much!" I tried to keep my voice down, but a couple of nurses at the nurses' station glanced our way.

"Beck, do you want me to prescribe a few Valium for you? I know that this has been a shock to all of you. You seem to be holding everybody together, but Valium might be helpful."

I crossed my arms. "No. I'll be okay. I just need to get Bob home. I can call my mother, and she can help out. Thank God, I can call my mother." The irony of my need for my mother right then as Bob's mother was wreaking havoc did not escape me.

"All right. You have my number if you change your mind. There is a bed for Ella available on the orthopedic ward for the night. Third floor. I suggest you two go home, take naps or at least rest, and come back this evening to see Ella. Visiting hours start at five and go until nine."

I was suddenly exhausted. "Right. We will do that. Thank you so much."

By the time we got home, Janey had received my text. There were brownies and hot chocolate waiting for us.

We sat in Ella's kitchen, nibbling. Neither one of us was hungry.

Janey put foil over the pan of brownies and put them in the cupboard. "Bobby, you can have one after supper."

"I won't want any supper. I feel sick to my stomach."

I did, too. Janey took matters into her own hands. "Bobby, you go upstairs and stretch out for a little while. You looked tuckered out. And Beck, go home and do the same thing."

Bob started to argue. "But visiting hours!"

Janey leaned over and kissed Bob on the cheek. "Honey, if you fall asleep, I promise to wake you up in plenty of time. You, too, kiddo." Janey rubbed my arm and gave it a pinch. "Now git out of this kitchen, both of you."

I walked into my apartment, lay down on the sofa, and fell asleep clutching my cell.

▷◁

Bob and I stopped on the way to the hospital and got her some butter pecan ice cream, her favorite. Bob also insisted on getting her a roll of cherry Lifesavers, "Gran's favorite," and a bunch of daisies, despite the fact that I reassured her that Ella would come home tomorrow.

"Doesn't matter. She can take them with her. She needs something to cheer her up."

The subject of Rowena did not come up until we sat beside Ella's bed, watching her dab at the ice cream in the cardboard cup. Ella set the ice cream on her rolling bed table and gently pushed it away. "What are we going to do about this?"

I stood up and began fussing with the flowers, moving them from the bed table to the windowsill. Stalling.

"Beck, honey. Sit back down. We have to talk about this."

Bob made her position very clear. "I don't want to see her. You can't make me." She pulled her legs up in her chair and clutched them with both arms. Her sneakers were untied. Her face was flushed. She flashed a defiant look at me. "I don't have to see her if I don't want to."

Ella looked at her great-granddaughter, wound up like a spring, threatening to uncoil at the both of us. "Bobby, I don't want to see her either. But think about it. She is your mother. She is so weighed down by her own troubles. She traveled a long way to get here, because she must have something to say to you and me. I worry that if we don't let her talk with us…" I thought Ella stopped herself just in time.

Bob's eyes widened.

Just then, the nurse came in to take Ella's vitals. It was a welcome interruption. She listened through her stethoscope and frowned. "Mrs. Bowers, your blood pressure is up." She made a notation on her iPad and turned to us. "I am afraid you two will have to go now. Mrs. Bowers needs to rest."

I was relieved, and I couldn't wait to get out of there, get Bob home to Janey, and haul ass over to Mom's. I watched as Bob unfolded herself, kissed Ella sullenly, and turned to go.

"Wait just a minute, Bobby! I want to tell you something!"

Bob swiveled back to her gran. "Closer, honey; it's a secret." Bob approached the bed and leaned over Ella, who whispered something in Bob's ear. Bob seemed to relax a little, and she kissed Ella on the cheek. "Okay, Beck, we can go now."

On the way home, Bob was silent. I turned on the radio and fiddled with the tuner.

"Can we just leave the radio off? I need to think about things."

"Sure, kiddo."

Janey was waiting for us. As soon as I pulled into the driveway, the front door opened, the light shining behind Janey's comforting bulk. "Come on in, honey!" She roared. "I have some soup and toast waiting for you!"

Bob undid her seat belt and scooted out of the car. "Janey! I am starving!" With that, Bob disappeared into the house, and Janey waved to me as she shut the door behind them.

CHAPTER THIRTY

Mom held her door open with one hand, and handed me a glass of beer with the other. "You sounded like you needed this. Now sit down and tell me what on earth is going on!"

It took me about ten minutes to tell her the whole story. As I recounted everything from the "forgiveness letter" to the saga of Rowena's heroin habit, Mom's expressions went from sympathy, to anger, and back to sympathy.

"And I get it, Mom. Who am I to judge? This woman has had a hell of a life. But I don't understand why she needed to drag herself across the country to inflict herself on Bob again. And endanger Ella, who is already so frail." I finished the final inch of beer in my glass with one swallow.

Mom shrugged. "You sound just a little bit on the defensive to me. Are you jealous of Rowena?"

I spluttered. "What are you *talking* about? The woman is a junkie and God knows what else!" I banged my glass down on the table so hard, it's a wonder it didn't shatter. "She's a disaster!" I was shaking. "What sort of woman does this? Imposes herself on her daughter out of the blue like this? A child who has been devastated by her irresponsible and immoral lifestyle. So she's temporarily 'clean,' and that justifies fucking with Bob's mind? Damaging her emotionally and physically?"

Mom puffed out her cheeks and let the air out gently. "For one thing, have you listened to yourself? We are talking about Bob's mother. I think the term 'junkie' is quite harsh. And you seem to be implying that Rowena is more than that. A prostitute? A thief? You sound as if you are judging her. And might there also be a little bit of envy of this woman who, despite her unfortunate situation, is so incredibly important to Bob and Ella?"

I let that sink in for a minute. Before I could respond, Mom continued, "Let's put this in gentler terms, okay? You have told me a story of a young woman who has had a tough life so far. She seems to have admitted just how gripped she really is by her addiction. But she is clean at the moment, having gotten herself on this drug that is controlling her craving for heroin. Am I correct so far?"

I nodded.

"So this young woman, who clearly loves her child, takes this opportunity to get herself all the way from Iowa to Framington on the bus. She does this, in her own words, so that her daughter can see her not as a person high on drugs or alcohol, but as a sober human being. Are you still with me?" Mom smiled.

"Yes."

"Well, then, Rebecca. It seems to me that Rowena needs your help. She isn't here to take her child away from her grandmother. She isn't here to turn over a new leaf, or make Bob and Ella think more highly of her than they do of you. The way you describe her, she is well aware of her limitations. 'Junkie' isn't the way you ought to be thinking of her. You are holding onto a very limiting stereotype when you call her that, aren't you?"

"Mom, who is the heavy, here? I am a Good Samaritan, for heaven's sake! Why the scolding?"

Mom slid her way along the sofa until she was right next to me. Close enough that I could smell her Chanel No. 5 and see the tiny hazel specks in her green eyes. She put her arm around my shoulders very softly.

"I am not scolding you, honey. I'm your mother. I'm telling it the way it is. What is the new phrase everybody puts on Facebook? '*I hate adulting*'? It seems to me that you are the adult in this situation, don't you agree? No matter how tough that is."

She patted my shoulder. I leaned against her, my eyes watering and my nose running. But I stifled any inclination to cry.

Things looked a lot better to me after I spent those few minutes in my mom's arms. So when I got home, I settled into bed and slept as if in a coma. I woke up the next morning with Simpy plastered, purring, on top of my head, and the need for a huge mug of coffee. I was also possessed with a new, strong sense of resolve.

Since it was a Saturday, I was able to text Rowena that I would see Bob before lunchtime. *Sit tight.*

She immediately texted back: *Will she see me?*

I was honest. *Not sure, but I will try.*

After I finished my coffee and snuggled with Simpson for fortification, I threw on a pair of cargo pants and an old Denison tee shirt and crossed the street. Before I could even clack the knocker, Janey opened the door and handed me a warm blueberry muffin on a paper towel. "I saw you comin', hon!"

"Is Bob up?" I took a bite of the muffin, its steamy sweetness a huge comfort.

"Yup. She's up and dressed. She has already talked with her gran on the phone this morning. You all can go pick her up as soon as they sign her discharge papers. Ella told Bob it would probably be in an hour or so. Bob is pretty hyped up. She's in the kitchen, working on her second muffin."

As soon as she heard me in the hall, Bob dashed out of the kitchen, her smile wreathed in crumbs. "Gran's fine! We get to go bring her home before lunch!" The old Bob seemed to be back, bouncing and weaving in the hall, splitting her freckles in half with a huge grin.

I put my hands on her shoulders to try to slow her down. "We need to have a conversation, kiddo. Serious one. Let's go into the living room and sit down for a few minutes."

Bob caught my mood and deflated on the spot. "This is about my mother."

She scuffed into the living room and sat down in Ella's chair. I would have preferred to sit beside her on the sofa, but Bob was keeping her distance. So I sat down in the center of the sofa and crossed my hands in my lap. Bob looked at me and blinked quickly, as if she had suddenly developed a tic.

"Your mom really wants to see you."

Bob drew up her legs again, as she had at the hospital last night. She clutched her knees as if to protect herself from an onslaught. "I know. *I* don't want to see *her.*"

I raised my palms and lowered my head in a gesture, I hoped, of peace. "Bob, I know you don't. But I spent a lot of time talking with your mother, and I think that she needs to tell you something important. No. Maybe to show you something important."

"I know. I didn't say I wouldn't see her. I just said I don't want to."

It was my turn to blink, more in shock than anything. "Wait. You are okay with talking to Rowena? How did you come to change your mind?"

"Didn't you tell Gran that she only wanted a few minutes with me?"

"I did; that's right."

Bob scrunched up even tighter. "So okay. I will talk to her for a few minutes. But you have to be with us. It can't be alone. I need you and Gran to be there. It's okay. She won't faint again. She's strong enough now.

My entire prepared opening statement was unnecessary. Somehow, this little tightly wound up pile of arms and legs had made up her mind to go with the flow. It didn't make any sense to me. Especially since Bob looked even more strained than she did last night.

"Bob, you don't seem very comfortable with your decision. You actually look like a turtle completely disappearing into its shell; I don't think you could hug your legs any tighter. So your words don't match your body language right now. Help me understand."

Bob let go of her knees and straightened out her legs in the chair. She looked at me while she stroked her thighs, as if to reintroduce the circulation in her legs. "Last night, before we left the hospital, Gran told me something."

I remembered. "She whispered something to you, didn't she?"

"Yes. She told me that she and I have to remember to make my dad proud of us."

It took every bit of self-restraint to keep myself from flying across to Bob and attempting to make the term "eat her with a spoon" somehow a reality. Instead, I must have choked, trying to get my own words out. "Bob, I can make this happen. One thing, though. Are you sure about your gran?"

Bob fished in her shorts pocket and pulled out her cell phone. She punched and swiped until a text message flashed onto her screen. It was from Ella (I had no idea she knew how to text; Bob was a better tech advisor to Ella than I realized). The text read:

Bobby. I am ready for her if you are. Gran ☺

"You taught your gran how to text?" Bob wrinkled her nose. "Yeah."

"AND USE EMOTICONS? This may just be the end of the world!"

Bob managed a single giggle. It sounded like harp music to me, I can tell you.

▷◁

Rowena agreed to meet me for dinner at Arby's. I got there first and ordered a Diet Coke. As I sipped it, I looked around at the other diners. There was a man with acne scars, greasy hair, and dirty overalls. Probably a laborer. He stuffed French fries and bites of burger into his mouth, hardly chewing. His companion looked about fifteen, her hair lank, her hands wrapped around a milkshake. She was at least fifty pounds overweight, and she was crying between sips. His daughter? His girlfriend who was pregnant, perhaps? To my left, an elderly woman sipped a small coffee. She looked at every person in line, as if hoping for someone to recognize her. Lonely, I guessed. Everyone in the place had a story. Arby's—full of roast beef, French fries, and human drama.

I caught sight of Rowena as she walked through the parking lot towards the building, her jeans torn into frayed slices, but most likely not due to some sort of fashion statement. Her matchstick arms hung out of the sleeves of a grayish tee shirt that said GET REAL across the front in black caps. As she approached, she glanced behind her, as if worried about being followed. She carried the same greasy, black backpack over one knife-thin shoulder. I waved at her through the window. She nodded and pulled the door open—it seemed to take all her strength to do so.

As she slid into the booth opposite me, I caught a whiff of marijuana. So she was "clean," but not completely. I stiffened at the smell. "Hi. Are you settled in at the Y?"

She raised one eyebrow. "That was *sincere*. But, yeah. I'm okay."

I stood up. "I'm getting a hamburger. Do you want something? My treat."

It was Rowena's turn to stiffen. She reared back, reached into her jeans pocket, and pulled out some bills. "I have money. I can buy my own damn food."

This was starting out well. We walked up to the counter together, and I hoped I didn't see anyone that I knew. I ordered a cheeseburger with everything, and Rowena ordered a roast beef sandwich with barbecue sauce and a Coke.

As we ate, Rowena kept watching the door.

"Are you being followed or something?" I asked.

Rowena threw her head back and laughed roughly. "It's a habit; hard to break. I am always on the lookout to score. Stupid, huh? When I'm straight? Shit." She looked down at her half-eaten sandwich and ran her finger through the barbecue sauce on the waxed paper. "This is the way it is with addiction. It's with you, reminding you, all the time." She crumpled up her napkin. "See this?" She held out the napkin wad, stained red with sauce. "This is what I feel like right now. A wadded up piece of trash. Being straight isn't glowing and bright. It's just me, Rowena. A loser. I am a loser when I'm high, and I am a loser when I'm straight—because when I'm straight, I just want to be high again." Her eyes flashed at me, challenging me to disagree.

"You have no way of even beginning to understand." Rowena lifted her thumb to her face and gnawed on her cuticle.

I pushed my hamburger aside and leaned toward her. "I *don't* understand this. You are, by your own admittance, a complete mess. You have no hope. So why are you here? Why are you inflicting all of this on your daughter and Ella?" I resisted the urge to punch her.

Rowena took her thumb out of her mouth and sneered. "Because Roberta is my daughter! Because all I can do for her is to see her right now, when I am able to make sense to her. I need to show her that"—she swept her arms down her torso as if displaying a prize in a quiz show—"THIS is not what she should become! That THIS is her mother!" Rowena shook her head. "I want to tell her that I love her so much that I want her to forget that I ever existed." Rowena's nose started running. "I want her to know that I love her, and then I want her to erase me from her life." She wiped her nose with the heel of her hand. "That's all."

I handed Rowena my napkin, and she blew her nose. I felt suddenly cold, as if the AC was on overdrive. I didn't know what to say. So I put my hand over hers and we sat, both of us gorged with emotion, in the midst of a mediocre fast food restaurant in America's heartland.

▷◁

Getting Ella home and settled was nowhere near as laborious as it had been with her hip. She still needed her walker, and the hospital insisted on a wheelchair. But once we got her home, she was relatively spry, getting herself out of the car and up against the walker. She only needed a bit of support from Bob.

Janey had made a delicious lunch of our favorites: grilled Velveeta sandwiches with tomato soup, followed by a wide assortment of cookies. I ate every bit. Ella picked at hers nervously, and Bob didn't take one bite. Since it was a beautiful day, Janey hustled us out onto the porch to have our "meeting."

Bob sat in one rocker, Ella sat in the other, her walker off to one side; and I sat on Ella's wicker ottoman. Janey made sure we had iced lemonade. "Now you all make a plan, and I will make myself scarce." The door popped closed behind her.

"Rowena says she can stay here a couple of days. She hinted that after that, her money will run out. She's at the YWCA downtown."

Ella smoothed her slacks, as if they actually contained wrinkles. "I think it's best if we get this over with, as soon as possible, or Bobby and I might just worry ourselves to death over it. Don't you agree, Bobby?"

"I have a lump in my throat after I swallow. Gran says it's nerves. I don't like feeling nervous like this. And I can't sleep. I want to get it over with, too."

I pulled my phone out. "I have Rowena's number. I'm sure she's waiting very impatiently to see you both. I bet she would be willing to come over this afternoon."

Bob stiffened. "And you promise you will stay with me and Gran?"

"I promise. Should I make the call?"

They looked at one another and said "yes" simultaneously.

So Rowena would be arriving in a half hour.

It seemed like an eternity. The way time slows down to a trickle—like when you are waiting for biopsy results or the letter telling you whether or not you got into college. Ella rocked in her chair for dear life, I paced, and Bob sat on the steps, tapping her heels until I could stand it no longer and sat down beside her and forced those skinny knees into the "down" position.

Just as we thought we might all explode from the combined tension, Bob pointed. Rowena walked down the street towards us. She looked quite different than the day before. Her hair was clean and shiny. What was mousy gray yesterday gleamed golden brown today. She wore a yellow headband that framed her forehead almost like *Alice in Wonderland*. Instead of the ratty leggings, she wore a clean, white tee shirt and a long paisley skirt. Her bright orange toenails peeped out of her Birkenstocks. She carried her grody backpack, and her steps were tentative, but as she got closer to us, she drew herself up and began to move more quickly, like an automaton. But I realized that there was a good reason for that.

As she turned up our sidewalk, Bob and I stood up and moved aside so Rowena could come up onto the porch.

Ella's voice never wavered. "Rowena. I won't get up. It's a little too difficult. But I want to shake your hand."

Rowena stepped up to Ella and held out a hand, awkwardly. Ella grabbed it in both of hers and squeezed, rubbing Rowena's hand as if to warm it. "Sit down, dear."

Rowena sat in the wicker chair beside me. She seemed at a loss.

"Beck said you wanted five minutes." Bob waggled her hand: *let's move this along.*

Rowena flinched. I leaned over and flicked Bob on the arm with my thumb and index finger. "We don't have to be rude. Sit down and listen politely."

"I will only use up the five minutes. I came here, Roberta, to sit in front of you today as a clean and sober person. No matter what happens to me from now on, I am the mother that gave birth to you, and nobody will ever love you more than I always have."

Bob's eyes clouded.

"Wait. I'm sorry. Bob. You want to be called Bob." She paused and seemed to gather herself. "Today, I feel good. I can eat, because now that I'm straight, I have an appetite. I'm taking a medication that eliminates my craving for heroin. I spent time in rehab, and I got clean cold turkey. You see, this drug I'm taking, Suboxone, is pretty expensive, and up until recently, it was experimental. There isn't a lot of it out there. Beck can explain all that to you. So yes, I am obtaining it illegally; I can't get it from a doctor."

Ella put a hand over her eyes. I wanted to cover mine, too—it was so hard to watch this. Not Bob. She looked unflinchingly into Rowena's eyes.

"This is why I am here. As long as I take Suboxone, I do okay. As I said, since I'm eating now, I have enough energy to maybe get a job. I might go back to waitressing. That's the goal of every addict. But that isn't why I'm here."

Bob remained rigid. She sat stock-still, her eyes boring into Rowena's.

"So *this* is why I'm here. Ro—Bob, I wanted you to see me now. Right now, when I am well. I want to tell you that you are a very good girl, just like your father. You are good, and smart, and beautiful. You are nothing like me."

Bob began to tremble. Her knees knocked; she grabbed them with both hands to still them.

"I want to ask a favor of you, Bob. I want you to promise me that you will remember that I love you, and that is all. I want you to forget about me and all of my mistakes. I am someone that you should never even think about from now on. I want you to go out there and do good things. I don't want you to have to remember what a disappointment I have been. I don't want you to think of me at all. Just go forward with your life, your gran, your father, and your friends. Please forget about me and be happy. Be happy." Rowena reached out as if to touch Bob's cheek, but stopped herself. Instead, she kissed her hand and put in on the top of Bob's curls, just for a split second.

"So that's it. The five minutes. And I promise all of you that I won't be back. You can count on that. As long as you can promise me, Bob. Promise to look forward, and not back at me."

Bob stood and backed away from her mother. She reached out blindly in my direction, so I took her hand and squeezed it.

Bob didn't look at Rowena as she said, "I want you to go now."

Rowena looked around at me and Ella as if she had just noticed that we were still there. She nodded to Ella, and smiled a weary smile at me. "I will. Now that I have seen you, I can leave town. There is a bus I have to catch in fifteen minutes. I have just enough time to make it."

Ella held out her hands again, but this time, when Rowena took them, she pulled her down into a hug. "You try to stay healthy and strong, dear. I am so glad to see you again. Bless your heart."

Rowena turned to me and held out a hand. I shook it, and then surprised myself by kissing her on the cheek.

"Bob, do you want to walk your mother down the block and say goodbye?" Ella looked hopeful.

Bob said nothing. She turned her back on her mother and hurried into the house, shutting the door firmly behind her.

Rowena's back was straight, her head held high as she disappeared down the street, her backpack bumping against her frail shoulders as she walked. At the end of the block, she turned and waved.

I waved back, my heart overflowing.

Just then, the door flew open, and Bob flew out, galloped down the porch steps, and hurtled down the block toward Rowena, calling, "WAIT! WAIT!"

Rowena turned. Bob sprinted up to her mother, stopped short, and they stood, seemingly in conversation. Then Bob handed something to Rowena, who held it up, and they both stared at it.

"What on earth are they doing?" Ella asked.

"It looks like Bob is taking a selfie." I was flummoxed.

It was over in a second. Rowena disappeared around the corner, and Bob walked towards us slowly, her head down. She stumbled up the steps. Ella held out her arms, and Bob got down on her knees and folded herself into her gran's arms, sobbing softly.

"Bob, why did you run after your mother like that?" I whispered.

Bob looked up into her gran's soft face, tears sparkling. "Just because she wants me to forget her, I didn't want her to forget me." Bob held out her cell. "So I had her take our picture. So she and I could both have it. I told her I couldn't promise to forget her."

Ella stroked Bob's cheek with her gnarled hands, gently wiping the tears away.

"But why do I still want to hate her so much? And love her a little bit, too?"

Ella ran her thumbs under Bob's eyes. "Because you are human."

Bob put her head down in Ella's lap. I left them together, went into the house, sat on the sofa, and shriveled.

CHAPTER THIRTY-ONE

That evening, back at my apartment, I looked over at the Bowers' house, lights blazing in all of the windows. I needed to do something. I needed to try to fix things for them. I wasn't exactly sure what I could possibly do. So I called my mother.

"What a heart wrenching story. Honey, I am so proud of you for helping Bob and Rowena."

I snorted. "Helping? It wasn't exactly catharsis. Rowena went back to her life of crap, I presume, and Bob is devastated. How did I help?"

Mom sighed. "Well, you were there for both of them. You know, they are each on their own paths. You can't wave a wand and fix either one of them. But you listened, and you made the meeting easier for both of them. Now you just have to continue being the best friend possible to both of them."

That didn't really make me feel much better. It was getting late, but I knew Gail would be up, so I called and started to tell her the whole story. She was kind, but interrupted me in the midst: "Honey, I would really like to hear you out, but Theo is here right now. Can I call you back tomorrow?"

I was thrilled for Gail, if frustrated myself. "Don't bother, kiddo! Have a lovely evening. Smooches!"

I had no choice. I called my sister.

In between sips of wine, I laid out the entire story. She did not interrupt once, which surprised the hell out of me. And when I finished, as I watched the lights go out in Bob's bedroom, D gave me her take on things.

"You know what they say in therapy? You have to get things out. Help Bob recognize what's churning around inside her right now. Love and hate. Anger."

"I am not a therapist, D."

She laughed. "Obviously. But you are a writer. Writers get rid of all sorts of angst through prose and poetry. And artists draw. Maybe you can get her to do art therapy or something with you. It can't hurt. Probably it could help."

"Diana, you are sort of a genius. This is a great idea. If only I can figure out how to make it work."

I spent the rest of the night trying to picture myself as an art therapist. No pun intended.

▷◁

I invited Bob over for lunch. I told her I had gone to Costco and discovered that they had raspberry Popsicles. She seemed mildy enthusiastic.

As soon as she arrived, Bob dropped to her knees and called Simpson, who padded in smiling, his fur now gleaming from all of the post-traumatic vitamins and special food we were giving him. He purred, and Bob scooped him into her arms. Thank God he was back. But as Bob stroked Simpy, she stared into space, her face devoid of anything. She was flat.

We had fried bologna sandwiches, which I slathered with mustard. They were incredibly delicious, but Bob just nibbled at hers. Although I waved the blue Popsicles invitingly in front of her, she declined. "My stomach is littler since my mother left," she explained. "It feels like there are spikes all inside me, poking me from inside. Everything's all mixed up."

Here was my opening.

"I have an idea, kiddo. You told me you are all mixed up together in there," I indicated the area around her head and torso. "The spikes are probably a combination of anger, love, and stuff like confusion, am I right?" I had my fingers crossed. I was hoping that Bob wouldn't self-destruct right in front of me.

Bob looked startled. She nodded vigorously. "Yeah! My insides are all mushed together with stuff! I can't concentrate at school, Hallie gets mad because I don't want to play, and Gran says I need to look for the sunshine in life, but I can't. I don't know what to do." Her fingers raced over the tabletop, her eyes blank. "I feel all empty."

"I have an idea. It may be stupid, but I thought we could try it. I have a bunch of things mushed up inside me, too. And I thought that one way we might get all that stuff out is to write some little poems. Have you learned about poetry in school at all?"

"A little. We studied it in school last year at Christmas. I know that it doesn't have to rhyme. And the teacher told us that good poems don't start with 'roses are red, violets are blue.' We wrote Christmas poems. It was fun. Let's go into the living room."

I got out the two pads of paper that I purchased that morning at the CVS, along with two newly sharpened pencils. I motioned for Bob to sit beside me on the sofa, and I placed a pad and pencil on the coffee table in front of each of us.

"You're right. A poem doesn't have to rhyme, and it can be really short. Poems explain how poets feel inside. I thought that we could each think about what is poking us from inside, and we could write a poem about it. We can share them if you want to, but that isn't necessary."

Bob looked dubious, but she picked up her pad and set it on her knee. With the other hand, she took the pencil and rubbed the eraser against her cheek. "We have to take time to think."

I picked up my pad and pencil. We sat quietly for a while, and then Bob began to write on her pad. It took me a bit longer, but then my poem appeared.

I titled it "Beck's Poem"

You drove away from us
My whole world went with you
We weren't good enough
Dad

I stared at it. Some of the spikes did stop poking me from inside. They were still there, just not poking quite so hard. I rubbed my forehead and looked over at Bob, who had finished writing and was staring at her pad intently.

"Do you want to share yours?" I asked.

"Do you think we should?" Bob rubbed her pad with her thumbs, as if to cover up her poem.

"Only if you think it might make you feel better."

Bob said, "I have another idea. Is your poem sad, or mad?"

"My poem is very sad to me." There was a catch in my throat for some reason.

Bob looked grim. "Well, my poem is MAD. I don't want to read it right now. You know what I want to do with it? I want TO STOMP ON IT!"

She ripped off the little sheet, carefully placed it on the floor beside her, and then Bob stood up and smashed it repeatedly, first with one foot, and then the other. She worked up quite a head of steam, leaping up and down at least ten times, grinding the paper into the floor with each stomp. She stopped suddenly, standing on top of the paper, and flashed a beatific smile in my direction.

"Oh, I feel so much better! What do you want to do with yours?"

I looked at her triumphant little face, wreathed in freckles, her deep blue eyes flashing.

I tore my poem off the pad, stood up, kissed it once, and then tore it into tiny shreds, throwing them into the air like confetti.

Bob laughed. "Yours must have been full of love with the sadness. Right?"

I laughed, held out my arms, and Bob jumped into them. We hugged for what seemed like hours. I made a mental note to send my sister some flowers.

Later that night, I found Bob's poem under my coffee table, gritty from all the stomping.

> *"Mother"*
> *You don't smell like flowers*
> *You have dark eyes*
> *Remember me*
> *I am good.*
> *Don't come back.*

Bob took to poetry like a duck to water, pardon the passé phraseology. She got into the habit of leaving me a poem in my mailbox on her way to school in the mornings. The first one said

>"Another poem to Beck from Bob"
>Life is hard, but you are my friend.
>I like to sit with you and have a treat.
>Please write me a poem,
>If you were a color
>You would be pink.

So since she requested a poem in return, I took this one over to Ella's and asked Janey to put it in Bob's lunch box:

>"Bob, Small but Big"
>When you are mad, even though you are a kid, you
>get very big and strong.
>Tough.
>When you are happy, you make me happy.
>When you grow up and get tall, I hope you get a cat
>To sleep on your head.

Ella reported that Bob put with that one under her pillow.

A few days later, I found this on the floor in front of my apartment door:

>"Beck the Beckest"
>Hallie is my best kid friend.
>You are my grownup one.
>You know my secret.
>Love and hate
>They can be together.

When I got that one, my breath seemed to leave my lungs temporarily. I had to sit down and try to keep from dissolving into ugly tears. I carefully put it into an envelope and put it into the drawer beside my bed, where I could read it whenever I needed to remember what a blessing I had in my friend Bob.

However, I requested a few happy poems, because I told Bob that I thought we needed some laughs. I asked Janey to put this one in Bob's lunch:

> *"Bobbo"*
> *You have so many freckles*
> *Your face looks like it has*
> *Chocolate sprinkles all over it.*
> *Remind me not to lick your cheek!*

This is the one I got back:

> *"Happiness"*
> *Gladness is watching TV and eating Fritos with*
> *Janey and Gran.*
> *Fun is riding my scooter really fast. And Hallie*
> *Happiness is having you across the street*
> *And Popsicles*

After that one, I told Bob we needed to take a little poetry hiatus, or else my heart might just burst. Bob smiled and said, "That's okay, because I don't feel anywhere near so spiky and mushed around inside, do you?"

"Bob, you're right. I am spikeless."

▷◁

I showed the poems to D. She read them all, set them in her lap, and gently stroked them. She sat, looking down at them as if they were alive somehow.

"I wrote one about Dad. But I tore that one up."

Diana didn't look up. "What did it say, if you will tell?"

I sorted through the images inside my head. There stood our father, so handsome, love for us radiating all around him. But there was something else there, too. His eyes. I remembered his eyes. How whenever he spoke to someone: us, Mom, the neighbors—his eyes were never totally focused on the person standing in front of him. He was always scouting, looking for what was just beyond range.

"I told him I loved him and missed him. Then I kissed him and let him go."

CHAPTER THIRTY-TWO

Things calmed down for a while. I thanked the universe for that. Bob and Hallie went back to being besties. Ella, although exhausted by recent events, tried manfully to resume her therapy routine. She actually graduated to the point where she could take a few steps without her walker inside the house. Her goal was to be able to get herself into the bathroom to take care of things, and then get herself back out without having to ask Janey for help. So far, she hadn't succeeded, and Janey reported that she wondered if Ella was "stalling out."

One afternoon, Janey's day off with her family, Ella sat in her kitchen, sipping tea and instructing me in the art of spaghetti sauce making, Ohio, non-Italian style. Her mother's recipe. We were cooking because Ella "just couldn't face taking another walk."

"Why am I not using olive oil, again?" I asked her, stirring the onions in the frying pan.

"Oh, honey, olive oil has such a strong flavor!"

Right. Italian. "I see. Is that also why I'm using garlic salt instead of actual garlic?" I looked at the jar of McCormick's on the counter beside the stove.

"Yes. We want the sauce to be subtle." Ella clinked her teacup against the saucer.

Subtle sauce. Basically crushed tomatoes, a touch of garlic salt, tomato paste and just a soupçon of onion. Absolutely nobody would get heartburn from this. As I shook just a bit of the garlic salt into the sauce, Ella cleared her throat.

"Rebecca, Bobby isn't perking up the way she should. I know she loves the poetry, and that is fun for her. And you have been so good to her, trying to cheer her up. But her teacher called me this afternoon and told me that she feels that Bobby is listless. I'm worried about her."

I turned down the heat on the sauce, poured myself a glass of water, and slid into a chair opposite Ella. "This has been a very tough year for her, hasn't it?"

Ella's face, usually pale but with a swath of pink across her cheekbones, looked especially dull, and there wasn't any sparkle left in her eyes. Defeated. "Rowena. I curse her for coming here. Bobby still has bad dreams."

"Ella, it takes time. She needs to work through her feelings about her mother. Give her time."

Ella nodded unconvincingly. "That isn't all of it. She keeps asking me how much longer before Janey can go home. She nags me that I have to start going upstairs. She seems so focused on having things back the way they were before."

Ella looked down at her legs. She raised them one at a time, straightening them out from the knee. "I'm doing the exercises as best I can. But Rebecca, I am eighty-four. I may not ever be able to go upstairs again. I'm afraid that Bobby carries around so much on her shoulders, with me and my hip, Rowena, Charles being away—she frets. I think she's afraid I might fall again, or worse."

I felt as if I had been struck by lightning. "Oh, no! You are so far from that scenario!"

Ella pulled on her earlobe. I poured her another cup of tea. As she stirred, her face brightened a bit. "Halloween is coming in a few weeks. That is always such fun for the children. Maybe we should make a special night of it for her, with decorations and lots of treats. Like a party right here. It would give Bobby something to look forward to—something new to focus on."

"This is a fabulous idea! Especially since Bob has mentioned that she doesn't want to go out trick-or-treating, because Janey would have to go, too. She doesn't want to leave you alone. Even with me here to keep you company. I will be glad to help with the decorations and things. We can carve pumpkins; I'm very good at that. It will be the Halloween event of the year!"

Ella clinked her cup against the saucer. "I'll talk to Bob and Janey about this. Oh, Rebecca, what would I do without you?"

We sat, Ella sipping her tea, me staring at my glass of water. Then the strangest thing happened. Ella suddenly sat bolt upright in her chair, grinned mischievously, and winked at me. "Yes! Halloween is just the thing! Now, Rebecca, get going on finishing that sauce and put it in the refrigerator for later. Then you can just go on home."

Ella handed her cup to me and reached for her walker. Gripping it tightly, she nearly *sprang* up from the table. "I have to start making a list, and when Janey gets home, we will have to get busy, won't we? A porch party for Halloween! With all sorts of decorations, and we can do cupcakes. Jack-o'-lanterns! The neighborhood children will all come. Bobby will be happy!" She paused, smacked the handle of her walker, her wedding ring making a loud *ding*. "And maybe there will be surprises!"

I watched as Ella, now suffused with enthusiasm and determination, clunked her walker on the linoleum and stumped out of the room after it. In the doorway, she paused and twisted back towards me. She chuckled and winked.

▷◁

"Doesn't he just look beautiful?" Bob stroked Simpson's fur. It was still growing back, but it gleamed. He purred loudly. "And all the scabs are gone. That hole in his neck is almost all gone, too."

I looked at the two of them, perched on my sofa, a skinny cat, kneading skinny little scabbed knees. "It was a miracle, wasn't it?"

Bob put her face against his side, to better hear the purr. "And your sister found him. So you aren't mad at her anymore?"

"Well, I stopped being mad at her long before that. But I was sure glad that she found this guy."

"He walks funny, but that's okay, 'cause he can get around just fine. And we have the collar on him now, for identification. But he won't get out again, will he?"

"No, he won't."

"I told Gran. I told her that Simpson was worse than she was. And he got walking again without physical therapy or anything. I think she listened. She is trying harder, don't you think?"

I didn't know how to answer. "Your gran is better. But we are coming to the end of her therapy. Bob, she might not improve much more. But I don't think, honey, that she will get worse! Don't you worry about that."

Bob adjusted Simpson on her lap, so that his legs didn't dangle over onto the cushions. I lowered myself onto the sofa beside them and continued. "Janey may just have to stay with you indefinitely."

Bob stroked Simpson, who kneaded her lap gently. "Gran says that I should be very excited about Halloween."

I watched as Bob rubbed Simpy's forehead with her index finger. He closed his eyes in rapture. Bob's forehead creased with worry. "She and Janey are making a big deal out of it. They think it'll be thrilling for me." Bob shook her head. "I'm not very thrilled."

"Bob, I get it. This has been a hugely eventful summer for you. Good grief. So your gran and Janey just want to cheer you up. Have you told Hallie and your school friends about the party?"

Bob continued stroking, but her eyes were faraway. "Nope. Not yet. I have to get into the mood."

She looked so defenseless. "There's plenty of time. Halloween isn't for a couple of weeks."

Bob closed her eyes. "I think about my mom a lot. I wonder if she's okay."

I cleared my throat, and Bob's eyes flew open. "But I don't want to see her again! I just wonder about her."

"You will probably always think about her, Bob. That's perfectly normal. And I'm sure that she is so glad that you were kind to her when she was here."

Bob sniffed. "I asked Gran if we should tell Dad about it. She said not to. She said that we shouldn't worry him over there; that he has so much to think about, and he needs to concentrate on staying safe."

My heart thumped. That porch party was sounding better and better. "Bob, sometimes we do have to just let things be. Let time smooth things over. Focus on the future, not what's behind us. This Halloween party is your gran's way of giving everybody something to look forward to. And kiddo, I am a *master* pumpkin carver!"

Bob hefted Simpson onto the floor and attempted to brush the volumes of cat hair off her lap. Her smile was just a bit forced. "Okay! I've never made a jack-o'-lantern with a knife, 'cause it was too dangerous. But this year, can I try one?"

"Bob, I don't know. We don't want to have to take you to the ER for stitches right before the big night. Maybe we should just carve one, and then do a couple more with permanent markers. You can draw a picture of Simpson's face on one."

"Okay."

"Hey, your gran said that there would be cupcakes. I bet Janey will let you decorate those!"

Bob put her thumb up to her mouth and bit at the nail.

And maybe you should write a special poem for Halloween. You can illustrate it with drawings of jack-o'-lanterns.

"That's a good idea. Do you think you could buy me one of those giant boxes of crayons?"

Thank God for distractions.

▷◁

Dr. Lauren called a few times to check up on Ella. She was as discouraged as I was. "Some people never overcome a bad injury. I hadn't expected this of Mrs. Bowers, but it is certainly not unheard of." She was glad to hear that Janey was in place, but she agreed with me that the days of Ella's independence were probably over.

D called me nearly every evening. We had established a ritual. After I popped in on Ella and Bob, Janey would send me off with a "night, Miss Beck," and I would sit outside on the porch, sipping a beer. Watching the lights go on in the neighbor's houses, I would imagine what might be going on inside. Were the Andersons having sex? Dave Anderson was extremely virile. What was that flickering upstairs at the Homans' house? Oh, that was the upstairs bathroom—I bet Louise Homan had candles burning around the tub. In the midst of my reveries, my phone would beep, and D and I would compare notes. Tonight was no different.

"Alex may be teething."

"Isn't he way too young for that?"

"Not really. According to Google, babies can get their first tooth as early as three months. He is drooling and whining, and his bowels are loose."

"Sounds fun. Don't invite me over for pizza any time soon."

"How are you holding up? How's the cat? What about the gang across the street? Is Ella still dragging her ass?"

I have to say that the new relationship I had with my sister wasn't perfect. I still found her to be annoying about seventy percent of the time. But the other thirty percent was proving to be very worthwhile.

"I wouldn't put it that way, but yeah, I guess. She's an old person, D. They don't always bounce back."

Diana sighed at the other end. "So this caregiver isn't the solution? The mighty Janey?"

"It's going to have to be. However, Janey is awesome, but she isn't like family. Bob thinks Ella hates being dependent. I have now come to accept the fact that Ella has tried her hardest, but she just won't ever recover fully. I don't think it's her fault. She has tried."

"Sounds like they're stuck over there. At least you said that Ella can afford this. They'll just have to suck it up and go with the flow."

"Oh, D. You can be such a kind and empathetic person." I hope she picked up on the sarcasm in my voice.

I heard Alex start grousing in the background. "That's right, sis. Just call me Mother Theresa." She laughed.

The lights started to blot out around the neighborhood. It was getting late. "I wish there was something I could do to solve things over there. Bob wants Janey to go. Ella *needs* Janey to stay. I told you about Halloween. Ella is hoping that making a big to-do out of it will turn Bob around. So Ella is planning a porch party for Halloween. As if that will accomplish anything. What a mess."

"Well, nobody said that growing up was easy. Every kid has to deal with the crappy things that life hands them. We certainly did.

And we're both okay, aren't we? We got over Dad throwing Mom under the bus. I'm getting used to the idea that Bryan and I are toast. You seem to be a happy old maid. So this little girl with all of her tragedy isn't all that different than most of the people in the world."

"D. Thank you for that insightful summary. It warms my heart and gives me hope."

There was a pause. "Yup—the entire human race is doomed to misery, right? So what's the answer? Maybe Ella is right. Beggars' Night Magic. Hell, it may just work. Ella may just feel the Halloween mojo and get hit by a bolt of lightning. Maybe a porch party is just what the doctor ordered. For all we know, she'll be running in the Boston Marathon next year. We gotta have faith, I guess. Hey, are Alex and I invited?"

"Of course! Hey, I have to hang up now. I need my sleep. Perhaps I will say some prayers tonight. Kiss Alex for me. And give him an ice cube to suck on."

"Okay, sis. Hang in there. And just be thankful that Janey is around. She is trained for things like changing Depends. You did the right thing hiring her. This is what is waiting for all of us, you know. Getting old sucks."

A little stomach acid welled up into my throat at the thought. "Thanks, D. Just what I needed. A reminder that someday I shall be wearing Depends."

She chortled and hung up.

I finished my beer. The leaves rustled, and a dog barked from somewhere in the next block. Then the Duncan's dog across the street joined him. The Chihuahua from the apartment below mine chimed in with his tiny yips. Some irate guy opened a window and yelled, "Pipe down, out there, for fuck's sake!"

Ah, the nighttime serenade of the Midwest. I rested my cheek against my empty can of beer and looked up at the sky. There weren't any shooting stars, but I made a wish anyway.

CHAPTER THIRTY-THREE

Once the subject of the porch party came up, Bob had certainly participated in all the preparations for Halloween, but not in a carefree way. Damn Rowena. Plus, Ella's condition seemed to be dragging Bob down, and Ella's over-the-top enthusiasm for the party wasn't having its desired effect on any of us.

I wondered if maybe Bob was disappointed that she was missing out on trick-or-treating.. Maybe that was what was behind her faked enthusiasm. "Bob, would you like to go out trick-or-treating with the neighborhood kids? You could do that for a little while, before the party gets really cranked up."

Bob was adamant. "Nope. I want to have the Halloween party with Gran. She will really like it. And I won't miss trick-or-treating, 'cause Gran and Janey and me can eat candy all night. You, too. I'm telling Janey to get extra candy," Bob declared with a sort of desperate intensity.

Despite the pall of doom, Janey and I decided to go *all out* for the porch party. I got orange crepe paper and glow-in-the-dark skeletons to affix to the porch railings. Janey got *full-sized* candy bars. According to Janey, word gets out very fast about which house has the best loot, and it would not take long before the Bowers' house became the Halloween hot spot.

I tried to talk to Ella about this. I was attempting to tape orange crepe paper over the top of the front door, but the masking tape I was using kept coming unstuck.

"Honey, that isn't working. Why don't you just drape it over the porch lights and let it hang? That will look fine."

I started draping. "Ella, this party is making everybody nervous. You seem so worked up about it. Are you placing a bit too much emphasis on this? Bob is going along with everything, but I'm not sure that the party is going to solve everything. Like POOF."

Ella sat in front of the end table, a bag of candy corn in her lap, taking handfuls and placing them in little cellophane envelopes, folding the tops over to seal them. "Rebecca, don't you worry. This will be a magical night." Ella lined up the little envelopes on the table. She leafed through a deck of Halloween stickers, choosing a sheet of bats with wings outstretched. Affixing them to the envelopes, she grinned and popped some candy corn into her mouth. "I just love candy corn, don't you?"

I hate candy corn. It makes my teeth ache. "But, Ella. It might not be what you expect. Bob is muddling through, but there is just so much on her mind these days. What if the party isn't a success? Shouldn't you be prepared for it to . . . well, *fail?*"

Ella looked startled at my choice of words. She folded her lips into a stern line and glared at me. "Believe me, Rebecca. The party will be thrilling. And that is all I will say about it. Now take that crepe paper off the porch lights and do something else with it; it looks terrible like that."

I did as I was told.

▷◁

Halloween in Ohio can be fickle. Some years, it is a golden evening full of fallen leaves and flashlights, parents escorting ninjas, tiny ghosts, scarecrows, and goblins. Other years, it is so frosty that all the trick-or-treaters wear overcoats, their costumes obscured by goose down and hoodies. But this was a golden year. The porches on our street were festooned. Jack-o'-lanterns had been burning nightly for at least a week. Mr. Fenway had out his usual corn sheaves and hay bales. The Davis's house had a graveyard in the front, complete with cobwebs and giant spiders. Halloween this year would be picture perfect.

I came over early to have dinner before things got started. Janey had made chicken soup and BLTs, but Bob and Ella were just picking at their food. I, on the other hand, adored everything and asked for a second bowl of soup.

"Bob, you need to eat something. If you just have sweets all evening, you might get sick," said Ella, who had taken exactly one bite of her sandwich.

"I can't eat. I'm not hungry."

In between bites of my sandwich, which was regrettably nearly gone, I said, "Bob, I really like your costume. You look just like Simpson."

Janey had used an old eyebrow pencil of Ella's to draw whiskers on Bob's cheeks and blacked out her nose. She had painted a few stripes across Bob's forehead, and Bob wore a headband with cat ears on it. "From Amazon," Janey told us. To complete the look, Bob wore black tights and a black leotard. A fuzzy tail was Velcroed to Bob's back end. Also found by Janey while shopping online. Bob looked cute enough to be edible.

Ella looked up at the kitchen clock and pushed her plate away. "It's almost time. We should go out on the porch now. The children will start coming. Where are the cupcakes? Rebecca, will you take the matches and go out and light the ghost candles on the railing? Janey, you might as well bring out all the extra candy." Ella was so wound up, her hands shook as she grasped her walker. She nearly tripped on one of the legs as she tried to pull herself up too quickly.

My stomach forgotten, I slid out of my chair to steady Ella. We walked out to the porch together, my hand on her arm. I wondered if I should take her pulse. I had never seen Ella so nervous.

We arrived on the porch just as the first few trick-or-treaters appeared on the other side of the block. I took a deep breath and shot a quick look skyward, pleading silently with whomever ruled the universe to let this evening pass without a tragic incident.

Diana and Alex arrived. Diana was apparently the *sexy* witch. She wore sheer black leggings, a teensy black skirt, four-inch heels, a black-and-orange striped top, mostly obscured by Alex in the baby Bjorn, and a peaked black witch hat. Her hair gleamed down her shoulders, and her lips were bright red. Alex was wearing skeleton pajamas. "Take him, Beck," Diana unfastened her son. "He is ruining the full effect here." D held her son out and shrugged off the Bjorn. "I mean, let's not deprive the dads around here of *this*." I took Alex as D thrust out her chest.

"Of course not. What dad wouldn't want to get a load of your boobs?" I pointed to the Bjorn with my foot where D had dropped it. "Bobbo, would you help me on with this?"

We were ready. The sexpot sister, Janey and her delectables, me baby-wearing, Bob faking cheeriness, and Ella, her jaw set with determination. I held up Alex's fists and waved them. "LET THE FESTIVITIES BEGIN!"

Trick-or-treating was scheduled for the hours between six and eight o'clock—for safety, before it got too dark. That was a shame, I thought. Trick-or-treating when I was a kid, in the dark, with no supervision, was much more fun. But that was then and this is now.

They came in clusters. The moms and dads, most of them in costumes, hanging back on the sidewalk as their kids rushed up to ring doorbells and demand candy. I loved the cries of "Trick or Treat!" My favorites were the tiniest ones; some even babes in arms, dressed up as tiny peas in pods, or mini superheroes.

Hallie giggled by, and after rushing up to hug Ella, grabbing a Hershey bar, and high-fiving Bob, she kissed Alex. Then she and her father rushed back into the fray to gather up more booty.

The streetlights came on at seven, even though it was 'the gloaming,' as Mom liked to call it. Not exactly dark, but shadowy. The children, their bags almost full, started to drag. Parents looked at their watches. The traffic was thinning.

Our candy was getting low. Ella's hip was bothering her; she shifted in her chair uncomfortably. I felt Ella had had about enough.

"Bob, we are almost out of candy. I think it's time to just leave the bowl on the porch and turn out the porch light. Diana's feet must be killing her in those heels. Your gran is tired."

"NO. I am not tired, not a bit." Ella squared her tiny shoulders. "We will stay out until the end. There are at least a half-dozen cupcakes left, for heaven's sake!"

So the party wasn't over. Bob and I sat on the steps, the bowl of candy on Bob's lap. She hadn't had one piece. I was at a complete loss. I reached over and helped myself to a Snickers. I offered Bob a bite, but she demurred. Yes, such a queer evening! We handed out two more treats to a small policeman who was holding hands with a princess. It was almost dark. We were approached by a clump of kids, followed by their dad. They were dressed as a ninja, a robot, a nurse, a skeleton, and yet another princess.

He was dressed like a soldier. Tall, erect posture. He certainly looked authentic, in tan and beige desert fatigues, the large duffle bag slung over his shoulder. It looked heavy, and I wondered why on earth any father would go to such lengths for Halloween authenticity. He even had on shiny black combat boots. Despite the heat, he looked comfortable. Whew. This was one hunky-looking father. As he got closer, I realized that he looked vaguely familiar; he must be a neighborhood dad. I wondered which of these kids were the lucky ones to have such a good-looking parent, but he didn't seem to be following any one of them in particular. D let out a low whistle.

As the children standing on our porch took their candy, Bob looked up and noticed the soldier. With a shriek, she shoved the boy in the skeleton costume aside, knocking him into the princess. In a tangle of arms, legs, and fun-size candy bars, they struggled to right themselves and retrieve their spilled candy. Bob paid no heed and hurtled down the sidewalk and right into the soldier's arms. He dropped the duffle and swept Bob up, burying his face in her hair.

As he carried Bob towards us, Ella pressed her hands to her cheeks and began to cry. "Charles. Oh, Charles. You came! I was not sure, not completely!" Ignoring her walker, she stood up and extended her arms. Janey gasped and put her hands out in case Ella fell down. But she didn't fall. She pushed her walker aside and took two very firm steps forward.

Bob struggled in his grip to turn to both of us. "GRAN! IT'S DAD!" She tried to whirl around in his arms. "EVERYBODY! THIS IS MY DAD!"

He carried Bob onto the porch and set her down. Taking a cupcake from the plate, he popped the entire thing into his mouth, consuming it in one munch. "Chocolate with candy corn icing. My favorite." Wiping the crumbs from his chin, he flashed a stunning grin at us all. "Now what is this I hear about somebody not doing her exercises? And not climbing stairs yet? Is that why you had me sent home? To be your personal trainer?"

He gathered Ella into his arms. Weeping, she ran her hands over his cheeks, murmuring "Charles. Oh, Charles!"

Bob was a living pogo stick. "YOU DID THIS, GRAN? You SUR-PRISED me!"

Ella disengaged Charles's arms and motioned toward Bob. Charles dropped and crouched in front of her. "Bob, you told me how hard it was for Gran. You told me you were discouraged, even though Janey"—he flashed a brilliant smile in Janey's direction—"is sort of like Mary Poppins."

Janey beamed.

"And when I heard about your mom coming, and how that turned things inside out, I felt just awful. But Gran had an idea. She asked me for the name of my commanding officer. And she sent him a very impressive email. EMAIL. Gran didn't know what email even *was* before this last deployment." He chuckled.

"And what happened with Gran's email?" Bob could not stop vibrating.

"Here I am! Gran's letter convinced the marines to let me go home. Early discharge! And I have my twenty years in. Bobby, I am officially retired. Here. For good."

Bob wrapped her arms around her father's neck and wilted, sobbing. Charles stood, holding her and swaying back and forth, whispering into Bob's ear. Then he turned to Ella and put his free arm around his grandmother. The three of them stood, embracing like a scene from an Academy Award winning movie.

Diana looked first at the soldier, then at me. She strode over to me, undid the Bjorn, and hoisted her son. "Time to go home, buddy." Before she went, D leaned over to me and whispered, "*Forget what I said about being a happy old maid.*"

He stroked Ella's hair softly with broad, strong hands, kissing her forehead and the tip of her nose. His dark hair gleamed in the light of the porch as he smiled with straight, white teeth. His black eyes glinted, and the edges of his eyes crinkled with his smile. He looked as strong as Superman. My God. This man looked as if he might have stepped directly out of one of my books for "lonely" women.

His arms full, Charles turned to fix me with those magnetic black eyes. "So you're Beck, the one-and-only? The one who dropped everything in order to take care of my gran and be my daughter's guardian angel?"

My heart popped like popcorn.

Acknowledgments

There are two distinct groups of people that I wish to thank for my writing life. The first is professional. I have to thank Lou Aronica for seeing my potential, mentoring me for the many years that it took for him to teach me how to write a novel, and then for being the wonderful publisher and editor who has never once let me down. Beth Hoffman has held my hand, calmed my fears, given me private tutorials, and become a close friend. Robin Black encouraged me to self-publish my first book of flash fiction. Catherine Ryan Hyde has been an inspiration and supporter. Andrea Peskind Katz and her Great Thoughts Great Readers blog and Facebook group are great cheerleaders. Ann Imig, Alexandra Rosas, the women of Creative Alliance, The Erma Bombeck Writers' Workshop, The Tall Poppy Writers, and every single author who has taken the time to converse, share ideas, and commiserate with me are deserving of my deepest gratitude.

The second group is personal, made up of the friends and family who have given me love and encouragement from the first blog post I ever wrote. Sheryl Chapman Kammer, who told me I should be a writer before it ever occurred to me. My husband, Charlie, who never stops applauding. My two daughters, Marion and Annie, who keep me grounded and tell me when I need to "change that outfit" before I go out. My darling grandson Charlie and my yet unborn grandchild (boy? girl?) whom I can't wait to hug. Bryan Sander, Trudy Krisher, David Lee Garrison and Suzanne Kelly Garrison, Dave and Jane Reeder, Hazel Dawkins, Lisa Rosenberg, Bob Rosenberg (my model for Bob Bowers, though I turned my Bob into a girl!), Suzy Soro, Amy Sherman, Bonnie Feldkamp, Lee Reyes Fournier, Dennis Fairchild, and all of my neighbors, who have to listen to me talk about writing.

To my medical advisor, Laurie Bankston, and my veterinary advisor, Joe D'Amico, who appear as Dr. Lauren and Dr. DeMarco in this book. Thank you for your help and friendship.

And finally, to my dear departed cat, Simpson, who stood in for all the cats in my life. I am indeed, one of those "cat ladies."

About the Author

Molly D. Campbell is a two-time Erma Bombeck Writing Award winner and the author of one previous novel, *Keep the Ends Loose*. Molly blogs at http://mollydcampbell.com. Also an artist, Molly's work can be found at http://www.cafepress.com/notexactlypicasso. Molly lives in Dayton with her accordionist husband and four cats.